ANDY REMIC

The Dragon Engine

BOOK I OF THE BLOOD DRAGON EMPIRE

ANGRY
ROBOT

ANGRY ROBOT
An imprint of Watkins Media Ltd.

Lace Market House,
54-56 High Pavement,
Nottingham
NG1 1HW
UK

angryrobotbooks.com
twitter.com/angryrobotbooks
Slicin' & dicin'

An Angry Robot paperback original 2015

Copyright © Andy Remic 2015

Cover by Lee Gibbons.
Set in Meridien by Epub Services.

Distributed in the United States by Random House, Inc., New York.

ISBN 978 0 85766 454 9
Ebook ISBN 9 780 85766 455 6

Printed in the United States of America

9 8 7 6 5 4 3 2 1

PRAISE FOR ANDY REMIC

"If Quentin Tarantino read a lot of Heavy Metal comics and played *Dungeons & Dragons*, and decided "Hey, I'm gonna write a book!", this is what he would write... *The Iron Wolves* is a vicious, over the top violent, and thoroughly vulgar ripping bloodfest of a fantasy... This book grabs you by various body parts and then punches you in the face when you try with all your weak little might to get loose."

  The Ghostworks

"For anyone who is missing their David Gemmell fix."

  iO9.com

"Remic has a very precise way with descriptions of battles and fights and with weapons of every type (including head butts). The scenes leap and snort off the page, making the heart race with anticipation about their outcomes ... *The Iron Wolves* seethes with action; indeed, it stomps across every page."

  Sharon Reamer, author of the Schattenreich books

"*Kell's Legend* is a rollercoaster ride of a book that grabbed me right from the first page and tore off at a rate of knots like I hadn't seen in a long time."

  Graeme's Fantasy Book Review

"Violent is really not the right word for this spare-no-detail fantasy monstrosity. Insane? Maybe. Really, the only way to describe Remic's *Kell's Legend* is with a phrase: a bloody, violent, fantastic journey through carnage, terror, and a downright epic tale that makes Underworld and every zombie movie look bad... Remic is the Tarantino of fantasy, and if that isn't a compliment, then I don't know what is."

  Fantasy & SciFi Lovin'

This book is dedicated to my amazing little boys, Joseph and Oliver. I always wanted children, and they have shown me how great kids can be – thanks for so much laughter and joy, guys!

Prologue
THE PIG'S HEAD

Dake Tillamandil Mandasar, former Sword Champion of King Yoon's Royal Guard, hero of the Second Mud-Orc War and heir to the Lordship of the House of Emeralds, Vagandrak's largest ruling family, squinted at the pig's severed head dominating the long feasting table laid out before him. Granted, the head had been cooked to perfection; skin crisp, meat succulent and steaming, the red apple lodged in its mouth both inviting and in a position for comedy banter; agreed, the head had been placed centrally on a huge, expertly etched silver platter, the edges worked with intricate care and skill by some master craftsmen at the pinnacle of his guild artifice; and yes, granted, the flowering garnish which surrounded the cooked pig's head like a generous forest of autumnal colour and culinary precision would have made all of King Yoon's eighty-five Master Chefs weep into their onion soup bowls, such was the artistry with which lettuce and onions had been skilfully carved, potatoes and aubergines arranged *just so*, carrots and broccoli meshing together to craft a creative tapestry of wonder, begging even the most ardent of carnivores to dive naked and drooling into this feast of lightly seasoned vegetables.

Dake stared. The pig stared back.

"But I... *I* never ordered that!" said Dake, his vision locked to the doll eyes of the dead pig. Its eyes were small and black as ink. He felt they were watching him... *carefully*. With an educated understanding.

By all the gods, they ARE watching me! His mind reeled under the influence of this sudden realisation, aided, no-doubt, by the eight frothing flagons of Fighting Cock Ale he'd managed to consume in a shorter time than was holy.

"THAT'S BECAUSE WE ORDERED IT FOR YOU!" boomed Beetrax the Axeman, pushing through the crowd of chatting guests and slamming another frothing tankard before the former Sword Champion. "And... I didn't want to mention it before, but it looks like your sister!" He erupted into roaring raucous laughter, thumping Dake playfully on the shoulder – to a wince – as others around the huge table burst into laughter and they lifted tankards in salutation to a great moment of comedy, each gaining a frothing moustache with their humorous toast.

"My sister, Beetrax?" Dake's voice was cool. The cool that had disarmed thousands of opponents both in the gladiator rings and in the real-world insanity of battle. "Damn it! But I reckon this pig looks more like your mother," he snapped, grabbing his tankard and taking a hearty swig, a goodly quantity spilling down his leather jerkin and fine, pink-patterned silk shirt.

"No, wait," beamed the axeman, pausing for comedy effect, "it looks *even more* like my hairy arse!" More laughter erupted, and Beetrax positively glowed through his bushy beard, showing a broken tooth, victim of a long-forgotten tavern brawl. "Anyway, anyway, settle down, settle down... I said SETTLE DOWN!" The laughter and cheering subsided as if launched from a cliff. Beetrax swept his gaze across the long table, where perhaps forty guests were seated, attention now focussed wholly on him. The remainder of the crowded ground floor of The Fighting Cocks lowered their voices to a murmur, as everybody turned towards Beetrax, who had climbed – somewhat shakily – onto a three legged stool. The roaring fire, in an ornate stone fireplace some seven feet high, pumped out heat and light and cast Beetrax's shadow against the far wall near the long bar, escalating his already impressive stature to that of a giant.

Beetrax puffed out his chest. "Time for a speech, it is!" he said, deep bass voice rumbling like a clash of titans entering battle.

"Gods, not another one," cursed someone from the crowd, as a good-hearted chuckle ran through the friendly, gathered throng.

"Careful, lad, lest I knock out your teeth," warned Beetrax sombrely, swaying a little, his tankard clamped in a shovel-like fist, the knuckles heavily scarred, the backs of his fingers and hands tattooed with military script.

"Looks like somebody already knocked out yours!" More laughter, which quickly subsided when Beetrax gave *that* stare.

"Anyways," continued the bristling axeman, "I'd just like to ask all you fine people and comrades here to raise your tankards, cups, glasses and soup bowls to my best mate, Dake, and his lovely wife, Jonti Tal – there she is, that slim and beautiful one over there," he hiccupped, "who, on this very day five years back, took the bravest plunge of them all –braver than any front-line mud-orc charge, braver than facing any horse-beast massacre, braver than cleaning any type of street-fed cesspit – yes, men and women o' the

Cocks, they decided to get wed!"

The entire tavern's populace cheered, and many patrons slapped their fellows on the back. There were a large number of hugs. Love was in the air. Love, and wine fumes. Dake grinned around like a man possessed, and Jonti Tal, slender, elegant, with long black hair tied back, her steel eyes sweeping the room, stood, and waved her hands for quiet.

"Thank you, thank you all for coming..." she began.

Beetrax belched, wobbled again on his stool, then plummeted to the ground in what turned into a rather comical half-dive, half-roll which saw him practically put his head *into* the roaring flames. More laughter chased woodsmoke and good humour around the large tavern room, and Beetrax scrambled back from the roaring blaze on all fours, his tankard lost in the throng, face as red as his big bushy beard and shaggy head of hair. Embers sizzled in his beard, and a friend suddenly threw ale in the large axeman's face. Steam sizzled. Beetrax lifted both his clenched fists in a traditional pugilist's pose until Talon leapt forward, his slender arm half-encircling Beetrax's broad shoulders, and he managed to achieve eye contact.

"Whoa, Big Man! Go easy there. You were about to suffer a head engulfed in flame!"

"Eh?"

"Your beard, man, it was smouldering! Your bush was about to ignite! A harsh way to achieve a shave, I'd wager, even though so many here believe you need it. This friend, here, was simply saving your dignity. And your pride and joy. So, go buy him an ale instead of pummelling his undeserving features. Right?"

"Aye, right then, Talon," nodded Beetrax, slapping the

worried-looking douser on the shoulder, "that I will, that I will."

Jonti was well into her tale by the time Beetrax regained focus, and was saying, "...chose the most romantic way to propose – under The Saviour Oak in Peace Lily Square, with the scent of flowers in our nostrils, the full moon illuminating everything with highlights of silver... I was blessed, and honoured, touched, and in love. Therefore, as he stared up with those big sad eyes, I felt compelled to say *yes* to his most honourable proposal."

"So, nothing to do with his huge fortune, then, eh love?" shouted Beetrax from the bar. He had a man sat on his shoulders now and was attempting to dance a dance from the knees down.

"Talon," smiled Jonti, her face becoming yet more beautiful with the clarity of her smile, "would you kindly put an arrow through the fat man's eye?"

"With pleasure, sweet Jonti." Talon bared his teeth in what could have been a smile.

"Anyway," Jonti continued, sipping from a crystal goblet of thick red wine more reminiscent of blood than juice of the grape, "I would first like to thank you all for attending, except maybe Beetrax, who is a loveable rogue but, on occasion, more effort than should be required. I know many of you have travelled from far cities and towns over a week's journey away, and both Dake and I are truly honoured you made such an effort. We've put ten gold behind the bar, which I believe, according to Old Dog Ben, should last well into the small hours for both food and drink; and we would both be thrilled if you could fill your bellies, drink yourselves senseless, and make this, our fifth wedding anniversary, a night to remember!"

A cheer went up, with lots of clapping and shouts of goodwill. The atmosphere was charged with lightning. The band in the corner set up a merry jig, drums pounding, lyres strumming, feet stamping, and the party patrons began swirling one another around in a mad dash dance of vigour and fun.

Dake grabbed Jonti around the waist, and pulled her screaming and not-struggling-too-much down into his lap. The giggling and slapping turned within moments to a long, deep, lingering kiss, and they stayed like that for some time, entwined, lost amidst the merry bustle of the gathering and the dance, cocooned in their own little world of softness, sweetness, love and purity. Minutes flowed into hours, and time slipped by like a water snake through lilies. Dake and Jonti drank a decanter of fine Vagandrak Red, nuzzling one another, and reminiscing on past events with small laughter and glittering eyes. They were soothed into an alcoholic, embryonic haze of gentleness. They snuggled together, half dozing as the party started to lose momentum, and slowed, and soothed itself into a calmer time. Members of the gathering drifted around Dake and Jonti, shimmering like ghosts. It was a most comfortable situation, which led to long moments of holding, and longer moments of kissing; not the urgent kissing with a lust for sex, but a rhythmical union, a togetherness, holding one another for the simple sake of it.

Finally, Jonti pulled back.

"You still have it, my lord."

"Ha! Don't call me that."

"But... you *are* the Lord of the House of Emeralds."

"No no no... *heir* to the Lordship of the House of Emeralds."

"Still. You'll always be my lord." Her voice was low, and husky, and incredibly sexy. He reached up and stroked her smooth skin, lost in her. Jonti leant forward and kissed him, sensuously, for long lingering moments, until they both became gradually aware of an intrusive presence and pulled away, frowning. Beetrax was stood, warming his back by the fire, staring at them.

"You going to pay for a ticket?" snapped Jonti.

"Eh?"

"You're staring, my friend. At us. During our intimate moment."

"Oh, that." Beetrax waved his hand, as if swatting away a fly, dismissing an uncomfortable moment he'd created with a gesture. "Don't be ridiculous. I wasn't staring. I was just watching. There's a difference, you know."

Jonti scowled, but Dake gave her a little squeeze. *Go easy on him*, that squeeze said. *You love him. We love him. He's a brother. And you know what he's bloody like!*

"You have something on your mind?"

"I do, as it happens." Beetrax took a deep breath, gave a wide grin, and scratched his bushy ginger beard with sudden vigour.

"You maybe require some kind of herbal infestation antidote?" suggested Jonti.

"No! I have called the others. They're on their way."

"What others?" said Dake, struggling more upright and rubbing his face and mouth. He looked around, as if waking from a deep slumber. He yawned. "Gods, what time is it?"

"Two hours after midnight," said Beetrax, and his eyes were shining under his broad, flat forehead. He rubbed his chin again, and took a generous swig of honeyed wine, straight from a clay jug. Golden droplets hung in his beard, and firelight from the hearth turned them into suspended jewels. "You remember that time, on the walls? We'd just held against another mud-orc attack. I had that beautiful serrated axe, and was picking bits of bone and mud-orc flesh from the steel; and I was feeling despondent, like, as if the shit would never end. And you stuck your arm around me, and said…"

"I said, 'Don't worry, Axeman. This horse shit won't last past the end of the week. Keep your chin up, brother!'"

Beetrax grinned. "Aye. And you were right. We *won*. We were *heroes*. And a month later you were married to that… *sword ghost*."

"Hardly a ghost," smiled Jonti, relaxing back against Dake. His arm encircled her waist, his fingers reaching out, stroking her inner thigh with a practised intimacy.

"Weeks of battle, not a single scar on you," said Beetrax. He frowned. "Woman, you fight like a demon, and you turn to spirit form when the enemy blades and claws are near. *That's* what I was staring at. Remembering, like." Beetrax sat down on a stool with a sudden jolt, as if surprised by his own momentum and weight, and took another hefty gulp of wine.

Dake inhaled a deep breath rich with stray tobacco and woodsmoke. "Savage days," he said. "Thankfully over. But hey! Now, it's a time of peace. We're all wealthy, happy, privileged. Heroes! Vagandrak salutes us. Celebrates us in literature and song. I performed yet *another* school visit last week. The children were crowding around, asking me how many mud-orcs I killed on the walls of Desekra; the cheeky little imps. I had to send them back to their chalk slates and learning. Still. It's good for them to meet their heroes." He spoke with no irony.

"But you're not happy, are you?" said Beetrax, leaning forward. His shift of position put his face in shadow, and his eyes became very, very dark. Dake frowned.

"Of course I'm happy. I'm married. We're celebrating. I'm *drunk*, by the Seven Sisters!"

"Where's the excitement gone, brother? The adventure? The… the bloody *challenge*!"

Jonti made an annoyed clucking sound, as Dake opened his mouth to answer, but Beetrax's eyes shifted – to a spot beyond Dake. Jonti jumped up, and stood with hands on her hips. She was smiling as she swept the room, eyes finally coming to rest on the three newcomers to their little gathering.

The ground floor of The Fighting Cocks was almost deserted; now the jigs were done, the band drunk, the food consumed. Ben the Bear slept in the corner, still wrapped in his shaggy bearskin despite the pumping heat from the hearth. He was snoring – a soothing, gentle purring sound, despite his size and ferocity of looks. In another corner six women in silks and chainmail played around a game table, throwing carved knuckle dice, their near-silent cheers and curses a testament to the seriousness of their bets which had no doubt increased in quantity in line with the amount of honeyed wine supped. Kendalol, one of the barmen, was polishing silver tankards behind a scarred stretch of stained oak bar. He was legendary for his lack of sleep, although the gossip was that his narrow-faced wife was something of a harpy, and he was as argumentative as she, thus necessitating alternating states of existence lest one throttle the other.

Here, now, in the hushed and ale-spent tavern, stood Talon, tall, elegant, with long ash-blond hair so fine it was almost white; high cheekbones enhancing a somewhat haughty appearance, and his well-balanced athleticism speaking volumes of his legend – that of skilled archer, perhaps ranked third in Vagandrak, perhaps first, depending where you placed your bets. As well as his skill with any target a warrior could present, the narrow-hipped archer was also a languages expert, being a graduate from Drakerath University, and had been known, on special occasions, to be hired as Chief Protector for the Queen; he was also notorious for his outspoken views on his love for men, which got him into occasional spots of bother, but enamoured him to King Yoon as a man to be trusted with the King's young bride.

Talon gave a single nod of his head, then pushed back an errant wisp of drifting hair, smoothing it behind one ear, his eyes fixed not on Beetrax or Dake, but on Jonti Tal. Her eyes posed a question but Talon blinked slowly, lips pursing into a narrow smile. *You'll find out soon enough*, that smile said, and Jonti returned his good humour with shining eyes and a curt nod. By some trick of the light, her eyes almost appeared full of tears.

Beside Talon stood Lillith, a self-proclaimed witch specialising in the positive magick of healing, her studies forcing her to take a path of celibacy, and her work in the Great Library of Vagandrak notoriously invaluable over the years, translating ancient texts from foreign tongues and contributing immensely to the Great Library's body of knowledge. She was a much-studied healer, her skin olive dark, her hair a cascade of thick woven strands which ran down her back to her hips. She abhorred violence of any kind, and yet found herself drawn to warriors for it was here she could practise her healing skills with regularity.

Now, her dark sultry eyes appraised the gathered group and she bared her teeth in a welcoming smile, her scent, that of the exotic, reaching Beetrax's nostrils and making him think of older, better times.

"Beetrax," she nodded, voice husky and deep, and for a moment Beetrax's cheeks flushed red.

"It's been a while, Lillith," he said, voice thick with emotion. "I am so glad you could come."

"My pleasure, my love," said Lillith, almost shyly.

Dake slapped Beetrax's leg. "Stop fawning, you dick; you're like a love-struck fool!" he laughed.

"Sorry," rumbled Beetrax. "But you know how it is."

"Yeah, mate. I do."

Lillith pulled up a stool and sat, arranging her white skirts. Around her throat and wrists were silver charms that caught the light of candles and fire, and glinted with a supernatural eeriness.

Finally, from the shadows, came Sakora. She was tall, and slim, and moved with an incredible grace, a natural elegance. She wore a mixture of silks and hazy gauze fabrics which swirled around her. Her hair was long and brown, tied back in a loose tail, and her feet were bare, nails painted a shocking red, each toe circled by rings of gold. She appeared more a dancer than a member of this group of warriors, and yet they all knew, were painfully aware, that in the realm of unarmed combat the beautiful Sakora was more deadly than any person they had ever met.

"Welcome, Sakora," said Jonti, with a broad smile.

Sakora nodded, moving to one side, leaning against the wall, one hand stroking down a section of flowing silk. "It's been a while," she said. "When he," she nodded towards Beetrax, "sent the invitation, I was immediately suspicious."

"Har har! You know my reputation far too well!" boomed Beetrax.

"Indeed I do," purred Sakora, eyes fixed on the huge warrior, "and sometimes the words *sex*, and *pest*, enter the same timeline within the frame of my mind."

"Ha! Sex pest? You'd be so lucky."

Sakora shrugged. "You have indeed pestered me before."

"I don't remember that," said Beetrax.

"You do. I broke your thumb."

"Oh, *that* little misunderstanding!"

"I believe you dribbled a good pint of saliva down my breasts before I had to resort to the physical."

"Love, you can resort to the physical with me any time!" beamed Beetrax.

"You wish me to break your other thumb?" she said.

"Ladies, brothers, let's get to the point." Dake waved his hands suddenly, attracting their attention. "I – *we* – are completely flattered, and honoured, that you all came. Brother Beetrax here is resplendent in his willingness to go that extra league in making our anniversary something special. However, the hour is late, and without meaning to sound crass in any way, it really is time me and my lovely wife relived our wedding night from all those moons ago. I assume you are all staying in the locality, and thus we should meet again tomorrow noon, and perchance seek joy in food, drink, lively banter and one another's happy reminisces." Dake beamed, as if proud he'd managed to utter the words through an ale-fug which clouded his brain.

"Wait," said Jonti, looking around. "There's something else, isn't there?"

Lillith nodded, as did Talon.

"You've not told them?" Sakora gave a sideways glance

at Beetrax, and made a clucking sound of annoyance.

"Told us what?" said Dake, frowning.

"Hey, hey, I wanted it to be a surprise, right? I wanted the old gang back together before I spilled the beans and got Dake and Jonti here all excited and buzzing about a good idea and our future adventures."

Jonti gave a narrow smile. "What future adventures would these be, my ambitious little Trax? Seems like you have it all worked out ahead of us... without actually bothering to find out if we'd be interested in the first place."

"No no, don't get like that," said Beetrax, pleading with his hands. "Don't be getting pissed about it before you've even given me a chance to speak. Because when I speak, trust me," he pointed with a stubby index finger sporting a blackened nail, "*trust me*, you'll want to be in on it." He lifted his hand and gave a little wave. One of the few remaining serving maids brought over a large wooden tray containing several flagons and bottles.

Sakora waved away a glass – she did not drink – but the others helped themselves.

"Go on, have some," muttered Beetrax, looming close.

"It is not the way of the Kaaleesh. It affects judgement, timing, power, speed, all of those things you believe you possess." She looked up from those dark eyes and Beetrax gave a little groan.

"Gods," he mumbled, "it's going to be a long night."

"Right," said Dake, standing suddenly. "Jonti, come on, it's time we called it a night. As I said, we're all pleased you came, but the time for drinking is now gone, and we can discuss Beetrax's 'future adventures' tomorrow over a proper full fried breakfast... Mrs Mangan's down the street does a wonderful fried black pudding, and when you crack an egg yolk it all soaks in, and—"

"Sit down," said Beetrax.

Despite his voice being low, almost unheard, Dake caught a tone he'd not heard in a decade. He looked at Beetrax again, and saw something in the big axeman's eyes that made him give a little shiver. He felt goose bumps run up his arms and tickle his spine.

"Hear him out," said Talon, settling down on a stool and folding his arms. The slim archer had a cool, detached smile on his lips.

Dake laughed it off with a boom, tilted his head, and then gave Beetrax a single nod, sitting himself back down and crossing one high, gleaming black boot across the opposite knee. "Go on then. Explain, Axeman."

"I've spent the last week in the Rokroth Marshes," said Beetrax.

"Doing what?" asked Jonti.

"I was helping an old friend escape from... his enemies. You may know him. His name is Fanakor Greeves."

"That old rogue!" grinned Talon, showing perfect white teeth.

"Old rogue my boot," said Dake, eyes heavy-lidded. "He's wanted by Yoon and the King's Guard for High Treason; smuggling dark magick texts, blood sacrifice... you name it. Beetrax, you mad bastard, Yoon will have you hanged if you're caught aiding Greeves. Worse, he'll have you tortured for a month prior, and have you squealing like a kitten in a bear trap. Have you lost all your senses?"

"Would *you* help *me* if I was in trouble?" countered Beetrax.

"Yes, but that's different. You're a brother. Despite the bad beard."

"I owed him, Dake. I owed him my life. But that's a different story for a different day. The point is, I helped him evade capture; I smuggled him out. And I used my... less than salubrious contacts to fashion Greeves with a new identity."

"Well, I still think you've taken a dangerous, unnecessary risk, my friend."

"In return, Fanakor Greeves gave me his greatest possession, acquired after fifty years of study and grave-robbing; earned after a lifetime's obsessive investigation into the dark arts, into Equiem magick; into the Harborym Dwarves."

"Go on," said Dake, and the room was deathly quiet. The fire crackled, coals occasionally popping in the glowing hearth. Talon took a gentle sip of some fine white wine sprinkled with crystals.

Beetrax looked about, as if suddenly frightened of being overheard. He lowered his voice.

"Greeves gave me a map; a page torn from the *Scriptures of the Church of Hate*, or at least, what fragments still remain."

"That is one ancient, deadly, cursed tome," said Lillith, her eyes narrowing a little, their cores flickering like dragon fire.

"It is indeed," said Beetrax, face solemn.

"Legend has it that book belonged to the sorcerer, Morkagoth. The evil bastard who summoned the mud-orcs from the slime and attempted to kill every man, woman and child in Vagandrak."

Beetrax nodded. "Apparently. Whatever its origin, Greeves acquired access to the book, and stole the map."

"A map to what?" said Jonti.

"It's a map," said Beetrax, licking his lips, looking shifty for a moment, "that leads to the Five Havens, the five dwarf cities under the Karamakkos Peaks. They were once ruled by the Great Dwarf Lords who mined untold wealth – I'm talking oceans of jewels, warehouses full of gold coin, lakes of molten silver! Enough to buy you a lifetime of whores, Falanor brandy and Hakeesh weed!"

"Wasn't there something about a dragon?" said Talon, eyes narrowed, rubbing his chin.

"Three dragons," said Beetrax, his own eyes wide. He took a hefty swig from his ale tankard, warming to his subject, and smacked his lips. "By the gods, that's good. Yes. The three dragons were slaves to the Harborym, their minds hammered and broken, or so the legend goes. They were locked away in three huge cylindrical pits, where they were used to light the furnaces. Or something. Anyway, that's all academic bollocks. The point is, the Harborym are long gone, extinct for ten thousand years, the Five Havens lost to the knowledge and thoughts of us mere mortal men. But all that treasure is still there, waiting for some hardy adventurer types to trot along and fill their pockets, and maybe even a few wheelbarrows, with an orgy of sparkling loot."

"I hate to piss on your fire, Beetrax," said Dake, frowning, "but unless you hadn't noticed, we're all affluent to the point of decadence. That's what being Vagandrak's Best Kept War Heroes did for our pockets. Why then, in the name of the Holy Mother, would we want to risk life and limb climbing mountains, fighting rock demons, and delving into long forgotten underground pits probably better left to the psychopathically demented Rock Fairies and all their little golems? Hmm?"

"Because of the three Dragon Heads," said Beetrax, eyes

glinting. "Tell them, Lillith."

"The Dragon Heads were colourless jewels found deep, deep beneath the mountains. It was discovered they had incredible healing powers – they could bring a man back from the brink of death; they could heal massive, open wounds, making flesh run together like molten wax; they could cure plagues and cancers and other diseases we couldn't even dream of. They are referred to in the *Scriptures of the Church of Hate* with reverence, as if they were bestowed on the Great Dwarf Lords by the Mountain Gods themselves. Indeed, it is the Dragon Heads that gave the Great Dwarf Lords their dominion and kingship."

"They can heal?" said Dake, voice gentle. He did not look at Jonti, but he squeezed her hand.

"Better than heal, boy," snapped Beetrax. "They promise immortality! The Great Dwarf Lords lived for a thousand years, ruling their underground realm with iron fists. That was because of these gems. Until..."

"Until what?" asked Jonti, almost breathless.

"There was a civil war. Between the Church and the Crown. The Harborym Dwarves murdered one another in their tens of thousands. Being a noble race, the survivors, borne down by terrible guilt at what they had done, cast themselves into the pits of Moraxx, Kranesh and Volak."

"Who?"

"They were the dragons," grinned Beetrax. "So the book reckons; so Greeves told me. Volak was the big dragon, apparently. The male." He shrugged.

There followed a long silence, where everybody considered Beetrax's words. The big axeman took another generous swig, and looked around the group with as much subtlety as he could muster. Talon: well, he had the archer. He

knew Talon was a restless soul, and no amount of money in
the coffers under his bed would stop him going on a reckless
adventure with his old war buddies. He was the easy one.
Beetrax's gaze shifted. Lillith. He had Lillith, too, because
to Lillith, her quest for knowledge and new abilities to heal
would outweigh any personal risk or possibility of death.
She was a good woman at heart; too good. Beetrax knew
that well, for once, many years ago, they were betrothed.
Before she found her good side. Before she pledged herself
to the spirits, the gods, and the greater good; damn them all
to the Furnace.

The others, though?

Beetrax glanced at Sakora. She was staring at him, cool
as anything, eyes unreadable, lips moist. She exercised her
wrists, circling her fists and then pushing her shoulders
back to stretch muscles and tension her spine. *By all the
gods, that's one amazing specimen of a woman*, thought Beetrax,
momentarily distracted.

Sakora smiled, closing her eyes. She caught images of his
thoughts, flashing at her like flickers of starlight.

You'd better believe it, she projected back, not quite sure if
he would be receptive to the thought, but willing to give it a
try. She opened her eyes and smiled. Beetrax frowned, and
turned to Dake and Jonti.

They were gazing into one another's eyes, and there was
something wrong there. Beetrax tilted his head. They were
supposed to be arguing with him, him trying to convince
them, but... there was something else. Subtle. Out of
context. Beetrax knew he was a big boorish lout, an axeman
with a love of frothing ale, long-legged women and waking
up in a pool of his own sick. But he was, surprisingly,
well-versed in the art of the subtle. He could read people,

and read them well. He was surprisingly intuitive, a fact which had probably gotten him into double the number of tavern brawls than should have been normal for one of his character. But now... *now* he couldn't read his old friends Dake and Jonti. There was something they were not telling him. They were holding back. Something serious.

Talon broke the silence, as Beetrax knew he would. "When do you propose we leave?"

"In a week's time, from the front doorstep of this very tavern."

"I'm in," said Talon, brushing back his long blond hair. "Now, if you'll excuse me, I have a hot young brunette warming my bed sheets, and I simply haven't *enjoyed him enough* to satisfy my ego for one evening."

He stood, a quick hard movement, and turned to leave.

"Are you not going to wait and see who else volunteers?" said Beetrax, bushy brows forming a thunderous ridge.

"Not necessary. They'll all come." Talon swaggered off, reaching the foot of the stairs, where he turned for dramatic effect, tossing back his hair just a little. "After all... why would they not?" He disappeared, and Beetrax looked around at the others.

"I knew he'd be the easy one. He always was."

"I didn't realise you two had got it on that way." Sakora winked.

Beetrax reddened. "Ha! He wishes, the spindly little maggot. Anyways. What do the rest of you think? Lillith? You recognise the healing potential, the quest for knowledge from something like this?"

Lillith considered Beetrax, then ran both hands down the olive skin of her face. "I recognise the healing potential you have for yourself becoming possibly immortal. Is that what you want, Beetrax? Really?"

"I want," said Beetrax, resting his hand on his chin in a studied philosophical pose, "ten wives, a hundred children, a warehouse full of fine wine, enough money to live like a king, and the chance to live for a thousand fucking years, my dear. Yes. I am that vain, I am that greedy, I am that selfish, and I am that hedonistic."

"And the prospects for all the other people of Vagandrak?"

"When I'm immortal, you can do what the hell you like with the gems," grinned Beetrax.

"I always thought your selfishness was an affected air," said Lillith, with considered gentility.

Beetrax deliberated on this. "No," he said, and turned to Sakora. "What about you, Ó unarmed combat expert with the bad social grace to get her stinking feet out at a party gathering? Eh? You up for a bit of an adventure with old Uncle Beetrax?"

"Although I would deeply love to reject your proposal on the grounds of spending any kind of trip with *you* being worse than an eternity of torture at the hands of the Torture Priests from the Church of Hate, I must confess: a) I have become complacent with my wealth, my lack of personal challenge, and a certain growing need to push myself once more to the limits of human physical endurance, and b) I have studied a hundred different combat systems from a multitude of cultures. This would give me a chance, perhaps, to broaden my knowledge base."

"You seek knowledge?" said Beetrax. "Bah! Well, anyway, whatever does it for you. Glad to have you with us. I know your, er, bare feet will be wonderful in any attack situations we might find ourselves in. Unless they're wearing armour of course!" He slapped his thigh and roared with laughter.

"Any time you wish to dance the cobbles, my big and excessively hairy friend, all you need to do is lead the way outside."

"Hah! Maybe one day, little lady. But not now. I have a quest to prepare! In fact, damn, I have a contract for us to sign. Lillith, be a love and nip upstairs, drag that wastrel Talon down here, by his foolish long hair if necessary."

Lillith growled something at Beetrax, but stood and moved to the stairwell. Her open annoyance was irrelevant. Beetrax had already turned towards Dake and Jonti. Jonti was pale, a weak smile on her lips. Dake was holding both her hands in his own.

"I suppose we're going to have that big argument now, eh?" beamed Beetrax. There was a certain optimistic rivalry in his expression.

"No," said Dake, voice gentle. And as Beetrax watched, he realised his old friend's eyes had filled with tears. "We've agreed to come with you on your foolish adventure looking for diamonds of immortality."

"Really?" Surprise, forcing Beetrax's bushy eyebrows up into an arch. "For the gold? The jewels? The fame and the fortune? To explore long lost caverns and have a bloody damn great fun time doing it?"

Dake gave a sorrowful shake of his head. "No," he almost whispered. He glanced at Jonti, who gave a single nod of her head. Dake fixed Beetrax with a powerful stare. "Jonti is dying," he said, his words emerging like cursed charms on a river of sorrow. "She doesn't have long left to live. No amount of money can save her. The best physicians in Vagandrak have given up trying – that's why you are all here, for this reunion, this party. We'd invited you here to tell you the news. This was supposed to be our last get together before... the inevitable happens."

Beetrax literally stumbled into silence. His mouth opened once, then closed again with an audible clack of teeth.

"So yes," said Jonti, voice soft. "We'll come with you, Beetrax. Because I'm out of options." She looked up, and gave him a beautiful smile, her eyes full of tears. "In one month from now, I'll be dead. And there's nothing I can do about it."

It was the early hours. The fire, once a roaring inferno, a fireball to equal the pits of the Furnace itself, had calmed, flowing down into molten embers which glowed, and pulsed, like fireflies gathered over a rotting corpse in the Rokroth Marshes.

The men and women who stood around the table were sombre indeed. Beetrax had unrolled a thick vellum parchment, on which, in surprisingly neat script, he had drawn up the contract. One huge hand held the scroll in place. His eyes moved around the table, meeting each and every member, until they came to rest on Jonti Tal.

"This is our contract," he said, with great authority. "Each man and woman here should sign their name, or mark."

"I don't understand why we have to sign it," said Sakora, voice silk. "We all know one another; we all trust one another."

"We all sign," rumbled Beetrax, eyes filled with a sudden passion; a blaze of anger and strength. "We find the Dragon Heads. We save Jonti. Or we die trying." His gaze challenged every person individually, and Dake reached forward, dipping the quill in ink and scrawling his name.

"We die trying," he agreed.

One by one, they signed, then moved to Jonti and kissed

her cheek. Tears were flowing, and there were hugs, and kisses, and more tears. Finally, Beetrax took the quill and gave his broad, untidy scrawl. He looked around.

"You are my brothers and sisters," he said, voice choking, "and this contract binds us. We will save Jonti; by the Seven Sisters and the Holy Mother, I swear it will be so!"

Skalg

"The Mountain gives... and the Mountain takes away," said Skalg, voice a rumble, as his woollen trousers dropped, gathering around his ankles, to reveal his engorged, throbbing, purple-headed cock.

Skalg was considered small in stature, even for a dwarf, but immensely powerful; broad of shoulder – *twisted of shoulder* – one dropping perhaps six inches below the other thanks to a crushed and bent spine suffered during a tunnel collapse in his younger days, and whereby the subsequent growth of disjointed bone had turned him into a hunchback. Oh, how he'd thought he was going to die in that cursed tunnel, way down deep below the Five Havens, as the world shook and screamed and collapsed around him, rocks thundering and crashing, dust choking, Skalg slammed to the floor by a lump of gold ore the size of a horse. The *irony*. His first genuine, incredible, life-changing find – and the lode pretty much nearly killed him.

Skalg blinked away memories of pain and suffering. And he gave a slow, wide grin. Those days were gone, now. How things had changed!

"Come here, my pretty. Don't be frightened."

He shuffled forward a little, kicking out of his trews

and struggling with the glittering diamond buttons on his black and purple tunic; this, he tossed aside, to stand fully naked, his gait unusual thanks to his hunched back, but his broad face with its neat black beard showing no shame or embarrassment. How could it?

Skalg was the most powerful dwarf in the Five Havens.

"Come here, pretty one," he said, and gestured with his finger.

The young female dwarf, small, slender, and wearing nothing more than a hazy gauze robe of silver chiffon with woven edge-strands of gold wire, cringed back in terror. Her smooth round features grimaced, and her eyes were like those of a frightened gazelle. "I- I do not wish to upset Your Eminence," she managed.

Skalg gave a wave of his hand. "Listen, girl," he snapped. "Who am I?" He patted his hairy chest with an open palm.

"You are First Cardinal Skalg, High Priest of the Church of Hate."

"Am I not the most powerful dwarf in the Five Havens?"

"As well as the king..."

"Yes yes, alongside Irlax, of course, is what I meant. But am I not all-powerful? Like a god, in fact?"

The young dwarf, eyes wide, licked her red painted lips and nodded quickly, several times.

"You are very powerful, First Cardinal. So I know what I must do."

Skalg took a threatening step forward, leering at the young female. "Then get on the bed and worship your god," he said.

Time passed. Servants had recently left after relighting candles and filling a bath full of warm water scented with lemon leaves, gathered from the world above; overland; *very* expensive.

Skalg lay on one elbow, staring at the quivering back of the young dwarf sharing his bed. Her skin was smooth and white, her shoulders narrower than he would have liked, but her hips wonderfully broad. Good, honest, childbearing hips. Hips to deliver an army of fine young sons!

Skalg felt himself begin to stir below, and quelled his rising passion. They'd already coupled twice, and now she lay, quivering, and sighing occasionally, as he reached out and stroked the smooth skin of her back. Like velvet, it was. Soothing to the touch.

Ah, the pleasures and privileges of religious office…

"Kajella, wasn't it?"

"Y- Yes, Cardinal Skalg."

"Did I please you, Kajella?"

There was a pause, *that* pause, the one which Skalg always found *so* entertaining – as they lay in unhappiness, attempting to formulate a lie in their tiny, infantile minds. Minds like donkeys, he mused. Minds like… *common people*.

"You pleased me very much, Cardinal Skalg." It was spoken with a considered neutrality that Skalg found impressive; highly controlled, for one so young.

"How old are you, Kajella?"

"Seventeen winters have passed since I was brought into this world." She spoke slowly, her words measured and careful. She was dealing with her situation well. Her shoulders were trembling only a little.

"Ah… seventeen. That is a fine number! A breeding age, to be sure! Well then, Kajella, I shall keep you here for seventeen days, with your permission of course, for you have pleased *me* very much. Is that a situation which finds your approval, sweet Kajella?"

He grinned as he saw her muscles tense, and imagined tears rolling down her cheeks to form stains on the pillow. *Oh such sweet sorrow. I wonder what your father would think of his daughter, beautiful, pure Kajella, now nothing more than Skalg's cheap mistress to be abused and tossed aside whenever he fancied.*

"That would be… my pleasure," Kajella managed, her teeth gritted.

"Good."

He shuffled closer, hand stroking down her arm, ignoring the murmur she emitted. He grew hard almost immediately, for Skalg was practically priapic. Whether it be females, politics or religious matters – most excited him in one way or another. His hardness pressed into her, and he heard a gasp.

"There there," he said, grinning, "we're going to have such a wonderful night, sweet butterfly."

Skalg had only just finished when the door burst open, and for a delicious, delicate moment Skalg thought this might be some enraged suitor come to claim his love, or an axe-wielding father arriving to take revenge on the plight of his daughter in the name of the church. *Oh how disappointing. It's only Granda, here with his boring face and his boring voice to deliver more bad news…*

"Granda! What an outrage!" came Skalg's bored voice. "Can you not see I am in the middle of something extremely important…? Well, *fucking* something extremely important. Can you not see?"

Granda's eyes narrowed, flicking to the naked female dwarf on the bed, her embryonic, curled figure one to elicit pity in the eyes of even the hardest of dwarves; then back to Skalg. His brutal flat face showed no emotion.

"I beg your pardon, Cardinal."

Granda, Chief Educator of the Church of Hate and Prime Protector of the Firelaw of Skaltelos, scratched his beard and frowned as Skalg disengaged, rolled from the bed, and started pulling on his black and purple robes of office.

"Yes yes, what is it?"

"There has been an attack, Cardinal."

"What kind of attack? On an Educator? On a common, petty dwarf? On a–"

"One of our churches is burning," said Granda, voice low.

"What?" shrieked Skalg, and still pulling on one boot, staggered comically, crab-like, towards the heavy shutters which guarded his high balcony. Skalg slammed into them, and they folded outwards, revealing...

Revealing Zvolga, the deepest of the Five Havens, the deepest of the five dwarf cities – and therefore most wealthy. It was in Zvolga that Irlax, Dwarf King, ruled from his Palace of Iron. It was the largest, the wealthiest, with the most refined and affluent citizens, and where the Church of Hate had its core buildings, its most loyal members, and of course, the stunning, thousand-yard high Cathedral of Eternal Hate. Skalg stumbled out onto the balcony carved from the very interior of the mountain itself, as was the entirety of the Blood Tower, the top five floors of which Skalg liked to call home. He hit the balcony, both palms slapping down on smooth stone, his gaze sweeping the vastness of the city chasm beneath him.

To witness Zvolga was to witness a feat of architecture so grand, there were no words available to describe the sheer vast, engineering brilliance. The whole city was part of the mountain, with perhaps half the structures carved from the interior mountain rock itself, the other half built, no, *sculpted* with the very finest engineering precision ever produced in vast acres of stone. The city swept away from Skalg's high vantage point (the highest in Zvolga, Skalg was always keen to point out when he was entertaining "important" guests), twenty thousand buildings, each of individual elegance and grandeur. Huge arched bridges connected roadways and paths, crisscrossing like spider webs in the comforting glow of the city burners – the fire-bowls. From thousands of burn portals, flames rolled gently, filling the cavernous city of Zvolga with a gentle, warm light, where long shadows highlighted the fabulous stone carvings on every house, every tower, every church, temple or palace, even on the dwarf blocks at the far end of the city away from the Palace of Iron and Cathedral of Eternal Hate.

Now, from his vantage point, where a cool, languorous breeze drifted, and he could smell a hint of sulphurous fumes from the Dragon Pits and their collector bowls and pipes, fuelling the city burners, so Skalg swept his gaze in a sudden panic, from left to right, passing the Cathedral (*oh thank the Great Dwarf Lords it wasn't the Cathedral!*) until his eyes settled on a tiny, distant inferno. Figures had formed a dwarf chain, little tiny blobs highlighted against the bright orange flames, and Skalg's face grew grim, eyebrows frowning, mouth turning into a scowl. His fists clenched on the stone parapet, and he punched downwards three times.

"How dare they?! HOW DARE THEY?!"

"Shall I order your carriage, First Cardinal?" But Skalg was beyond listening, as his rage grew inside his breast, in a beautiful parallel with the fire accelerating and consuming his Church of Hate.

"Blasphemers! Heretics! I'll fucking see them *burn*," he hissed, spittle on his lips, soaking his beard. He suddenly seemed to gain focus and grabbed Granda, shaking the Chief Educator, a sudden move which made Granda jump. Skalg might have a twisted, hunched back, but he was immensely strong. A fact many of his enemies – now dead – had failed to take into consideration. "Who was it, Granda? Who did this to my church?"

Granda stared at Skalg with a stoic expression. Then he gave his lips a single, quick lick. The gesture of a shark.

"*Who fucking did this*?" screeched Skalg, shaking his Chief.

"There was a symbol," said Granda, choosing his words with care. "It was painted on the church steps... in blood."

Suddenly, Skalg's voice dropped to a growl. His eyes flickered like demon souls. There was danger there. Real psychopathy.

"What symbol?" he said.

"The one that has been plaguing you," said Granda, words coming out in a rush. "The sign of the Army of Purity."

Skalg's face was colder than a tomb. He opened his mouth to speak, but he was cut off before he could begin.

"You dirty... filthy... stinking, crippled old bastard!" came the words, and they were soft, and feminine, and dripped with a dark honey of hate.

Skalg refocussed on Kajella. He blinked. He bared his teeth in half smile, half grimace. She was holding a small crossbow. The one he kept under the bed to deal with intruders, assassins, ex-wives...

"I see you found my secret weapon," said Skalg, voice dry and level. "I thought you would have had enough by now."

"You ugly, dirty, perverted, evil... *whore*..."

"No need to get personal," said Skalg, and flicked a gaze to Granda. Granda had taken a step back. Skalg frowned. Was that a *step backwards because I'm about to leap into action,* or was it a *step backwards because now you're on your own and I don't really want to get a bolt in the neck*?

Skalg saw Granda's hand inching towards his belt, and a huge array of knives which hung in neat, oiled leather sheaths.

Kajella saw the look. The crossbow swung on Granda, but to his credit, the big dwarf did not flinch. Granda had been stabbed, burned, broken and impaled before. He was the toughest, meanest bastard Skalg had ever met. Skalg knew no crossbow quarrel would stop the killer.

Skalg relaxed a little. He forced a smile. "Kajella. Kajella! My sweet. Why are you doing this? I am the Cardinal, the fucking *First Cardinal* of the Church of Hate – appointed by the Great Dwarf Lords. Appointed by our *gods*, little lady. What you do is heresy. If you fire that crossbow, you will burn in the nine levels of the Furnace. You know this. So be a good little dwarf, and put the crossbow down."

Reflected in the glass to either side of Kajella he watched his church burn. He breathed deeply and sank into a low, calm place. The throbbing of this slow pulse beat through his broken back; through the hunchback which tortured him now, and to the end of his days.

"I... I hate you!" she said. Injured. Embarrassed. Degraded.

Skalg lifted a hand, palm outwards.

"Don't do anything hasty," he said.

The crossbow wavered now, swinging between Granda and Skalg, then back again. Suddenly there was a click and a whine and a *thump*. The thump of steel in flesh. Skalg's hands frantically pummelled his own belly, and came away so he could stare down in horror. But there was no blood. No stain. His head cranked left. Granda dropped to one knee. Blood poured out in a quick stream, then stopped. Drips pattered onto a glossy platter illuminated by distant orange flames.

Granda groaned.

The crossbow swung back to Skalg. He grimaced. Now there was an edge of panic to his voice.

"Come on, Kajella. What are you doing? Your father is High Born. All you have to do is serve me for a number of weeks, and your family will be *blessed*; your House will be honoured by the Church! By doing this, *this*, you bring dishonour on an ancient clan, the clan of Karik 'y Kla. What, in the name of the fucking Great Dwarf Lords, do you think you are doing?"

"You took me as only a dwarf should take his wife," spat Kajella, face scrunched into a snarl. "I feel dirty inside! And if my father and mother and clan allow this *wrongness* to continue, then they can all rot in the Furnace for all I care…"

Skalg eyed the crossbow. It was a Steir & Moorheim. The best of the best. A *double-shot model*…

"Kajella! Please, girl! Think of the gods! Think of the church! Think with your head, not your battered quim…"

"You're going to die, Skalg," she hissed. The crossbow tracked him.

Like a coward, Skalg cringed back, then shuffled left and shuffled right, trying to avoid the swaying eye of the crossbow. Suddenly, there came the terrifying click and whine, and Skalg truly believed he saw events in a flickering of static images. Kajella, face contorted in rage and hate, pulled the trigger. The crossbow kicked. The quarrel sped towards him, and whisked over his shoulder, a thumb's breadth from ripping his left cheek from his skull. Skalg felt the passing of the steel bolt. A hiss ejaculated from his bearded lips. And his face changed slowly from fear to... something else.

Kajella made a high-pitched sound, more animal than dwarf, and charged at Skalg in a sudden sprint, both hands on the crossbow, hoisting it high to bring it down and crush his religious skull.

Skalg, an expert in avoiding pain, staggered to one side, ducking and twisting. Kajella, carried forward by the weight of the swung crossbow, hit the waist-high barrier and flipped over with a scream. The crossbow sailed into the vast landscape of the mountain interior below, end over end, disappearing into distant black. Skalg imagined he heard a tiny clatter as it disintegrated on stone flags some several hundred levels below.

Skalg checked himself. He breathed. *Donkey shit. Not only does another church burn, a fucking prick-rider thinks she can assassinate the First Cardinal of the Church of Hate... is there a poison in the mine water?*

Skalg realised he was on his knees. He gave a laugh like a dog bark. Damn. How did that happen? Skalg knelt before no dwarf, man, nor god.

Slowly, he grabbed the carved stone rail and hauled himself to his feet. He stood on tiptoe and peered over, expecting to see a vast blank canvas; or at the very best, a distant splatter of Kajella's broken corpse.

Instead, he looked down into the young dwarf's face.

She stared up at him, fingers flexing in agony, blood under her fingernails. She blinked rapidly, breath coming in short bursts, chest heaving.

Skalg sighed, and grinned, and leant both elbows on the stone balustrade. "Well well well," he said, smiling down at the distraught and desperate dwarf. "I thought you had fallen to your death; I thought your arms and legs had separated from your plump but very sexy little body."

"Please..." she gasped. "Please help."

"Didn't you just try to kill me? Didn't you put a bolt in Granda's belly? Look at poor Granda kneeling there. Wheezing and bleeding. How are you doing, Granda?"

"It hurts," he grunted.

"I'll see to you in a minute." He returned his gaze. "You see, sweet Kajella? You injured poor old loyal Granda. And that just won't do..."

"I'll... I'll be good. Anything you ask. Please. I don't want to die."

Skalg stared at her. Kajella's desperation was palpable. Here was a young dwarf who would happily perform his *every* whim. No matter how depraved.

"What do I get out of it?"

"I'll do *anything*, Cardinal Skalg. I promise. Absolutely *anything*. No more complaints. Just... don't let me fall..." She glanced down, and gave a little shriek of terror.

"Hmmmmm," he said. Then brightly, "You see? There are worse things than spending time in my bed."

"*Pleeeeease...*"

"If I'm honest, young Kajella, I'm not sure I can trust you any more."

"I will swear on my blood, on my honour, on my House."

Skalg stared down at the young dwarf. "You are very beautiful," he said.

"My father said I was blessed," she panted.

"Hmm. Yes. Yes of course. That was why you were picked." He considered, one finger on his lip.

"Yes, yes, yes," she said.

"But then, of course..."

"Yes?"

Skalg stared at her face. Large, beautiful eyes. Heavily lined with ochre. Fine square jaw. High cheekbones, like the Great Dwarf Lords themselves. Pretty. No. *Beautiful, classically beautiful*, like the princesses from the *Scriptures of the Church of Hate*.

Kajella yelped, and one hand came free. She was seconds from death.

Skalg smiled.

He reached over, reached down, and grabbed the hand which still held on. Blood had run from under broken fingernails, cracked and split from the pressure; now it ran down her fingers and dripped onto her breasts.

Skalg's throat was dry. *Blood. Breasts. Quim. Screams, long into the night. I will do anything. Anything, First Cardinal. Anything you can fucking imagine in your most depraved fucking heaving sweating dreams...*

He licked his lips. His eyes gleamed.

Skalg took Kajella's weight, and he held her over the abyss. His head lifted then, catching the scent of fire. His eyes narrowed. The church was burning furiously. Howls of wind drawn into the pumping furnace wailed from the city far below. Smoke billowed, making the whole of this underworld city seem... hazy.

She caught his gaze.

"Please," she mouthed. "You said I was one of the most beautiful young dwarves you had ever seen!"

Skalg nodded. And smiled. "However, I see *hundreds*

of the most beautiful young dwarves in the entire Five
Havens," he said. "You are nothing special, other than the
fact you tried to kill me."

He opened his fingers, and enjoyed the look of shock on
Kajella's face, as he watched her accelerate quickly into the
landscape.

Wearily, Skalg pushed back his shoulders. His hunched,
broken back gave a *crack* and he shuddered, but felt a little
random relief. He stared down, tilting his head slightly,
listening. Finally, there came a distant *thump*. There was no
scream. Skalg imagined her bloody, pulped carcass, and gave
a little shudder. "The Mountain gives, and the Mountain
takes away," he murmured.

Skalg turned, and ran a powerful hand over his face,
stroking his dark beard. He fixed his gaze on Granda,
who was lying on his side now in a pool of blood. He was
groaning softly. Skalg hobbled over to his Chief Educator,
and sat the man up from his sticky platter with a grunt.

"How do you feel?"

"Is the little bitch dead?"

"In separated pieces on the ground far below."

"Good."

"We'd better get you to the infirmary."

Granda nodded, face grey and lips quivering. Then he
grabbed Skalg's sleeve. Skalg looked down at the grip, eyes
narrowing at the lack of formality; but he managed to stay
his words at the impropriety.

"There's something else," Granda managed, through his
pain.

"Yes?"

"My Educators. They caught one."

"Caught who?"

"One of the fire starters," said Granda, blood speckling his frothing lips.

With Granda transported to the Hospital of the Sacred Church, Cardinal Skalg, in full church robes, escorted by twenty of his most trusted Educators, powerful men and women armed with spike-headed maces, clubs (known in the business as Peace Makers), and crossbows painted in church colours, smart of dress, stern of face, descended on the still burning church. This particular treasure was a two thousand year-old edifice on Red Stone Street, and as Skalg led the formation of Educators, their eyes lifted to see the still raging inferno now at the heart of the church, as if some great dragon had broken into the core and was burning the religious building from the inside out.

Skalg stopped. His Educators halted also, boots stamping. They were in a perfect inverted V formation; almost military in its structure, precision and synchronicity. Skalg looked up, and tears ran down his cheeks.

"How *dare they*?" he murmured.

A dwarf came running forward. He was soot-blackened, boots caked in slurry, fire protector uniform torn, soot-stained, the polished gold buttons tarnished. "Cardinal Skalg!" He saluted.

"Give me your report."

"We have the fire under control, Cardinal. Now as you know, a church doesn't burn easy. This act of arson was very well executed by people who know their art. As far as we can ascertain, the culprits covered the lower storey windows with fire blankets to allow the fire time to take hold without discovery. They set barrels of tar at every single timber support strut, and ignited them simultaneously. That is why," he turned, glancing up at the destroyed church where thick plumes of black smoke poured from the ruined tower, "their fire has caused so much damage."

Skalg's eyes were hooded. He sniffed. "The Scriptures?"

"Rescued by the bravery of my fire protectors," said the dwarf, swelling with pride. "Our first act, as instructed, was to breach the fire-damaged structure and rescue that which the Great Dwarf Lords gave with such generosity; the Sacred Chest is now under the guard of church wardens. We only lost eight dwarfs recovering the chest, with another twelve seriously burned and on their way to the infirmary now."

"Good, good," said Skalg. "The church will look after them and their families for their sacrifice." Skalg's eyes narrowed slightly. "I was told one of the, ah, culprits, was captured?" The gentility of his voice should have been a warning. Skalg was so far beyond anger he had entered a new realm of emotion.

"Yes, he is under close guard by church wardens until the Educators arrive; it took six of them with clubs to pacify him. He has been taken to the closest firehouse."

Skalg nodded, and walked forward towards the great arched doors – or the charred, blackened remains of what *had been* incredibly rich and decorated arched doors. His boots crunched on shattered glass shards, on chunks of charred charcoal, and he kicked something, a blackened coin of church gold, which rolled away and chimed as it performed a sad, lonely series of jumps down five stone steps before rolling in a circle and singing itself to a halt.

Skalg glanced at the two lead Educators, a great hulking dwarf called Blagger, and a slender female with a scarred face and one eye, notorious for her ferocity and lack of mercy. Her nickname was Razor, a nickname which had stuck, and not for pleasant reasons.

"Blagger, Razor, come with me. The rest of you, I want house-to-house searches. I want more information about who committed this sacrilege; you are allowed to use maximum persuasion." His eyes swept out over the dark city. Flames flickered in fire-bowls and curve-burners, and the cobbled streets were damp. He looked up, at the towers and the arched bridges high above, glowing softly like gold, and he felt completely part of this damp mountain underworld. He felt like he was part of the rock; part of the mountain's soul; an integral cog in the machine, in the engine that powered the dwarves and their society.

"Yes, First Cardinal!"

"We will get to the bottom of this," he said, turning, purple and black robes sweeping behind him as he marched, somewhat crookedly, down the damp stone street with Blagger and Razor in close proximity behind.

Skalg halted before the huge doors of the firehouse. He adjusted his robes, and reaching out, pounded a complex rhythm of knocks. Fires burned in iron brackets to either side of the great studded door.

Behind, Blagger rolled his huge head on thick neck muscles, and there were a series of cracks. He glanced at Razor, and she was stood, cool, relaxed, and almost nonchalant. Her face was expressionless, her one good eye impassive, her milky, ruined eye like a glass bauble in a dead doll.

Razor looked at him, a quick movement, like an insect. She caught his stare and grinned, showing blackened teeth. Blagger looked away, looked back at the door and the patiently waiting twisted figure of Skalg, feeling himself redden a little. Razor wasn't somebody you wanted to upset, and she'd made it plain, on many occasions, often backed up by violence, that she didn't like to be looked at. She'd slit throats with her "razor knife" for much less.

Skalg glanced back at the two Educators, but his face was unreadable. Blagger gave a single nod, as if to say, *we're here, Cardinal Skalg, we have your back.* Razor offered no such securities, simply stared ahead, face impassive.

"When we go in," he said, words so soft they were barely audible, "you follow my instructions, instantly, and to the letter. Do you understand?"

"Yes, Cardinal," rumbled Blagger.

Razor gave a curt nod. A simple acquiescence.

Skalg felt himself being inspected through the spy hole, and slowly, the door creaked open. Three wardens stood with crossbows levelled, and Skalg gave a nod, then hobbled inside. The Educators followed, and the church wardens backed away a step, licking dry lips, fingers suddenly slippery on crossbow stocks. To be a church warden was to have an unprecedented level of power throughout the Five Havens, but to be an Educator was something else.

"Who's in charge here?" snapped Skalg, as the heavy door boomed shut.

A portly dwarf in smart uniform stepped forward. His buttons were polished gold. His boots gleamed. A long moustache had been waxed to perfection, and despite his age, he had a military bearing and utmost seriousness.

"Cardinal Skalg. Thank the Great Dwarf Lords you have arrived! I am Fire Sergeant Takos."

"You have a prisoner for me?"

"We do. He is causing us some concern."

"Why is this?" Skalg's eyes were iron.

"He has threatened that all of us, and all our families, will be exterminated within the next twenty-four hours. He is a frightening individual to behold!"

Skalg nodded. "Take me to him."

Takos led the way down a complex set of corridors, all gleaming with military cleanliness. Everything was sterile and white. Even the polished stone floors gleamed.

Skalg limped on, his hunched back aching like the devil, and sending secondary pains down his spine, and bizarrely, into his balls. That's when he knew he'd seriously overdone it. Pain in the bollocks. And he knew it would last until he smoked gangga, sucked on crushed malwort, and had twelve hours sleep. He rubbed at red-rimmed eyes and for a fleeting moment pictured Kajella disappearing from the high balcony of the Blood Tower, broad, beautiful dwarf face gone in a flash.

"Damn."

He paused, flat hand against the cool wall, panting. Blagger stepped forward, and almost, *almost*, touched Skalg. "Are you well, Cardinal?"

"Apparently not," snapped Skalg, and regretted his anger. He took several deep breaths. Fire Sergeant Takos had also halted, turned, and had his fingers steepled before him, waiting. There was a nervous sweat on his broad brow. "Give me a minute."

Skalg took several deep breaths and waited for the pain to fade. He pictured Kajella's face again. Imagined the howling grief puked from her mother. Skalg snarled at himself, and a drool of saliva fell from his mouth, and removed an ounce of dignity from his black and purple robes.

So they see me as a dwarf suffering real and terrible pain?
Fuck them. They will see an echo of reality, then.

I might have been blessed by the Great Dwarf Lords, but I was cursed, also, by the Mountain. Cursed, I tell you.

Regaining his composure, he signalled distractedly for Takos to continue. The Fire Sergeant did so, looking back every few seconds to check he wasn't in some way inconveniencing or embarrassing the First Cardinal. Because that was a very dangerous thing to do. Skalg's evil reputation preceded him by a thousand leagues.

They moved down more white corridors.

Eventually, they arrived at a door. There were two more pale-faced church wardens with mounted crossbows, safety triggers off.

"Point them the other fucking way," snarled Skalg, tiny flashes of pain almost blinding him. The wardens obeyed immediately, terror etched into every crease of their faces, fear a live worm wriggling inside their brains.

"Cardinal Skalg, the prisoner is in there."

"What am I dealing with?"

"A man, heavy build, singing and screaming religious doctrine." He saw the look in Skalg's eyes. "Although no religion I've ever heard of," he added quickly. "He is, I fear, insane."

"Does he have a name?"

"None we could beat out of him."

"We shall see," said Skalg. He half turned. "Razor? Blagger? Ready?"

"Yes, First Cardinal."

The wardens pushed open the door, to reveal a fire wardens' locker room. It had tiled floors and walls, white and sterile. Against one wall there were wooden shelves for uniforms and equipment. In lines across the ground were thick wooden benches. Two had been pushed together, and on these, lying on his back, was a heavy built dwarf with thick black beard and shaggy hair. He had grey eyes, like steel, and clenched teeth, and was straining at his tightly tied rope bonds.

Nobody who has succumbed to the throes of insanity attempts to escape, thought Skalg.

He moved forward, kicking a boot out of the way which skittered across the tiles. The man strained forward, looking at these new actors on the stage. He snarled a stream of obscenities in *old tongue* and Skalg smiled.

"Razor. Put out one eye."

"Yes, Cardinal Skalg."

In a fluid movement, and to the shock of all present, she strode forward, unclipping a sheath on her hip. A shining silver blade reared in the air; it was curved slightly, and etched with fine runes. Razor reached the prisoner, and cut down, a diagonal slash, *so*. The fine steel cut a grove across the prisoner's eyebrow, popped the orb with a spurt of vitreous humour, and carried on down the cheek. The man went rigid in shock, suddenly screamed, and continued to thrash and strain at his bonds.

The church wardens stood uneasily, shifting from one boot to the other. Fire Sergeant Takos stood, stunned, as blood pitter-pattered to the clean white tiles of this makeshift holding cell.

"I…" he said.

"Yes?" Skalg turned.

"King Irlax…"

"I operate on an equal footing to the king; for the church, under the rule of the Great Dwarf Lords, *was given equal power and authority*."

"But I—"

"Yes?"

And Skalg knew what the good, honest, proud, noble Fire Sergeant wanted to say. He wanted to say, *But King Irlax has made it be known there is to be no torture, no punishment without trial, no unfair treatment of prisoners until every shred of evidence has been investigated.* And Skalg grinned, because he lived in the real world, operated in the dark underworld, where criminals didn't play by the rules so why the fuck should the Church of Hate? He wanted to *educate* Fire Sergeant Takos, and explain that the Church of Hate had been created *by* the Great Dwarf Lords as a secret weapon, an underground cadre, an organisation formed to root out the evil which threatened the Five Havens. Hence equal power. Equal authority. One could not go against the other, for both were at the opposite ends of the same scale.

"Be quiet, and know your place," said Skalg. He moved forward, and knelt by the prisoner. Very quietly, he said, "Tell me what you know."

"I would rather die!"

"That can be arranged. However, would you rather be tortured?"

"Torture is illegal in the Five Havens!"

"And so it is, as all good citizens believe."

The man turned his carved-up face towards Skalg. Muscles were twitching, and tears had formed in the good eye which remained. "You cannot do this to me! I am a legal resident of Zvolga. I pay my taxes. I have a job, a family..."

"And yet you were part of the unit which torched the church on Red Stone Street."

"No!"

"Yes!"

"You will have to prove it."

Skalg rocked back on his heels, and stepped away. He turned his back on the prisoner. Then he glanced sideways, and gestured for the wardens to remove the Fire Sergeant – who complained as he was manhandled out – but not too much. Skalg had that kind of effect on people.

"Blagger?"

"Cardinal?"

"Castrate him."

"Really?"

"Do I have to say it a second fucking time?"

Blagger frowned. "Er. No, Cardinal."

"What?" screamed the prisoner. "You can't do this! I demand to see the Head of the City Watch! I demand my rights! I demand an audience with King Irlax, you… you fucking heathen bastards, look what you've done to me," he wept. "I cannot believe this is happening…"

"Razor?"

"Cardinal?"

"I'm sick of his noise. Gag him."

"Yes, Cardinal."

It was later. Much later. The prisoner lay, limp, eyeless, his stomach carved open, several fingers and toes lying forlorn on the floor like lonely, discarded toys.

News had arrived. The fire had finally been extinguished.

It was morning.

Good dwarves were on their way to work in the mines, in the merchant houses, in the guild houses.

Blagger sat in the corner, face grey.

Razor sat on a bench, slowly sharpening her curved, razor-sharp blade.

"So what have we learned?" said Skalg, half looking at

the limp, tortured corpse on the bench.

Razor shrugged. "He wasn't part of the Army of Purity."

"Or he was very good at keeping secrets."

"No man could have gone through that," rumbled Blagger from his corner. His normally brutal eyes looked just that little bit haunted.

Skalg breathed out deeply, and got to his feet. His head was pounding, and his bed was calling.

"We should call this a night."

"Morning," said Razor.

Skalg shrugged, an odd and exaggerated movement with his hunched back.

"We are no further forward towards finding out who did this," said Blagger.

"Yes," said Skalg.

"If this man *was* innocent..." he began, then saw Skalg's look, and stuttered into silence.

"He was a well-trained arsonist working for the Army of Purity," said Skalg, face grim. "You both heard him confess."

"Yes," nodded Razor.

"His family will also be put to death," said Blagger.

Razor stared at him.

"Yes," said Blagger.

"There's another loose end."

"There is?"

Skalg looked sideways at Razor, as if to say, *where the fuck did you find this one?*

"We'll take care of it," said Razor, and moved to Blagger, helping the huge Educator to his feet. "Come on. We need to give Fire Sergeant Takos a ride home."

"A ride... oh, I see."

The Educators moved out of the room, and Razor closed

the door with a heavy click. Skalg moved to the eyeless corpse, and lifted the head by its blood-drenched hair. He stared into the mangled, bloody, eyeless sockets, and said, "We'll find you, you bastards. We'll find you and fucking destroy you. See if we don't." He let the head fall with a sodden thump, and limped, almost crab-like, from the blood-stained room now so reminiscent of a cattle slaughterhouse.

Making Friends

Beetrax stood with fists on hips, breathing the chilled morning air, having enjoyed a full fried breakfast of pig slices, five eggs, black pudding and mushrooms, with huge chunks of toasted black bread smothered in fresh butter and damn near a gallon of over-sweet tea. He belched, and rolled his neck, and scratched his bushy ginger beard.

"Ach, life feels good!"

He beamed at the frosty clear sky, then ambled over to the stables, patting his overlarge belly, and gave a nod to the stable boy. A few minutes later his boots were planted on the gravel, as he fitted a brush over his hand, and started to groom Bella, his grey mare, with long, sweeping strokes. She whinnied, head coming round to nuzzle Beetrax, and with his free hand he patted her velvet snout. "There there, good girl. You know who looks after you, eh lass?"

"They say when a man talks to his horse, he has truly gone mad."

"I went mad a long time ago, brother."

Beetrax turned and smiled at Dake, who stood in the entrance of The Fighting Cocks, wearing baggy trews, a ruffled white shirt, with braces hanging down by his sides. His cavalry boots were scuffed and face full of dark stubble.

He held a tin mug of tea, from which steam slowly rose, and he took a sip and touched his forehead gently with the splayed fingers of his left hand.

"Gods, how much did I drink?"

"Enough to drop a Shire horse."

"That's why I feel like this!"

Beetrax brushed Bella. The mare gave a gentle whinny. "You have a good night, Dake?" He gave a leering grin, and Dake shook his head. "You know, after you left us, and went to bed, like?"

"Yeah, I had a good night. What about you?"

"I woke up on a bench with a full flagon of ale balanced on my chest. Damn, but I hurt my shoulder. Must've slept funny."

"You left a full flagon? That's not like you, Beetrax. Must be getting old."

"No worries. I drank it right down for breakfast. Lined my stomach for the pig slices and eggs." He belched again, as if to emphasise just *how much* he had enjoyed the fine breakfast dining at The Fighting Cocks.

"I can't believe you ate breakfast." Dake looked ill, tinged with green.

"Ha! It's the only way to mop up the ale."

Beetrax stopped his brushing and took a step back, admiring his handiwork. Then he studied his fingers for a few moments, before looking up at Dake, then glancing away. "Look, Dake. About last night…"

"Don't worry. We're still coming with you. One week from now."

"Yes yes," he waved a paw, "I know that. I just wanted to say, you know, sorry, like, about what we was talking about."

"I don't want to talk about it."

"None of us had any idea."

"I *really* don't want to talk about it."

"Yes. Yes. Sure. It's only–"

"Beetrax!"

Beetrax looked at his friend.

"Yes, Dake?"

"This is why we never told anybody. It's not a topic for discussion. And every time you mention it, you make the pain feel that little bit more real. So please – just treat me and Jonti like normal. We'd appreciate it."

Beetrax strode forward, and grabbed Dake in a hug, spilling hot tea down both their shirts. Through his beard, he mumbled, "It's just, I love you both, and I want you to know I'd die for you both."

Crushed by the huge axeman, Dake wriggled. "Yes, thank you, I already know it. Now please get off me, you stink of ale, eggs and black pudding! And sweat. And... *horses*? Gods, Beetrax, do you *ever* bathe?"

"Got one lined up! Er. In a few days."

"I advise sooner, rather than later," smiled Dake kindly, stepping backwards.

There came a sound from the tavern, and small man stepped out pulling on a heavy overcoat. He had short hair, spiked irregularly, a narrow, angular face and sharp dark eyes. He was modest of stature, but moved with a purpose and poise that showed he could handle himself. His eyes cast over the large axeman, and settled on Dake. He gave a narrow smile.

"Well met, Dake."

"And you, Weasel. Are you keeping well?"

"As well as any man can," he said, and buttoned up the

heavy coat. Again, his eyes roved over Beetrax, eyeing up his massive physique, brutal flat face and military tattoos.

"Friend of yours?" said Weasel, with a casual air that wasn't.

"I certainly am," rumbled Beetrax, "and if you don't stop talking about me like I ain't here, I'll come over give you a good shake, just to show you I'm real, like."

"A bristly one as well, eh Dake?"

"Right," snapped Beetrax.

"Whoa, big fella," said Dake, moving in front of Beetrax and placing a restraining hand on the axeman's huge bicep. "Weasel here helps run the fighting pits; he's always on the lookout for new talent, isn't that so, Weasel?"

"I certainly am." He smiled, but it was a smile with little humour. "If you can fight, a big man like you could make some real money in the pits."

"But not as much as you, eh Weasel?" Beetrax grinned like a corpse. "Listen. I done my time in the pits before you was a nipper. Now, I am a man of independent means, and don't need to crack skulls to prove anything."

"A shame," said Weasel, with that same narrow smile. "You fought under Tanker Kal?"

"I did."

"So you'd know Dek, then?"

"Aye, I know Dek. We had a couple of disagreements, me and that cantankerous bastard. He's the one knocked one of these teeth out."

Weasel looked impressed.

Dake coughed. "I seem to recall it was late one night, after considerable wine, and you said his wife had the face of a horse's bollock sack?"

"No, no," Beetrax held up his hand, shaking his head.

"She wasn't his wife."

"Well you did well then, sir."

"Well?"

"To still be walking. He broke a man's spine last week."

Dake winced. Beetrax's eyes showed no emotion. "'Tis the risk you take when you fight in the pits. But then, Dek did well to walk away from me." He smiled.

"He did? How so?"

"He didn't win."

"You sure, lad?"

Beetrax grinned, and continued to groom Bella. "We fought each other to a standstill. Three times we went back into that mud-slippery shit-hole, after the bruises had gone down, after the bones had mended; each time we fought each other to exhaustion and neither of us could beat the other."

Weasel cocked his head. "Ah. *That* Beetrax. *Trax*. I remember your name, now. I heard the tales."

"No tales, little fella."

Weasel gave a long, sly grin. "Less of the 'little fella', if you don't mind. In these parts I'm a respectable businessman. Last man to call me a 'little fella' got a blade between the ribs."

Beetrax shrugged, and turned his back on Weasel. He continued to groom Bella, presenting his broad back as if to say, *there you go, little fella, stab away as much as you like.*

Weasel pulled on a pair of gloves, and gave a shiver against the cold. "Not very friendly, is he?"

"He grows on you," said Dake, smiling.

"Well, tell him if he changes his mind I can be found here, usually on a Sunday afternoon."

"I'll do that."

"Oh yes. Dake. A word of advice for an old friend. A couple of merchants came in yesterday. All cut up. Said there's a new batch of bandits on the road north out of Drakerath. Just if you was travelling in that direction. Yoon is supposed to keep the roads free, but with more recent cuts to the army…"

"Thanks for the warning, Weasel. We're heading northeast."

"You got business in Rokroth?"

"No, we'll be heading up towards Skell Forest."

"You becoming a woodcutter, my friend?"

Dake grinned. "It's a long story."

Weasel gave a short wave, and disappeared from the courtyard, down the cobbled street. There was some life outside on this bitterly cold morning, the clatter of iron-bound wheels, some chatter; but the city seemed sluggish in coming to life, as if a shroud of weariness had dropped over its ancient stones.

Beetrax moved back to Dake, scratching at his chest. "What did he say?"

"Bandits, on the north road."

"Ach, horse bollocks. They won't be no trouble for the likes of us."

"I'm sure the City Watch will have sorted it out before we pass anywhere near." Beetrax was staring at him. "What?"

"Have you had any breakfast yet? Come on, I'm going back inside. I'll buy you a feed fit for a king!"

Dake looked aghast. "Beetrax, you've *already* eaten."

The big man loomed close. "I'm a growing lad, ain't I?"

For Beetrax, the next few days were spent gathering together weapons, provisions, and checking the packing of his saddlebags. Beetrax wanted to travel light, and yet knew they had a substantial journey and therefore had to take a goodly amount of provisions. The roads north of Skell Forest *were* used for some small amount of trade, but eventually the villages ran out and various treacherous mountain passes had to be traversed. Due to the hostility of the terrain, few travelled north towards the Karamakkos Peaks; there was no reason other than insanity.

Beetrax, however, had been there before. He knew it was tough, but it was doable. And he had a secret weapon. He *knew* about the bridges – the Ice Bridges of Sakaroth – and how to reach the long deserted underground ruins of the Five Havens. That was the irony; the Five Havens were only accessible during the winter months, the very time most would decide against battling the mighty Teeth of the World. In the summer months, the Grey Chasm was impassable. Utterly and totally.

As the following weekend approached, Beetrax was getting worried. He sat in The Fighting Cocks growing more and more nervous; and the more nervous he became, the more he drank. And the more he drank, the more chance of a fight and injury that would halt his little adventure in its tracks.

They might not come.

Of course they'll come!

Dake and Jonti, for sure. Talon, yes. But Lillith and Sakora? You're not exactly their favourite bearded axeman of the year...

Beetrax sat in a corner, nursing his ale and fretting. This made him angry, because he wasn't the sort of rough-and-tumble headcracker who fretted about nothing; and yet here he was, mumbling to himself like a teenage virgin at the first sight of ready moist quim.

Damn, what's wrong with you, Axeman?

Shut up. It'll be all right! They'll come! Trust in your friends.

I trust in no man, woman or god. They might not turn up!

Damn…

"You staring at us?"

Beetrax blinked, and looked up. The young man was clearly the worse for wear, swaying and holding a flagon of ale, most of which appeared in an inverted V down his tunic. It was the material of the tunic which made Beetrax narrow his eyes. Vagan silk, edged with silver thread. A noble's tunic. Ah, but damn. Beetrax took in the pockmarked face, the neatly trimmed hair – not done with a freshly sharpened short sword, like Beetrax's own shaggy mop, but with a *proper* razor – and small goatee beard which sheared neatly into curved sideboards.

Gods, that sort of facial sculpting, that kind of narcissistic blade-work, it must take him ages! What's the point, eh lad? When you have a face like it's been trampled by a diarrheic donkey?

Beetrax smiled, shook his head in the negative. "What, little old me? No, friend, I'm simply sitting here minding my own fine business, like. Thanks for calling over to say hello, though. I appreciate your attempt at brotherhood." He beamed, and waited.

"My lady friend, Jallenta, she reckons you were staring at her." He gestured vaguely behind himself with his flagon, to where a woman who had the extruded face of a horse, was lying across a table, head resting on one arm, snoring. She, also, wore a fine embroidered dress of red and purple. Beetrax's eyes dropped to her boots. Fine soft leather. No scuffs. No mud.

Beetrax took a deep breath, eyes searching for the landlord. But The Fighting Cocks was filling up fast and he was lost somewhere in the throng at the bar. *By the Seven Sisters, how do I manage to attract trouble all the time? Eh? Why does it come looking for me like a bull after a flapping, slack-jawed idiot?*

"Look, friend, turn around and go away. I don't want no trouble."

"She said you were staring at her bosom." The man bared his teeth, in what Beetrax thought was a snarl.

"Right. For a start, I can't even see her tits from here. And if her face is anything to go by, I'd be more after grooming her horse mane than trying to fumble with her nipples. But that's by the by, *friend.* You need to turn around and *fuck off* before I break your stupid nose. Then your jaw. Maybe a few fucking teeth."

Beetrax stood, suddenly, and loomed over the well-groomed youth. The man looked up, swaying a little, and Beetrax was annoyed that his sheer size didn't make the little scamp run for his mother's milk tits.

The man wagged his finger, and belched. "My name is Daron. I'll be back." He turned and slid into the crowd.

"Right," mumbled Beetrax. "Time for a swift exit." He downed his flagon, belched, rolled his neck and pushed his way through the throng.

This was the end of the working week for most, and the Cocks was full of mostly labourers, smiths, hard-working men ready for a few ales after a week of breaking their backs. They were boisterous but mostly friendly; Beetrax's sort of men.

He passed the table with the snoring woman wearing fine boots, and then made for the stairs. They had a long journey ahead of them on the morrow, last thing Beetrax needed was a belly full of ale, broken knuckles and three nights in the city cells. He passed the bar, shouldering a couple of rough-looking men out of the way with a muttered apology, down a narrow corridor, then right to the stairs leading up to the accommodation on the floor above. He started up, wincing a little as his knee and hip twinged with pain, legacy of an old injury, a fall from a cantankerous stallion during a cavalry charge, way back, years ago, nothing more than a hazy dream from older, better days.

Five stairs. Eight. Halfway. A voice from above.

"Where are you going, old man?"

Beetrax cursed, glancing up. It was Daron, with his silk tunic and trampled face. He seemed a little more sober, and this was odd. What was *not* odd was the short dark blade in his fist.

"Listen son, I did nothing wrong," said Beetrax, turning at the sound from the bottom of the rough-sawn stairs. Two broad-shouldered men. Both carrying blades.

Beetrax gave a narrow, bloodless smile.

"I beg to differ, you unwashed, common scum," said Daron, advancing slowly down the steps. Behind Beetrax, the two large soldier-types began to climb. Beetrax weighed up his options, sighed, and charged up at Daron.

The charge was a surprise, and the blade came up as Beetrax batted it aside with his left forearm, grabbed Daron's bollocks in a meaty grip with his right, and delivered a bone-crunching headbutt that broke the young man's nose.

Beetrax stared at the squealing face beneath him, blood-drenched, jaw working sporadically as Beetrax's iron grip crushed his testicles, and images flickered and flashed into the axeman's brain, older days, darker days, on the walls at Desekra, slamming his axe into a mud-orc's face, watching brains splatter over the battlements, watching his friends squirming in their own blood and sloppy puddles of disembowelment. And then it was gone in a flash of relief and Beetrax cannoned back to the present.

His left hand grabbed the man's windpipe, and by throat and balls, he picked him up and hurled him down the narrow stairwell. A tossed ragdoll, Daron cannoned into his companions and all three went tumbling down the hard wood steps. Beetrax fancied he heard some bones break. He charged down after the flailing limbs, jumping from the mid-point, not caring where his boots landed, or whom he crushed. His boots thudded home, one against a skull, another against ribs, and then he was on his knees punching all three men in a squirming mass of limbs and bodies and faces. A knife flashed past his face, but he nudged back, the steel carving past his eyes. He grabbed the arm and broke it with a crunch. More punches, and then suddenly everything was still in the dimly lit corridor.

Mumbling and groaning, Beetrax grabbed one man by the legs and dragged him along the corridor, backkicking the door open and pulling the man onto the icy cobbles. The cold hit Beetrax, and he shivered, but now he had a clear mission before him. If anybody called the City Watch, there'd be questions, and arrests, and pointless wasted time. Beetrax didn't have time nor inclination for none of that.

Methodically, he dragged all three men out onto the cobbles and they lay, unconscious, like three cadavers. Beetrax checked they were all breathing, which they were, and that was a good thing. Beetrax killed men too easy these days, and it was a struggle to restrain himself when the blood was up and boiling, and the anger and bad memories flowing.

Beetrax breathed softly, and calmed himself, and looked

around. Lit by the moon, the courtyard was eerie, spectral. He noticed a couple of leaning sheds behind the stables, and dragged Daron over to them, kicking down a door and peering into the inky blackness. It seemed to contain some huge, rusted machine, with several large cogs and wheels. Grunting, Beetrax pulled Daron inside, then went back to the other two men, pulling them inside also.

A short trip to the stables and one length of old rope later, Beetrax bound the men by ankles and wrists, then tied all three to a huge old cog as big as he was, like some disused component from a dismantled water wheel.

He stood, admiring his knots.

Daron began to stir, and slowly his eyes flickered open, white and wide and frightened by the light of the moon spilling through the shed door.

"What have you done, you monster?" His words were distorted by his broken nose and, no doubt, several broken teeth.

"Er, me?" Beetrax cracked his knuckles and moved forward, kneeling behind the stricken man. "What have *I* fucking done? I was minding my own business, as it always is. And you were out to impress your horse-faced woman, so you tried to pick a fight with me, and then brought in your heavies to back you up when things weren't going your way. Spoilt little rich prick, you should have stayed up in the hills."

"They… they weren't my heavies…"

"What were they, then? Your fucking sisters? Or just *fucking* your sisters?"

"They were my bodyguards…"

Beetrax frowned. That didn't sound good. That didn't sound good *at all*. "Why would a little squirt of horse spunk like you need bodyguards?"

"Because I am Lord Daron. *Lord* Daron. Great nephew to King Yoon of Vagandrak!"

Beetrax considered this for a while, then rocked back on his heels. "Hmm," he said, his eyes fixed on the broken men before him.

"You must let me go immediately, you vagabond! Yoon will see you swing high for this!"

"Vagabond, is it?" Beetrax crawled close, so that his mouth was only a thumb's breadth from Daron's own, as if they were lovers about to kiss. "You came to me looking for a fight, great nephew of King Yoon, and I fucking gave you one, so I did. The question you need to ask yourself now, is this: you're so busy threatening me with a hanging, you are not focussing on your immediate situation. What motivation have I got to keep you alive? If I cut all your throats, you can't sing to the City Watch. But if you give me your word, on your mother's deathbed, that you will remain silent – I may just leave you tied up awhile. It's your choice, *Lord* Daron. Shall I go get my axe, or no?"

Daron was trembling, and foam speckled his lips. His eyes were wide as pig-roast platters. He seemed to consider his options, although Beetrax wondered what he really had to consider.

Eventually, the man breathed, "I'll keep my mouth shut."

"Good lad!" boomed Beetrax, rocking back on his heels and standing. He wiggled his feet. "Damn but that gave me some cramp. Now listen, lad, I'll leave you three here tonight, then let you go in the morning. No hollering, like. My room's just up there," he pointed, "and I'll hear you. Be here quicker than you can say 'axe blade decapitation'. You got that, little Lord Daron?"

"Yes," he whispered.

"And one last thing."

"Yes?" Eyes suddenly hopeful.

"I don't like being attacked with blades," said Beetrax, without a glimmer of compassion, and kicked Daron in the face, watching him slump down once more into bloody unconsciousness.

Beetrax slept well. Probably down to the extra eight flagons of ale he drank after tying up his attackers. *Well, it was thirsty work, wasn't it? All that violence?*

As a late winter dawn broke through the cracks in the shutters, Beetrax rolled from his crumpled sheets and pulled on his trews and boots. Then he sat there for a moment. Some fleeting idea teased him, something which had seemed so solid in sleep, and yet now danced away like dragon smoke. What *was* it? Something about threads. String. No, *loose ends*. But... *what* loose end?

Beetrax shrugged, and heard the stamping of hooves in the courtyard. He threw open his shutters and beamed down at Dake and Jonti. "Glad you could join me!" he boomed, voice practically cracking the ice on the puddles.

"You're late," snapped Dake. "You'd be late to your own bloody funeral."

"It's just a matter of a few moments. I am packed and ready to go. Any word from the others?"

"Lillith is on her way. We've not seen or spoken to Sakora or Talon since last we met."

Beetrax nodded, dressed, grabbed his pack, and pounded down the stairs. He settled his bill with the landlord, and took a fond look around The Fighting Cocks. It had been a home to him these past few years; a place to drink, eat, party, brawl, a home from home (and indeed, mostly his home, as his home was a humourless cold place run by servants with whom he had no affinity; he found it easier to "slum it" at the Cocks after a hard night of drinking; ironically, he decided, some people should really not be blessed with riches because all they did was squander their good fortune).

Stepping out into the cold air, he gave a wary glance to the shed. The shed where he'd locked, well, damn him, the great nephew of King Yoon, King of Vagandrak. Beetrax gave a nervous grin. *But shit, I didn't see that one coming!*

The stable boy brought out his horse, Bella, and she nuzzled Beetrax's bruised knuckles. Dropping from his own mount, Dake nodded to his fists. "Trouble?"

"No. No trouble. Too much ale. I fell."

"Yeah, and horses can walk on water."

Jonti turned in her saddle, and pointed. "Lillith is here."

A small, grey mare cantered into the courtyard, and Lillith, dressed in white skirts and a thick white fur, dropped from her own mount. She cast a quick glance over the gathered group. "So, I see we are still about this madness, then?"

"You turned up," pointed out Beetrax.

"I am simply thinking of the greater good to the world of medicine." Her dark eyes fixed on Beetrax. "You are well, Axeman?"

He caught her scent, and his lips were suddenly dry. "I am, Lady," he said.

"Ha! I am nobody's Lady. Now, I have herbs and powders with great healing properties. I have my diary, a quill, and enough ink to compose a thousand pages of letters. The Head Librarian from the Great Library has given me his blessing, and unlimited resources for tracking down ancient texts…"

"You told him where we were going?" said Beetrax, aghast.

"Of course! He is an old and trusted friend."

"It was supposed to be a secret adventure," snapped Beetrax.

"If I know you, every whore within a two league radius knows of our plans! Anyway. Do we know when Talon and Sakora will arrive?"

Jonti pointed, to where a clatter of almost panicked hooves were striking sparks from the cobbles. Around a bend came Talon, pushing his horse hard and screaming for people to clear a path from the middle of the frozen road.

"He… looks in a hurry," observed Dake, exchanging a glance with his wife.

"I wonder what he's been up to?" said Beetrax, feeling a trickle of apprehension worming between his shoulder blades.

"*I* wonder if he's opened the eyes of yet *another* young sexually innocent noble…"

Talon slammed through the gates to The Fighting Cocks' courtyard, and leapt from his lathered mount. Talon was flustered, seemingly out of breath. He whirled, and stared hard at Beetrax.

"*What have you done?*" he gasped.

"Er. Me?" said Beetrax, eyes wide, all innocent.

"King Yoon's *great fucking nephew* is missing, along with two of his bodyguards. His girlfriend, Lady Arsehole something-or-other was drunk in a tavern – she does not remember which – but she does remember a huge man with bushy ginger hair, bushy ginger beard, and military tattoos on his neck and hands and probably his arse… Beetrax? *What* did you do?"

"What? WHAT? Why are you all looking at me? I didn't do nothing."

"Beetrax?" said Lillith, in the tone that always made him blab.

"Well," he preened, "I don't see how they could pin anything on me, like. Those spoilt bastards came to me – to me! – looking for a fight. How was I to know it was Yoon's bloody nephew, eh? And that girl was practically unconscious. How could she circulate my description? She was fucking asleep!"

"Well she did," snarled Talon, face filled with fury. "And *your* description, *your very specific* description is being circulated right now. Sakora has gone ahead to check out the gates, but we need to get out of the city real soon before it's crawling with Watch."

Beetrax mumbled something, and Dake slapped him on the back. "Never a dull moment with you, you mad ginger bastard."

"Yes. Yes, I seem to bring trouble to me like flies…"

"…to horse shit," Lillith completed, lips narrowed. She watched Beetrax move to his horse and prepare to mount. "Well? What did you do with them? I trust you didn't *murder them*?"

"Of course not!" scowled Beetrax. He nodded to the shed. "Tied them up in there, didn't I? I ain't letting them out, though. Brought me enough trouble, they did."

Jonti strode to the shed door and threw it open, revealing three bruised, battered, broken men squinting at the bright daylight. Her sword hissed from its sheath and cut through their bonds. She turned back to Beetrax.

"Better mount up. I think we need to ride."

Secret Weapon

King Yoon reclined on a vast bed of silk sheets, his long, shaggy black curls oiled and lank, his smooth, pale skin glistening. His face was painted white, his lips red; the stench of his perfume hung heavy in the air, like rancid fish oil, and his nails were painted with intricate detail, scenes of great battles and historic moments, whilst on each finger he wore a gem of considerable wealth, each finger sporting a different coloured stone. He wore a gauze lavender scarf around his throat, but that was all, and with eyes closed, he lifted both hands in the air as if conducting an orchestra as the generously proportioned whore, dressed in nothing but strips of stitched leather, took his cock in her mouth and began to delicately, enthusiastically and skilfully ply her trade.

"Oh yes," said King Yoon, tongue flickering between painted lips. "That's good. That's excellent, in fact, my dear. You certainly know your cock. We are most impressed. Indeed! We are most totally delighted!"

Also on the bed were three naked ladies and two young men. The men, lesser nobles of Vagandrak, wore staggeringly different facial expressions. One was enjoying this scene of fellatio with open admiration, his own hand moving to his genitals where he began to cup and squeeze, working himself quickly into a frenzy. The other, with close-cropped black hair and a goatee beard, wore a shocked mask, as if he was stranded on a beach, trapped between the incoming tide and a vast wall of treacherous cliff. He didn't quite know which way to turn or where to look, and he did *indeed* look stunned, shocked, unable to get comfortable. He looked like a man who wondered how the hell he had arrived, naked and unwilling, in the king's bedchamber – for what looked like an impending evening of considerable orgy.

The three naked ladies were all experienced. From their hard eyes and professional, made-up faces, to their perfectly toned bodies and strategically placed clothing of lace and leather. They watched with the same kind of idle languor normally reserved for the honey-leaf addict. Which they may well have been.

King Yoon was reaching his own frenzy of excitement, when a thundering came at the door. Yoon's eyes flickered open, and the snarl was not a pretty sight. He grabbed the whore's head with a handful of hair, and dragged her roughly from his erection with the bellow, "Who is it dares interrupt THE KING?"

The door opened slowly, and Zandbar, Captain of the King's Guard, stood in full plate armour. His face was grim, his eyes dark and hooded, his military bearing ramrod straight and specifically non-judgemental.

"I apologise for the interruption, Sire," came Zandbar's deep rumble, "but this is a matter of grave urgency."

"What is it?"

"Your great nephew, Lord Daron, has been beaten to within an inch of his life."

"Did he deserve it?"

"Most probably," said Zandbar, hand on sword hilt, and without a flicker of emotion.

Yoon sighed, and crawled across the bed. His naked companions scrambled to get out of his way.

Yoon kicked into velvet slippers, and an aide stepped from the shadows of the fire-pit illuminated room, hanging rich red robes over Yoon's shoulders. Yoon rolled his head, releasing cracks of tension, then stepped in close to Zandbar.

"We better go sort it out, then. For an attack on the royal bloodline is an attack on the king. And that cannot be tolerated. Summon Chanduquar."

The long cobbled street was a private one, with twenty foot high iron gates at either end, each manned by three armed guards, and bearing a high watchtower mid-point down the street, this time manned with four archers bearing powerful longbows.

At this late hour, torches burned on street corners, but the shadows were long, the cobbles slick with ice, and the group that approached the iron gate brought all three pikemen to bear with lowered weapons and shouted challenges rattling through the dark.

"Stop! Who goes there? We will inflict violence!"

"Relax," said Zandbar, oozing from the shadows. He wore a dark wool cloak over his armour. "Shanga, Mellith, Talor. We have business within. Open the gate."

"Of course, Captain." Shanga saluted, and they stood up their pikes, stood to attention, eyes staring straight ahead and definitely *not* at the small group, including a man with a black silk hood over his head, who stood stamping boots on the frozen cobbles.

The gates opened without sound on well-greased hinges,

and the small group of mostly hooded figures stepped through the portal. They walked down the cobbles, between towering buildings of ancient black stone, and stopped at some seemingly random point on the street by a small, black door of iron.

One of the figures foregrounded himself, and looked left, then right. Producing a long, slender iron key, with intricate filigree work around the shaft, he unlocked the door and one by one the figures entered, the final person to cross the threshold being Zandbar guiding the hooded prisoner, a stocky figure, hands bound before him with steel wire.

A torch was lit from a low-burning brand on the wall, and then the door was carefully locked behind them. The group moved away, down narrow, shadow-haunted, high-ceilinged corridors, into a maze of yet more corridors where they turned left and right at several gloomy intersections to finally arrive at another anonymous door. Here, King Yoon threw back his hood and shook out his shaggy black hair. Here, in this place, his white makeup and red lipstick should have looked comical, clown-like. But did not. They looked more like the affectations of a madman, and this place the basis for his physical and mental asylum.

Yoon unlocked the portal and they stepped through into a plain, high-ceilinged room. There was a large table of dull oak, surrounded by perhaps thirty chairs, each hand-carved and antique.

"You may remove your hoods," said Yoon, licking his painted lips. All removed their hoods, except for the prisoner, who was unable, and Yoon looked at each face in turn, weighing up the gathering he had summoned in the middle of the night.

There were various solid men, each loyal to Zandbar and

Yoon, and there as protectors. Then there was Lord Daron, his nose bent, nostrils still bloodied, his face bruised and battered, eyes swollen, lips quivering at this seemingly important clandestine activity – all on his behalf.

One of the group was a small man, his skin the darkest of ebony. He threw off his cloak with distaste, and stared with an intense frown corrugating his ageless face. "I do not like to creep around in shadows," he snapped, tone disrespectful, body language aggressive.

This man who challenged the king wore very little, except for many body piercings which, on close inspection, could be discerned as the polished bones of a wide variety of animals. His hair was close-cropped to his seemingly over-large skull, his eyes yellow from years of alcohol abuse, his thick lips tattooed with delicate script. He wore soft leather boots and had a long, wicked, curved knife at his hip.

Rather than take offence at the little man's brash and aggressive behaviour, Yoon adopted a different strategy. "Chanduquar, my friend, I have brought you here because of a most delicate matter. This is a case of gross disobedience, of violence against my bloodline, which as you know…"

"Yes yes, is a dishonour to the king. I know this horse shit. Let's get on with it."

King Yoon bit his lip. His face contorted a little, and Zandbar, Captain of the King's Guard, studiously looked away lest his face crack into a smile. Nobody spoke to King Yoon that way – not unless they wanted their severed head on a spike decorating Desekra Fortress. But this little man… this little *shamathe*, corrected Zandbar, was a tool King Yoon decided he needed.

And if the tool became expendable?

Zandbar gave a little shiver. *He would not like to be the little black man if Yoon, in one of his moments of insanity, decided he no longer had dire need of the magick-maker.*

"This is my great nephew," said Yoon, gesturing broadly and vaguely in the direction of Lord Daron, who was shivering and looking up at the high vaulted ceilings. "He was beaten to within an inch of his life by some heathen bastard, by the name of…" Yoon looked towards Zandbar for confirmation.

"Beetrax," said Zandbar.

"Beetrax," said Yoon, turning back to Chanduquar.

"The Axeman," added Zandbar.

"The Axeman," smiled Yoon, running a hand through his shaggy hair.

Chanduquar looked at the group, from one to the other, then focussed on Yoon. "You have brought me here, to this place, to do what I know you want me to do, for *one man*? You want to unleash this creature back into the world because of *one man*? Because of *one disagreement*? *One beating*? *One tiny insignificant moment of dishonour against yourself*? Are you… insane?"

Yoon's left cheek twitched. He gave a little, polite cough. "This is a serious matter, Chanduquar. I would like to respectfully remind you how much gold coin I deposit at regular intervals at your temple. And I would also like to remind you that my family honour, my bloodline, my *family* mean more to me than all the good citizens of Vagandrak put together. So. This is going to happen. So make it happen, or I will find myself another… *serving* shamathe."

Chanduquar scowled, but gave a single nod. "So be it. Who is this hooded man?"

Zandbar tugged the hood free, and a late middle-aged man, with grey at his temples, squinted in the weak light of the burning brands. He looked around, quick and nervous, at the group before his eyes finally settled on King Yoon. He had been beaten, both eyes blackened, his lip split in three places. He was shaking. He seemed to realise he was in deep over his head.

"This is Kendalol, lately barman at The Fighting Cocks tavern where our little sordid problem began."

"I- I- I would like to beg forgiveness, from His Highness... Truly, I did not see anything of this so-called fight, I..."

"Quiet, simpleton," snapped Yoon. He clicked his fingers, and one of Zandbar's soldiers upended a bag onto the tiled ground. The stained sheets stank, and King Yoon prodded the offending items idly with the toe of his velvet slipper.

"Tell me..."

"Kendalol."

"Yes, whatever. Tell me, peasant, my men say these are the bed sheets from the room where Beetrax the Axeman slept for more than a week. Can you confirm this?"

"Yes, yes, Your Highness, I took them there, when they came to the tavern asking questions. I remembered. Because Beetrax had been there for a while, and he drank ale and slept up in that cheap room, the cheapest we have because it's next to the brothel and you can hear humping through the wall all through the night..."

"Hmm. Quite. Maybe that's *why* he hired the room? Anyway. I fear I must warn you, peasant bar man, that if these sheets turn out *not to be what you claim*, then Zandbar here, my wonderful Captain of the King's Guard, will chop off your head and place it on a spike. Do you understand?"

"Oh yes, yes, Your Highness. Totally. I swear by the shade of my late mother that this is the case! Oh I swear–"

"Yes yes. Shut up now. Chanduquar?"

The small black shamathe gave a grunt.

"Over to you."

Chanduquar nodded, and instead of turning to Kendalol, he moved across the large chamber floor until he reached the end of the room. Here, practically the whole wall, thus far concealed in shadow, was revealed to be a huge, iron-slatted door. As Zandbar's men came forward with their flickering torches, so the intricacies of the door were revealed. It was ancient, and carved with lines and angles, with swirls and triangles. Huge roller-hinges stood to the left, and to the right there was a huge bar attached to a pronged wheel. The bar was made up of three forked segments, each interlocking through massive iron loops. It would take a hundred men to force the door from the other side. Maybe a thousand.

Three of Zandbar's men moved to the wheel and took their positions, bracing themselves. King Yoon gave three little claps of his hands, like an excited child about to open a birthday present.

"Oooh, I do like this bit," he said, face genuinely alight with pleasure, and the men, muscles bulging, started to heave on the large, iron wheel. It moved, slowly, grinding heavier than any mill grindstone; the men strained, faces turning purple, and slowly, *slowly*, the huge intricate iron door started to shift to the left, inch by inch, huge panels stepping forward and sliding past one another, halving itself, then quartering itself, to reveal... a pitch black chamber within.

Eventually, the grinding stopped, and the three men stepped back, bathed in sweat.

Yoon took a small series of steps forward, hands clasped before him, face framed in fascination.

Chanduquar stood perfectly still. Then his hands came up, forming a complicated pattern with fingers and palms turned out.

Lord Daron gave a small whimper, and clutching his damaged ribs, took a step back.

"Nobody *moves*!" hissed Chanduquar, suddenly.

From the inky pool of darkness beyond the iron gate, something rumbled. It was a deep, bass noise. Nothing human could make a sound like that.

Chanduquar began to chant, and dropped to his knees, eyes closing. His lips writhed and words in a different, ancient tongue poured from his mouth. No longer was he a slightly comical bone-pierced black man from the far south jungles; now, he commanded a sudden, awesome presence. Now, they felt the *power* nestling within him, like a mollusc in its shell, just waiting to be coaxed out with the right provocation... and this *was* the right provocation, because the rumbling sound grew louder, and there came a noise, a twisted mewling that set every man present on edge, made hairs stand up on necks and arms, made throats tighten, mouths go dry, hands go to weapons—

"No—body—move—" growled Chanduquar, voice emerging as if dragged from a thousand leagues away, a pitiful human voice eased free as if forced from a different plane of existence, of reality, a place of nightmares and demons and an eternal, burning furnace...

Something large and bulky shifted in the black. Then it moved forward, a heavy rattle of chains following as the tethered creature limped into the light from the burning brand and made all — all except Yoon and Chanduquar — give a little gasp.

It was bigger than a horse, although of different

proportions. Indeed, it was like a horse, but not like a horse, for no foal could have been born so deformed and yet lived. It was huge and uneven, stocky, with bulging lumps of distended muscle emerging from its torso, seemingly at random – as if it had been broken in places, and forced back together again. It was a rich chestnut colour, uneven skin patched with horse hair in segments, as if it had suffered burns from an awful fire; and although it limped forward on four legs, the front right did not touch the ground, for it was too short, and bent forwards at an irregular angle.

Yoon licked his lips in obvious pleasure, as his eyes rose from the great, heavily muscled body, from thick horse legs with twisted, iron hooves – up the uneven chest to the head, the great misshapen head that was too large to be right, too bent to be living. And yet live it did. The head was a broken equine skull, long and pointed, but with the mouth pulled back, jacked open too far, showing huge blackened fangs. The eyes were uneven on the head – one yellow, one blood red and double the size – and from one side of the bent skull curved a jagged horn, easily the length of a short sword but fashioned from yellowed bone, showing many notches and nicks where battle had scarred it. That twisted horse head lowered, and turned, revealing the blood red eye, which blinked as it surveyed the group of men standing in awe – and horror – before it.

It leapt then, a near-human scream like that of a woman dying in childbirth smashing from quivering lips on a trajectory of thick phlegm. Chains rattled, grey and taut, dragging the beast back, straining at its heavy leash. Its head smashed left and right, that great horn carving a figure of eight before the gathered men, a challenge, and a promise. A promise of death.

Lord Daron urinated down his leg, forming a little puddle. One of the guards placed a reassuring hand on his shoulder, then saw the puddle and stepped deftly to one side.

"Unchain it, unchain it!" quivered Yoon, mesmerised, stepping forward again, seemingly oblivious to the awesome power of the hostile beast before him.

"Highness, please, slow down," muttered Chanduquar, eyes open, staring at the king. Then he returned to his chanting, and the twisted horse-beast surged against its chains once more. Iron links rattled, chains twisted together, and there came a whine of stressed, unwinding steel.

"I think one is about to..." said Daron.

There came a tremendous screech of stressed steel as a chain the thickness of a man's wrist snapped and lashed across the room. It caught one guard across the chest, tossing him backwards across the room and pursuing like an eager metal snake, where it continued to crash through chairs and table, and left a huge groove in the stone wall with a shower of sparks before coming to rest beside the broken, dead body of the man it had just slaughtered.

Daron turned to run.

"Run, and you die," said King Yoon, without turning, his words very quiet, but menacing all the same. Then he held up a hand. "Wait."

Chanduquar continued to chant, eyes closed, hands vibrating before him. And then – a transformation took place.

The horse creature suddenly went still, trembling. It lowered its head towards the small, black-skinned *shamathe*, and very slowly, knelt, as if in obeisance.

Chanduquar ceased his chant, the final words leaving his mouth like dark smoke. Ancient sigils writhed across his lips, a fluid tattoo, which gradually faded along with the sound. Now, all that could be heard was the uneven rumbling of the giant, pacified beast.

"Fascinating," said King Yoon. "So, it does work!"

"Halt pointless noise," barked Chanduquar. His head snapped round. "You. With the bag. Come here."

The guard stepped forward, and Chanduquar took the black canvas pack, upending it to dump a disarray of bed sheets on the tiled floor. Leaning forward, he pushed them towards the beast, which still regarded the little man with the blood-red eye. Its panting was deep and rhythmical.

"You understand me?"

The beast gave a nod, and Yoon licked his lips in excitement.

"You understand the binding spells I have cast?"

Again, the twisted equine gave a nod.

"This is the scent of your quarry." He turned at stared at Zandbar. "You may release the chains."

Zandbar stared, hard. "You realise, if it attacks, we will all die?"

"And if you stand here gibbering like a slack-bowelled idiot, we will also die. *Do as I instruct.*"

Slowly, with creaking joints belying his age, Chanduquar climbed to his feet. He moved forward, within the boundary of restraining chains, and reached out, laying his hand on the creature's quivering muzzle. Its head shifted, and it gave a little whinny, a sound of affection not too unlike a horse. At that moment, Chanduquar felt his heart go out to the corrupted beast; this was no evil entity, but a living, breathing organism despoiled and degraded by the evil of Orlana's magick.

You should have stayed in the Furnace, he thought.

Zandbar released the chains, and ran them through loops, stepping back as the creature rose to its full height. Its head swung round, the tusk making a hissing sound, and the guards – as one – leapt back.

"Remember what I can do for you," said Chanduquar.

And then it spoke. And the room was filled with a hushed silence, like falling ash after a great fire. "I… re… member… Mast… Master," came the disjointed, hissed words from that great, jacked open maw. The beast plunged its snout into the bed linen – into *Beetrax's* bed linen – and then lifted its head.

The head turned to Chanduquar, as if asking a question.

"Show me," said Chanduquar.

With a squeal, the beast charged the door, smashing it from its hinges and knocking the frame out of its position in stone. Huge slabs of stone block were torn from the wall to accommodate the beast's bulk, and dust billowed into the air. As if fuelled by its own violence, the creature suddenly bellowed and charged down the corridor, smashing through another locked portal. And then it was gone.

A silence followed, interspersed by distant shouts.

"Shouldn't you have warned them?" said Zandbar, voice neutral.

"Let them earn their pay," said Yoon, inspecting one slightly damaged fingernail. "But damn, I will have to have this repainted." He turned. "Chanduquar? Would you escort me out?"

"Yes. You realise Beetrax is a dead man, sire?"

"Of course. No man can stand against such an incredible creature. And we have… how many?"

"More than a hundred have been rounded up and penned, Your Majesty."

Yoon smiled. "That is impressive. Inventive, even. Please. Carry on."

They moved towards the destroyed door. A guard coughed on the dust.

"Er. Great Uncle Yoon? Majesty? Er…"

Yoon paused, and turned. "Yes, Lord Daron?"

"So, our bloodline will be avenged for the dishonour done to me?"

Yoon smiled, a wide and generous smile. "Of course, my boy. Now, clean up your piss before you follow us out, there's a good lad. It's starting to stink something horrid."

Civil Unrest

Skalg lay in his firm, specially designed bed, pain wrenching through his twisted back and the hump of broken bone which nestled under his dark skin like some kind of piggy-backed evil twin. He licked his lips, where he could still taste the honey-leaf infusion, and closed his eyes, fists clenched, each holding a handful of satin covers as he waited for the dancing bright lights of pain to gradually, eventually, fade.

Through the pain-filled corridors of his mind he walked, and each street was a street from his city, Zvolga, and each civic edifice was a triumph of stone engineering, each dwarf a citizen under *his* law and *his* rule, and this filled him with an intense pride for his race, and his Church of Hate, and the Law and Religion of the Great Dwarf Lords.

But I cannot understand how a group of lowlife degenerate brigands calling themselves the Army of Purity could turn against the church? What, in the name of the Harborym and everything holy, were they thinking? Why would they target the church? And me? Five attempts on my life had been made, ably thwarted by my Educators… but who, WHO would fucking DARE?

Thoughts and ideas raced around his pain-riddled brain, but slowly, his administered infusion began to have an effect and, if any casual observer had been allowed into Skalg's private, personal chambers at the top of the Blood Tower, or within his seven personal homes throughout the city, they would have witnessed his fists gradually relax, and a narrow crease of pain, and concentration, and frustration, ease from the ridges of his broad, strong face.

Ah, but I am cursed.

Sometimes, he believed his hunched back, that mass of broken, twisted spine and shoulder blade which had then grown even when the rest of his body had ceased to grow, was indeed some kind of malevolent spirit, some individual entity which had taken residence in his body, and which he carried around as a female dwarf might carry a child; only Skalg's womb was on his back, and the umbilical which fed his evil, cantankerous, pain-giving *bastard* was his spinal column. Occasionally, in the lonelier, darker hours, Skalg even fancied his dark hump spoke to him.

And Skalg's only chance of aborting the evil foetus he carried on his back would come with his own death.

Skalg's face had gone pale with the pain. Now, some colour returned, and awkwardly, helped by the odd camber of his bed, he climbed to his feet and pulled on a black, glossy robe, sliding the silk-like material over his burly arms to cover his heavily haired chest. He padded to the steel sink and gripped the rim, staring at himself in a battered silver mirror with a polished brass frame. He spat in the sink, and rubbed his mouth with the back of his hand, then turned and moved to a low metal bench of exquisitely finished silver, the entire surface carved with swirls and symbology, including the clan signs of all three Great Dwarf Lords, and crests linked to the three dragons which heated the cities of the Harborym Dwarves.

Skalg stared at these crests for a while.

Moraxx, Kranesh and *Volak.* Imprisoned for millennia, mindless, useless, broken wyrms which inhabited the lower shafts beneath the Five Havens, and provided heat and fire for the cities, and also for smelting in the furnaces of the Great Mines.

Oh how we'd struggle without your fire, thought Skalg, and poured himself a large silver goblet of *fire liquor* from a silver decanter. The liquor warmed his lips and scorched his throat and, as its name suggested, put fire in his belly, which he welcomed. He stared at his broad flat face in the brass-framed mirror, and admired the flat forehead, strong ridges above his eyes, a flat nose and prominent jaw. A fine face for a dwarf. But from the corner of his eye he caught sight of the bone hump, poking up past his shoulder which, as he analysed, was higher than the other, the lower one pulled down by his twisted spine. His mouth warped into a snarl.

He reached to one side, picking up a well-worn letter hand-scribed on yellowed vellum. At the top was stamped a wax seal for the Guild of Medicine, and his eyes skimmed down through the polite opening paragraphs to the lines, which, as always, drew his dejected gaze:

> *We regret to inform you that, because of your injuries*
> *in the mine collapse, and the length of time allowed to*
> *pass before seeking our medical expertise, the fused mass*
> *of bone which has grown outwards, creating what you*
> *referred to as your "hump" or "hunchback", is, we*
> *very much regret, inoperable. Shards of bone from your*
> *shoulder blade and clavicle have become entwined with*
> *your spinal column, growing outwards – and pulling*
> *your spine out of its true line – but also merging into*
> *one almost solid mass of bone. This is a most unusual*

*condition, never before seen, but one thing is for certain:
our investigations can confirm that to remove part of
your bone hump would be to interfere with your spinal
column. This, in our educated medical opinion, would
cause you a total and permanent paralysis. We can
operate on outlying sections of fused bone to reduce mass,
but again, there is a high risk of paralysis.*

*It is with great sadness, Cardinal Skalg, that we must
inform you that your injuries are permanent.*

A rage swamped him, then, for just the blink of an eye,
and he tensed to crush the letter in his fist. But, as always,
he resisted the urge, and carefully smoothed out the vellum
and laid it to the left of the silver decanter.

*Would you have become the First Cardinal of the Church
of Hate without your injuries to power you forward?
Would you have become the most powerful dwarf
in Zvolga without the aid of anger, and hate, and
determination given to you, like a gift from the Great
Dwarf Lords, by this injury which brought about a
singular fucking clarity of purpose? You were mocked,
and shunned, and despised. You joined the Church of
Hate in lowly ranks, and clawed and bit and scratched
and tore your way to the top over the bleeding eye sockets
and sundered rectums of a thousand destroyed peers.*

The voice was an echo deep within him. *Deep* within his
embryo of bone.

*Would you have become First Cardinal Skalg without the
constant pain to fuel you? I think not, brother of bone, brother of*

flesh, brother of spirit.

"Shut up," muttered Skalg, and finished the goblet in a single swallow, sending fire scorching down his throat. His belly ached. His head thumped. He groaned, and his groan merged with a gentle knock at the door.

"You may enter!"

It was a young lad in the royal livery of King Irlax. He gave a modest bow, then met Skalg's questioning gaze.

"The Great King Irlax commands you attend him immediately."

"He does, does he?"

The young dwarf coughed. Then he suddenly lowered his eyes, remembering exactly *whom* he addressed. "He, er, that is, King Irlax, demands an update on progress towards the apprehension of the Army of Purity, who, er, he states, have been targeting his churches."

The messenger risked a glance up. Skalg's gaze was ice cold and fixed on him filled with razor daggers.

"Er."

Skalg gave a short cough. "You may inform His Majesty that I have received his *request*, and I will attend his court in due course." Skalg gave a narrow smile. "Now run along, before this silver decanter," he gestured, vaguely, "connects repeatedly with your fucking face."

"Taking my leave, Cardinal." The messenger hurried out.

In foul mood, Skalg began to dress.

Methodrox sat in the corner of The Slaughtered Warrior, a flagon of ale in his grip, his dark, intelligent, glittering eyes watching the ebb and flow of tavern patrons. The Slaughtered Warrior was situated in the darkest, most undesirable quarter of Langan's Dock, affectionately known to its inhabitants – with dark irony – as the Pit. The Pit was not an actual pit, but a metaphor for perhaps how low it had sunk in a social context; here, nothing was contraband. In fact, every contraband was available, and only the Pit was the safest place to buy and sell. Even Skalg's Educators were wary of travelling the Pit. It amused Methodrox greatly to see them enter in threes or more.

Now, Methodrox waited for his contact. He sipped his ale, barely taking any in, despite the intoxicating and addictive flavour. Ale was part of his blood, but not today, not on this night, not with this mission. This mission was everything.

Methodrox watched the dwarves in the tavern, and some watched back. All were armed, many armoured. By the bar there came uproarious laughing, which erupted immediately into violence. Fists were flying, at least five or six people involved in the sudden vicious brawl. An axe flashed in the lamp light, and a head was detached from shoulders with a sodden thump. In a few minutes it was over, and two dwarves dragged the headless corpse from The Slaughtered Warrior and dumped it in the street.

Methodrox watched, hand on his own knife, eyes narrowed lest he in some way become dragged into the fight. Unlikely, but always a possibility. Fights in the Pit had a way of getting out of hand extremely quickly.

A slim figure slid in through the door. He was hooded, nothing suspicious there, and tall for a dwarf. He had to stoop a little to avoid bumping his head on the beams. He moved quickly, neatly, a dwarf who was a master of his own actions.

Methodrox leaned back a little, eyes following the newcomer who made his way to the bar, good boy, and ordered a flagon of ale. The man glanced around with interest, and Methodrox felt his eyes glance over but show no emotion. And yet the connection was there.

He took his ale from a rough-looking barman with arms the width of most dwarves' thighs, and tattooed heavily with blurred images of female dwarves showing breasts and open quims. He sipped, casual, and moved through the raucous crowd until he reached Methodrox's table.

"You have a spare seat. Can I sit?"

"Be my guest."

He sat. Sipped ale. Pretended to not be interested in Methodrox.

"You enjoying your evening?"

"Good fight before. Shame the dwarf had to lose his head."

"Occupational hazard."

"In a tavern?"

"In Zvolga. In the Pit."

Methodrox nodded. "I'll second that." He paused and studied the newcomer. "You seem like a handy fellow. Are you looking for work?"

"A labouring dwarf is always looking for work."

"I have a delicate task. How are you with precious stones?"

"I have a delicate hand."

"For this, you will need to be delicate and yet brutal."

"I can be both of those things."

Methodrox finished his ale. "Count to a hundred and meet me outside."

The streets were warm, the cobbles dry. It was five minutes since the last Dragon's Song, and warm air still pulsed, lantern flames bright.

The newcomer emerged, and Methodrox set off, not checking behind himself. He moved into a narrow maze of four-storey high, leaning slum buildings, the left-hand side carved from the mountain, the right free-standing at a variety of shifted angles. Cheap. Dangerous. Abandoned. Dwarves crowded the streets, dressed in poor garb, many clutching bottles. The Pit was nothing if not a den of poverty, violence and alcohol. Young dwarves with scabbed faces, dressed in rags, sat in doorways, begging, daggers with dried blood in their boots. Whores stood in other doorways, promising they were clean, lips painted bright red, eyes dead like those of a corpse.

Through all this Methodrox weaved, hand on his knife, axe on his back. He made a series of complicated cut-throughs, down narrow dark alleys, under bridges, over stinking, open sewers which got worse, more polluted, the deeper into the Pit one travelled.

Eventually, they came to an old DumpShaft, from a time before "civilisation" was brought to the Harborym by the Great Dwarf Lords. It was a wide well, a low wall of stone defining the perimeter – perhaps thirty feet wide, a natural shaft deep, deep down into the bowels of the Karamakkos. It had been used as an industry tip for centuries; now it was used more to dispose of unwanted corpses. It saw a lot of business. Most DumpShafts had been sealed by the church; here in the Pits, nobody seemed to care.

Beside the DumpShaft stood a warehouse. Big. Old. Falling down. By the narrow entrance leaned two serious-looking dwarfs, both carrying evil, well-worn maces. Methodrox stopped beside these two individuals and looked back. The dwarf following did not pause, but came in close, trusting, confident, eyes meeting Methodrox's.

"Watch the street," he said, and ducked inside. The newcomer followed.

They moved through various corridors, eventually coming to a small room. Again, there were five large and very serious-looking dwarves. Their eyes glittered, their faces grim slabs. Here, Methodrox finally stopped and dragged up a chair, sitting himself down. The newcomer was left standing.

"State your name."

"Echo."

"Can you prove this?"

The newcomer shrugged, and looked at the five dwarves who spread out before him, pushing in front of the seated Methodrox. A wall of muscle. A wall of bristling weapons.

"Do you need me to?"

The five stocky dwarves attacked in a sudden rush. Echo ducked a club, dropping to one knee and delivering a right-hand straight that broke the dwarf's knee. He screamed, rolling to one side as Echo rolled to the left, grabbing a second attacker's groin and dragging down on his balls. Another scream.

They backed off for a moment, finding new positions. Echo was relaxed, features neutral. Then he attacked. Three strikes in three seconds, leaving them rolling on the floor with various breaks and dislocations, groaning the way only big, tough killers can groan from an unexpected violence.

Echo glanced up. "You wish me to kill them?"

Methodrox stood, and held up a hand. "No. Follow me."

More corridors, more narrow apertures to squeeze through. They came to a big space, bright with a thousand candles. A thousand dwarves were seated around tables, food and drink before them. As they entered through a side door, Echo looked genuinely surprised. "The Army of Purity?"

"A sample," smiled Methodrox. "We grow stronger every day."

"The Church of Hate truly has something to fear."

"A wise observation. Follow me." They moved between the tables, where serious faces regarded Echo and he returned their stares, face neutral. Finally, they came upon a table at the far end of the chamber, around which were arranged eight grave-looking dwarves, with neatly trimmed beards and black, polished armour. They stood, and nodded at Echo, and then they all sat – except Methodrox who gestured to an empty seat. Echo sat, looking around at each face slowly, as if memorising the features for future reference.

"You want me to kill Skalg?" said Echo once more, quietly, placing both hands flat on the table. The backs of his hands were crisscrossed with narrow white scars.

"No," said Methodrox. "We want something... a little more elaborate."

Slowly, Methodrox outlined his plan.

"There is... considerable risk."

"And we offer considerable reward."

"I require no payment."

Methodrox looked taken aback, and he rubbed at the bristles of his beard thoughtfully.

"You would do this out of principle? To free the dwarves of the tyrannical rules of the Church of Hate?"

Echo shrugged, and looked off, as if into the distance. "Let's just say that bastard Skalg and I go way back; and

I have an old score to settle." His eyes were gleaming and he locked his gaze to Methodrox. "Let's say I do it for the memory of my sister."

Skalg sat in his plush, donkey-drawn carriage. The curling ironwork was gleaming black, edged with gold as befitted the First Cardinal of the Church of Hate. As they rattled through the dark streets of Zvolga, the carriage was flanked by six Educators, which kept the pace slow. This pleased Skalg, at the thought that every passing second would be infuriating King Irlax to the point where Skalg could be guaranteed an argument. As Skalg's father used to say, *the only good king is a dead king.*

As they moved their way through the streets, some dwarf citizens stopped to stare at the carriage. Skalg's procession often had this effect on people, after all, he *was* the *First* Cardinal, and as such, demanded the respect of the populace. On this occasion, however, the six Educators also probably helped to draw stares; it wasn't often such brutality was openly courted.

They rattled down various side streets, and flicking back a curtain, Skalg glanced out; Razor was walking, her body fluid, her head turning continually as she searched for any possible danger.

The other Educators also looked fearsome, with their collection of unsheathed weapons, scars and no-nonsense faces. Skalg felt quite proud at that moment, that he could summon these – and hundreds of other – psychopaths.

They reached the gates of the Palace of Iron, a towering, black iron structure, all spikes and towers and turrets. The fence surrounding the large, paved grounds was twenty feet high, with body-thick iron bars, each capped with a sprouting of razor spikes. Two guards stood on sentry duty outside the gates; inside were two squat guard houses, in which Skalg knew another ten guards waited.

Recognising Skalg's transport, the gates were opened on smooth, silent hinges, and the carriage rolled through as the guards stood to attention. They trundled down the smooth central causeway, the Palace of Iron looming eerily above them against a backdrop of the savage, jagged rock of the mountain's carved and shaped interior.

The carriage halted, donkeys stamping, and Razor opened the door for Skalg with a tiny *click*. He struggled out, leaning heavily on Razor and feeling the solidity of her muscles. Then he straightened, as much as a man with a bent spine could straighten, and hobbled towards the great iron doors.

The Educators followed in silence, and the huge door swung open showing a long corridor, lit by roaring fires on large, iron stands. Skalg was met by a small, neat dwarf, clean shaven and looking very odd for it. Rumour had it the dwarf was also a eunuch; indeed all of King Irlax's male personnel got the snip, in order to protect his collection of queens, mistresses and casual lovers.

"Welcome, First Cardinal Skalg. The king is most urgent to share your counsel."

"Lead on, then. He should have called upon me sooner."

Skalg followed, limping, and shortly was presented before King Irlax. The hall was large and impressive, with glass cases surrounding the vast space containing a thousand artefacts of Harborym heritage. From weapons of war to clever mining devices; from items of formal regal dress and precious stones, to items which, historians claimed, had once belonged to the Great Dwarf Lords themselves!

King Irlax was leaning forward on his throne, and Skalg

could sense his impatience. As a result, he slowed his limping approach yet more, grinning a little beneath his beard. Finally he stopped, and glanced around, and finally alighted his eyes on his king.

"Well met, King Irlax. Apologies for the delay. I had some short business to which I had to attend."

"You kept me waiting more than a fucking *hour*!" hissed the king, his eyes flashing with fury.

"Excuse me," said Skalg, meeting his monarch's gaze, "but I think you forget to whom you speak."

Irlax stared at Skalg, his right eyelid twitching, and this gave Skalg time to study the King of the Harborym Dwarves. He was big, for a dwarf, and barrel-chested – very, very powerful, as he liked to prove in wrestling tournaments where he would get drunk and pound some unfortunate into pieces. He had a bushy black beard, run through with streaks of silver, and his hair was a mane, again black, again showing evidence of his progressing years. His hands were big, heavy, powerful from wielding a battle-axe, and he wore black iron armour under his regal robes of kingship.

Irlax took a deep breath, and Skalg was humoured to see him attempting to control himself.

Irlax peered down from his raised platform, but Skalg did not let this worry him. He knew, in terms of power, in terms of popular support even, that he wielded just as much authority as the king. In many ways, the Church of Hate was even more feared, for in many forms it predated even the Great Dwarf Lords, and it had been the church that helped subdue the three dragons, Moraxx, Kranesh and Volak, using long-lost spells of Equiem magick from the elder days. From before the wars of men and dwarves.

The Church of Hate also had a reputation for being...

nasty. Thanks in no small part to its sadistic First Cardinal.

"Cardinal Skalg."

"King Irlax."

"I believe we got off on the wrong foot."

"I believe so," said Skalg, with a narrow smile. "Please, sire, let us begin again. You requested I attend you to discuss…?"

"Let's begin with the church fires you've been so recently suffering. What information have you come up with concerning the perpetrators?"

"I believe they call themselves the Army of Purity, or some such nonsense. Although how they believe their purity can come about by burning priests to death and causing sacrilege against the altars of the Great Dwarf Lords, I cannot quite fathom."

"I believe you have a suspect?"

"Yes."

"Where is he now?"

Skalg smiled. "He expired."

"He expired?"

"That's what I said."

"In what way did he expire?" There was an edge to King Irlax's voice; an edge that Skalg knew well. An edge he did not care for.

"My Educators attempted various forms of persuasion in order to extract information about the fire, and indeed, the Army of Purity itself. After all, we cannot have thugs running around the streets burning down churches. Maybe soon they would turn their attention to the monarchy, and you yourself, sire, might find yourself on the blunt end of their anarchic fire-starting behaviour."

Irlax stared at Skalg. "Tell me he confessed."

"He did not confess."

"Did he tell you *anything*?"

"No. I believe he was innocent."

Irlax stood, then, a sudden movement, and began to pace before Skalg. His fists clenched and unclenched once.

"Cardinal Skalg, can I remind you – with respect – that you cannot go around my city *torturing* suspects. Especially when they turn out to be bloody innocent! What about this dwarf's family? His children? His friends?"

"It was a necessary act." Skalg cleared his throat. "I would also like to remind Your Highness – with respect – that the Church of Hate acts externally to the monarchy. We – and I – are not answerable to Your Highness in any way whatsoever. It could be said we are symbiotic." He smiled.

Irlax's face darkened. "You may operate outside my rules," said Irlax, his voice suddenly soft and laced through with poison, "but I am an honourable king, and I will not stand, *will not fucking stand* for the murder of innocent citizens. Do I make myself clear?"

"You make yourself crystal clear," said Skalg. "As clear as a mountain sky. However, you are not in a position to tell me what I can and cannot do, and in pursuit of these… these *villains* I will use every technique at my disposal in order to discover their identities. Do I make *myself* clear?"

Irlax turned to face Skalg. He stepped in close. "You play a dangerous game with me, Cardinal."

"This is no game, Your Highness. This is a group of your so-called precious *citizens* challenging the church with all-out war. I will not stand for it, do you hear? I will not have the Church of the Great Dwarf Lords desecrated in such a manner – and any who stands in my way is a heretic.

Surely, you do not challenge the Will of the Three Gods, do you, King Irlax?"

Irlax smiled, and relaxed back. "Of course I do not challenge the Will of the Three Gods. As you say, that would be foolish indeed – especially for one in my position." He moved back to his throne, and seated himself, his eyes turning on Skalg with a cold, calculating steadiness. "Why, if this sort of madness progressed, then our population might find they had to make a choice between church and king. And that would rip our world asunder, would it not? There would be a bloody civil war. That eventuality would benefit nobody."

Skalg nodded, and twisted a little, seeking comfort.

"It still pains you?" Irlax smiled then, a warm and friendly smile. "I could recommend you to my personal surgeon. He trained in Vagandrak, at Vagan University, and is skilled beyond the comprehension of most of our people."

"No, no, that's quite all right," said Skalg. *Because how long would my life expectancy be under the scalpel of your most loyal physicians? How many minutes? Less than I would care to wager!*

Irlax waved his hand, then rubbed it down his beard. "Anyway. Enough of this kind of talk. I have several other matters I need to discuss. Shall we retire to the library? I have some fine port that needs attention, and there we can discuss the current shortage of slaves in the Great Mine. I believe we are going to send teams out again, scouting; our shortage of criminals of our own kind is getting quite disconcerting. It's almost as if," he laughed quietly, "word of church cruelty has spread. Almost is if people fear the church more than serious crime itself!"

Skalg nodded, and scowled a little when he realised his

presence was going to be required at the Palace of Iron a lot longer than he had first anticipated.

"It would be my pleasure, Your Highness."

Four hours later, and with his hunched back screaming at him in pain – *damn, I did not bring a honey-leaf infusion!* – Skalg limped down the steps and climbed wearily into his carriage. Fires burned along the roadside as his carriage trundled from the gates, and dwarves bustled along both sides of the busy thoroughfare, going about their everyday business. As usual his Educators drew wary glances, but Skalg was in no mood for such minor enjoyment. He drew the curtains, leaving himself in a comfortable, maudlin gloom.

That bastard Irlax is going to have a few surprises in store over the coming days, weeks and months; this, I promise, thought Skalg sourly as they progressed, wheels rattling, his Educators alert. *He thinks he can tell me what to do, tell me how to run the Church of Hate! He thinks to order me, the First Cardinal, because in his feeble dwarf mind he is at the top of the food chain! Well, he is not.*

Skalg leant forward, back screaming fire, and put his chin on his fist, grunting in pain. He felt the sway of the carriage, and then the tilt as they started down the steep descent of Smith Street, and the donkeys strained backwards, taking the weight of the carriage against their harnesses. Skalg heard the hiss of the brakes.

One day, somebody will teach Irlax a lesson.

One day, somebody will remove him from the throne.

And on that day, the Church of Hate will be the only power in Zvolga – indeed, for the whole of Harborym Dwarves!

The carriage laboured down the steep hill, iron-rimmed

wheels rattling on cobbles.

A shout sounded outside, and Skalg, ever-cautious, flicked one of the curtains. A swarthy dwarf on the pavement was pointing back up the hill, and shouting. Others turned, and more shouting rang out. Several female dwarves screamed, and a panic rippled through the crowd on the pavement.

A cold chill gripped Skalg's chest. He shifted in his seat, slapping open the rear curtain to stare up the curve of the sloping cobbled road. His mouth dropped open, eyes growing wide.

Thundering towards his carriage was a huge barrel, rolling on its side, the whole thing roaring with flames. Reflected orange danced from the slick dark walls of the buildings lining Smith Street, and dwarves were leaping out of the barrel's path with shouts and growls of anger and fear. A noise came to Skalg, a thundering, pounding, roaring sound. The donkeys could smell fire now, and became suddenly skittish, pulling against one another. Skalg banged on the window, but his Educators were staring in horror at the speeding, flaming barrel.

It's going to hit, thought Skalg as fear coursed through him. *It's going to fucking hit!*

He looked behind again; a dwarf was ploughed under the barrel, which barely shifted as it crushed him, such was its weight. And realisation struck Skalg like a helve blow and left him reeling.

Assassination…

He reached for the door's handle, but the donkeys bolted, dragging the carriage with them. The door swung wide and noise rushed in, shouts and the ominous thundering sound. Skalg could smell fire and smoke, and fresh dung from the panicked donkeys. The door banged against the gloss of the carriage bodywork, denting the fine lines. Suddenly, the donkeys veered left, but too sharply, and the carriage turned, one wheel cracking with a sound like snapping bone. The carriage tilted onto its side and, in a shower of sparks, slid down the cobbles, grinding, the momentum and weight dragging the donkeys over onto their backs, legs kicking, strangled by their own harnesses as they were now pulled over, and down, kicking and screaming over the cobbles. Skalg was tossed about inside the carriage, and just as it came to a rest, the barrel struck, driving the carriage further down the slope of Smith Street, snapping the wheels and grinding at the undercarriage. Inside the compartment, Skalg cowered back as the floor buckled in towards him, and flames roared and screamed, and he grabbed hold of the cracked and bending seat as they were slammed down the road once more. The donkeys were screaming, kicking feebly with broken legs. Dwarves were shouting. The world seemed suddenly black and filled with smoke and sparks.

Please let it end. Oh no. Will it ever end? Will it ever end?

Skalg cowered, choking on smoke, eyes streaming, the roar of flames in his ears. Then came a long, low grinding sound, louder than a tunnel collapse in the mines, and Skalg's hands – laced with cuts from the smashed glass of the carriage's windows – covered his ears, his face contorted with a mixture of terror but also rage; rage at this attack, rage at this assassination attempt.

I will show them!

I will not die in such an ignoble manner!

The grinding increased, the barrel no doubt rotating against the buckled underside of the carriage. Stars exploded in Skalg's mind as his skull bounced from a bulkhead. His thoughts were spinning. He vomited onto what was now the floor, but was the broken frame of the carriage's side body.

Slowly, slowly, the carriage eventually ground to a halt.

The flames continued to roar, and with horror Skalg realised the carriage was burning. He reached up, grasping the door above him. His fingers were sliced by shards of broken glass. He shoved, but the door was firmly wedged shut in a buckled frame.

"Help!" he cried, from this burning womb. "Help me! It's..." he had a fit of coughing, "it's Cardinal Skalg! Your cardinal is trapped in here! Somebody help! Help your cardinal! The church needs him!" *Those fucking useless Educators, I'll see them lose the skin off their backs for this!* he thought.

Skalg's boots clattered on splinters of seat, and he managed to poke his head through the hole where the window had been, careful lest some stray splinter of glass gouge out his eyes.

The world beneath the mountain seemed to have descended into chaos. Further up the slope of Smith Street, three more flaming barrels were rumbling on an accelerating trajectory. Flames roared and smoke billowed. Several buildings lining the street were in flames. Dwarves were running around like ants in a pile of sugar, in seemingly random paths, to Skalg's eyes. The barrel which had taken out his carriage had shifted to one side but was still burning merrily – as was the majority of his carriage. Within a few seconds, he would be on fire.

Through smoke, he managed to locate his Educators... and his mouth fell open for a second time, for they were fighting a battle with axes and clubs against a large force of stocky dwarves – a force advancing on Skalg and his burning carriage. Even as he watched, Blagger went down under the strike of a club, and three dwarves laid in with boots, rendering his face and head a smashed-in pulp.

Only Razor looked calm and collected, dancing amongst the attackers, a short blade in each hand, cutting throats and stabbing groins.

"Help!" cried Skalg, weakly. His hands shook the door in its frame, and his eyes swivelled frantically.

Will I fit? Will I fucking fit? He strained to pull himself out of the window slot. Glass cut into his upper arms and chest, making him squeal. But he would not fit. His hunched back, source of many a curse, made him too bulky to squeeze free.

"*Damn you!*" he screamed, frothing at the mouth. "*Damn you all to the Furnace!*"

"I find that unlikely," came a cool voice, and Skalg looked up into a face that filled him with terror. He knew that face, for it was the assassin, Echo, wanted by the Church of Hate and the monarchy for endless crimes of murder against the Harborym Dwarves.

There was a click, and Echo dragged open the carriage door, reaching down and hauling Skalg from the burning carcass. He threw Skalg, who hit the cobbles hard, like a sack of compact horseshit, and lay very still as pain lanced through him; through his crippled spine, through his tangled limbs, through his battered skull. Blood-filled stars spun in his eyes. *This is the end*, his mind reasoned calmly.

Echo leapt smoothly from the carriage, which continued to burn. The sounds of clashing sounds rang out through the streets. Others were arriving now, City Guards, King's Guards, Church Wardens. All came with their particular brand of robes and weapons and helmets. With the many fires, the street was now a thriving chaos through which various factions fought. But on this side of the burning carriage, it was cool, and dark, and safe for a few moments. Populated by only two people.

Skalg. And his would-be assassin, Echo.

Skalg rolled, twisting with his hump, and managed to get on his hands and knees. He began crawling across the cobbles.

"Where are you going?" laughed Echo, and leapt past the cardinal, drawing a short black knife and allowing firelight from the burning carriage to dance along the dulled blade.

Skalg, who'd rolled over and was resting back on his elbows, dirt-smeared, smoke-stained, blood-spattered, with his robes torn and in disarray, looked up at Echo – a face from distant nightmares – and gave a narrow grimace.

"Don't kill me," he said. "I have money. I have influence! I have it all at my fingertips…"

Echo leered down at him, and grinned. "Your money won't help you now, you murdering crippled bastard," he said, as his knuckles tightened on the blade.

Journey

They rode north.

Beetrax formed the point of the wedge, as he always had in the past, as he always would in the future. It was a pride thing, it was a warrior thing, it was a man thing; nobody objected. It kept him from moaning.

Second came Dake and Jonti, at ease atop their mounts; Lillith came next, at the centre of the party, the safest place – in theory – for one who abhorred violence of any kind. To the rear came Talon, the most talented archer in Vagandrak, alongside Sakora, who preferred silence to talk and thus made her a questionable companion for Talon, who liked to regularly verbally express the concept of his own physical perfection.

Over the next few days they skirted the Rokroth Marshes, unwilling to get dragged into the misty, stinking realm; many better men and women had died in that unloved place. Beetrax knew the paths, as did they all, for they were Vagandrak ex-military and the army liked to train its soldiers hard.

They rode over undulating grasslands, littered with huge rocks, and saw the towers of the abandoned Skell Fortress in the distance to the west. They had the same old conversations, of war, and horror, and the ghosts of old soldiers; or hauntings and evil and how some abandoned places were abandoned for a reason.

A flurry of snow caught them in the open, but they pushed on through sad grey days, knowing the journey had to be like this, because the Ice Bridges of Sakaroth would allow access during only a short window, and without this crossing their mission, their adventure, their exploration, their treasure hunt, would stall in the water before it had even begun.

As their horses picked their own, gentle route through the rolling grasslands, Beetrax looked over the distant towers and battlements of Skell Fortress. He gave a deep sigh, and rolled his neck, the cracking sounds of released tension making Talon groan.

"I hate it when you do that, Axeman."

"I hate it when you take noblemen to your bed."

"Oh, we're on that old topic again, are we?"

Beetrax leaned back in his saddle. "I thought it was your favourite?"

"Beetrax, men can love men, just as women can love women."

"Well, it ain't right."

"How's that?"

"Well, sex, like. It's for a purpose."

"Go on."

"It's to make babies, ain't it?"

Talon chuckled, both hands on his saddle pommel, his face broad and beautiful and filled with good humour. "Axeman, if that's the only reason you fuck, then not only are you doing it wrong, you have some serious mental issues."

Beetrax flushed a little red. He scratched his beard. "Well, we... enjoy the company of a lady... to make babies. Surely? That's our... biological purpose. A man's legend lives on through his children. That's his immortality, that is."

"And what about women?" said Lillith.

"Eh?"

"What about a woman's immortality?"

"Do women even seek immortality?"

"Of course not! You are right. We simply exist to sit at the feet of our heroic men, gazing up with wide, adoring eyes, clutching feebly at their well-muscled legs, and thanking our lucky stars we managed to find such a perfect specimen of masculinity."

Beetrax frowned. "Well, *I*'ve never met a woman who wanted immortality."

"You've been keeping the wrong company then."

"Horseshit!"

"Tell me the last time you had a meaningful conversation with a woman."

Beetrax thought about it. "This one?" he said.

"Ha!" Lillith smiled, and pushed back her heavy locks. "You should come to the library more often, Beetrax. You have an amazing body, but your mind is... shackled. I will help you expand your mind. I will help unlock the inner you."

They rode on for a little longer. A few flurries of snow snapped at them, like annoying dogs. The wind howled through a forest to the east, low and mournful, a fresh widow's lament. The ground was peppered white, rocks cast with frost. The sky was a huge wide pale blue bastard, streaked with serrated daggers of ice cloud. The horses stamped occasionally, smoke snorting from nostrils, iron shoes striking hidden rocks with cold sparks.

Beetrax dropped back, slowing his mount, to ride beside Talon.

"You hear that, lad?"

"What's that?"

"Lillith made comments about shackling me."

"I thought she meant your mind was locked down, and she would help you unshackle your prejudice; to make you mentally free?"

"Er. Is that what she said?"

"Look, Beetrax, the world is changing. People are changing. You're stuck in an outmoded place. Why don't you let me educate you?"

"I don't need no education from you, lad. I was on those battlements whilst you were still suckling milk from your mother's tits!"

"Beetrax. I fought on the same battlements, remember? That mud-orc was going to skewer you on a spear, and I put an arrow through its mouth. The point popped out the top of its head on a shower of brains, and we laughed about it in the mess afterwards."

Beetrax stared at him. Then he glanced off, towards Skell.

"I feel, sometimes, that I am older than the world. I feel, sometimes," he eyed Talon thoughtfully, "that everybody in the world is mad, and I am the only sane person who walks between them. I spend my nights in the tavern, and people want to fight me, or joke with me, or fuck me – usually just after I've beaten somebody senseless. I'm confused with the world, Talon. I feel like I don't fit in. I feel like..." He struggled for words. "I feel like people are *strange*. Or, I acknowledge, that maybe *I* am strange. Maybe I'm the insane one." He lapsed into a brooding silence.

Talon smiled easily, and reached over, patting Beetrax's

leg. Beetrax stared at his hand, with its long fingers and perfectly manicured nails. "Axeman. You know what your problem is?"

"Go on."

"You need to relax."

"You see! You see! That comment makes me want to take out my axe and split your fucking skull in two like a ripe melon. Why do you do it? Why do you and all those other fucking bastards goad me into violence all the time?"

Talon sighed. "I believe," he said, "that there are breeds of men. Just like you have breeds of dog."

Beetrax stared at him. "You're not making this better, you know?"

"Hear me out. Some men are yappers, little annoying whelps who nip at your ankles until you give them a good solid kick. Some are born fighters – like yourself – who raise their hackles at the first affront and won't back down until they're both bloody and battered and wishing the fight had finished an hour ago."

Beetrax frowned. "So which one are you, lad?"

Talon grinned. "I'm the intelligent one at the back, watching the idiots fight and deciding on rich pickings afterwards."

"Hmm," said Beetrax. "I will think on what you said."

"Good! Good!"

"Although you made an error of judgement with your choice of mongrel."

"I did? How's that?"

"Because you're the pampered fluffy poodle, sat in the middle thinking it's top fucking dog, when in reality you are the one soon to be… supper." Beetrax grinned, showing his broken tooth. "And you don't ever want to be supper, lad."

•••

They made camp within a circle of huge, house-sized boulders.

It was snowing, and Dake had eventually got a fire going. Talon had been out, brought down a stray deer with a single shot. Beetrax skinned and gutted the beast, and Dake set large flat stones over the fire, greased with fat scraped from the hide. He was frying venison steaks and the smell had filled the circle, amidst the flickering orange light, making it feel homely, warm, friendly. Beetrax pulled out a bottle of brandy.

"Drink?"

"Bad idea," said Jonti. "I thought we were on your amazing mission to find immortality and eternal wealth?"

"What's that got to do with a drink?"

Jonti shrugged. "I thought, after the contract, that this was supposed to be professional?"

Beetrax stared at her. Hard.

"Yes, well, I confess," she continued, "I recognise that you and professional exist on a different level."

"Listen," said Beetrax, gesticulating with the bottle, "when we stood on Desekra, and those mud-orcs came howling towards us, I was the most professional soldier in that whole fucking army. When I was down in Zakora fighting off bloody bastard tribesmen and their insane squealing women, and we got trapped in a gulley and had to face a wall of steel – I was professional. When I had to fight this horrible twisted horse-creature, with only a dagger and a broken shard of wine goblet, I was the most professional soldier you'd ever met. But now, here, now, in this shit, on my terms, in my world, there's nothing wrong with having a neck of brandy to ward off the bloody snow, like. You get it?"

"I get it," said Sakora, grabbing the bottle from his hand with one lightning-strike gesture. She popped the cork and took a sip. "Good. Twenty years, I reckon."

"Hey! How did you do that?"

Sakora grinned at him. "Training. And... lack of alcohol."

They ate, and huddled under blankets, and enjoyed the heat of the fire. There was friendly atmosphere, gentle banter, and Beetrax found himself relaxing for the first time... since he'd stood on the walls of Desekra Fortress, awaiting an attack by Orlana's mud-orcs. They shared his brandy, and talked about the coming journey through the Karamakkos – the Teeth of the World.

"I knew five men who did it, and returned to tell their tale," said Talon.

"How many set off?" asked Dake.

"Eight. Three got caught in an avalanche. But five survived."

"What was the purpose of their quest?" said Lillith, sipping a cup of water and lifting her hand to turn away the offered venison steak. "Sorry. I do not eat meat."

"They climbed mountains. For fun," said Dake.

"Why?" asked Beetrax.

"Because they could? Because they enjoyed it? A challenge, maybe? I don't know. You'd have to ask them."

"Er. So there was no gold, nor whores, at the end of it?"

Sakora coughed.

"Apologies." Beetrax held up his hand. "So there was no gold, nor throbbing ladies of the night, at the end of it?"

"It was a challenge," said Dake. "They battled the mountain. And won. Well. Five of them did. An avalanche is a terrifying thing."

"I remember," said Beetrax, voice soft. "Anyways!

Enjoyable and morally uplifting though this conversation is, I have had my fill of brandy and venison." He chuckled. "I must confess, I didn't think this quest would be quite so difficult! I am going to turn in for an early night." He stood, and paused, and then looked to Lillith. She looked back.

"Yes?"

"Would you like to accompany me for a conversation?"

"Not particularly."

"I insist."

Lillith sighed, and gathering her wide black skirts, stood. She crunched across the snowy ground and followed Beetrax out beyond the rocks, where a chill wind was biting through the darkness. Away from the fire it was blacker than a dwarf mine-pit, and Beetrax crunched into the snow, his broad, athletic, fat frame forming a huge black mass against the star-filled turquoise sky.

Lillith halted. "Beetrax? What's bothering you? It's been a long day, and I'm more used to libraries, research and reading, than travelling; I'm tired."

"I just wanted to say." His voice was a deep rumble.

"Say what?"

"I miss you."

"Oh, Beetrax."

"I'm sorry. I can't help it. What we had was... amazing. And I miss it. All of it. Even the arguments. And I miss you."

"I've moved on," said Lillith, as gently as she could. "And you should, too."

Beetrax took a little step closer, then stopped, as if unsure of himself. "I miss you. I miss holding you. The sex was amazing, yes, I grant you that, but I miss holding you. Holding you naked, in the long hours before dawn; just feeling the smoothness of your skin. Just touching you. I miss that more than anything."

"I changed, Beetrax," said Lillith, and she had edged closer to him. She stood in his awesome, huge shadow, like a young doe before a stag.

"Why did you change? Why did you leave me?"

"I needed... something else."

"What?"

"I became a different person. I no longer craved humanity. I craved education, and medicine, and a burning desire to help people less fortunate than myself. I am a healer, Beetrax, not a warrior."

"Horseshit. People less fortunate? They thank you at the time, but people are selfish by nature. Except for those you love and who love you. You left me, Lillith, and I still don't truly understand why."

"Neither do I," she whispered.

Beetrax stepped in closer. He leant forward. He smelt her hair.

"No," she said.

"No what?"

"We cannot go down this path again."

"Why not?"

"Because I will not allow it."

"You allowed it once before."

"And I am a different person now. I told you. I'm a better person. My aim is to help all people, not shackle myself to one man in a selfish and vain attempt at pleasing my own vanity, my own base desires."

"Base desires are good," whispered Beetrax. "They define us. They make us human."

"They are a challenge to overcome. To show we are in control of our own minds."

"Then maybe I am no longer in control of my own mind. Because I want you, I want you more now than I ever did; and I love you, Lillith; love you more than life itself. I will kill for you, and I will die for you."

"I desire neither outcome," she whispered.

"You have no choice in this matter," Beetrax said.

"I could walk away. Abandon this quest."

Beetrax paused. "As you wish," he said, voice incredibly gentle for such a big, aggressive man.

There came a moment of calm, of quiet. Beyond them, within the rocks, they could hear quiet conversation. A laugh. The crackle of burning logs.

"Can I ask you one thing? One favour? You may say no."

"For old time's sake," said Lillith, and ran her hands through her long thick hair, her face lifting, coming up to focus on Beetrax.

"Can I hold you? One more time? Please?"

Lillith considered this, her breath coming in short bursts. "You may hold me," she said, her voice tiny.

Beetrax stepped closer, and reached down, and took her in his arms, encircling her. And he breathed in the aroma of her hair, and he breathed in the scent of her skin, and he tasted her again, tasted her for the first time in a million years, and a raging inferno roared through him, and she was everything, she was the world and the universe and life and death. Her arms encircled his waist and they stood there for a while, like young lovers in a first embrace.

When she pulled away, she realised Beetrax was crying.

"I am sorry, my love," she said. "I never meant to hurt you in any way. I just chose a different path to follow; a different journey to the one which was forced upon me, by my parents, by my friends, the one I was *expected* to pursue.

I have a craving in my heart, and I had to pursue that need."

"I understand that. I respect you for that."

"Will you let me go, now?" She looked up at him, at his face and beard, pale under the wan moonlight, under the dazzling starlight.

"No," he said.

"Never," he said.

"I cannot," he said.

"You make it almost impossible for me to travel with you," she said.

"Then that is something we both must suffer."

"You will suffer more than I," said Lillith, kindly. "And that is not something I wish to bear on my conscience."

"I will bear it," said Beetrax. "Go back to the fire, now."

Lillith moved towards the circle of rocks. She stopped. She turned back, hair describing a floating arc. "Are you coming?"

"No. I will wait out here for a while. The cold air is good for me."

Lillith disappeared, and Beetrax stared up to the stars, and then the massive black silhouette of the rearing, distant mountains. Tears were on his cheeks and he scrubbed at them savagely. He pulled out the remains of his brandy. He drank it in one vicious movement, then threw the bottle down in the snow where it shattered on a half-hidden rock.

"I'll miss you," he said, and closed his eyes against the majesty of the vast, sparkling heavens.

Jake Crade cracked his knuckles, took up his bow, notched an arrow, and sighted down the shaft. His men, most of them lounging on the ground, or on fallen trunks in the deep silence of the velvet forest, gave a low ripple of heavy, cynical laughter.

"Try not to kill him," growled one.

"Anyway, not right away, Jake, please!"

Jake shrugged off their mumblings, and steadied his aim. It was quite difficult after a full flagon of wine, and he was aware of the tip of the arrow wavering, moving from the lad's head to his groin and back again.

"For the love of the Seven Sisters," wailed the young man, "why are you doing this?"

"Shut it, before I shoot an arrow through your ball sack!"

"Please, let me go! I won't tell nobody…"

The bandits laughed, and passed around the grog, and watched this evening's entertainment with dark eyes and savage smiles. There was no compassion there. No humanity. Just pleasure in watching a fellow human being suffer. Some men were like that. Some men enjoyed the badness.

"You don't have to do this! I'm an honest woodsman…"

"Shoot him through the quim. That'll stop the bitch whining."

Jake released the string, and the arrow whined through the air, missing the lad's head by a hand's width and rattling off through the trees.

"Damn," muttered Jake, and accepted another flagon. He took a long drink.

A hundred feet away, a fern shivered, and the forest slowly regained composure.

"There's sixteen of them," said Talon, squatting down before the group. "Nasty bastards, by the look of them. Ex-soldiers, I'd wager. They may lounge around like scum drinking wine, but their weapons are clean and oiled, their kit packed and ready to move in a moment. Professional."

"We'll plot a way round," said Beetrax, scratching his beard. "If we move a quarter league east, then head north again, that should keep us out of their immediate territory."

"There's a complication," said Talon, glancing up. His eyes met Beetrax's.

"What's that, lad?"

"They've captured a young woodsman. They've tied him to a tree. I fear he is their evening of entertainment."

Beetrax stared at Talon. "Like I said. We move a quarter league east, head north, plot around them."

"But they've captured a young lad."

"So? They've captured a young lad. He should have been more careful."

Talon scowled. "Is this what the great Beetrax has become? A coward, frightened of standing up for the innocent in need?"

"How do you know he's innocent?" countered Beetrax. "Maybe he's a pig thief and they're teaching him a lesson?"

"Horseshit," snapped Talon. "They were drunk and toying with him. Hurting him."

"I've seen you toy with and hurt many people."

"This is not about me!" snapped Talon. "This is about doing the right thing!"

Dake put his hand on Beetrax's shoulder. Beetrax looked up. Then he looked at Jonti, and Lillith, and Sakora.

Sakora was shaking her head, and Lillith turned away.

"What? *What*? We're on a fucking mission here, or hadn't you noticed?"

"Yes, for gold and your fucking immortality," said Sakora, face a snarl. "And every moment we sit here arguing with an idiot, a young lad is being tortured by forest brigands. Well, I'll go on my own if I have to."

She stood, and clenched her fists.

Talon moved beside her, and strung his bow.

"Ha!" Beetrax stormed upwards, unhitched his axe, and scowled. "How many did you say?"

"Sixteen," said Talon, quietly.

"Well, they're in our way, then. Let's go clear us a path."

The forest sighed, like a satisfied lover. The trees shifted, conifers settling pine needles into the carpet. A gentle wind eased between solid boles, shifting ferns, as if the forest itself was breathing.

Beetrax emerged from the trees, and the head of his axe made a *clunk* as it hit the forest floor. The brigands turned towards him, as one, and he saw their eyes narrow, then move around, searching the forest to see if he was alone.

"You all right, lads?"

"What do you want?"

The leader foregrounded himself immediately. He was a big man, scruffy and professional at the same time. He held himself upright, broad chest protected by an old silver-steel breastplate. His hair was knife-cut short to the scalp, greying at the temples, a five-day shadow bearded his face, and his eyes were dark and calculating.

Beetrax glanced at the captured lad, slumped against bonds which secured him to the ancient oak. The lad had passed into unconsciousness, and his blood showed bright on his face, alongside bruising and a split lip, blackened eyes. Possibly a broken nose.

"Who's that?" Beetrax gestured.

"None of your business."

Beetrax gave a broad smile, and pushed back his shoulders. His axe came up, to rest comfortably in his hands, and he rocked back on his heels to give himself balance; the balance of a warrior.

"Do you know who I am?"

"Amaze me," snapped Jake.

"I am Beetrax the Axeman."

"Never heard of you. All I see is a fat old man with broken teeth and a ginger beard that needs a trim. Now fuck off, before we fill you full of arrows."

"Old man, is it?" said Beetrax.

The axe left his hands with some force, and made a *thrum thrum* sound as it turned end over end, and split the bandit's skull and breastbone down the middle. The man was punched backwards, where he quivered on the ground for a full minute, his blood and brains leaking out to soak the forest carpet.

Beetrax put his hands on his hips, scowling. "Any other cunt think I'm a fat old man?"

The bandits surged to their feet as Talon, Dake, Jonti and Sakora drifted from the trees like ghosts. One bandit ran at them, screaming, sword raised. Talon's arrow smashed through his eye, the steel tip emerging from the back of his skull in a shower of brains and skull shards. He hit the ground, fitting, frothing pink, legs kicking.

There was a moment, where everybody was poised. Balanced scales. Nobody shifted. Then the bandits, fancying their odds, screamed and charged, swords hissing from oiled scabbards. Beetrax stood at the forefront, with Dake on his left, Jonti on his right. Jonti's sword snaked from her scabbard and she smiled.

"Just like old times," she said.

"Let's break some skulls," said Beetrax, cracking his knuckles.

They leapt forward. Jonti's sword took a man in the throat, cutting out his bobbing Adam's apple. Blood flushed down his chest accompanied by a silent, necessary scream. Dake ducked a sword swing, moving like an athlete, fast, supple, sure, and rammed his blade into his attacker's groin. A bandit leapt at Beetrax, who had both hands wide apart, like a preacher, unarmed, easy meat. A sword hacked down. Beetrax shifted, arm lashing out, deflecting the flat of the blade. He grabbed the man's tunic, pulling him onto a savage headbutt which dislodged teeth and cracked a cheek bone. Three times Beetrax headbutted the bandit, into unconsciousness, took his sword like sweet cakes from a child, and hacked off his head in two hard savage blows. They clashed together, and Beetrax, Dake and Jonti surged forward, weapons rising and falling. Talon fired off a dozen arrows, shafts punching into chests, legs and throats. Sakora waited patiently in the wings. A bandit charged her, sword raised, blackened teeth emitting a foul stench. She slid away from his three, four, five strikes. Her hand struck out, flat blade connecting with his windpipe. He staggered back, choking, dropping his sword, falling to his knees. Sakora watched impassively as he choked, and turned blue, and gradually toppled onto his face, dead. His windpipe was crushed by a single blow.

In a few moments it was over.

Beetrax strode forward and pulled his axe from Crade's skull and caved-in chest with a crunch. It took three tugs, and he had to put his boot against the dead man's ribs, but it came at last, and Beetrax observed the blood on the blade – like a hundred thousand times before – and gave a narrow smile which had nothing to do with humour.

"Bad choice," he muttered.

"Any injuries?" shouted Lillith.

Beetrax cast around. Dake nodded. "We're good," said Beetrax, and turned his attention from the slaughtered bodies to the young lad tied to the tree. Beetrax sighed. He shook his head.

The lad was watching them, analysing the slaughter. He looked green.

Beetrax sighed.

"Talon, go see to him."

"You go see to him. This became your slaughter the minute you stepped from the forest!"

"I was trying to avoid a bloodbath!" roared Beetrax.

"No. You were milking your ego. You *encouraged* a bloodbath."

"What? WHAT? So, you fancy fucking archer, what would you have done?"

"Picked them off one at a time from a safe distance."

"What? You fucking brought us here! I wanted to sidestep this whole mess."

"Well, it's a mess now all right," said Lillith, moving past the arguing men and walking to the tied youth. She used an arrow blade to saw through the ropes and he slumped against her, blood drooling from his mouth. Gently, Lillith laid him on the ground and made a pillow for his head. She lifted his tunic and winced at the bruising.

"He's been badly beaten," she said.

Beetrax ambled over. He'd pulled free a strip of dried beef and was chewing on it thoughtfully. "Will he die? And I'm being hopeful here. We don't need no dead fucking baggage on this quest."

The lad's eyes opened. He smiled, then winced, and his hand went to his broken ribs. "You're Beetrax. From

Desekra Fortress. The hero!"

Beetrax's face brightened. "Yes! Did we fight together?"

"No. I learned about you in school. We had a picture book."

Beetrax frowned. "I was in a picture book?"

"Yes. You were slimmer. And more handsome. But it was you."

"By the Seven Sisters!"

The lad coughed, and spat blood on the ground. "To answer your question, no, I won't die."

"Er. Good."

"My name is Jael."

Beetrax shrugged. "So what, lad? Tell me again in a month's time. If you're still alive, then I'll make the effort to remember it."

The Hunt

Ellie had built a fire in the hearth, and as the flames flickered, outside the small cottage, distantly, a wolf howled. She gave a shiver, as if suffering a premonition, but shrugged it off and stood, knees creaking, to smile at little Ailsa, in her pretty red and white dress, sat in her special high chair and kicking her legs as she waited for supper. Janny was sat staring at a small wooden puzzle on the table before him, brow creased in concentration, his seven year-old fingers turning the pieces over and over as he tried to work out how to fit them together.

"Are you hungry, little ones?" said Ellie, smiling, tugging her shawl tight. Outside a frost had peppered the land, and until the fire was roaring, she could now feel the effects of the creeping winter.

"I hung, hungree," grinned Ailsa, eyes shining, and Ellie crossed, rubbing the little girl's mop of golden curls.

"When Dada gets back."

As if invoking her husband, Troma, the door opened and a large man stepped through, arms piled with logs, his bearded, kind face glowing red with the cold. He kicked shut the door and deposited the logs beside the hearth to warm, before turning and hugging Ellie, like a bear enveloping a child.

"By the Seven Sisters, I swear the snow will be here tonight."

"You look freezing, my love. Come, sit by the fire."

"In a moment." Troma crossed to his little boy, and picked up the lad, hugging him deeply. Then, carrying the giggling boy in one arm, he plucked Ailsa from the high chair and snuggled into both his children, eyes closed for a moment, Ailsa pulling at strands of his bushy beard.

Ten minutes, the fire was roaring and the small cottage filled with heat. Ellie had slow cooked a beef broth during the day whilst Troma was out cutting firewood for what they both knew would be a long winter ahead. Now, as Troma mopped up the last of the gravy with a thick slice of coarse bread, a contentment settled on the family like warm honey. Troma laughed at Ailsa's stew dribble, and set to working out the wooden puzzle – which he had carved himself – with Janny, who was complaining it was too difficult, and even the teacher at school in the village had been unable to solve it, and he was an expert at maths.

"Kabor called round today," said Ellie, voice gentle as she nibbled her slice of bread.

Troma looked up. The big man's eyes narrowed. "What did he want?"

"He said there was work for you on the firewood team. He said he'd never seen a man work so well with an axe."

"Well." Troma took an old worn bread knife, which had once belonged to his mother, and his grandmother, the wooden handle worn smooth with decades of use, and slowly sliced himself a chunk of bread. "I don't care for many of the men he employs. Rough types with vulgar mouths. Always yapping. They give me a headache."

"Troma." He looked into Ellie's beautiful dark eyes.

"We'll struggle. We cannot afford to live if you have no work. I know you broke that man's jaw, but Kabor can see past that. He's willing to put the past behind you."

Troma toyed with the bread, but did not eat. "I don't like that man coming to the house. I will have words."

"Please don't threaten him. One day we may need his coin."

"Don't you worry about money, my love. I will get work in the quarry over in Hisbeck. My back and shoulders are strong, and you know I am as powerful as a Shire horse."

Ellie opened her mouth, then closed it again. The cupboards were starting to look exceedingly bare, and Troma, despite being a gentle giant, could display a fierce temper if any man made comments about his wife or children, as had been displayed several weeks back when his fury overtook him and he had lost his job.

Troma sat in thought for a while, as Ellie cleared the dishes and wiped Ailsa's face with a damp cloth. His contemplation was disturbed by another wolf howl, closer this time – which was suddenly cut short.

Troma frowned. Ellie glanced at him.

"That was odd."

"Maybe a woodsman killed it?"

"Perhaps. But at this time of night?"

Troma stood, and strode to the door. "I will go and check around the cottage. Stay inside. Bolt the door behind me."

"What do you think it is?"

Troma shrugged, and pulled on a thick bearskin jerkin, once his father's. He strode outside, carefully closing the door and waiting, listening for Ellie throwing the bolts. Just so he knew his family was safe.

The moon was out near-full, casting a cold, pale glow.

Troma moved to the woodshed, where his large axe squatted, steel head embedded in a huge log. His hand curled around the polished shaft, and he tugged it free with a smooth, practised action. He turned and walked slowly down the slope to the lane, which led further down to the village. Walking up the lane, one carrying a shovel, the other an iron bar, came Jeg the Smith, and Woolard, a self-appointed busybody who masqueraded as the village councillor now he had retired from proper work. They stopped, offering narrow smiles.

"We think there's a pack on its way over," said Jeg. "You want to lend a hand?"

"I reckon yonder way." Troma pointed, and he saw both village men's eyes drop to the axe carried in his free hand.

"So, you're expecting trouble as well?" said Woolard.

"Maybe." Troma gave a single nod.

They trekked up a narrow track, the mud frozen solid now, and within minutes hills rolled to either side. Woodland to the left was a dark ink blot under the light of the moon, and where it was a place village children played during daylight, now it seemed eminently foreboding.

"Don't normally get wolves this far south," said Troma, after a while.

"Maybe it's slim pickings, what with the early frost?"

"Maybe," said Troma.

They came to a steep section of track, and began to climb. Woolard was panting hard; an unfit man, and greying, it was well known he liked his ale, and since the death of his wife some years previous, the councillor had increased his drinking pace and consumption. He paused halfway up the slope, bending, hands on his knees, then shook his head at Troma, and pushed himself up and onwards.

They breached the rise, and stopped.

Ahead, through the darkness, under pale moonlight, came a... creature. It was large, bulky. Almost a horse. Almost. Its gait was uneven, curious, as if it were lame. But one of its shoulders also moved... oddly. As if its bones had been broken and reformed... wrong.

Troma stared, and licked his lips.

"What the hell is that?"

"It's a horse," squinted Woolard.

"That's like no bloody horse I've ever seen!" snapped Jeg the Smith, and hoisted his solid iron bar.

The creature saw them. A deep growl rumbled across the coarse, knee-high grassy folds that separated them – a distance of perhaps a hundred yards. Suddenly, it accelerated into a gallop, a twisted, broken gallop, and Woolard made a strangled noise, turned, and ran for it, disappearing over the brow of the hill and away from view.

Troma and Jeg exchanged glances. Jeg licked his lips.

"When it's on us, we separate, strike from both sides."

"What in the name of the Holy Mother..."

"And watch that bloody horn!"

The sounds of the beast's hooves thundered across the grass, indicating the beast's weight. As it grew near, Troma blinked, suddenly appreciating just how *big* it was. Much, much bigger than a horse. He swallowed dry, and realised his hands were slippery with sweat on the axe. The great, broken horse head reared, quivering lips pulled back over black fangs, and it was nearly upon them. Suddenly it jacked back its shoulders, rearing up as Troma and Jeg snapped apart, their weapons slicing through the air – to bounce off the creature's hide. It screeched, hooves pawing the winter air, then slammed down at Jeg, huge mouth engulfing his head and twisting sideways, wrenching the head free trailing neck tendons, flaps of torn skin, a shower of blood and a tail of his broken spinal column. Jeg's knees buckled and his corpse hit the long grass. Everything was ghostly pale under the moonlight, Jeg's blood black as ink.

Troma staggered back, mouth open, filled with a total, all-consuming shock and terror. Then the beast whirled on him, and he lifted the axe which felt like a toy in his big hands. It leapt at him, moving faster than anything that size had a right to move. He slammed the axe sideways in a savage, tree-felling cut, and it embedded in a thick band of corded muscle; the beast shifted sideways under the impact, and the axe was dragged from Troma's slippery hands. He staggered back again, unarmed now, and the beast glanced right, down the slope, then lowered its head and started to walk towards him.

Troma stumbled backwards, his hands coming up.

"What, in the name of the Seven Sisters, *are you*?" he gasped.

The beast suddenly stopped. Those eyes fixed on him. The twisted equine lips, black and slick and quivering, seemed to be laughing. And it spoke. The creature said, "I am... your dark... ness."

It leapt, head slamming down, twisting sideways, and the horn skewered Troma through the chest, erupting from his back in a shower of blood and broken chunks of rib. His hands slammed down, grasping the tusk which had impaled him as the beast lifted him easily from his feet, gasping, choking out blood, and shook him like a doll.

Troma was blinking rapidly.

This was all a dream. A bad dream. A nightmare.

And he pictured Ailsa's face, covered in sweetcake. And

Janny, fumbling with the puzzle his Dada had made for him. Tears filled his eyes. Rolled down his cheeks. And he remembered meeting Ellie. She had flowers in her red hair, and was sat under the Marriage Oak in the Lower Meadow, waiting for him, for their first date, for their first kiss. She had looked so, so beautiful...

The beast grunted, and tilted its head, and the steaming corpse slid from its horn.

It turned, and limped to the summit of the hill, gazing down the slope at the white-haired man who was running away, as fast as he could, panting and grunting. He had dropped his shovel halfway down the slope, and there were several muddy skid marks where he must have fallen and slid.

The beast reared its head, and a huge, screeching, twisted whinny erupted, cutting through the night like a razor.

The man turned, saw the beast silhouetted against the moon, screamed something, then stumbled, falling flat on his face. The creature galloped down the slope after him, and he heard its approach, rolled onto his back, saying, "No no, please no, please no," as those great, uneven eyes watched him with something akin to amusement.

Then he stopped his muddy scramble, and lay still, and watched, and waited, and piss stained his pants.

The beast took a step forward, lifted one front leg high in the air, and planted an iron hoof through the centre of Woolard's face.

"When will Dada be home?" asked Janny. Ellie helped him into his woollen pyjamas, an arm, another arm, then a leg, and another leg, as he giggled and sat on the edge of the low bed which Troma had built. Janny then crawled into bed next to Ailsa, and Ellie pulled up the blankets to ward off winter chill.

"He won't be long, my darling," she said.

"I miss him already. Will he be going back to work soon?"

"I am sure he will," said Ellie, with a smile.

She tucked the children in tight, then moved to the door, only half closing it so the light from candles and fire would give them comfort. Ailsa was sucking her thumb, eyes closed tight. Dreaming the dreams of an infant.

Ellie crept around the cottage for a while, listening for the return of Troma. When a half hour had passed, she frowned and moved to the window, drawing back the curtain. The moonlight turned her garden into ink and shadows, dancing softly. Her eyes strained, searching for her husband, but to no avail.

She closed the curtain. A chill wind blew over her soul.

Outside, there came a *thump*.

Ellie turned and stared at the dual bolted door. The bolts were thick iron, made by Jeg the Smith. They were not toys, not playthings, but heavy duty, fitted during the siege of Desekra Fortress when rumours told of the country being near-overrun by mud-orcs.

Again, there came a *thump*.

Ellie backed away, grabbing a hand-sharpened bread knife from the rack.

With a tearing sound, wood being ripped asunder, and a screeching of twisting, separating iron, the door – in its entirety – was ripped free from the doorframe and tossed backwards. What stooped and stared in at Ellie was a twisted horse creature from cheese-fuelled nightmares. Blood stained its broken hooves and quivering black lips.

The eyes bore through her with an alien intelligence she found both amazing and terrifying to her core.

The creature pushed, but its bulk was too big for the doorframe.

"Get back, you evil scourge!" she hissed, brandishing the bread knife. It trembled violently in fingers that shook.

The creature rumbled, in what could have been a deviation of laughter, then heaved its bulk through the gap, breaking the doorframe which crumbled to either side like tinder, and taking out several stones from the wall. The roof beams shook, and dust floated down, twirling patterns by the lights of the flickering candles.

A cold breeze flowed in, buoyed on a current of stench. The stench of rotting meat, of carrion crows feasting on a long-deserted battlefield; the stench of maggots in eye sockets, of opened bowels long coagulated, of part-digested flesh vomited back to the earth by those who feasted on death.

The beast advanced, hooves shaking the floorboards.

"No," whimpered Ellie. "No, wait, stop! I know you. I know what you are!"

The beast halted. Steam rose from its wide open maw. Great fangs gleamed, stained with blood, caught with little strips of skin and muscle.

"What... am... I?"

"You are *splice*," said Ellie, voice trembling, tears running down her cheeks. "You were created by Orlana the Changer – the Horse Lady! She merged you, a man, with a horse, to create this terrible thing you have become."

The beast tilted its head, listening to her. Its great chest rose and fell, and steam oozed from its nostrils.

"It's not your fault," said Ellie, taking another step back.

"But you… you don't have to do this!"

"I need… to feed."

Hating herself, Ellie whispered, "Find others. Not here. Not my children. Not my babies. There are others in the village." She gestured with the shaking knife. "There are… old people. Near the end of their lives. Take them! Not my children."

The creature shifted, its head turning in the direction she pointed. For a moment, an eternal moment, which took just the single beat of her heart, she thought the splice was going to retreat, take her advice, and seek older, sour meat. Those who were already dead. Condemned by the cages of their aged frames.

Then its head swung back to her on bulging, uneven muscles. It shook its head, as a horse shakes its head and mane, then lowered its great maw a little and those terrible eyes met Ellie's.

"I am cursed. I am… sorry. But you have seen me."

The splice leapt, crashing *through* the table and chairs and ending Ellie's life with a single bite. Blood surged across the boards, dripping between gaps, staining splintered chairs. A terrible silence fell, and the splice tilted its head again, listening, its breath snorting from its horse snout.

"Dada?"

Janny stood at the door in his woollen pyjamas. His hands came to his mouth.

The splice met the little boy's frightened gaze.

And it started forward

Karamakkos

It was the night following the fight with the forest bandits. Beetrax and the group had made camp after pushing hard, riding north, distancing themselves from collected brigand corpses. The lad, Jael, doubled up with Sakora on her mount, as she was the lightest, her horse less burdened and thus able to suffer two lighter riders.

They made camp in a quiet woodland, where the wind whispered seductively between brown leaves and pine. After Dake had built a fire, Jael lay beside the flames, wincing, murmuring, and Lillith tended him, administering powdered pain killers which she ground with a small pestle and mortar, and mixed with warm water.

"Drink this."

Jael sucked it from the bowl, and scowled at the flavour, a bigger scowl than even his injuries had produced.

"That is, truly, the worst thing I have ever put in my mouth."

"Widow Pouch, Snukkit and Dark Root. They will ease the pain and help in the healing and building of bones."

"Thank you. You are very skilled."

"Very experienced. I've had lots of practice." Lillith smiled, and started pottering, packing away her equipment.

"You were with them, weren't you?"

Lillith stopped. "What?"

"At Desekra Fortress. You were with Beetrax, and Dake, and Jonti and Talon. I've read all about you. You were heroes. You *are* heroes!"

"Yes, I was there." She did not meet his gaze.

"Was it exciting?" His eyes were shining. Lips wet.

Lillith remembered the screams of the injured as they writhed on the stone cobbles trying to hold their massacred bodies together. She remembered the glazed looks in the eyes of the dead. She remembered the pleading and whimpering from fathers who would never see their baby daughters, from newly-wed husbands who would never see their young wives. She remembered the tears. The begging. The blood. The agony. The screams. The piss. The shit. The humility of the cut, the broken, the severed and the dying.

"Yes. It was exciting," she whispered.

"I would like to be a great warrior, some day," said Jael, and winced, grabbing suddenly at his broken ribs.

"Talk to Beetrax." She smiled kindly. "He will train you. His vanity won't let him do anything else."

"Dake. May I have a word?"

"Er. All right then." Dake nodded, and frowned, and stretched his shoulders, and followed Beetrax off into the trees away from the group. He glanced up, where towering evergreens swayed, creating a gentle, background hissing. Their boots crunched old pine needles.

Beetrax stopped, and paused, then turned around, hand resting on the head of the great axe holstered at his hip.

"What are we doing, Dake?"

"I thought we were on a mission." Dake's lips narrowed

into a humourless smile. "To get rich. Or die trying."

"And don't forget the immortality," nodded Beetrax, grinning suddenly. "And healing Jonti, obviously. That has become a priority." His face turned serious.

"Yes. A priority," said Dake, distantly. He looked off through the forest. His grey eyes seemed dreamy, detached.

Beetrax coughed. "It's this lad we rescued. Er…"

"Jael."

"Yes. Jael."

"What about him?"

"We should cut him loose. Get rid of him. He'll slow us down."

"Only for a little while. Until his wounds heal."

Beetrax stared at Dake. "Damn you man, do you need me to spell it out to you? This was our contract. Our agreement. Our mission. Our quest. We never agreed for no… no *seventh party* coming on board. I'm very sorry this young lad was captured by forest bandits, I am sure. But I ain't his fucking dad. We can't be responsible for every fucking waif and stray we find wandering around the forest getting themselves into trouble. What are we? A fucking charity?"

"Didn't you hear his story?"

"What story?"

"About the bandit attack on his village?"

"I didn't hear no story."

"Ah yes." Dake looked down his nose at Beetrax. His lips curled a little. "You were asleep, curled up to your best friend, the wine flagon."

"Nothing wrong with a wine flagon," frowned Beetrax. "Like I've always said. A wine flagon is one of the cornerstones of civilisation, along with the gold coin and the happy whore. Now, what's this story you're clucking on about like an invigorated chicken?"

"An invig..." Dake's hand rested on his sword hilt. "Beetrax. Sometimes, you go too far. Take back that comment before I show you what damage an invigorated chicken can do with a blade as sharp as any razor." He half-drew his sword, and fixed his gaze on the big axeman.

"All right, all right, don't get your pants all twisted with vinegar. I take it back. For old times' sake, like. Now then. What this lad's story?"

"He wasn't just wandering around the forest aimlessly, picking fights with bandits. Those bastards attacked his village and killed damn near everybody. He resisted, using his wood-cutting axe, but they were professional soldiers. Hit him to the ground where he watched his mother and father murdered, watched his sister abused and then her throat slit." Dake shivered. "Sometimes, I lose my faith in humanity, for I believe we live in savage times."

"We need to send a message to the king's guard. We can't have scum like that roaming Vagandrak."

"At least we taught them a little lesson," smiled Dake. "But, as you can see, this lad is damaged goods. I suggest we at least look after him until his wounds have healed. Then he can make his own choices."

Beetrax scowled. "I suppose we could write him into the contract, so that if he continues with us on this quest, he is not eligible for any share of the treasure..."

"Beetrax!"

"What?" His eyes went wide. "*What*?"

"It's not about the *share in the treasure*, you ginger bastard. It's about a basic humanity. About looking after an injured youth in need."

Beetrax sighed. He nodded. "Oh. All right then." He rolled his neck and cracked the tendons, releasing tension. He took a few steps back towards the group, then turned and stared hard at Dake. He unhitched his axe, and pointed at the warrior with the gleaming twin blades. "But let's get one thing clear. He ain't anything – *anything* – to do with me. He's your fucking burden, soldier. And your fucking *problem*. So don't talk to me when he starts crying for his mama's milk tits."

Dake watched Beetrax saunter down the narrow trail, as if didn't have a care in the world.

They called it the White Lane, which cut a line up the western edge of the White Lion Mountains. Once, in years gone by, the army had used it for training, along with the testing ground of the mountain summits themselves; but with recent cuts to the army made by King Yoon, it had become an abandoned valley, three leagues long, perfect ambush ground and doorway to the northern edges of Zalazar, Elf Rat lands, and the Karamakkos beyond.

They stood in a line, eyeing the narrow channel ahead of them.

"It's been a long time," said Sakora, licking her lips.

"Happy memories," rumbled Beetrax, resting his axe on his shoulder.

"*Happy* memories?" Jonti stared at him. "I remember risking my life, training hard, carrying rocks, risking avalanche, crevasses, and death."

"As I said," rumbled Beetrax. "Happy memories. It is such training that made us the soldiers we are today. The warriors. The *heroes*."

Jael, who sat astride Sakora's mount, face bruised and

swollen, wincing with every movement, turned to Beetrax.

"This is where the army trained?"

"Aye. Not just the army, though. This was the training ground for the Iron Wolves. The elite."

"The Iron Wolves…" whispered Jael.

"They were hard bastards," said Dake, nodding.

"I knew Kiki, one of the captains," said Lillith, smiling, and running her hand through long hair.

"You did?" Beetrax looked at her. "When?"

"Shall we say we both had a love of the same herb lore."

"Eh?"

Dake nudged Beetrax, and gestured to Jael, who was still staring at the axeman. The young lad struggled, and slid from the horse, and approached, limping. "I have a request, Great Beetrax."

Dake chuckled. "The only thing *great* about him is the girth of his wine belly."

Jael shook his head. "In school, we were taught repeatedly about Vagandrak history. Your name – all of you – your names came up many times. Around the time of Orlana. And the mud-orc invasions at the Pass of Splintered Bones. But what caught my attention, the stories that made me gasp, were about Beetrax, and his amazing Axe of Death."

"Oh, Axe of Death is it?" said Dake, elbowing Beetrax in the ribs.

"Shut up," muttered the axeman.

"I wondered, if I might hold the great weapon of these legends?" Jael looked up at Beetrax, eyes pleading from a puffy, swollen face. One eye was nearly swollen shut, and the lad's nose was bent, nostrils still bloodied.

Beetrax sighed. "All right. I don't normally do this. But understand this, there is no Axe of Death bollocks; she has a name, yes, a name only I know and which I will never share. And it's... unusual for another man to touch my axe. You could say it's a bit like touching my cock. It's something you just don't ask to do."

Talon gave a little cough.

"Shut it, you bastard." He turned back to Jael. He scowled. He seemed ruffled, suddenly out of place; uneasy. "Here. Take it." He thrust out the weapon.

Jael took the battle axe in both hands, eyes widening in awe. "This is the same weapon that slew mud-orcs on the walls of Desekra Fortress?"

"That'd be it, lad."

"One day, I will be a great warrior like you! I will join the army. I will find evil woodland bandits. And I will slaughter them. I will protect the innocent from the evil strong." He thrust the axe back towards Beetrax, and turned away from the group, tears coursing down his cheeks.

Lillith moved over to him, as Beetrax stood looking uncomfortable, and she placed her arm around the young lad's shoulders.

"Everything will be all right," she soothed.

"Listen." Beetrax stood, red-faced. Jael's shoulders were shaking. Beetrax looked around the group, then watched as Jael turned. He was snivelling, and presented a pretty pathetic specimen of a man.

"Yes, Great Beetrax?"

"I, er, well, I heard you have suffered, like. With your family, is what I mean. And I realise you want to do some good."

"Yes, Great Beetrax?"

"Well, lad, seeing as you're so enamoured with this battle axe, and we're going to have a bit of free time on our hands,

I thought I might teach you a few of the basic moves. You know, so if forest bandits come at you again, you can chop off their heads, and suchforth."

"Oh, that would be amazing, Great Beetrax!"

"Yes. Well. Anything to help out a young lad in need," he rumbled, and grabbing the reins of his horse, marched ahead, surveying the White Lane and the huge boulders which littered this jagged avenue through the mountains.

Dake followed, leading his own mount. "Beetrax! Wait up!"

Beetrax did not turn.

"What?"

"That was a good thing you did, man. A noble thing."

"Yeah. Well. I expect extra wine rations. Or something."

"He's just a feeble woodcutter. He won't take up much of your time."

Beetrax shrugged. "I hate to see a young lad cry like that. It's not right."

"Still. You did a good deed today. Be proud."

Beetrax turned and eyed Dake carefully. "I will then, Dake. Thank you. Sometimes, I remember why you are like a brother to me. Sometimes." Beetrax strode forward, leading Bella by her reins.

"One last thing, Great Beetrax."

Beetrax stopped dead. "Yeah?"

"It's not like you to make new friends…"

"Fuck off."

"Be gentle with him. We'll be watching and scoring."

"Fuck off."

"I'm amazed you're going to let the lad touch your axe!"

"Dake? Fuck off."

Beetrax strode ahead, kicking rocks out of his path.

•••

They travelled the White Lane without incident. It was silent in that narrow gulley, and dark, each side towered over by sheer icy walls of rock and snow. The grey light that filtered down was ethereal, the atmosphere ghostly, seemingly from another, more innocent time, a time before the rise of Man.

Jonti rode alone. She was surrounded by her travelling companions, cocooned by her friends; and yet she rode alone.

She remembered this place, remembered like it was yesterday. Sections had changed, new rock falls, different formations of fake wall sections which they, as newly recruited soldiers, had to defend and attack in mock battle situations. She stopped her mount by one such temporary defence – she remembered helping to build it, down to shorts, smock and boots, sweating with the others as they scouted for rocks and added them to the pile.

Sergeant Dunda had bellowed at them, waving a short black stick which he called the "Recruit Fucker", and they'd all worked so much harder, not wanting that chunky black stick across the back of the head.

Jonti blinked. And breathed. So long. So long ago. And yet here, now, replayed in this moment of time.

She surveyed her companions, face impassive, moving from Talon to Beetrax to Lillith to Sakora, then Jael, clinging on tightly to the horse and looking like he was going to be sick. Finally, to Dake. Her lover. Her husband. Her man. Her loyal man. Her soul mate.

Snow started to fall, a light sprinkling, and she looked up, enjoying the tickling feeling of snowflakes caressing her skin. She closed her eyes for a moment, and enjoyed the sensation. It was beautiful. It brought her life… whilst inside her body, the corruption, well, that only brought her death.

Jonti grimaced. And smiled.

That's the way the dice roll.

"There's a barracks up ahead," said Beetrax. "Good place to make camp for the night. I don't fancy another night in the rocks; my piles are bad enough as it is."

"You should get them seen to," said Talon, giving him a narrow smile. "A man as rich as you can surely afford the best in medical expertise! After all. You don't want the wrong fingers poking away up there, do you?"

"Fuck off, Tal."

The barracks was a large, old building of rough-cut stones and blackened timber. It sat snug against a rock wall, and had been roofed with slate taken from the surrounding mountain detritus. The windows were small, signalling the harsh climate, and the door was open a little, showing old leaves and a scattering of pebbles.

Dake scouted inside, sword unsheathed, ever wary of bandits, but the old barracks was empty.

"There's even a fire laid," he said, grinning as he emerged.

"I'll stable the horses," said Talon. "Beetrax?"

"Aye, lad?"

"Can you muster some of your famous Vagandrak stew?"

Beetrax beamed suddenly. "Oh yes, lad! By all that's holy, I can do *that*!"

Snow fell, along with the mountain night. A savage wind howled down the White Lane, bringing with it yet more chill and ice. A fire roared in the hearth, filling the main room with heat, and warmth, and an easy, amiable light. Beetrax had fished out an old iron pot from the store cupboard, and after cleaning it with handfuls of snow, soon had his stew bubbling over the fire. He mixed in dried beef, wild onions, small potatoes, wild mushrooms Lillith had picked back in the forest, then added plenty of salt and a mixture of his own special blend of herbs – Beetrax's "special recipe" as made "by his mother, grandmother and great grandmother for the past one hundred and twenty years". Or so he claimed.

The room was filled with an amazing aroma that soon had everybody's mouths watering. As the door slammed open allowing Talon to stagger in, Jael close behind, both laden with logs for the fire, Beetrax scowled.

"Come on, come on, you're letting the snow in!"

"Feel free to help bring logs," snapped Talon, dumping them beside the hearth. "After all, it's more than a two-man job to heat this bloody place for the night!"

Beetrax, who had just tasted his stew and was holding a wooden spoon, wagged the spoon at Talon. "Listen, archer, I don't tell you how to fire your arrows, or string a bow. I don't need you interfering with the culinary art – *art*, you hear? – of perhaps one of the finest chefs in Vagandrak."

"Art now, is it?" growled Talon, eyes narrowed.

"Lad, without meaning to sound arrogant, you don't have an artist – that's me – break away from a masterpiece – that's the stew – to do some simple, heavy, manual labour, like what you is doing. Right? I mean," he chuckled with incredulity, "who *else* could cook such an amazing meal?"

"Manual labour," said Talon, in a strangled voice.

Lillith moved over to Talon, her thick hair swaying, her scent strong, eyes smiling, and placed her arm around his shoulders. "Ignore the self-important axeman. You *know* what he's like."

"I know he wouldn't be able to wave that spoon at me

with a yew shaft through his hand."

"Threats of violence, lad. I like that. Like that a lot! But you'll still want to eat my stew when it's ladled onto a plate before you, so keep your threats to yourself, or you won't be eating from my pot."

Talon frowned. "I won't…"

"Shh," said Lillith, turning him around. "Dake wants to speak with you. Over there, in the other room. About Jonti."

"Where is Jonti?"

"Tending the horses. Go now. I think he needs your… support."

Talon nodded, and without looking at Beetrax, picked his way across the room and disappeared into one of the several other chambers leading from the main common room of the old barracks.

Lillith moved, and sat beside Beetrax.

He looked at her.

"Why do you goad the man?"

"Keeps him on his toes."

"I do believe Talon does not need to be kept on his toes. He is as accomplished as any in this company."

Beetrax shrugged, and looked at Lillith. "He looks down at me, I think. He thinks I am scruffy, and common, and vulgar."

"You are."

"I fucking know that! I just don't want some man-loving dandy with hair like a woman to keep reminding me." He scratched his beard vigorously. Then looked sideways at Lillith. "Anyways. It didn't stop you, did it?"

"Eventually."

"Yes, but whilst it lasted…" He coughed, and found a

sudden interest in his stew. "Why, er, why did you like me?"

Lillith smiled, genuine, pleasant, and honest. "You touched me. You affected me. You changed me. I was in your aura, and like a moon caught by a planet, I was in your sphere of influence; in your... *gravity*."

Beetrax considered this. "Wow. Nobody has ever been in my gravity before."

"That day we met, in the woods, you changed me. With your power and aura. Your presence. The warrior within."

"Why did you not stay with me?"

"Always we return to that damn question. A question, truly, I cannot answer. Only know this. There have been none after you. Not one man has touched me since you. And I love you, Beetrax. You know that. I always have, and I always will."

Beetrax was fighting himself. He looked at her then, with an intensity, a passion so deep it burned right through him. "Come to my bed, Lillith," he said. "I want you. I need you. Like the sapling needs sunlight. Like a babe needs its mother's milk. Come to my bed, tonight."

Lillith pursed her lips, and smoothed out her black skirts. "You should not think of me in that way. It is over." Her words were gentle and she stared into the fire, refusing to meet his gaze.

"But... I do think of you that way," he said. "I watch you. Every movement. Every hand gesture. I watch your fingers, want you to put them in my mouth, to taste them. I watch your face. The sparkle of your eyes. The curve of your mouth. The slender taper of your nose. I remember your long pale limbs. I remember your breasts, your nipples, I remember tasting you, my tongue inside your mouth and inside your quim; sandalwood, that's what you taste like. I could drink you like I would drink well water–"

Talon gave a small cough from the doorway, then walked forward. He sat beside Beetrax, and glanced at Lillith. "Not very private, these barracks, are they?"

"Not when you're here," snapped Beetrax.

The door opened, and Jonti entered, bringing with her a blast of freezing winter chill. "The snow's getting heavier. We'll have to turn the horses back soon. No sense in killing them out in the wild. They'll find their way to warmer pastures."

Lillith nodded. "The Karamakkos beckon."

Jonti smiled, but it was a smile without humour. "Indeed they do. As do the Ice Bridges of Sakaroth."

"Let us hope they have formed, or we'll have a long wait in bloody miserable freezing conditions."

"Only the Mountain Gods know the answer to that."

"STEW'S UP!" bellowed Beetrax, suddenly, and stared at Talon. "What?"

"Hell, man, you made me jump."

Beetrax grinned. "I'll remember that for next time."

"I'm going to die, aren't I, Dake?"

"Nobody is going to die, my love."

"I am. I'm going to die, without ever having children, without ever seeing my babies grow up into fine young men and women. What did I do wrong, Dake? What evil gods did I upset? It's so damn unfair."

They lay, curled together under warm blankets. Outside the wind howled, and snow fell, smothering the world. Dake's hand rested on Jonti's hip, and slowly he ran his fingers across her smooth, warm flesh, up, until his fingers rested just beneath her left breast. Jonti gave a low groan, and pushed her face into his neck. He could feel her tears on his skin and it killed him. Killed him there and then, and for all eternity.

"We're going to find these jewels, and they will heal you," whispered Dake into her long, dark hair. He smelled her musk. Her natural scent. He inhaled her, and knew that he'd be lost without her.

"You know what the doctors said. What the *surgeons* said. This *thing* inside me, it will eat me, I will grow weak, and then I will die. There is no cure."

"There is magick," said Dake.

Jonti snorted. "Magick is so much horseshit. Charms and chanting and invisible spells. Next you'll be telling me fucking dragons exist outside of a child's bedtime story!"

"What about the Horse Lady? What about the mud-orcs? The demons we fought. That is proof of magick. Surely, you have not forgotten so soon?"

Jonti considered this. "I think... there are some things we don't understand. I believe there is a power in the earth; in the mountains, the rocks, the soil, the trees. But I don't believe there are sparkling baubles that will shine and sing and take this cancer away. It's inside my *bones*, Dake, my love. And I appreciate your sentiment; all of you. I appreciate it. But this, for me, is one final adventure. One last chance to do something... great. Special. Different. Call it what you will. But to be here with you, and all these other bastards – well, it will make my final days worthwhile."

"Don't talk like this, my lady. I cannot bear it."

Jonti sat up, suddenly, and took his head in her hands. "Stop being maudlin! Stop whining. You are a man, Dake. A warrior. So fuck me now, make me scream, because I want to feel life lived to the full." She took his balls in her hand

and squeezed, hard, holding him in place. Dake groaned, and blinked, fell deep down into his wife's magick wishing well.

Beetrax sat, staring into the fire. He took another slug from a wine flagon, and welcomed the feel of alcohol pulsing through his veins. He had welcomed it far too much these past decades… a source of constant regret. And yet there was nothing he could do about it. Drink was drink. And some things were just meant to be.

"Well met, Beetrax!"

Jael had emerged from a bunkroom, and sat down beside the large axeman. He was smiling and friendly, but Beetrax frowned. Beetrax was not smiling and friendly. In fact, the last thing Beetrax wanted was idle chatter.

"Your stew was magnificent!"

"Thanks."

"I was paying you a compliment, Axeman."

"I know."

"You don't sound very happy, Beetrax? Have I done something to offend you?"

Beetrax turned his head and stared at the youth. The swelling had gone down a little in his face. His eyes were shining; young, and bright and alive. Optimistic. Hopeful. It filled Beetrax with piss and bile.

Offend me? Of course not young man! I am here to entertain you, and offer you words of wisdom on becoming a great axe warrior like myself. Then you, too, can defend the walls of Desekra Fortress against a common evil that seeks to invade your land and kill your women and children… and you'll watch your best friends die on the battlements, arms lopped free, throats cut, bowels emerging from long sword slashes, spilling to the stone as men scream and weep and beg to die, their blood freezing in crimson puddles as we step on their wailing bodies in an attempt to halt the same horror happening to us! You want to hear the glory of battle, boy? Well, in all honesty, you can fuck off. There is no glory in battle. Only corpses and regret and rich generals drinking port.

Beetrax coughed. He focussed; a little. "No, lad. Not at all. I was just feeling... mawkish. Remembering old things, like. Old times. Friends who are dead. Lovers long past."

"We could raise a drink to them?"

"Not tonight, lad. Not tonight."

They sat in silence for a while, flames crackling, with the smell of woodsmoke strong in the air. It was comfortable and comforting. Beetrax settled back a little, alcohol buzzing him, and took a gulping swig from the wine flagon. Then, without a single word, he held out the flagon to Jael.

Jael paused, then took the flagon, and took his own dribbling drink. He spluttered, nearly dropping the flagon, and Beetrax tutted, grabbing the clay flask back from him. "What's wrong with you, boy? If you drop it, there'll be none left!"

"It's strong!" wheezed Jael.

"Aye. That'll be the liquor I add. Just to fortify it a bit. You know. Puts hairs on your chest. That sort of thing." He grinned then, and leaning forward, slapped Jael on the back. "That was your first time, wasn't it? Eh? Go on, own up!"

Jael's cheeks were flushed, his eyes wide. "Yes. Yes it was."

Beetrax loomed close, great shaggy brows frowning, bushy beard making him appear even more aggressive – evil – in the small, fire-lit space. "You been living in a fucking cave, boy?"

"No. My parents did not drink. And there was never any liquor in the village. The Elders used to complain mightily if any alcohol was discovered!" He grinned, rubbing his mouth with the back of his hand.

"Ah. Elders, eh? Fuck me. Wise men so full of the need to satisfy their own pleasures and expanding purses, they rarely think of the greater good. Like politicians. All in need of a sword blade sawed through the neck." He paused, and stared hard at Jael. It was a disconcerting stare. "So then. Was it good, lad?" he said suddenly. "Get more down you!" He thrust the flagon, and Jael took another choking drink, handing it back to Beetrax who roared with laughter.

"Beetrax? I have a question?"

"Go on then."

"I was looking at your axe." He gestured with a nod, to the weapon which never lay far from Beetrax's bear paw.

"Aye?"

"It has all those metal bands down the shaft. I've never seen that before."

"That's because you're used to woodcutters' axes, boy. Mine is a weapon of war." He saw Jael frown. "What I mean is, a woodcutter does not have somebody swinging a sword at him. The metal bands are called langets. They make it more difficult for an enemy warrior to cut the shaft during battle."

"Ah. I see. Because an axe with no shaft…"

"Is a lump of useless steel, lad." Beetrax grinned. "I'll tell you something else. A good axe-maker uses his skill to carbon-edge the blades. You can sharpen them a lot keener, then. Makes a proper mess of a mud-orc's neck."

"Or a forest bandit."

"Yes."

He settled back yet more, and took another long draught of wine. He sighed, and scratched his ginger beard.

"Were you in many battles?" asked Jael, voice gentle, eyes shining in the light of the fire. Demon fireflies sparkled, as if surging upwards, attempting to be free of the killing jar.

"Too many."

"Poets used to come to our village all the time; they would recite ballads about... you."

"Yes, well, I hope your Elders stoned the bastards. I fucking hate poetry."

"Beetrax?"

"Hmm?"

"You are not like what I imagined."

"And what did you imagine? Now, be honest boy?"

"Somebody more... polite. Noble. With good manners. Somebody who did not drink and fight so much."

"Well, that's heroes for you. All of them a shower of horseshit, in my humble opinion. Noble? Ha! I wouldn't know noble if it bit me on the arse. And neither would the nobles!" He roared with laughter, slapping his leg at his own comedy.

"You still laughing at your own jokes, Beetrax?"

Lillith stood in the doorway, like a ghost. Her dark hair framed her soft, gleaming olive skin. Her eyes were hidden. Silver charms glittered on her wrists in the firelight. Her form was alluring, without meaning to be so.

"Always," said the axeman, without looking round.

"Could I speak with you?"

"I thought that's what we were doing." He lounged back, glancing at her, as if he didn't have a care in the world. Which they both knew was a lie.

"In private."

Beetrax sighed, and looked at Jael. "Better get a move on, lad." He nudged him.

Jael stood, wincing, hand on his broken ribs, then disappeared down a short corridor to his chosen room.

Lillith came forward, and sat opposite Beetrax.

"You require my counsel, lady?"

"I was thinking."

Beetrax opened his mouth to make some smart retort, but some primitive instinct took over, some spark kicked his mind into sobriety and he recognised this meeting was subtly different. This was no fireside banter. It had become, worryingly, serious.

"Yes?" He took another drink. A mote of apprehension drifted into his mind; a sliver of excitement pushed into his breast. Suddenly, the bitter wine tasted sweet. The acrid fire-smoke was perfume. The very fucking air was a drug.

"I... I feel I very much wronged you. When we were betrothed, all those years ago. We were so close. And then I finished it, and I devastated you. I realise that. And, truly, I am sorry."

Beetrax nodded. "It's fine, Lillith. I never deserved you."

"Oh, you deserved me."

Beetrax frowned. "I was a fighter, a drinker, uncouth and brash and vulgar. And you floated into my life like an angel. It was almost like we were opposites, Lillith. You love medicine and herbs, animals and people. To me, animals are something you eat, not rescue. People are bastards – *sorry* – who simply get in my way, and then I have to clear a path, usually with my axe. How did I deserve you? What gentle aspect of my soul brought you to me?" He gave a rumbling chuckle, and rubbed at his thick red beard.

"You undersell yourself."

"Oh yeah? How's that, like?"

Lillith lifted her knees before her, and placed both hands around them, hugging herself. The fire crackled and popped, then settled into a glowing, humming hearth. Occasionally, a flame shivered upwards between the two, a dancing, flirting demon.

"You wish to dissect my mind?"

"Er. Yeah. If you like."

"What would you like to know?"

"Why me?" Beetrax grinned, but his eyes were deadly serious.

"Why you?" She considered this, dark eyes glittering in the firelight. "Ask my core, my chemical makeup, my soul. You are smart and funny, strong and... honourable, despite your claims to the contrary. You make me feel like I'm the only person in the room. Nobody has ever made me feel like that before. Not ever."

When Beetrax spoke, his words were low, and tender. "You are using the present tense," he said.

"You think things have changed? You think I fell out of love with you, just because I refused to marry you?"

"You said you did. You stood there and *told me* you'd changed. Become a different person. Gone chasing education and medicine, helping people, and shit."

"I had to say that. I had to break free. For both of us. Sometimes, the greater sacrifice is the only way it can be."

Beetrax considered this. He shook his head. "Ha! You fuck up my mind, woman."

"Beetrax?"

"Hm?"

"Come to me. Come to my room. Now."

Beetrax stared at her. His hands were trembling. "Lillith,

now you are truly making no sense."

"Does it have to make sense?"

"You cast me aside, woman! And now you want me back in your bed? Why?"

"You're asking me to explain something I don't fully understand; but I will try. When I first met you, Beetrax, it was something I didn't ask for, something I didn't look for. I was studying hard. I was in love with medicine. And then you were there. I didn't ask for our connection, I didn't expect it or even want it. It was just *there*. And it was immediate. I'm not going to give you crazy similes. From the moment I first met you in Vagan Library, you looking all flustered and lost, like a big oaf, well, you accepted my help. And after you left, I knew you would be there again the next day; I couldn't wait to get back. I wrote you a letter, and you read it, and soaked up the words and the meanings, and I loved that. Loved this big brutal warrior who took the time to read my words. My bloody *words*. And up until the time I told you I was drawn to you, that you had affected me, that I believe we had connected, every moment apart from you was needles of pain in the centre of my brain."

"Er. You never told me that before."

"I'm telling you now."

"Dissecting your brain?"

"Trying to explain."

"Er. Wow."

"I knew you'd say that. I knew you'd use that word."

He frowned. "Well, you know me too well, then."

They stared at one another across the fire. Lillith licked her lips, and the sensuous moment was not lost on Beetrax.

"You are mad," he said, finally.

"Don't call me mad."

"You're *fucking* mad."

"Beetrax, that's worse!"

"I mean… because of your intensity. Because you never told me before. You waited all these years, until now, until this place, this time in our lives. Why? *Why*?"

"I feel self-conscious now." She looked away, running her hand through her long, dark hair.

Beetrax stood, and moved around to her. He sat, close, and their legs touched.

"Don't do this," he said. "For I am weak. And I am lost."

"I have never been anything but honest with you."

"I know. But you left a lot unsaid. For all those years. You ripped a hole in my heart when you left. I thought I would never be whole again."

"I am sorry, Beetrax. Truly, I am."

"What you just said to me, now, that was beautiful and touching. I might be as rough as you can get, but I appreciate your honesty; I appreciate you talking to me like this." He reached out, and brushed a stray hair from Lillith's forehead. "I've missed you, you know? Missed our… intimacy."

"I, also. For months I convinced myself I had done the right thing. Now, I wonder."

"Why didn't you say something sooner? I told you, back in the forest how I felt. How I'd never let you go. How you were… in my heart."

Lillith sighed. "I feel… vulnerable, where you're concerned."

"Vulnerable? You hurt me!"

"And by doing so, hurt myself."

"But now you're back?"

"Yes."

"Horseshit. Anyway. You never answered my earlier question."

"Which one?" Lillith appeared a little flustered, which was unlike her. She leant in closer to Beetrax, their arms applying pressure to one another.

"Why wait all this time? Why say these words *now*?"

Lillith turned her head, looked into Beetrax's eyes. "I believe this is our last mission together," she said, words little more than warm, sweet breaths. "I believe we will die under the Karamakkos."

"That's not possible," smiled Beetrax, as they inched closer, and their lips brushed, and Beetrax closed his eyes, and her lips were warm and sweet and tender, and she kissed him, and he tasted her, and he remembered that taste like a dream, like a bad drug, like chains wrapping around his brain and heart and soul. It triggered a beating in his heart and in his core. He sank into her. He worshipped her. Their tongues entwined. Her hands came up and held his head. And then they were apart and Beetrax was breathing, cheeks flushed, and Lillith stood, a surprisingly fluid movement, her hips twisting, and she reached down and took his hand and led him past the fire.

Beetrax followed. Like a dog. Like a slave. He had no control. He had left that behind with his sanity.

It was cold away from the fire, and the shadows lengthened into black velvet as she led him through the darkness of the old barracks in the mountains. Despite the alcohol in his blood, or maybe because of it, Beetrax felt he was floating. Lillith moved before him, her hand reaching back, holding his large, solid, scarred and tattooed fingers. The walls around them were cobwebbed, ancient stone, and Beetrax breathed in their history like perfume, revelled in every image that stuttered before his panic-reeling brain. And then they were there, at the doorway leading to... her room.

"Come in," she said, voice husky, pushing at the old timber door. It creaked open, and they stepped through the portal. Stepping behind him, she closed it again.

A single candle burned, its light flickering like a beacon.

Beetrax felt as if he moved through honey, a spectator watching his own dream. She moved to him, pressing herself against him, and he smelled her, and remembered the taste from inside her. It was sandalwood. She tasted of sandalwood. It drove him wild.

"Kiss me," she instructed.

He kissed her.

"Hold me."

His arms encircled her slim waist, edging up her shirt, connecting with her naked flesh, savouring her warm skin. Their lips brushed once more, and Beetrax gave a low groan, and Lillith bit his lip, her tongue sliding into his mouth, her arms around him now, her naked flesh under his fingers. They fell back to the bed, which creaked, and where the blankets smelled of her.

"You're in my room, now," she said, voice husky.

"I am your slave," he said.

"I know," she said.

"I am your prize," he said.

"I know," she said, and she undressed him, and he let her, for he had lost all his freewill, misplaced his control, and had ultimately fallen under her dark witchcraft spell – again. Or so he told himself. In reality, he allowed himself to be mesmerised. Welcomed the abuse, the pain, the pleasure, the guidance, the mastery.

They were naked together, and the room was cold, but neither felt the chill for their flesh was tingling, their minds spinning. They kissed, lying side by side, and her hand touched his chest, and travelled down, taking his cock, squeezing it gently, dropping down to his balls, and squeezing them as well.

"Tell me if I hurt you."

"You won't hurt me," he said.

And she kissed his lips, and kissed his neck, and kissed his chest, and dropped lower, taking him all in her mouth, taking him deep, and his hips pushed forward and his mind went bright as if fever had torn his mind free; her hair fell like a curtain onto his belly, and he reached down, pushing it to one side, so he could see her beautiful face, see the work of her lips and tongue upon him.

He came, suddenly, an explosion that ripped through him, and she swallowed him, drank him all down inside her, took every drop for herself. And then they lay together, and he stroked her breasts, stroked her belly, his hand dropping further, his fingers moving in slow circles. His fingers slid inside her, and he crawled down the blankets, and pushed his face into her quim, and worked on her with a delicate passion as she writhed beneath him, and he tasted sandalwood, just like before, and now it was his turn to drink her down, and these images, this passion, merged with what once had been; and he remembered, remembered it all as Lillith's passion rose before him, and his hand reached out, took her breast, squeezed the nipple, and she moaned and her fingers curled through his hair and he felt her shuddering, shuddering, vibrating like a tight-wound machine, lost in another world, a world of pleasure, and memories, and unity.

Later, they fucked, and she lay beneath him, enraptured face framed by her dark hair, and they gazed into one another's eyes and joined together, worked together, came together. And everything focussed on a pinprick moment of absolute intensity; and she clutched him until it was over, and the stars died, and the world died, and finally, the sun went out.

They lay under the blanket, curled together, a perfect fit. It was near dawn, and cold light filtered through window shutters.

"Come on. I want to show you something," she said.

They dressed, and Beetrax pulled on his boots, watching Lillith cover her nakedness with regret. He did not speak. For a few moments speech had left him, for this impossible dream had come true, and she was back here, with him, like he thought would never happen. His mind felt fractured. He did not understand. But he welcomed it all the same. It made him more gentle. Lillith calmed the savage beast in his soul. She tamed his primitive nature with an inculcated instinct; by a presence of will, of possession, of dominance.

They walked through the deserted barracks holding hands, past the embers of the fire, and outside into the snow. More had fallen. It was crisp and grey, the sky smeared with blue. The far horizon of the mountain walls was rimmed with a copper glow. A cool draught drifted down the White Lane, bringing promises of ice and death from the north.

Lillith stared to the south. She ran a hand through her luscious hair, then turned to Beetrax. "We could turn back. Turn away from this foolish, pointless journey. We could head back to Vagandrak. Forget the Karamakkos. Forget this pointless quest for riches and immortality. It will never happen, you realise? There *is* no immortality."

Beetrax shrugged. "What about Jonti? This has grown bigger than our simple quest. There is a greater need, now."

Lillith sighed. "I know," she said, staring south, lips narrowed into a grim, resigned line.

The breeze stirred the fresh powder of snow on the ground.

Beetrax took her in his great arms from behind, encircled her, pushed his face into her hair. "I'm glad you came back to me. You have made me whole again."

"I have made myself whole."

Distantly, far south, drifted a long, drawn-out, mournful sound; it was a howl, but stuttering, as if formed by a throat and lips that were far from animal. It was quite possibly the most terrifying sound Beetrax had ever heard, and he felt the hackles rise on the back of his neck, felt goose bumps race up his arms.

"A wolf?" said Lillith, going rigid in his arms.

"That's no wolf," said Beetrax.

"But if it wasn't a wolf…"

Beetrax let go of his woman. She turned to him. His face was grim.

"I know exactly what it was. I just hope, by the Seven Sisters, it's not looking for us. Let's wake the others. We need to move."

"Beetrax? What is it?"

"It's a splice," said Beetrax, voice the lead of a tomb door. "Left over from the war. One of Orlana, the Horse Lady's, terrible, deformed creatures; one of her *weapons*. They hunt, and they kill. That's what they do. That's *all* they do. Now *come on*!"

The Engineers

Skalg focussed on the black blade. It had become the centre of his world. The centre of his universe. Everything that was left, all his dreams of power and conquest, all his wealth, it all devolved into nothing more than a tiny thrust from a sharpened point. *How did it come to this? How the fuck did this happen? And where are my fucking Educators? What do I fucking pay them for?*

Suddenly, a terrible anger infused Skalg. He had worked so hard, scrambled and clawed and bit his way up the pyramid pile of vanquished enemies, amassed a fortune in gold and jewels, riches which, technically, belonged to the Church of Hate's coffers, but in reality formed financial wells for Skalg's own private and personal use.

And now this? To end it, like this?

"Don't kill me," he managed, voice hoarse.

Echo seemed to consider this. His dark eyes were bright. Finally, he spoke. And Skalg deflated a bit. For words... words were better than sharpened steel in his throat. "Do you want to hear what I have to say? Do you want to listen to the words of the Army of Purity?"

"Well you answered one question. Who sent you?" He saw Echo's face, and held out both hands. "Wait, wait! Let

163

me assure you, I can pay you a whole lot more than those church-burning radicals. Ten times more!" No response. "*Fifty times more*! But for this, I must remain alive. You understand, Echo?"

"Ah, so you recognise me. Good. That saves time. I have a message. So you need to listen good, *First Cardinal Skalg*, for as you have just seen, we can get to you. I could kill you right now, if I so desired. But I will not."

Skalg relaxed back a little. His eyes hardened. He allowed himself to breathe, and even the pain in his hunched back could do nothing to detract from this moment.

"I thank you for that," said Skalg, voice gentle. "What is your message? What will it take for the Army of Purity to stand down their attacks on my churches and wardens? What is it they actually *want*?"

"They want the three Dragon Heads," said Echo.

"You know those are not mine to give."

"But you have access."

"Even I cannot remove them from the Iron Vaults in the Sacred Pit of the Cathedral of Eternal Hate. Not even King Irlax himself would be allowed to remove them, for they were placed there by the Great Dwarf Lords themselves."

Echo considered this.

"Then you must allow us access," he said. "And we will find a way to steal them."

"You will perish in fire," said Skalg, voice hard.

"Then we will perish in fire, trying," said Echo.

Skalg stared at him. The sounds of battle had come closer. Echo's eyes glinted.

"Why, in the name of Skaltelos, do you want them? You seek immortality? It is not true, Echo, the legend is false—"

"We will make that decision!"

Razor came leaping over the carriage, crashing into Echo and they both went down in a flail of limbs and slashing steel. Then they were up, and spun apart. A cut bled across Razor's upper arm, and her good eye was bright, alive with the thrill of battle, with the thrill of killing.

"I know you," she said.

Echo attacked, a blistering assault with two long knives. Razor fought back, her own weapons similar, and they clashed in the air striking sparks. They spun apart once more, like dancers, and leapt to the attack with more clashes of steel and showering sparks from razor edges. Skalg watch with a mixture of awe, and horror, at this wild and primal dance, at this display of almost unbelievable skill. Suddenly, Echo delivered a side-kick that caught Razor in the chest, powering her backwards with a grunt, to land on her arse on the cobbles.

And then Echo was gone, sprinting up a side street through long shadows, knives sheathed... vanished.

Razor climbed to her feet, wheezing, holding her chest. She came over to Skalg and helped the cardinal to his feet with some difficulty. Skalg smiled, and patted her on the shoulder.

"You did well today, Razor."

"Than...k yo...u, Cardinal."

Skalg looked up the road. His wardens had formed a cordon. There were forty or so corpses in the street.

"What about Blagger?" he said, as pain came flowing back into his body now the adrenaline of the moment was wearing off; an old friend; a returned lover.

Razor shook her head. "He didn't mak...e it."

"That's a shame. I liked him. There was one dwarf who did what he was told."

•••

Chief Engineer Skathos stood on an arched bridge of gold above the Central Cavern of the Great Mine, and looked down in wonder at what they had achieved. What the Harborym Dwarves had achieved.

The vast space of the Central Cavern could fit an entire city within its massive hall, and had been the First Dig, that is to say, the first excavation when the dwarves originally tunnelled down looking for precious metals and jewels. Since then, they had been working their way upwards – creating the newer cities, also known colloquially as *the slums*, and also further down, deeper down.

"Time to check the pits, Chief," said Jengo, his Second Engineer, and the small, neat figure of Skathos nodded, stroking his combed beard. They moved across the perfectly smooth, stone-engineered surface of the bridge, dropping down through various levels of the Central Cavern. Around them was a constant bustle, as engineers moved about their shift work. Normal mining was undertaken by the Harborym Dwarves themselves, and they were proud to follow in the footsteps of their ancestors. However, new safety measures brought in by King Irlax meant that in dangerous tunnels, toxic mines and life-threatening digs, only convicted criminals (and by this he meant criminal dwarves convicted by a court, as opposed to some random unfortunate who got in the way of Cardinal Skalg) were forced into slavery to work the more dangerous sections of mine. Convicted criminals, and outsiders. The dwarves had eighteen different words for "outsider", or "not of dwarf origin". Many of the words doubled with enemy, traitor, or simple foul language difficult for a human throat to recreate. It had to be said, the dwarves were not keen to expand on human/dwarf relations.

Reaching the base level of the Central Cavern, they moved onto a nearby platform where a series of underground trains ran, powered by steam hydraulics and chains. The steam was superheated by the dragon engines, which, interestingly, was where Chief Engineer Skathos was heading for the ritual twice-a-day Dragon Pit examination.

After all, without the dragon engines, the entire mining system of the Harborym Dwarves would grind to a halt.

The platform was smooth black granite, and Skathos peered down onto the tracks, as he always did. The iron rails were polished on their surface, the rest of the track grime-smeared and littered with pebbles, rocks and old, black oil.

At the centre of the track, suspended at waist height, was a thick chain – about the width of a dwarf's thigh. It vibrated softly, and then suddenly burst into life as points changed, gears engaged, and a train was due.

The chain hissed past, humming. It seemed to go on forever, and then a series of carriages zoomed past, loaded with chunks of mined rock. Skathos counted, despite knowing how many there were; he observed this scene ten times a day.

With clanks and thunks, the carriages whizzed and hummed, iron wheels rattling on iron tracks. Skathos stood, impassive, but Jengo, as always, was suitably impressed.

"I will never get over our feats of engineering," he said.

"We have excelled ourselves," admitted Skathos.

"Our jobs would be a million times harder without the network."

"I agree. And a billion times harder without the dragon engines."

The chains suddenly halted, flexing and humming. Three

minutes and one second later, they started again, from a different direction, flying past at an incredible speed. The scent of steam and hot oil came to Skathos, and he closed his eyes for a moment. To the Chief Engineer, this was a hot oil perfume; not just the scent of the mountain, but the incense of the mines, the aroma of machines, the fragrance of engineering.

The next carriage slammed to a halt, rocking slightly. Steam curled. It was the same design as one of the mining carriages used to transport rock, ore, mined silver; except this one had been fitted with bench seats for transporting miners, engineers, convicts, slaves. The entire stretch of carriages was empty, as it should be. This was the middle of a working shift.

Skathos and Jengo stepped onto the carriage and sat down. Jengo clicked shut the door. They set off at instant high speed, flowing down the rails, through narrow tunnels then wide halls, through wide tunnels and narrow halls. Rock flowed past, fractured by precious lodes. Marble, granite, diorite, basanite, nephelinite, obsidian, quartz, scoria, basalt, harzburgite. This section of mountain was igneous, former volcanic, and Chief Engineer Skathos was an expert, as was only right. Sight, texture, smell, he could detect every variant from a hundred paces. Or so it was rumoured by the under-engineers. This made him smile and rub his neat beard. He liked ridiculous stories like that.

They sped on, occasional pools of fire from the furnaces lighting the way and providing a little heat in this deep, dank, cold place. This bowel of the mountain. This underground depth which, some said, should never have been mined.

The tracks moved up and down, twisting on different cambers as they sped on this insane journey through leagues of tunnel. Suddenly they stopped, carriage rocking, excess steam ejecting from hydraulics with spurting hisses. Both Skathos and Jengo jumped out. It did not do to wait, or be slothful, with the network system. As the saying went, "the chains wait for no dwarf". And seeing a miner cut in half by the power of the chains only ever happened once. In such a powerful automated system, it was a very real danger.

The carriage sped off, clanking. Chains vibrated. And finally, stopped.

This was it.

The Dragon Pits.

"Come on," said Skathos, and led the way. They moved down huge tunnels – more curved halls than tunnels, so vast were their polished heights. Fire-bowls stood at regular intervals, allowing long shadows to rule between pools of light.

They walked, boots echoing, and came at first to a massive iron gate. It was guarded by ten dwarves in full hardcore battle armour: The Dragon Guards. They allowed Skathos to pass, and he was stopped at five more gates, each one with bars as thick as a dwarf's arm. Each time Skathos was allowed to pass, and Jengo stared at suspiciously by bulky guards between slit-helmed battle-dress. All weapons were unsheathed and sharp and oiled. These were not unpractised guards, but veterans. The toughest of the tough, their regiment put in place – so it was claimed – by the Great Dwarf Lords themselves. They were insular, almost masonic, and answerable to neither the king nor the church. After all, they protected the dwarves' greatest treasure.

The Dragon Engine.

On moved Chief Engineer Skathos, and came to the first viewing portal. Jengo was still early in his training, so was made to stand outside. Skathos, on the other hand, stepped into the capsule and pressed the button operating hydraulics. The capsule was slung across on steel cables, and Skathos peered out of the small window... and as always happened, felt his heart climb up his throat and perch in his mouth.

This was Moraxx.

She lay, curled at the bottom of the Dragon Shaft, one-third of the Dragon Engine which kept the five cities above heated, lit, her power such that with her two companions, she could power the cities and the mines and the interior of the mountain itself.

Skathos stared, in wonder, at the brass-coloured scales, overlapping, each scale the size of a church door. His gaze travelled along the neat, powerful body, ridged with needle spikes, each the length of a spear, atop the long, tapering head and snout. The eyelids were shut, now, as they had been for several millennia. But Skathos was privy to the knowledge that the eyes beneath Moraxx's eyelids were black. Black, like the darkest night. As black as the Chaos Halls. Curved horns arched up from Moraxx's mighty skull, and the wings were folded along her back. Spines of armoured spikes ran down from the head, back, and to the tail which was curled around the body. The tail was the width of a road in the city, and tipped by a huge triangular spike capable of smashing buildings into splinters with a careless flick.

All in all, Moraxx was the size of a modest street. The head was the size of a house. And the eyes, had they been open, would have been great dark pools into which Skathos could have dived, and swam... all the way down to a splintered oblivion.

Skathos shuddered, and shivered, and then pulled a lever. The capsule swung back on cables and pulleys, and then out into a second chamber. Here, Skathos admired the bulk of Kranesh, the scales this time silver, the facial structure different, with the same curved black fangs, but higher cheekbones. Skathos liked Kranesh very much.

"How are you, my girl?" he whispered, the awe and the magick never leaving his voice, his eyes, nor his soul.

First he analysed the dormant dragon, checking for missing scales, wounds, anything out of the ordinary. But as usual, as there had always been, there was no change. His eyes fixed on the ever-so-gentle rise and fall of the mighty chest. Below, half out of sight, he could see the mineral feeding pit, from where the dragon would imbibe some of her fuel.

"Magical," whispered Chief Engineer Skathos.

His eyes roved the vast Dragon Pit one final time, before he pulled another lever and was swept away, out of the Dragon Shaft and towards the final, largest cylinder, the main power source for the cities, and indeed, for the Harborym Dwarves.

The capsule swung into the Dragon Pit.

Skathos found it hard not to curse.

Here she was, the largest of the three, the leader of the dragons, and the most powerful component of the Dragon Engine.

Volak.

Beautiful Volak!

Matte black, her scales dull like fire-scorched steel, she lay, tail curled around her body, head lowered as if in submission.

Skathos found tears rolling down his bearded cheeks.

"Oh how you must have looked magnificent, roaring through the skies! A Mistress of the World!"

Volak was breathing, her huge chest rising and falling like the changing of seasons.

Swiftly, for Firesong would soon be upon them, Chief Engineer Skathos checked Volak for damage, for injury, then lifted his eyes, checking the integrity of the Dragon Shaft. If this was to fail, in any way, it could blast the cities above it with an all-consuming inferno. A disaster of epic proportions.

Satisfied, he pulled another lever and his capsule swung back into the safety of the chamber walls. And, as he always did at this time of the day – and three others – he waited for the Firesong.

Firesong started as a feeling in the pit of his stomach, and rose through vibrations, gradually, until his entire body was trembling with the repressed power, the sheer withheld energy of it all.

At this moment, Chief Engineer Skathos could not think, could not breathe, and the one thought which powered through his mind was…

I am truly honoured to witness this miracle.

Slowly, and in perfect time, each dragon lifted her head on a long, arched neck, graceful, and with great majesty. Gradually their heads lifted, writhing like water snakes in a stagnant lake, and their huge snouts rose to the heavens, to the cities above, to the summit of the mountain, and in absolute silence, they appeared to roar–

Fire erupted, huge blasts of incredible energy, powering up through the three Dragon Pits to be harvested above, thousands of channels piping away various flames and energies, five thousand giant boilers on the "Fire Route" slammed immediately to boiling point, their cleverly formulated oils bubbling and storing the energy of the Dragon Engine.

Chief Engineer Skathos watched this spectacle, his face glowing with green, blue, yellow, orange and finally white flames, and the whole world seemed to be engulfed in sheer pure power which went on, and on, and on...

Until suddenly it stopped, leaving glowing after-images on Skathos' retinas.

The three dragons slumped to the ground, spent.

And darkness bled in, like ink spiralling down through pure spring water.

Skathos stepped from the capsule, to see the concerned face of Jengo. Always, his face was filled with concern. Always, his eyes were wide and awe-filled, despite never having witnessed the true beauty of the Firesong... the most beautiful miracle Skathos had ever, and would ever, witness.

"Did everything... go to plan?"

"Of course," said Skathos, brushing an imaginary speck from his tunic. "Now come. There have been reports from the 597 Mine, odd configurations of geological strata, according to the engineers there. Mining has been halted until I investigate. It is time to resume your training."

"With pleasure!" beamed Jengo, like an eager puppy.

"Follow me," said Skathos, and they returned to the oily platform, their job there complete.

The carriage to 597 Mine rattled along, finally stopping at one of the farthest, deepest outreaches of the current mining operation – one of seven currently being worked in various directions and at different depths, each searching and mining for different elements. Chief Engineer Skathos stepped free, as did Jengo, and they watched the carriage retreat leaving them in a wide, low-ceilinged corridor of black granite.

"End of the line," said Skathos.

"Yes?" Jengo smiled, a little nervously.

"Old dwarf mining joke," said Skathos. "Come on, we have a considerable walk ahead of us."

As this was a survey, as opposed to an actual active dig, no further infrastructure had been put in place until mine wealth could be confirmed. "No point wasting precious resources when there is no profit to be had!" was the mantra of every dwarf engineer from Janya down through all five cities.

They walked through the rough-hewn corridor, or what Skathos thought of as a *survey corridor*, or in common slang, a *slave shaft*. Hacked by prisoners, convicts, slaves in search of… something. Something of value. Something of *more value* than the lives of those who performed the hardest and most dangerous of physical labour.

It was dark down here, and very cold, having not been piped into the Dragon Engine. Skathos pulled up the collar on his woollen cloak, and stomped onwards, boots clacking a rhythm not unlike a soldier's march. It took them nearly an hour to reach the corridor's terminus; during the journey, seven times they came to side-corridors and vertical exploratory shafts which had revealed nothing. Now, as the corridor ended, so it opened into a modest-sized chamber which had been opened up by picks, axes, and small chemical blasts fashioned by the dwarf engineer apothecaries; small charges formed from metals and minerals, which could be ignited to burn with a ferocious white light. These seams of high-powered cutting were at the forefront of dwarf mining techniques, but something of which Chief Engineer Skathos did not approve. There had already been several instances of explosions when burning metals met with pockets of gas, and the threat of toxic fumes could also be great. Oh no. Skathos was old school; you cut a precision section, allowing the weight of the rock to break itself and be removed in pieces. Accurate, and providing already sculpted building materials – if done right. None of this fancy high-power chemical reaction nonsense.

The chamber had jagged walls, and to one side was huddled a gang of chained slaves. Mostly dwarf, but with a single miserable-looking human mixed in, his flesh dust-smeared, his frame shrunken, weak and bruised. Skathos' gaze passed over the human; the man would be dead within the week.

"Chief Engineer!" panted a stocky dwarf, running over to Skathos. He was bare-chested, except for various studded straps, and wore leather trews and a leather apron, hung with various very specific tools, different sizes of rock picks, chisel-tip hammers, crack hammers and rock chisels, with a hand-lens protected in a belt-hung leather case.

"It has been reported you have some kind of geological abnormality? Take me to it."

"Yes, Chief Engineer Skathos."

Almost bowing and scraping, the under-engineer led the way and Skathos followed, past the subservient slaves and dropping down hand-chiselled steps to the crude floor. Across this floor they moved, until they came to a blank, smooth wall amidst the rugged, hacked sections.

Chief Engineer Skathos stared at the wall, and frowned.

"Why," he said, feeling his temper rising – and only an abuse of mining technology could do that to the dwarf – "*why* have you hand-smoothed a section of random wall, may I ask? This is a pointless operation; it's…"

"Chief Engineer. We didn't do this. A previous section was cracked away," he gestured to the stone detritus on the floor, "but it revealed this."

Skathos frowned, and stepped forward, touching it. The stone was curiously warm.

"And if I may be so bold, Chief Engineer," said the bare-chested dwarf, "you will note this is a different composition of granite. The grain does not run in the same direction."

"So it was placed here."

"Yes, Chief Engineer."

"It looks like…" but he frowned, and could not force himself to the say the word, because the idea that down here, after mining for thousands of years, they would suddenly come across a *door* was ridiculous beyond belief.

Skathos whirled on Jengo. "Jengo. Go back. Assemble my trusted team: Hiathosk, Denko, Lellander, Yugorosk and Kew. Tell them to bring all their equipment. Remember to stress *all of it*. I think we're going to need it."

Several hours later, with the slaves and minor engineers ushered out, and three fire-bowls burning brightly providing copious amounts of light, they began their examinations. It took them only twenty minutes to find the hidden mechanism which, when levered out, revealed a device they had never before seen. Tentatively, Denko released the mechanism, and in silence, the great slab of rock folded down, hitting the coarse ground with barely a thud.

The engineers peered into a massive hollow chamber.

It was a dome, with a perfectly symmetrical arching roof of polished obsidian, gleaming black under their collected firelight. Skathos advanced, his boots echoing hollowly through the vast space.

"What is it?" asked Jengo, his voice lowered in awe; still it came booming back, the echoes reverberating around this vast auditorium.

"I'm not sure," whispered Skathos, "but it is not natural, and it was not hewn by the dwarves."

With some primal instinct, he walked across the floor until, by his reckoning, he stood at the direct centre of the chamber. The floor was layered with a fine powdering of dust; looking back, Skathos could see the trajectory of his boot prints.

"Bring me more light, over here!" he hissed, and the sounds went spiralling around the perfectly smooth cavern, and came whipping back at him like a barrel full of hissing snakes.

Hiathosk carried over a fire-pit, shadows dancing around them, and Skathos got down on his hands and knees. He smoothed away the dust to reveal a pattern in the rock. His hand-sweeps widened, revealing the pattern extended outwards, in a complex set of spirals that grew wider and wider. At the very centre there was a small circle, no larger than the Chief Engineer's thumbnail.

"Pass me a No 5 round point stone chisel," he said, "and a crack hammer."

They were handed down to Skathos. He placed the point against the circle, looked around at the others for a moment, who all had gazes fixed on him, mouths open in anticipation. He gave the chisel head a whack.

Nothing happened.

A few dwarves let out a breath.

"Well, that was a pointless exercise," muttered Hiathosk, just as a very distant, muffled grinding sound came to their ears.

"Is grinding good?" asked Jengo.

Skathos stood, and took a step back.

The ground started to tremble, the floor vibrating, dust rising in tiny puffs as they felt the building tremor beneath their feet.

"What is it?" cried Jengo, panic flooding him. But before he could speak, the central tiny circle sank into the ground and disappeared. Suddenly, the spiral slabs started to drop, one by one, flooding outwards in a spiralling circle, each one dropping like a falling domino. Down they sank, accompanied by vast booming and grinding sounds, as if some titanic and ancient machinery had come to life. Skathos and the others stumbled back, as the sinking slabs of shaped stone fell away and two of the fire-pits went tumbling down into the stone whirlpool left in the wake of the dropping, downward spiral...

The engineers were scrambling back, but the falling stones seemed to accelerate, swirling outwards in an ever-increasing fan of widening, sinking stone. Chief Engineer Skathos tried to get away – but the disappearing, black circle suddenly reached him, caught his boots, and dragged him down into a whirlpool of hissing, showering dust and grinding rocks.

I will die, he thought.

This place, it is a place of devils, a place of demons, and it will take me into its bowels, into its machine, into its engine, and chew me up into flesh and bone shards. I am lost. Who will comfort my wife? Who will nurture my babies?

Skathos felt himself tumbling, whacking his limbs and torso and head on stone edges. Dust poured on him, into his eyes and mouth and throat. It was a chaos, and he was toppling down, rolling, bouncing. And then, suddenly, the grinding sounds stuttered to a halt. Still, there came a hissing from pouring dust, which he thought would never end as it filled his eyes and spluttering mouth.

Silence.

Blessed silence.

Skathos rubbed grit from his eyes, coughing, amazed he was still alive.

He was blind.

He heard others coughing, gravelled, penetrating sounds the in Stygian gloom.

His hands stretched out, to be met by smooth stone, with hard ridges, hard edges. He was lying upside down, head descended. He rotated himself, with some effort and grunting, and then rolled onto his knees. Stone edges bit into his bones. He coughed again, and was close to vomiting.

"Skathos?" hissed a voice through the hazy gloom. "SKATHOS?"

"Yes, yes, I'm here." It was Hiathosk.

"Have you seen it?"

"Seen what?"

"Clean out your fucking eyes, and look!"

Still wary of a mountain of rubble coming down on his head, Skathos spat into a corner of his shirt, and scrubbed at his eyes. Gradually vision returned, and it was a bright vision, shining with silver.

"What?" he muttered. And rolled over, sitting on his rump with a bump.

"Look!" Awe. Wonder. Amazement.

Chief Engineer Skathos dragged open his eyes. A world spread out before his open vision. It was an underground world, lit by a soft golden light. There were massive square buildings, pyramids, towers with intricate designs. And Skathos suddenly realised – they were all made from silver, made from gold. It glimmered dully, like glowing coals; a city of precious metals. There were massive, towering arches of filigree silver, a league high, and crisscrossing in the distance. There were glittering roads of golden cobbles, weaving between the buildings like scaled snakes. There were palaces fashioned from precious stones, which shimmered in different, hazy hues. There was a river, cutting the city in two. It flowed with a sluggish demeanour. It was a river of molten platinum.

"By the Great Dwarf Lords..." whispered Chief Engineer Skathos.

He glanced sideways, at where Jengo sat, dust-smeared, his mouth open, tongue flapping.

"What did you find, Chief Engineer?" he whispered, lost in awe; as were they all.

"It is Wyrmblood," croaked Skathos, palpitations racing through his pounding heart. "The lost city of the dragons."

The Mountain Gives

The company rode north through the White Lane during the morning, and Beetrax rode at the rear, axe out in one scarred fist, constantly looking over his shoulder and squinting through the light falling of peppered snow. Three times more they had heard the mournful wail; like a song from some terrible demon crying for its lost love.

It made them all shiver.

And one thing was certain. Whatever it was, it was getting gradually closer.

The ground had started to rise, and as the afternoon wore on, the valley, or road, known as the White Lane came to an end. They dismounted, and each shouldered packs and slapped horses into a gallop back the way they had come.

"Goodbye, Bella," said Beetrax sombrely.

"You love that horse, don't you?" grinned Talon, although his eyes were narrowed, and he appeared strained with tension.

"More than you." Beetrax gave a death's-head grin. "Keep that bow strung. I worry we may need your skills sooner than I anticipated."

Jael shouldered a light pack, claiming he was feeling strong enough for the climb. Beetrax shook his head. *It*

would have been better to leave the lad behind, back at the forest.
Now what horse shit has he got himself into?

All members of the company pulled on hats, and stared up at the steep trail ahead. It was formed, at this point, from slabs of stone, working its way via switchbacks up the steep slope ahead of them. The slabs were treacherous with ice, and Beetrax gestured to Dake, who nodded, and set off up the stone ramp.

Jonti followed him, then Sakora, Jael and Lillith, with Talon staying at the rear alongside Beetrax.

They trudged up the pathway, legs burning at this sudden increase in ascent. It was steep. Near as steep as a man could comfortably walk without resorting to scrambling. Within minutes Beetrax felt his lungs burning and he cursed his lack of fitness. It wasn't like this in his younger days, when he could drink all night, shag all morning, then run up a mountain and still have strength to wrestle at the top. *Ach. Those were the days.*

Talon walked beside him for a while. The climb was having little effect on the effete archer.

"You struggling, old man?"

"I am *one* year older than you. *One fucking year.*"

"Granted," said Talon, "however, your *fitness* is fifty years older than I. Why did you let yourself get so out of shape?"

"Fuck off, will you?" he wheezed.

Ahead, Sakora said to Jael, "See how your famous axeman suffers?" She gestured back, to where Beetrax was now red in the face, brow dripping sweat, shirt soaked.

Jale shrugged. "He is still my hero," he said, simply.

They climbed for two hours, and cliffs dropped away beneath them so the ridgelines of the land began to open up, the landscape, the world, unfolding like some vast and breathtaking map. They paused for a breather, to drink water and eat a hurried snack of dried beef strips.

Beetrax dropped to a rock and struggled out of his pack. He took off his furry hat and ran hands through his sweat-streaked hair. Jonti moved to him, offering water.

"You all right, Trax?"

"Yes," he snapped.

"You sure?" asked Dake, chewing on a strip of beef, and grinning over at Talon who was inspecting his shafts, checking them for true.

"Will everybody stop bloody asking me how I am, right? Yes, Beetrax the Axeman has put on a bit of weight. Yes, Beetrax the Axeman has not been running for the past few years, and now has the stamina of a little girl. And yes, Beetrax the Axeman is suffering like a fat raw recruit on the climb. But what I'd like you all to do is *fuck off*, and let me suffer in peace, and stop grinning at me before I lose my temper and knock out some teeth, like."

Lillith hurried over, and sat beside him. She looked into his eyes, and stroked back his hair. "Remember? What you said?"

Beetrax stared at her. Angry. Then subsided. Meek. "Yes. Right. Sorry. I'll... try." The last word was from behind gritted teeth.

Talon and Dake exchanged a glance, wide-eyed. A glance that said, *didn't expect that to happen? Where did that intimacy come from?*

When Beetrax had regained his breath, he clambered up a large, cubic rock and stood, hands on hips, gazing down into the valley they had so recently vacated. The snow had abated for a while, and his eyes tracked the path they had climbed, zigzagging up the side of... he searched his memories for the name. *Talkanoth*. The first, modest peak of the Karamakkos, and the initial summit they would have to breach in order to cross the Ice Bridges of Sakaroth. That path would then lead them deep into the Karamakkos – and towards the ancient, deserted lair of the Harborym Dwarves.

Beetrax followed the White Lane with his eyes. He could just distinguish the old barracks where they had slept, and then his gaze travelled further south. But he could see nothing; no enemies, no mud-orcs, no… *creatures* of the night.

Talon climbed up beside him, and slapped him on the back.

"Any monsters?"

"None I can see."

"Relax, Axeman! Even if it *was* a splice, which I very much doubt, as King Yoon had them all hunted down by the Iron Wolves and killed, even *if it was a splice*, why would it be hunting us? It's just as likely to eat our horses. Yes?"

"I have a bad feeling."

"Ha! I'd forgotten this about you, Beetrax. Everything is a bad feeling; every fallen tree is the gods trying to scupper your plans. Every raven is a promise of death, every swollen river an attempt to get between you and your gold. I *remember*. Shit. How did I ever forget that?" He looked incredulous.

"No, Talon, you heard the sound. The wail. That was a splice."

"I'm not so sure. I've drank a lot of wine since back then. And *you've* drank way too much brandy."

"So, what was it then?" Beetrax wore his famous scowl.

"I don't know."

"Exactly! You don't know!"

Talon yawned. "Listen, you're jumping at shadows. I didn't appreciate being rolled from my bloody bed at the crack of dawn by a raving lunatic gabbling on about bloody horse monsters; and I don't appreciate you pushing this hectic pace – a pace, I might add, you can't keep up with due to your ever-expanding ale gut – when we were supposed to be on a more… *relaxed* outing."

Dake shouted up, "Talon! Leave the big man alone. He needs to get his breath back."

"Yes, sir!" Talon saluted, a smart military *snap*, and climbed back down the big cube, leaving Beetrax alone and muttering and scanning the trails, eyes sweeping back and forth like a madman; a man possessed.

"I know what I heard," he mumbled, and scratched his beard, brows furrowed. "I bloody know what I heard."

Darkness started to fall as the company neared the summit of Talkanoth. The air was curiously alien and still, and with altitude the temperature had dropped to a brittle chill which numbed fingers. The path erupted upwards from a narrow fissure filled with a silver, frozen stream, in which they had to kick steps. It was a long, laborious process, but the ice was too slippery to climb. At the top of the ice stream, the path suddenly opened into a broad mountain-top plateau, a virgin snow sheet of purest white, peppered by several modest boulders. Beside one such boulder there was an old cairn, and a shelter built from rocks carried up by soldiers training for the Vagandrak Army over a period of years during decades past. The shelter's original function had been that of life-saver for soldiers lost on the mountain; a shelter to hide within during a sudden storm. Now, it served Beetrax and the others as a place to camp for the night –

and they were very thankful of its simple, thick stone walls.

There was no wood for a fire, but each made a space for their blankets on the hard-packed earth. There was a narrow aperture for a doorway, and no windows; that would defeat the object. But as darkness flooded the summit of the mountain, and stars twinkled high above, shimmering and hazy, so Beetrax stepped outside and breathed deep the fresh mountain oxygen.

Sakora prepared a cold meal for the group, grumbling about the lack of a fire and how this was no way to live, and they huddled together, the temperature within the small space rising due to their combined body heat. They were eventually able to remove hats and gloves, but not much else.

"It's going to be a long cold night," said Beetrax, squeezing back through the entrance.

"I'm sure we can find a way to keep warm," said Lillith, voice soft, her eyes meeting Beetrax's.

Jael sat, a bowl on his knee, looking around the group, picking idly at the dried beef, sliced cheese and black bread. His mind was still spinning at the coincidence of it all; at the sheer... *adventure*.

Only days earlier his village had been attacked by bandits. The memories seemed distant and unreal, as if he had endured a bad dream. He shook his head, looking down into his bowl, and tears formed in his eyes, running down his cheeks…

Bandits!

Taylan, his father, ran from their cottage carrying his wood-chopping axe, but the attack came fast, and the lead bandit reared his mount, steel hooves pawing the air, then Taylan's chest and face. He hit the ground, bloodied and unconscious. Jael watched from the window with the potted purple flowers, mouth open, as the horse reared again, hooves coming down to crush his father's head. No, screamed Jael, running outside and everything was a sudden blur, moving through treacle, leaving smears through the air, and arrows were whistling through the village, punching men and women, even children, from their feet. A club whistled from behind, cracking Jael on the head and he went down like a sack of shit, mind reeling, and watching from the mud as his sister, sweet Alina, peeped from the doorway and a bandit dismounted, grabbing her roughly, forcing her down onto the ground where his hand grabbed between her legs and she suddenly started screaming, kicking, and the bandit punched her into silence. His mother came out bearing a bread knife, blade silver and gleaming, hand-sharpened, and as the bandit mounted the young girl, the knife slammed into his back between his shoulder blades and he went suddenly rigid, slumping forward. An arrow slashed through the air, taking his mother in the throat. Both hands came up, clasping the shaft in disbelief, and Jael watched as blood bubbled around the wound and she opened her mouth and frothing blood came out. She dropped to her knees, then toppled to her side, and Jael looked into her dead eyes and knew that the world was going to end, knew that nothing would ever be the same again. It went on. And on. The killing. The rape. And then fire, flames taking to thatch in seconds, the roar of fire demons striding through the village, the laughter of the bandits as they loaded stolen wares onto their horses and a broad cart. Then words. As he drifted into a well of despair. Here... we have a live one. Let's keep him for a little entertainment after supper! Laughter. Cruel laughter. Movement. Travel. Slumped over a horse. Then tied roughly to a tree. He struggled, and a big shape moved in, fists pounding his face and ribs. More laughter. He hung against his bonds, hands numb, ribs on fire, and vomited onto the needles of the forest floor as he felt completely useless, completely worthless. Time passed. He did not know how much. But one thing he did know: he was going to die there, tied like a pig to a tree. Die, just like his father, just like his mother, just like little Alina.

Then the trees moved. Branches creaked. A man walked from the forest, a big man, carrying an axe.

You all right lads?

What do you want?

The words drifted to Jael like a dream, and despite his pain, he struggled to open his eyes because suddenly, as adrenaline kicked through him, he realised this was not a dream. This was real. And the man was Beetrax the Axeman, subject of so many stories, poems and books. Beetrax! The Hero of Desekra! Jael reeled, lounging against his bonds, and he knew they thought him unconscious but he could hear, and see, and taste the fear of the bastard brigands who had brought misery to his entire fucking world.

Who's that?

None of your business.

Do you know who I am?

Amaze me.

I am Beetrax the Axeman.

Never heard of you. All I see is a fat old man with broken teeth and a ginger beard that needs a trim. Now fuck off, before we fill you full of arrows.

Old man, is it?

And then the scene surged into violence, and the others from legend were there, real as stone, killing the evil bandits in the blink of an eye. Just like heroes. Just like the heroes from his story books.

They saved my life, he realised.

And now I am with them, on their next adventure. Their next legend.

Jael dried his tears on his sleeve, and settled his mind, and ate his food. Then he looked up, in that cold shelter, surrounded by the heroes of his childhood, and he took a deep breath.

"I would like to thank you all," he said.

"Aye, lad?" said Beetrax.

"That's good of you," said Dake, kindly, and reached forward, patting Jael's arm.

"I mean…" he stumbled, and reddened in the darkness. "I mean, for saving me. Sparing my life. I'm nothing but a humble village woodcutter, and I suffered a great injustice; but then, then… to be rescued! By such amazing heroes!"

"It was nothing," said Sakora, kindly. She reached forward and took his hands in her own. She was surprisingly warm. "We are just human, you know? Just like you. And when Talon scouted ahead, and discovered you were being tortured by those brigand bastards, it was something we had to do. We couldn't allow you to suffer like that. We had to take steps against the evil strong."

Jael nodded, lowering his head. "I thought I was going to die," he said. Then his head came up, eyes burning bright. "And I watched Beetrax, greatest of heroes, stride from the forest and I thought it was all a dream! I could not believe what I was seeing! I knew, when I saw him, despite you being outnumbered, that you would end the evil."

Jonti looked sideways. "You hear that, Beetrax? He knew we would end the evil."

"I hear," rumbled Beetrax, uneasily.

"Funny thing is," said Talon, coughing to clear his throat, "and the truth as it lies, is that we had a bit of a debate."

"You did?" said Jael.

"Shut up," said Beetrax.

"Yes," continued Talon. "You see, *I* scouted ahead. I saw you tied to that tree. Took this information back to the company. And we had a… discussion."

"A discussion?" said Jael.

"Shut up," growled Beetrax.

"Aye," nodded Talon, turning his head sideways and staring hard at Beetrax. "We had a discussion."

"What kind of discussion?"

"Well," said Talon, as Beetrax sank lower, and lower, and lower in his blankets, "I reckoned you were a handy-looking lad, and I said that if we rescued you, you'd obviously be injured; but *Beetrax* agreed that if we rescued you, it would be amazing, and that he'd train you up as a warrior with the axe. So you could protect yourself in the future. Isn't that right, Beetrax?"

"Tha's right," mumbled Beetrax. "Protect himself."

"So the minute you feel able, you just give Beetrax the nod. And Beetrax here, fucking amazing hero that he is, will teach you everything you need to know about chopping off bad people's heads."

"That's amazing," beamed Jael, eyes shining in wonder.

"Amazing," said Talon, grinning. "You hear that, Beetrax? The lad thinks it's amazing."

"I heard," said Beetrax.

Jael leapt forward, and threw his arms around Beetrax, pushing his head into the big man's shoulder. "Thank you, Beetrax. Thank you so much! You don't know what this means to me. It is… *everything*!"

"That's all right, lad," said Beetrax, pushing the youth away. "Now… you just go and sit down over there, and eat your food, like. There's a good lad. I think I'm going to try and get some sleep. That climb did me in, and I know it's only going to get harder."

•••

Talon sat on a boulder, staring up at the stars. Sakora stepped out into the cold moonlight, and crossed to him. She was smiling as she looked up, her almost painfully regal face, with its high cheekbones, highlighted in starlight like finely chiselled stone.

"You look beautiful tonight, my lady," came Talon's musical voice.

She ran a hand back through her long, brown hair, and dazzled him with a shrug. "You are biased, I think, Talon."

"Not so. I see every creature as they really are, for I am not prejudiced against the male or the female form; to me, they are both equally stunning, and to me, everybody has a gift they can offer."

"I have a question." She settled down, cross-legged on a flat rock above the snow, and looked up at Talon on his pinnacle.

"For me? Oooh, I am intrigued. Shoot."

"Why did you come?"

"That's easy. The wealth, the glamour, the oiled-up young men begging to hear my story afterwards..."

"No, really, Tal. Why?"

Talon stared up at the stars, and rolled his head, stretching out his neck muscles. Then he looked at Sakora and grinned. He shrugged. "Who knows?"

"You had a lover? Back in Vagan?"

The smile went a little crooked at the corners of Talon's mouth. "Yes," he said, voice wooden.

"A flash in the pan, a one-night stand, or something more... serious?"

"We had been together a while," said Talon, voice gentle.

"And yet you were willing to leave him?"

"He left me."

"For another?"

Talon paused, then jumped down from the rock. He sighed. "Yes. For another. Don't they always leave? Don't they always find something more exciting, younger, suppler, harder, and more dirty?" He shrugged. Tears glistened in his eyes. "I loved him, Sakora. This time, it was real. I loved him to the bottom of my heart; to my beating, acid core. But he betrayed me. He was seeing another."

"You found out?"

"How could I not? I read people well. He wore the fresh lust on his sleeve like a new perfume."

"So what did you do?"

"I was crying. I was drunk. I took my bow, and a long knife, and I followed him through the streets. Watched him climb white marble steps, and knock on the door. His new lover was young, beautiful, his skin oiled and golden, his stench of flowers reaching me even across the street. He had golden curls. Bright blue eyes. More like a woman than a fucking man. More like a woman…"

"What did you do?"

"I crept around the back of the house, climbed up to the third floor. I peered in. They were kissing on the bed, giggling like children. Hatred swamped me. Truly, I saw fucking red; I saw them strung out, their skin peeled by a razor blade wielded by my hands. I watched them for a while, the bastards, then I leapt across the balcony, slipped the lock on the bedroom window next door, and dropped to the thick, soft carpet."

"Gods, Talon, what did you do?"

"I padded through that rich bastard's house, my mind set on murder. They want to fuck together? Well, they can die together. I'll fuck them with my knife. A single blow, pinning them together forever. I came to the door, pushed it open. Candlelight spilled across rich tapestries. They were naked now, holding one another's cocks. This was my man, my lover, my best friend. Holding another man's cock, then dipping his head and sucking another cunt's cock. I moved forward, padding oh-so silently. My blade was in my hand, and I stood beside them, and they were so entranced, so lost in the moment they did not even see me. They were lost in the moment. Like dogs." He looked at Sakora, then. Tears had rolled down his cheeks, and glistened in slick trails under the starlight.

"You killed them?"

"I turned, and I left the room. I went back to my house, packed a bag with essential belongings, poured lantern oil across my bed, and set the whole fucking place alight. I believe it took three days until the fire was finally extinguished. It could be seen from all four quadrants of Vagan."

Sakora looked at him, pale in the moonlight, his hair a shimmering fan. She smiled.

"I understand," she said.

"You do?"

"It doesn't always have to end in murder. Sometimes, we can just walk away."

"Like now?"

"I am uneasy," confessed Sakora. "I believe this… quest is foolhardy."

"And yet we both agreed to come."

"We did."

"So, what's the solution? To return, head back south, before we cross the Ice Bridges of Sakaroth?"

Sakora shrugged, a delicate gesture. "I feel for Jonti. I

believe I want to help, no matter how slim the possibility."

"And it is slim indeed."

"Beetrax's quest is based on greed, not saving the woman we all love."

"And yet it could produce the same outcome."

"Possibly. Hopefully. Although I'll believe it when I see it."

Talon sat next to Sakora, snuggling in close. They held each other for a while, sharing body warmth as the cool, random breezes of the chilled mountain summit drifted around them.

Talon wrapped his arms tight around Sakora, and they hugged.

After a few minutes, he pulled away a little, and stared into her face.

"Are you well?"

"I am very well."

"You enjoy my hugs?"

"Very much."

"Good. I enjoy hugging you."

"Is this where you ask for sex? Because if you do, you might find me compliant." She smiled, a warm smile under cold stars.

Talon put his head on her shoulder. "Not tonight, my dear. Tonight... well, tonight is a night about mourning."

And they sat under the stars, and watched the universe slowly spin by.

Sunlight gleamed from the blanket of white snow, as they headed down from the shelter onto a steep slope which led from the mountain summit. No more snow had fallen, and the air was cold and crisp, with a biting wind which blew in from the north, stirring the powdered surface. High above, against a pale blue vista, an eagle dropped into a glide and rode the thermals, circling slowly.

"This way," said Dake, and as they crossed the plateau, the world opened up into one of the most stunning views any of them had ever seen. The Karamakkos. The Teeth of the World. They stretched away, filling the horizon, a seeming infinity of peaks extending off northwards, glinting with ice and snow, threatening with deep chasms and towering violence. The silence to this vast backdrop was terrifying. It was holy.

They trudged through snow, Dake leading the way.

Jael shuffled alongside Beetrax, who had seemed to acclimatise a little to the strenuous effort of travelling through snow, and was now taking long, loping strides, his axe strapped to his pack on his back, his furry hat, with drooping ear covers, seeming to merge with his beard and turn him into a ginger and brown bear.

"Where are we actually going, Beetrax?"

The axeman glanced down at the youth. "Your face is looking better. The swelling is nearly gone."

"Yes, but it's still tender."

"That will fix, lad. It'll fix. Well. We're heading for the Ice Bridges of Sakaroth."

"And what are those?"

Beetrax gave a nod, ahead, to the vast wilderness of jagged peaks ranged before them, staggering ahead like a thousand massive black and grey teeth. "You see that? That vast playground is known as the Karamakkos. But access is severely limited. There are no roads, no easy pathways. If you are an expert with ropes and climbing up vertical sheets of ice, you can find yourself a path; but for us mere mortals, we need a bridge. Sakaroth is the next peak, but a vast chasm lies between Talkanoth and Sakaroth – impassable. Except for a few months of the year, when a bizarre natural occurrence of various mineral streams from overhead ledges, wind from various caves, and other shit I no doubt would never understand, create these ice bridges that cross the chasm. They are unstable, and more slippery than a bent whore in your wallet, but they will provide us passage."

"Where do they lead? What is it we seek?"

The words *treasure hunt* came to Beetrax's lips, but he pushed them aside, and coughed, and said, "You see Jonti over there? She is ill. We are seeking a cure for her."

"A noble quest, then!" beamed Jael, innocent face lighting up with brightness and honesty. "This is like many stories we read at school, of heroes and quests and saving the land. It is an honour to be caught up in such a quest, Beetrax!"

"Er. Sure." Beetrax turned away.

They travelled through morning, losing height from the summit of Talkanoth. Dake picked a superb route, across fields of steep snow and boulders, and high walls reared around them once more as they came to the Fingers – twin pillars of perfectly smooth stone, each pillar maybe fifty or sixty feet in height and naturally formed.

They stopped here, and had a brief lunch, sitting on their packs. Jael stared between the Fingers, to where a flat, rocky path stretched away between vertical walls of jagged black. At the far end, Jael could see, by squinting, that something glittered.

Snow started to drift down, gentle puffy flakes.

"This place is beautiful," said Jael, voice soft. "I never

realised such a world existed!"

"You've never been in the mountains before, Jael?" asked Jonti, moving over to stand beside him.

"I'd... heard stories. And even though you could see the peaks from my village, nobody chose to explore. I suppose day-to-day life was hard enough, just cutting wood for fires, and growing food to survive."

Jonti nodded. "The Karamakkos, the White Lion Mountains, the Mountains of Skarandos where the Pass of Splintered Bones cuts through; they are all incredibly beautiful, but also, without exception, incredibly deadly. These are not places for the reckless. The Mountain – she does not take prisoners."

Jael gave a little shiver. "I hear you," he whispered. Then changed the subject. "Beetrax said you were ill, and our quest is to save you?"

"He did, did he?" Jonti narrowed her eyes, and glanced over to where Beetrax's booming laughter rolled between the Fingers.

Jael sensed her annoyance. "Was it supposed to be a secret? All I wanted to say was that I was glad to come along; glad to be part of a quest for such a worthwhile cause. I am happy to help, that is all."

"That's all right, Jael. And thank you for your sentiments. It's just... Beetrax is renowned for having a big flapping mouth. I bet that's something the saga poets don't sing about when they sit round the fire, begging for their supper?"

Suddenly, their conversation was broken by a distant howl; the same long, wavering sound which had haunted them back at the barracks. The note held, a stuttering whine, and then died to oblivion silence.

Beetrax shivered. They all looked at one another.

"Believe me now?" said Beetrax, quietly.

"I think we should move out," said Dake, voice hard.

"I reckon that was by the shelter."

Beetrax shook his head. "Too far. It was closer."

"Not good."

They walked between the Fingers, onto the wide rocky path, and increased their pace. Beetrax loosened his axe from his pack, and carried it resting against one shoulder. The walls to either side, maybe two thousand feet in height, were sheer and jagged, unforgiving; they sported long, spear-like icicles and a cold wind oozed mournfully down the narrow crevasse. Jael squinted again at the glittering, and as their boots kicked rocks, crunched ice, and they progressed through the narrow channel, so he realised what he could see was snow glinting from a dazzling array of ice.

"We need to move faster," growled Beetrax.

Jael was limping, holding his ribs now, face lined with pain. Beetrax shot Talon a glance, as if to say, *there, I told you he'd slow us down.* Talon stopped for a moment to string his bow, and his hand shifted behind his head, checking his quiver of steel-headed shafts.

They reached the end of the chasm, and the world opened into a bright, glittering array of sunlight bouncing from ice. Ahead was a towering mountain, with various cave mouths staggered up the vertical wall, containing overhanging promontories of black rock. But what made the company gasp were the Ice Bridges of Sakaroth – there were seven of them, each of varying widths. They curved away in random directions, most with a slight dip towards the centre where huge icicles had formed beneath, dropping away to some bottomless pit far beneath; some terrifying chasm of infinity and death. The narrowest bridge was the width of a man, and spiralled towards the centre, with a rainbow of mineral colours trapped in the glittering ice. The widest, just off centre to the right, was perhaps the width of a narrow, cobbled road in Vagan, down which one cart could comfortably pass.

They gleamed.

The company stood, staring in awe.

"It changes every year," said Jonti, glancing over at Jael. Then to Dake, "The widest?"

Dake nodded, and to everybody, said, "Look at the camber; there is a slope. We'll have to take it slowly. If you have a dagger, keep it to hand – they make an impromptu ice axe. If you go over, dig the knife into the ice until somebody can help."

"And if we all go over?" rumbled Beetrax.

Dake scowled at him, and chose not to reply.

The howl came again; the howl of the splice, long, and wavering, followed by a crunch of ice and rocks, scattering across the rocky floor with hollow clacks like loaded knuckle dice across a corrupt gaming table.

Beetrax's head whipped round, and he growled a curse. The huge, twisted, deformed horse creature stood between the Fingers, reared up on hind legs, front legs dangling before it with great, twisted iron hooves, scarred and bent from battle. The equine head, with lips pulled right back displaying layers of fangs, quivered. The creature's uneven head and lop-sided eyes, one yellow, the larger one blood red, stared at the company of adventurers.

"Shit," muttered Beetrax, getting a good hold on his axe.

The creature's front hooves hit the rocks, and it lumbered into a charge.

"Get across the bridge!" screamed Dake, suddenly, as

every member of the company drew weapons with hisses and clatters of steel. Jonti passed Jael a long blade, slightly curved and wickedly sharp.

"You might need this," she said, sombrely.

Jael swallowed, eyes wide with fear.

Talon leapt alongside Beetrax, withdrew a shaft, and notched it.

The beast was bellowing as it galloped down the rocky valley, shoulder-charging huge boulders out of the way with snorts of steam and blood, its head weaving from left to right, twisted side-horn glistening with some kind of mucus.

The closer it got, the uglier it got.

"Fucking shoot it!" snapped Beetrax.

"I don't want to waste arrows."

"So speaks the best fucking shot in Vagandrak? Fucking KILL IT!"

There was a snap and a whine, and an arrow sped across the space. It deflected from the beast's shoulder, clattering off amongst the rocks.

"Great fucking shot!" snapped Beetrax. "You missed!"

"I didn't *miss*, it's got a hide like plate armour!"

Behind, the others had stepped out onto the widest of the seven ice bridges. They slipped and slid, regaining balances. Jonti looked over at Lillith and Sakora. "It'll be a miracle if we get across!"

"We have to try. We have no option!" said Sakora, eyes on fire. "Link arms!"

They linked arms, and with each member steadying one another, began a slow crossing of the ice-slippery bridge, moving inch by inch, boots sliding out every second step, faces contorting in pain at stretched tendons and muscles.

Another whine, and an arrow embedded in the splice's side. It made not one iota of difference to its charge. It was nearly halfway down the valley now, and it was looking more furious with every passing second.

Beetrax turned full on, and grasped his axe in both hands, and readied himself.

"I hate to say this, old horse, but I think we're going to need more blades." Another arrow slashed at the beast, disappearing in the thick mane. Again, it had no effect.

"Fucking SHOOT IT!" screamed Beetrax, beginning to realise just how big the creature was. He swallowed, hard, mouth dry with sudden fear. It wasn't just big. It was BIG, ugly, and appeared fucking annoyed about something.

Talon held out his bow, fixing his cool gaze on Beetrax. "I swear on my life, Axeman, one more bloody word and you can kill it yourself."

"Just do something!"

The space between them was rapidly closing. They felt the very rocks beneath their feet shaking.

"Gods, it's nearly the height of two stallions!"

Talon started firing shaft after shaft, aiming for eyes and throat, but the beast was weaving, odd disjointed legs smashing rocks as it carried itself forward in an almost random trajectory; certainly one hard to anticipate. Arrows struck from its head and shoulders now, and it reared suddenly, staggering on hind legs, and let out an almighty roar that reverberated around the mountains, the canyons, the valleys, the crevasses, booming and grinding, screaming a created sound of animal hate rarely experienced in the realm of Vagandrak.

Dake, helping Lillith and Jael, glanced up as a shower of small rocks and ice pattered onto the ice bridge. They were half way across, but looking back, he knew they wouldn't make it. And what was Beetrax going to do?

"I can't leave them," he muttered, and drew his sword.

"You mustn't!" hissed Jonti, grabbing his arm, face fearful.

"But... just look at the beast!"

Jonti stared, stared in horror, and drew her lips in a tight line. "Go back to them," she said. "Go back, now!"

Slipping and sliding, Dake reversed his progress, and started heading back for Beetrax and Talon.

Talon glanced left at Beetrax. The beast was nearly upon them.

"Well?" snarled Beetrax.

"Better use that bastard axe. I'm out of shafts."

It loomed close, eyes insane, mouth drooling blood and saliva, great head turning on Beetrax, for whom it made a direct charge. As it came close, Beetrax felt his arse clench in fear as it reared over him. There was a slither of steel as Talon's sword sprang free of its scabbard, and he rolled left under a crushing swing from an iron-shod hoof. Beetrax took a step back, the glittering heads of his great axe slashing through the air. The beast made no attempt to avoid the blow, but twisted, taking the blades on one leg as it heaved its bulk forward, almost sending Beetrax slipping backwards from the ledge into the chasm beneath the bridges. Off balance, he ducked a whirring hoof and jabbed his axe forward, opening a wound in the creature's chest. It bellowed, and Beetrax rolled right but the beast moved fast, rearing, hooves coming down to crush a section of rock a few inches beside Beetrax's head. He stumbled to his knees and feet, and circled around the beast. Talon circled the other way as it whirled about, fixing an evil gaze on Beetrax.

"You… die first, Axeman," it managed through squirming lips and quivering fangs, as pus and blood drooled from a mouth filled with strips of human flesh.

"Beast, you are one ugly son of a cunt," spat Beetrax, anger rising within him to overwhelm the fear. "I'd hate to meet your mother or your sister; although that's probably the same fucking nightmare beast, ain't it?"

The splice roared and charged, and Talon leapt from the side, sword slamming at its head. The blade cut a line but bounced free of armour and the creature whirled on Talon, turning faster than anything so large had a right to – and charged.

Talon skipped back, sword jabbing, and with a roar Beetrax charged in behind, axe coming down on the creature's back, cutting a huge, ragged hole. A leg punched out, iron hoof hitting Talon in the face and sending him spinning across the snow, dazed, sword clattering away. Then Dake was there, between Talon and the creature, his sword up, his eyes bright, his mouth a grim line.

"Come and taste some Vagan steel," he said.

Beetrax came in from the other side. He could see splatters of blood across the snow, and gestured to Dake, who nodded, circling away from Talon.

Suddenly, the splice roared, rearing up, and both Beetrax and Dake rushed in. A hoof caught Beetrax in the chest, picking him up and accelerating him across the ice, where he slid to a stop, wheezing, groaning, and a single foot from where the chasm fell away.

Dake's sword cut a long groove down the beast's hide, but it spun on him and advanced, huge maw opening wide and ready to bite off his head. His sword came up but was batted aside. Nothing could stand in the way of the splice…

On the snow, head pounding, Talon grabbed a stray

arrow which had been dislodged during the fight. He brought round his bow, notched the arrow, and in one smooth movement, fired.

The arrow whined, and embedded in the splice's big, red eye, popping the orb in a splatter of pus and fluid, and driving deep into the elongated horse skull.

The effect was incredible.

The splice went insane, rearing up, spinning round, screaming and roaring, tusk slashing randomly at the air, hooves slashing at invisible foes.

On the bridge, Jonti, Lillith, Sakora and Jael had reached the safe path across the ice. The ground, however, seemed unstable; there was a deep rumbling, a shaking, and looking up, Jonti realised the mountain itself had started to complain.

"Dake!" she screamed. "Dake! I think there might be an avalanche!"

"Shit," he muttered. "Talon! Trax! We need to get across that fucking bridge, NOW!"

Weapons in hand, and ignoring the spinning, gouging, roaring splice, they ran for the ice walkway, hitting the edge and each going over, sliding along on bellies and arses. More rocks and splinters of ice fell from above. The ground trembled, a tremor of terrifying proportions.

Beetrax slid to the very edge of the bridge, and peered down, heart in his mouth. Below, there were several much wider ledges, but then the chasm spun off into infinity. An eternity of deep, dark blackness.

"By the Holy Mother," he said, and sat up, spinning around on the slick, slippery ice. He accidentally nearly pitched backwards over the ledge, and rammed his axe down, blade lodging in the bridge surface, and saving himself from toppling off. He dragged himself back to his feet.

"This is not a good day," muttered Beetrax. "Dake? Talon?"

"I'm good," breathed Dake.

"I'm not, the bastard broke my nose!" snarled Talon.

"Er, gentlemen, I think we have a problem," said Dake, nodding to behind his two companions. The splice had suddenly stopped spinning, and turned, orientated on the ice bridge containing these, its enemies. It snorted blood, a crimson spray against the snow. It pawed the ice, and started forward, shoulders hunkering down, head dropping almost to the ground, like a hound scenting its prey.

"Whoa boy!" shouted Beetrax, gesturing at the bridge. "You'll collapse us!"

The single remaining eyes focussed on Beetrax. The creature snarled, lips curling back, fangs quivering, then clashing together at high speed, gnashing, as if anticipating his flavour, the taste of his flesh.

"Trax, it'll take us down with it!"

The ground was shaking; indeed, the very mountain itself seemed to be shaking. More snow and rocks tumbled from above, larger this time, hammering down around the trio. There came a staccato rapid-fire series of cracks, and the bridge shifted uneasily, like a ship on a rolling ocean.

"Get back," growled Beetrax. Then he turned and stared hard at Dake and Talon. "Get to the fucking ledge!"

The splice came onto the ice bridge. Beetrax snarled something incomprehensible and charged, axe in both hands, blades glittering like diamonds as shafts of sunlight painted their carbon-hardened razor edges. The splice stamped forward, head shaking, and lifting its head, roared up at the mountains, the shaft of Talon's arrow jutting from the left side of its twisted, uneven head.

The splice leapt at Beetrax, as lumps of ice and rock rained around him, and his axe thundered down, cutting a great cleft in the beast's shoulder. But that didn't stop the splice, and its head lunged forward, headbutting Beetrax and sending him staggering back. Then it leapt at him, a deadly strike, and Beetrax was punched backwards, sliding across the bridge on his arse, face contorted in pain at his crunched ribs.

"Now… you die!" gurgled the creature, head low against the ice-bridge. Falling rocks and ice were bouncing from its hide as Beetrax lifted his axe, and struck a mighty blow to the bridge. Steel and ice met, and Beetrax dragged himself to his feet, backing away, his axe striking down, three, four, five blows. Ice cracks zig-zagged in crazy lines across the bridge, accompanied by great tearing, cracking sounds, as if a mighty oak had been chopped at its base and was now tearing its narrow heartwood core apart.

The splice howled, and leapt forward… as the bridge at Beetrax's boots opened in a yawning chasm, and fell away. Huge chunks tumbled down, some landing on the wider ledge below, some bouncing away into the darkness of infinity. The splice, hooves clattering on ice, a half-scream, half-whinny grinding from its throat, was dragged away in a sudden downwards rush of tumbling ice.

Beetrax teetered on the edge, then a hand grabbed his belt and hauled him back.

He turned, to see Talon, grinning at him.

"Thanks," mumbled Beetrax.

"My pleasure, Axeman."

The cacophony of the roaring, falling bridge gradually subsided. All on the ledge stood, breathing deep, eyes wide in shock and fear.

"That was fucking close," snarled Dake, sheathing his sword on the third attempt. "Why did the bastard come after us? They're usually primed to hunt."

Jonti edged forward, peering down.

"I hate to piss on your fire," she said, "but it's not dead."

"What?" snapped Beetrax, and moved forward. Jonti was right. Perhaps a third of the bridge, huge chunks of jagged ice, had landed on the road-wide ledge below. Beetrax followed this ledge with his eyes, and it passed around, hugging the mountain, disappearing into a large cave with an entrance like a dark mouth. Amidst the chunks of rock, the splice was moving feebly.

Amongst the mountains, there came a terrible, deep, booming sound.

More ice and snow came falling from above. A white, coruscating waterfall.

"We need to get off this ledge," said Lillith, looking up.

The splice roared, and the mountain roared back, and several huge chunks of rock, each the size of a cottage, came tumbling down from above – and with them, an avalanche of snow that roared and screamed, thundering down from the higher slopes. Huge billows of snow, like smoke, blossomed outwards, like the vast white petals of some titanic rose unfurling.

Snow showered the ledges, and took out the remaining Ice Bridges of Sakaroth, destroying them utterly and casting them down into the bottomless chasm.

Eventually, the roaring and shaking subsided. The tumbling of snow slowed, and then became nothing more than trickles of powdered white sliding down over newly formed slopes.

On the ledge, the company had gone.

Predicament

Beetrax had a recurring nightmare. He would awake, to find himself in a coffin. He'd open his eyes, but nothing changed; everything was black. He would reach out, but find his arms pinned by his sides. He would try to move his legs, but find them similarly restricted, so that all he could move were fingers and toes. His breathing would become shallow, chest rising and falling rapidly as he felt panic build quickly within him, feel his entire body and mind become a pressure cooker as the world spun around him and he realised he was *trapped* he was fucking *trapped underground*, buried alive, and he'd open his mouth to call for help but no words would come out, nothing would come out, and he tried to speak or cry or wail or scream, but *no sound would come out* and he was mute. "Help me!" he wanted to scream, "I'm not dead, help me!" But nobody was there to help him, because he was six feet under the soil. And as panic flooded him like a shower of red hot razors flowing through his veins and brain, and panic welled in his throat like a fist, he would awake, into a cold grey morning, bathed in sweat, panting, fists clenched, sometimes with piss staining the sheets. It had always been this way. Ever since he could remember. And though he would never admit it, Beetrax was afraid of the dark.

Now, here, in reality, as consciousness finally came to him, at first he thought – believed – he was trapped back inside his nightmare. It was little comfort, being buried alive, but at least some small recess of his brain *understood*; yes, he would go through the usual agony but at least at the end he would wake up, change his bed sheets, burn his pissy mattress, and get on with his life.

This time, however, it was different. It *felt* different.

This time there was no black. Just a fuzzy white; an off-grey.

His eyes flickered open, and he was hot, and yet the world tasted cold. He turned his head to the left, and tried to move his arms. The left was trapped, but his right one came up before his face and he stared in wonder, in confusion, at his rough, tattooed fingers, with their chewed, broken, dirt-ingrained fingernails.

"What?" he mumbled, and his voice emerged as a cracked croak. "What happened?" Nothing more than a whisper.

Why has the dream changed? What is this new place? What is this new terror sent to mock and haunt my deepest nightmares?

And then he realised. And it chilled him to the very core of his soul.

He was buried.

He *really was* buried alive…

Beetrax started to scream, struggling, his right fist pounding the snow around him, the compact white shell which had formed like a protective cage to bury him, *bury him*, and everything was a swirling rage which growled like raging fire through his brain, and this was it, this was the end and his death would come and he would suffocate or be slowly crushed into a thin platter of pulped bones and leaking blood which would freeze, and he would spend forever here.

Eternity, under the ice.

He thrashed, struggling, head slamming from side to side. His arm beat until it could beat no more, and then he lay, paralysed in terror, his mind spinning away into oblivion, and he lay for what felt like eternity, although it was probably only an hour or two, and gradually he fell into an exhausted sleep where he dreamed they were lowering his coffin into an eternal pit, deep underneath a mountain where the dragons slept; and then it was blackness, and then there was no more.

Daylight. Sunlight. A weak, watery grey sky. Movement. A swaying.

Blackness.

The clank of chains. The stomp of hooves. Water on his lips, dribbling cold down his neck. He coughed and spluttered. White light. Gritty darkness. Swimming down into a welcoming ink pool of unconsciousness.

He could smell horseshit. It troubled his nostrils. The world was swaying, as if he were on a ship. It made him want to heave, and he groaned, and leant to one side, and tried to vomit but nothing would come out.

He realised there was a rhythmical clacking sound only when he stopped. A trotting horse? Was he on horseback?

He opened his eyes – into darkness.

Firelight came close, an intensely bright flare that made him shuffle back, his bound hands before him, chains digging into his flesh.

He looked down, focussed on those chains; there were black iron manacles, clamping his hands together. Confusion entered his mind, along with a low-level panic. They had been... on the bridge. Fighting the splice. And then an avalanche, bridge collapse, buried alive. Now manacles?

"Hello?" he managed, at the wavering, flicking firelight which came even closer, as if somebody was examining him. Yes, Beetrax got the definite feeling he was being observed.

"Why manacles?" he managed through dust-dry lips.

"Shut your mouth!" came a harsh, gravelled voice.

"But, I..." The blow was unexpected, and shocked Beetrax into silence. His head was spinning, and he felt blood dribbling down his nose. *Gods, that hurt; what was it? A fist? A club?*

The fire retreated, leaving Beetrax totally blind. He heard movement up ahead, then a cracking sound. Hooves clopped on stone, and they began to move.

His senses swimming, Beetrax struggled to get up, and managed it into a sitting position. He looked about, but all he could make out was some kind of underground tunnel. He dabbed his nose with the back of his hands... and suddenly felt movement beside him. Another body. Another human being.

The figure wriggled, until it was up close against him, and he leant sideways instinctively as lips pressed towards his ear. "Beetrax," whispered the voice, tickling him and making him shiver, "this is Sakora. The others are unconscious. Don't speak aloud, or they'll beat us with clubs."

Beetrax turned his head, putting his mouth to Sakora's ear. "Who will?" he whispered.

"The dwarves who dug us free of the snow," she replied,

voice a gentle murmur. "There were ten of them. With axes, helmets, battle armour."

"Where are we now?"

"The ledge on which we fell; beside it was a tunnel. We have been taken into that. Taken under the mountain."

Beetrax sat back, his head throbbing, his mind reeling. *We have been rescued? By dwarves? But the dwarves in these parts are extinct! They haven't been seen for thousands of years! All the academics agreed, the Five Havens were abandoned, the Harborym Dwarves long dead and bone dust in the massive tombs they had built. Hadn't Riorthrax the Taylor gone on a privately funded expedition and come back with tales of abandoned mines and mountains of jewels? He'd written a book about it. And Falanor Greeves, who gave me the map leading us here... why, he believed it enough he would have travelled with us, if Yoon hadn't wanted his head on a spike.*

Beetrax considered this as they trundled along. He could hear the squeak of an axle now, and the stomp of boots up ahead, beside the clopping of the – donkey? Mule? Surely a horse wouldn't survive down here in the...

In the mines?

Beetrax shuddered. Realisation sank in, like a corpse through the oil swamps of Laleska.

If the Harborym Dwarves still existed, and the Five Havens were real – how friendly would they be towards a group of Vagandrak heroes intent on robbery?

His mind turned grim, and he rubbed at his beard, tasting blood there, and calmed his breathing, and gathered his strength; he had a feeling it would be needed soon.

They emerged into a small circular chamber, the walls coarse and bare except for two brackets on the walls, in which weak-fires burned. It was as if even fire had no energy in this place. As if all the life had been sucked out.

The series of carts, for that was what carried Beetrax, Sakora, and the unconscious bodies of Dake, Jonti, Talon, Lillith and the young lad, Jael, laid out as corpses – gods, maybe they *were* corpses? – came to a stop, rocking on wooden wheels bound with rims of iron.

Beetrax and Sakora turned, staring up ahead, into the chamber. There were about ten dwarves, short, stocky, swarthy, just as Sakora had described. In full black and grey armour, and carrying weapons in meaty fists.

The dwarves seemed to be arguing about something, and then squatted down in a circle, rooting in packs.

"Are the others all right?" whispered Beetrax, gesturing to the figures of their companions. His chains jangled and he frowned, for shackles were something abhorrent to him; he would rather die than be captured; would rather be a corpse than a slave.

"I don't know," said Sakora, and he met her gaze, and Beetrax read the agony in her face. They had been so cocky, so confident, so sure of their own abilities; and at the first hurdle, it would appear they had failed.

Dake groaned, and stirred. He came to life gradually and Beetrax shuffled as close as he could get to his friend. "Shhh," he soothed, as Dake's eyes flared open in sudden panic. His chains jangled, and Beetrax turned. One of the squatting dwarves glanced back, then said something to his companions. They laughed, booming, harsh laughter that made Beetrax's heart sink further down into his boots.

"What's going on?" said Dake, coughing, and sitting up.

"We have been taken prisoner," hissed Beetrax. "And our captors don't like us making any noise!"

"Why?" snapped Dake, rubbing his face with both his shackled hands. "What the fuck are they going to do about it? *Trax*? Come on, let's teach them a fucking lesson."

"You there!" The voice was harsh, rough, deep. A dwarf stood up, and approached them. He carried an evil-looking black club, which he waved in Beetrax's face. "You all shut up, you hear? No talking amongst the prisoners."

"Listen," said Dake, "there has to be some mistake. We are heroes of Vagandrak! Take us to your masters, and..." The club struck him across the nose, a lazy, back-handed sweep that sent Dake crashing onto his side. The dwarf squared himself against the cart wall, and leaning forward, smashed the club down twice against Dake's head, knocking him unconscious.

"Bastard!" snapped Beetrax, surging forward against his shackles, but the club swung at him. Beetrax dodged the first swing, but the dwarf was quick, and the powerful return smash put Beetrax down. The next four blows to temple and jaw rendered the big axeman unconscious.

It took four. Beetrax was stubborn like that.

The dwarf turned slowly and grinned at Sakora with blackened teeth. His face was broad and brutal, with a scar under one eye and a thick black beard, peppered with silver. He wore a simple round steel helm, and a steel breast-plate with a complex crest. He lifted his club threateningly, eyes glinting with humour.

"You want some?" Sakora shook her head, lowering her eyes. "Good. My name is Krakka. I'm in charge of all Mine Slaves. I am the Slave Warden. You humans will learn real fast what it's like under my rules, in my mine. If you are awkward, you will die. There are always plenty more slaves where you came from. After all," and his smile broadened, showing several gold teeth, "the Mountain provides!"

He moved back to his companions. They had a small fire burning and were cooking something. Sakora's nostrils twitched. It was meat. It smelt *really incredible*. She tried to work out how long it had been since her last meal, but could not. She watched Krakka unstopper a small metal flask and take a hefty drink, then passed it round. Soon, their laughter was booming.

We have to escape this place, she thought. Despondency took her in its fist and tossed her down a well of despair.

The journey was a long one, down constantly descending tunnels. It was a maze, filled with a thousand junctions, many with ten or fifteen separate choices, from which they always seemed to veer in random directions. As the company came awake, one by one, they soon realised they had to keep silent, exchanging only glances or hurried, whispered words when they thought one of Krakka's guards wasn't listening.

Now, everyone was awake, eyes tired, faces grim and strained with exhaustion and a little fear.

During their first real conversation, the donkey-towed carts had been pulled to one side of a large chamber. There was a building – a kind of barracks – and the ten dwarves disappeared into the low-ceilinged abode, slamming shut an iron door with a clang. The companions looked at one another, and waited, wondering if this was some kind of trap to get them talking, thus necessitating another beating. During the two days of travel thus far, each had received at least one clubbing into unconsciousness, and they had been offered nothing to eat, not even water. Their misery was a live thing, a captured essence in a jar. They could smell, taste, and hear their own misery. And deep down, they suspected it was only going to get worse.

After five minutes, when the door did not reopen, Beetrax made a deep sigh, and muttered, "How did we end up in this shit?"

"More importantly," said Talon, brushing back his bloodstained hair over one shoulder, "how are going to get out of it?"

"We need the manacles off first," said Jonti. Her nose had been broken, and both nostrils were rimmed with dried blood. As they beat her, Dake had attacked – as best his chains would allow. It took three dwarves to subdue him; and three dwarves to beat him down. It had taken a long time for him to come round, and Jonti had wept over his unconscious body for hours, thinking him dead. "We can do nothing with these bastard irons binding us!"

"They have to move us from the carts at some point," said Lillith, her voice gentle. "But I fear they will only unshackle us one at a time."

"Then that person has to strike, and strike bloody hard," said Beetrax, scowling. "This is no way to treat a man! Bloody slavers!"

"But these are not men," said Lillith. "These are the Harborym Dwarves. Extinct, for thousands of years, so wrote the scholars. How little they truly know!"

"Pah! Bloody academics. They should come out here and do their own damn research! Not use us as a bloody bait trap to find out the bloody truth."

They sat in gloomy silence for a while, staring at one another, and wondering what to do.

"Do you think they plan to starve us?" asked Beetrax eventually.

"That would be counterproductive," said Lillith. "If they really have us down as slaves."

"What do you mean?"

"They want us to work the mines," said Lillith, staring kindly at Beetrax. "Don't you realise? To break out the rocks in the tunnels. That seems logical. Even these carts, look, filled with rock dust and pebbles. Used for transporting rock waste. The whole thing screams a mining operation."

"They want us to break rocks?" rumbled Beetrax, frowning. "That's just not right."

"Better get used to it, soldier," said Talon, sombrely, easing himself into a more comfortable position with a grimace. "These are dark days we face. They'll feed us. And water us. You'll see. They'll need us to keep up our strength."

"I ain't working in no fucking mine breaking fucking rocks," scowled Beetrax.

"We shall see," said Jonti, voice almost a whisper.

As Talon had predicted, before long the door to the barracks opened. Three dwarves stepped out, bearing plates and metal cups. They approached the group, who watched with burning eyes.

At the front was Krakka, grinning from ear to ear and showing his mixture of gold and black teeth. Behind him were two dwarves; one was relatively tall and slim, with a narrow, evil-looking face. He wore his beard close-cut, he had a long, pointed nose and black eyes, no emotion, like glass eyes in a stuffed fox. The other was a hulking, brutal creature, broad-shouldered, with massive, stocky arms and long braided red hair that fell down his back to his waist.

Krakka halted, and their boots kicked pebbles. "Right then, slaves, this here is Val," he gestured to weasel-face, "and this one," he nodded vaguely at the hulking monstrosity, "is Galog. They are my deputies, and whatever instructions they give, you obey instantly. You understand?"

The Vagandrak companions stared at him. His grin widened.

"I think they understand, all right," said Val, who had a slightly whining voice, as if he partially spoke through his long, thin nose. His attention seemed riveted to Lillith and Sakora. Slowly, his eyes moved over them, and then shifted to Jonti, whose lips became a compressed smile.

"Hng," grunted Galog, and they noted he carried a variety of hammers at his belt. They seemed more than simple tools for geological exploration.

"Tell me, human ladies," sneered Val, stepping a little closer. His eyes narrowed, and seemed to twinkle with humour at some personal joke. "What do you think of your first real dwarves, eh? We're a handsome bunch, ain't we?" He roared with laughter, as if this was some great comedy recital.

Lillith focussed on Krakka. "May we eat and drink, Krakka? We are close to exhaustion, and have not drunk for days, now. I am assuming you would rather we were strong, than weak shells unable to work?"

"Oh you'll be strong enough, lady," said Krakka. "But first, we need to learn you the rules, for the rules need to be learned. And that first rule is this – we control the water and the food down here, nobody else. If we say you starve to death, you starve to death. If we punish you with three days without water, then that's what you get. None of them *up there* care about what goes on in the mines, as long as we're meeting our quotas and the fire keeps flowing. You understanding me, all of you bastards? We have your lives

in our hands. You are now our *possessions*. You left your
freedom behind when you decided to come exploring the
Karamakkos." He laughed out loud, and leaned over the
cart, handing out the tray with cups and plates.

Val and Galog handed over their trays, one of which
Beetrax accepted, and he was dismayed to see Val's eyes still
lingering on Lillith. A look of thunder crept across Beetrax's
face.

"You can stop bloody staring at her," he snapped, and
Val's attention drifted, slowly, as if torn away. He looked at
Beetrax.

"Or what will you do, fighting man?"

"I'll break your fucking neck, is what I'll do."

"You reckon?" whined Val, and grinned, showing several
blackened teeth. His foul breath wafted over Beetrax, who
readied himself for another beating under the head of a
savage club.

Instead, Krakka stepped forward. "Val, Galog, go back
to the barracks. I need a quiet word with our Vagandrak
heroes here.

Grumbling, Val tore his gaze from Lillith, and padded
alongside the stomping figure of Galog. They disappeared
into the low building, door slamming shut.

Krakka moved closer, and flapped one hand, signalling
Beetrax to settle back down. "I just wanted to offer you
some advice. You obviously know nothing of our culture, or
our people. You have come here treasure hunting – as quite
a few of your kind do. What I'd like to point out is that you
all end up in our mines. Nobody ever escapes. Some live
out a long life of servitude; some," he glanced at Beetrax,
"are either killed, or we have to put down like rabid dogs.
Now, the decision is really yours. You choose how you

behave. And this is the last time I'm going to give you any such warning, but you – Big Man – if you ever threaten my deputy like that again, I'm going to have you beaten so badly you won't work for a month. And if you don't work, you don't fucking eat. You hearing me?"

Beetrax stared at him, single eye narrowed. "I hear you, Krakka. But I'm still going to kill him first."

Krakka stared back for a moment, then erupted into booming laughter. "Oh you Vagandrak bastards! You have such wild imaginations and a sense of humour. It has been a while since we had some of your kind here for sport; I look forward to seeing how you progress in our world. Truly, I do."

Krakka whirled, and strode back to the barracks, still laughing, rubbing his beard, and disappeared.

"Beetrax!" hissed Lillith. "Why are you antagonising them? You'll wind up dead quicker than you can blink."

"I'm not having that dirty dwarf staring at you like that. I'm just not bloody having it," rumbled Beetrax.

Talon grinned. "They can chain you up, manacle you, beat you with clubs, but you'll never change, will you, hey Trax? Always the hard head, always the stubborn attitude; nothing will break you, will it?"

Beetrax grinned, showing his less than perfect teeth.

"We shall see," said Lillith, her eyes hooded and dark.

They travelled for another full day, down deep tunnels, some narrow, some big enough to fit several houses inside. Most were coarse, jagged and black. They passed over high arched bridges, where the light from the brands fell away into a seeming infinity of darkness, so deep the spaces beneath appeared as black lakes, oil pools, way way down

below. The prisoners peered from their donkey-pulled cart
with grim faces and a gradual feeling of despair. The further
they travelled inside the mountain, the deeper under the
rock they journeyed, the less likely they were of ever seeing
daylight again.

Occasionally, they passed other groups of dwarves in this
deep, damp place. Sometimes they were groups of ten, like
this one, with donkey-pulled carts. Their greetings were
always brief, harsh words, snapped out like barking dogs.
Sometimes, they met squads of guards or soldiers, and
Beetrax and Dake observed various different uniforms, and
a multitude of weapons, from war hammers, axes – both
single and double-headed – to nasty little short swords,
some straight, some curved, all with modest blades. No long
swords down here in the mines. Not enough room to swing
a long blade.

Eventually, weary from the jerking of the cart's iron-
rimmed wheels, the rumble of wheels and clop of hooves,
they turned down yet more tunnels, deep within the maze
of the mountain interior, and emerged from an inverted
funnel into–

"That's the biggest damn mine I've ever seen," said Dake,
sitting upright, his shackles jangling.

"Look at the slaves," said Jonti, her voice small, and her
eyes met Dake's. They were filled with despair.

The roof sheared off above, and to the Vagandrak
heroes, it was like standing at the base of a mountain. A
mountain within a mountain. Ahead, there was a large
area; to the left various low wooden barracks, surrounded
by a compound of wire attached to posts drilled into the
rock. To the right there were more barracks, but of higher
quality and obviously belonging to the wardens. Behind

these, there was a slope to a large, underground lake; black as ink, slick as ice. Straight ahead was the mine face – at least three thousand feet, an upwards slope cut with a winding road, and various sets of steps. Against this face were various vertical steel towers, and swinging cables and rails on which carts rumbled, filled with rocks. A soundtrack became apparent: the *ching* of iron on rock. The smacking of rock hammers. The thump of sledgehammers. The distant, eerie jangle of chains. Against this slope of activity could be seen the working slaves; perhaps a hundred of them, all wearing rough grey smocks, their faces, although distant, downturned, concentrating on their tasks. Various dwarves patrolled the pathways, switchback roads and rough-cut steps. They carried whips and clubs.

"Let's get you lot out of the carts," snapped Krakka, and gestured to Val and Galog, who moved with practised ease, dropping side-gates and gesturing for the bound prisoners to jump down, an act made more difficult by the chains around their ankles.

Val held up a hand to help Lillith, but she scowled and leapt down, landing lightly, although clumsily thanks to the added metalwork.

"Welcome to Gold Mine 79. The most profitable of our enterprises for quite some decades now, and owned by the Church of Hate."

"The Church of..." Lillith bit her lip. A scene flashed through her mind. A cosy tavern, roaring fire, honey mead, good company, hasty agreements. It felt like a hundred years ago. It *felt* like a thousand years ago...

Greeves gave me a map; a page torn from the Scriptures of the Church of Hate, *or at least, what fragments still remain.*

That is one ancient, deadly, cursed tome.

It's a map that leads to the Five Havens, the five dwarf cities under the Karamakkos Peaks. They were once ruled by the Great Dwarf Lords who mined untold wealth – I'm talking oceans of jewels, warehouses full of gold coin, lakes of molten silver. Enough to buy you a lifetime of whores, Falanor brandy and Hakeesh weed!

Wasn't there something about a dragon?

The three dragons were slaves to the Harborym, their minds hammered and broken, or so the legend goes. They were locked away in three huge cylindrical pits, where they were used to light the furnaces. Or something. Anyway, that's all academic bollocks. The point is, the Harborym are long gone, extinct for ten thousand years, the Five Havens lost to the knowledge and thoughts of us mere mortal men. But all that treasure is still there, waiting for some hardy adventurer types to trot along and fill their pockets, and maybe even a few wheelbarrows, with an orgy of sparkling loot.

And now they were there. For real. And Beetrax's words had been so ill-informed it would have been laughable, if the whole sorry situation wasn't so tragic. And Lillith had a feeling it was going to get much, much worse…

They stood, in their shackles, looking at one another, gazing about. More dwarves arrived, perhaps twenty in total, armed with axes and war hammers. Their faces were grim, but a few smiled, their dark eyes glittering.

"New meat?" growled one.

Krakka nodded. "Time for them to be given their first lesson before we put them to work."

"Yes."

"Listen, you southern heaps of horse shit. You are now slaves of the Harborym Dwarves. There is no appeal. You will work in these mines, and you will die in these mines. You will do as you are told, or you will be beaten and whipped. If you die during such a beating, your corpse will be flung into the Dragon Engine where you will be eaten, or incinerated, depending on how they see fit. Now, you will be shown to your bunks."

"Let's get to it," said Val.

They were split up, and each manhandled by a group of dwarves towards the barracks on the left. They passed through various gates, and noted the perimeter, surrounded by ten-foot-high posts with horizontal spans of razor wire; getting over that would cut a person to ribbons. The barracks loomed ahead, to a backdrop of rough mountain walls and fire burning in iron fire-pits. To each man and woman of Vagandrak, it seemed like a dark dream, and they were powerless to resist being sucked into its whirling centre…

Party Time

Beetrax was hurled forward into what could only be described as a cell. It had bare timber walls, a blanket on the floor and a bucket. Beetrax stared around, and grinned back at Krakka, who stood in the doorway. He was carrying a solid club. He stepped forward, and three more big dwarves squeezed in behind him. They all stared at Beetrax, then Krakka nodded, and one moved forward with a huge bunch of jangling keys. Beetrax's eyes lit up. *This could be it. This could be my chance.* Suddenly, a club flashed in the air, striking Beetrax between the eyes. He stumbled back, but the dwarf kept coming, raining down blow after blow and putting Beetrax down on his knees, panting, blood in his eyes, blood pouring from his nose. Only then, did the dwarf stoop and unlock the ankle shackles, and then the wrist shackles. They jangled to the earth floor.

"Get undressed," said the dwarf.

"Fuck you," snarled Beetrax, and with a roar leapt from his kneeling position, charging the dwarves. A right cross put one down, but a blow to the temple stopped Beetrax in his tracks and he hit the dirt, panting, stars in his skull. When, gradually, they cleared, all four dwarves were there, Krakka grinning.

"We can do this the easy way, or do it the hard way," said Krakka.

Beetrax crawled onto his knees, drooling saliva and blood, and groggily, got to his feet. "Well, gentlemen," he managed, rubbing his beard, "I fear it will have to be the hard way." He lunged forward, both fists flying like whistling clubs of iron, but he missed his targets and all four dwarves put him down with their clubs, beating him unconscious.

Finally, panting from his exertions, Krakka looked back to the doorway, and said, "Better get the Ball Cracker."

Beetrax swam through a sea of red and black, and he remembered Lillith with flowers in her hair. He kissed her, and they sat under Lover's Oak, sunshine dazzling rays through the high branches, and they held hands, and she told him about her dreams, to work in medicine, to study herb lore, to help people less fortunate than herself, as the nearby stream tinkled music and the sun showered them with diamonds of light.

"I have written you a poem," said Beetrax.

"You have? How wonderful! Will you recite it to me?"

"Yes, yes of course." His bear paws fumbled inside his shirt, and he pulled out a scruffy, tattered, crumpled sheet of paper. "Now, don't laugh please, it's the first poem I've ever written, so it's not that good, not like those posh ones written by those fancy people at Vagan University, like."

"I'm sure it will be amazing," said Lillith, giving a gentle smile and running her hand through her hair.

He began to speak, his voice cracking and unsure at first as he glanced at her, but then falling into the words, and becoming entranced in the rhythm of the words he had laboured over for so long. He spoke slowly, softly, and Lillith listened in silence…

She stood upon the beach,
Naked.
She curled her toes in the sand,
As the ocean sighed the remains of a dream.

Her eyes were topaz.
They sparkled like breathing gems.
She understood infinity.
The hydrogen sparkle of dying stars.

The waves crashed like seashells gently weeping.
The ocean spoke to her, in tongues of the Wild.

You wish to swim in my cold waters? quoth she.
Well... I want to be free.

The ocean sighed. A mermaid's sexual union.
There is no free. Only a perception of free.
She considered the words,
Of a world gone wild,
Of a world gone strange.

Images flickered like stroboscopic memories,
Burning down the world.

I don't understand?
You are not expected to.
In her nakedness,
She walked forward and enjoyed,
The cold wind blowing in from an endless infinity.
Roaring waves. Surging.
It chilled her to the bone.

You wish to understand how the world works? quoth
she.

You want to know the mechanics?

The way people work?

The way a mind processes emotion?

I do, she said.

She curled her toes in the sand.

Her nakedness thrilled her,

For it was forbidden.

And yet she defied the Law.

She defied that which was not allowed.

Because she had to.

She stood before a million accusations,

pointing at her with twisted fingers,

Whilst she refused to hide her

shame.

You want to know the truth?

There is no truth.

What is there, then?

Only the Moment.

How do people work?

They are chaos.

And life?

Chaos.

And love?

Chaos. Madness.

An indecipherable poetry of a beautiful insanity.

I am the Ocean.

You wish I should give you an answer to your woes?

I am eternal. Omnipotent. I will die
when the stars die.
And yet I will answer you; if you require my counsel?

I do.

She sat in the sand. It was warm.
Her toes curled. Her fingers played with
Streams of consciousness.

There are no woes, quoth she.
There is no pain.
There is no struggle.
There is no right, nor wrong.

There is only a Perception.
There is only the Moment.
And the Moment, if you insist, will last for a Million
Years.

Beetrax stumbled to a halt, and refused to look at Lillith.
"I, er, I had a bit of help with some of the harder words.
Stroboscopic. The sergeant in the mess hall told me that. And
omnipotent, that was Gakes from down in G barracks. But
most of it is my own. Er."

Lillith reached out, and her finger curled under Beetrax's
chin, and she lifted his eyes until they met hers. "That is
wonderful," she said, and leant forward, and kissed him on
the lips, where they stayed for a while, lingering.

"Is that the moment you had in mind?"

"Er. Yeah. Something like that."

"Well let me show you another moment," she said, and

reaching down, grabbed the hem of her dress, lifting it over her head to reveal her nakedness. "Come here," she said, and Beetrax shuffled closer... and fell into her.

There is only the moment.

There is only the moment.

There is only the moment, and he came awake into the moment and his eyes flared open, and he realised he'd been tied to a steel chair. He struggled, snarling, his mind a swirling chaos not understanding where he was or what was happening. He was a wild animal, snarling and spitting and struggling, but he was bound tight with wire and chains, his legs tied tight to the chair legs, his arms behind him, muscles bulging and straining at his bonds as his head thrashed from side to side and he screamed; until his energy and rage were spent.

"Can we talk now?" said Krakka, stepping forward.

Beetrax looked up, drooling saliva and blood to his naked chest. *Naked*? He glanced down, realising in shame that the bastards had stripped him of clothing. Even his fucking boots. *What sort of man strips another man of his fucking boots? Eh?*

"What do you want?" Beetrax's words were thick, his tongue swollen and not working properly. He spat out a sliver of tooth.

"We want your obedience," said Krakka. "And I think I know how to get it." He stood, and stepped back, revealing another dwarf. This one Beetrax had never seen before. He was small and slender, almost effeminate, which was an amazing sight because the dwarves were so brutal in a natural, aggressive way.

"Hello, Beetrax," said the slender dwarf, and smiled,

and took another step forward. There was something about that smile that sent shivers down Beetrax's spine, made the hairs on the back of his neck stand out. He carried a small steel box with a hole in it, and various T-shaped handles emerging from the side. "My name is Tallazok Mentir. And this," he proffered the steel box, as if it were a gift, "is the Ball Cracker."

Beetrax went cold inside. He said nothing.

Tallazok, flanked by two stocky dwarves, approached and Beetrax started to thrash. Tallazok knelt at his feet, chuckling, as Beetrax struggled, trying to kick the slender bastard in the face but severely restricted by his bonds.

"Don't you touch me!" screamed Beetrax. "Don't you fucking touch me!"

"Oh but I have to," chuckled Tallazok, opening the steel box to reveal a complex set of machinery inside. "Now, then," he lifted Beetrax's cock and balls, "we just slide this under here," the steel was cold against the axeman's flesh…

"What are you doing to me? Get the fuck off me! I swear I'm going to rip off your head, I'm going to tear out your fucking spine with my fucking teeth…" He was trying to headbutt Tallazok, but the dwarf wasn't in range. A dwarf slid past, behind Beetrax, and grabbed the axeman's head between two powerful hands. The chair quivered with transferred rage, legs clattering and thumping on the ground, as if the chair had come alive.

"And now, we just reposition you… like *so*, and that fits in there…"

"Will you get off my cock!" screeched Beetrax.

"… and then we attach this clip, like *so*," Beetrax went suddenly very, very still, "and we close the lid, like this." There was a neat little *click*.

Tallazok looked up, directly into Beetrax's face, and he could see the big man had gone pale; gone deathly cold. "You see, my brave and hardy hero from the southern lands of Vagandrak, we are *very used* to dealing with tough cases down here in the mines. Let me explain it a little, so your simple brain may truly understand. We are handed the hardiest criminals of the Harborym Dwarves – and are expected to turn them into willing, obedient slaves who do not inhibit our yield of precious metals and jewels. We are bound by politics, alas, for we are judged on ounces of gold produced, compared to numbers of slaves we are given. We have a little leeway with such as yourselves, found in the open, for they tend not to be strong miners, although we still have to declare them to the Church of Hate and they are still taken into consideration when working out our yield quota. What I suppose I am trying to say, Beetrax the Axeman, who may be a very tough nut out in the soft wilds of the south, is that *I am given the difficult task of taming many of our most unruly slaves, who are usually here for murder and crimes against the king or church.*" He smiled.

"What have you done to me?" said Beetrax, his words very low.

"I have attached what we call the Ball Cracker to your private gentlemanly parts, although I do confess, the device has three main functions, which I shall now explain." He beamed, as if he were a helpful tutor passing on meaningful knowledge to a willing student. Beetrax stared at him with the eyes of a mass murderer. "The first function is that if I turn the right handle here," he gave it an idle tweak, "plates inside begin to come together, and we have what I like to call a 'crushing action' which gradually increases until your testicles are as thin as a Vagandrak gold crown."

"I get the picture," muttered Beetrax, sombrely.

"The second function, here," he twiddled another T-shaped handle, "drives a spike, or what I like to call a 'serrated skewer', through the centre of each carefully cupped testicle, and depending on the configuration of your gentlemanly private parts, also through the base edge of your penis, if that is the way you fall." He beamed again, obviously proud of his device, his technique and his teaching delivery.

"And the third function?" said Beetrax, weakly.

"You will note," Tallazok pointed, "the rocking lever on the summit of the Ball Cracker." He stared at Beetrax.

"Yeah? And?"

"It is a castration mechanism. It completely removes both your balls."

"Ah." Beetrax looked down again, then at Tallazok, then at the grinning figure of Krakka, and the other dwarves, who seemed gently amused, dark eyes glowing as if awaiting a perverse entertainment. "I can see, now, that you have me." He watched Tallazok stand. "Got me by the balls, so to speak."

"Very good, very good, do continue," said Tallazok, and removed his mail jerkin with a little jingle of tiny steel links.

"Er. You have made good your demonstrations." A frown crept over Beetrax's face as Tallazok removed his heavy leather jerkin, a layer designed to stop his chain mail chafing, and passed it to another dwarf. "I know now that I must be a good boy, and follow the rules, and not kick off again like that." Beetrax swallowed.

Tallazok turned towards Beetrax. He was unbuttoning his shirt, which he removed. His body was lean and powerfully muscled. Nearly every inch of skin, from his neck to his waistline, from shoulders to wrists, was covered in the most intricate and detailed tattoos, all black ink, all delicate thin lines, showing a hundred different images, a hundred scenes of people, of people…

Beetrax squinted. Tallazok smiled. "Welcome to my artistry," he said, as Beetrax recognised the images as those of dwarves, men, and children, all being tortured by some technique, device or instrument.

Beetrax felt his soul turn cold, as Tallazok moved forward and knelt before Beetrax, one hand on each of the axeman's knees.

"I feel like you need a more practical demonstration," he said, taking hold of one of the handles.

"No!" said Beetrax, eyes suddenly wide.

Knuckles clenched white on steel. The handle turned. And Beetrax began to scream a scream that was barely human.

Lillith backed into the chamber, followed by Val, who closed the door behind himself. They stood there, staring at one another, and Val's narrow, pointed face broke into a smile.

"There's no need to be nervous," he said.

"Not for me, no. But for you, maybe."

"You are Lillith. I have been watching you for a long time."

"I know. I have seen your eyes on me. But you have nothing to worry about, I am a gentle person; I abhor violence of all kind. I will be no threat to your little mining operation, or indeed, to obeying whatever instructions you give."

Val considered this. "I think you are a threat." He moved a little closer, hand on a sheathed dagger at his waist.

"Why?" She frowned, moving her arms. Charms jangled amidst the chains as she observed the dwarf before her. "You will not need that weapon, so do not even think of drawing it."

"Because of the big one. The Axeman. Beetrax, you call him."

"He may be a threat, but I am not."

"And yet I see in you a controlling mechanism. He listens to *you*, like he listens to no other."

Lillith considered this. "I will help you control him," she said, at last, feeling a bite of shame for her words; as if she were betraying her lover.

"I know you will. Come here. I have the key for those shackles."

"Why would I need to remove the shackles?"

"Because I am going to fuck you."

Lillith stared at the dwarf in disbelief, and noted the sudden bulge in his trews.

"Over my dead body."

"I can do it that way, if you like." He drew his dagger. The blade gleamed. "I have before."

She stared at him then, aghast as to what to say. Suddenly, she felt like a child again, immobile, helpless, at the whim of some greater power, some god-like effigy which had total control over her naivety. She forced her mouth into a grim line and shook her head, in a shower of dark hair. *You are not a child*, she recited to herself. *You are not helpless. You were put on this world to help people less fortunate than yourself, you were put here to study medicine, herbs, the curing of cancers. You are a good person, and because of this, the Seven Sisters and the Holy Mother will protect you.*

Suddenly, spells filtered through her mind. They were

good spells, white spells, magick used for healing and cures. But there, lurking in the back, were the dark spells, the evil spells, the tangled tails of Equiem magick which she had sworn she would never use; could never use, because to use this dark magick would make her no longer human; it would be to give up to a lifelong battle for purity and self-worth. To use the dark magick would be to twist her into another person. Non-human. A demon...

Val leapt forward, suddenly, striking her a blow to the nose. With a cry, Lillith stumbled back, stunned. He came after her, and through confusion she was unsure of what was happening; until the shackles were off, and he was there, his mouth on hers, his stink invading her nostrils, blotting out her own exotic aroma.

"Get off me!" she cried, and slapped him across the face. And then she stopped, as the dagger point under her chin nicked up, drawing blood, *like so*. His hand slid up her leg, under her skirt, and stroked the velvet flesh of her thigh.

"Don't do this," she said, tears flowing down her cheeks. "You don't have to do this."

"But I want to do this. And I promise you, you will like it, medicine woman. I will give you a cure for your loneliness..."

Lillith panted, like a cornered animal. Her lips were wet with fear. Her eyes looked hunted. Inside her, dark smoke swirled and she knew, if she could summon enough hate, she could unleash a spell that would rip this bastard apart...

and be lost

lost to the dark arts...

Equiem magick, the magick of the furnace, the magick of the chaos halls...

Suddenly, a noise went up. It was a terrible high

screaming, and Val lifted his pointed face, like a ferret sniffing the air. He grinned then, and when his head came down he stared hard at Lillith, eyes shining.

"What is it?" she said, voice filled with horror. "What is that sound?"

"That is Beetrax being tortured," said Val, with obvious enjoyment.

"No!"

"Listen, and listen good. You know I do not lie."

"Please make them stop," she wailed.

"Well then, you know what you have to do."

And Beetrax's song of agony hung in the air like the high, piercing note from a tortured animal.

Dake Tillamandil Mandasar, former Sword Champion of King Yoon's Royal Guard, hero of the Second Mud-Orc War, and heir to the Lordship of the House of Emeralds, Vagandrak's largest ruling family, paced up and down in the dark room of the mine barracks, his shackles jingling, his face contorted with suppressed rage and a need to do something, anything, but without any capacity to help. They had tossed him in, like a useless sack of horse shit, and the iron-reinforced door had slammed shut. He heard thick bolts thrown, scraping, and shouted to be released. He stood, with his mouth to the edge of the crack, and screamed, "Do you know who I am? Do you *fucking* know who I am? I am Dake Tillamandil Mandasar, heir to the Lordship of the House of Emeralds, and when my father hears about this outrage he will send a thousand skilled warriors to murder you and all your families! He will grind your fucking bones into dust for all eternity!"

He sank to the floor, panting, exhausted, filled with a quiet terror.

Have you heard yourself? whispered a little demon in the back of his mind. *Daddy's fucking boy. Hasn't got the bollocks to sort out his own problems, ooh no, he needs the Lord of the House of Emeralds to turn up rattling his sabre hilt on the door of the dwarf mines, threatening to burn down the cities of the Harborym Dwarves if they don't let his little squeaky clean bastard free... because that's what you are, Dake, you're a bastard, and the day you inherit the title of the Lordship of the House of Emeralds will be the day the Furnace opens its gates and invites all the good people of Vagandrak in for a little tea party, including cakes, with the flaming demons...*

"Shut up, shut up," he muttered, and climbed to his feet, banging on the solid portal once more. "Let me out, please, or at least, let me speak to my friends…"

Everything during the entirety of your life has been handed to you on a silver fucking platter. Hero of the Second Mud-Orc War? Don't make me puke down my scaled skin. Brought up on a distant estate with an army of nannies – each one being fucked by your father, I might add – looking out for your every pointless little whim, endless summer days playing in rich estates, climbing trees, entertaining your diseased little friends, eating with a silver fork and silver knife and silver spoon. In fact, there, I've done it, puked into my very fucking boots, you spoilt little fucking syphilis-riddled prick…

"No, no, it wasn't like that…"

Only the very best schools for Daddy's little bastard, with strict warnings to the teachers that if anybody so much as laid a finger on your pretty little head, Daddy would withdraw the funding and Vagandrak's second largest family would turn the school into a social wasteland, into an abandoned place. Ah, the privileges of power and wealth to fuck over those without any.

Dake slid down the door, and exhaustion swept through

him, and he put his head down between his knees, and grasped his hair with both hands; he could still smell remnants of the expensive oils he used to run through with his fingers.

What the hell had they been thinking, cocksure and dumb as donkeys, heading out into the Karamakkos on some foolish pointless fucking treasure hunt?

But... it had been more serious than that, hadn't it? A cure, for Jonti. A miracle to help save her life!

Or was it for your own benefit? sneered his private mocking demon. *Of course it was! Because you knew, deep down in your soul, that the little rich bastard was about to be cut off from the family fortune, that's what Daddy said to you, for marrying a common solider like Jonti; he said she was common scum, and deserved her cancer, that it was the punishment of the Holy Mother for being a soldier and a whore... and you held that knife to his throat and it felt so sweet, didn't it, little bastard? And that's why you're here, nothing about a noble fucking cure for your wife, oh no, but to secure your own personal wealth for after she's dead and fucking buried with the fucking wriggling worms...*

"No!" screamed Dake, clawing his own face, and he suddenly stopped as a wail rent the air and tears coursed down his cheeks, for the sound was animal and yet human, and filled with a terrible pain. "That's Beetrax," he panted, climbing to his feet. "Must help him, must help my friends..."

He crawled to the door, clawed his way up it, started to bellow through the crack – and was stunned into backward footsteps as the bolts were thrown wide, the door swung open, and a dwarf stood there, looking at him. He was neatly dressed, without armour of chainmail; just simple dark shirt, woollen trews and boots. Behind, were three wide shadows, but this dwarf was smiling and pleasant.

"Hello," he said. "My name is Nak. If you would follow me, please, I will take you to your wife, Jonti."

"Really?" gasped Dake, breathing deep. "You will let me see my wife again?"

"Oh yes," said Nak, frowning. "Just because we are dwarves does not make us some kind of barbarians!"

He backed away, and Dake stumbled from the room. Nak led the way and Dake followed, shackled hands before him, ankle-shackles making him stumble. Behind followed the three big, silent dwarves, their dark eyes fixed ahead, hands on sheathed swords, faces emotionless.

They walked to the far end of the barracks, and moved into a large, bright chamber, well lit by many firebrands. The floor was tiled, the walls lined with gleaming steel benches, and racks gleamed with a variety of tools.

"What is this place?" said Dake, confused.

"This is the hospital," said Nak, smiling. "After all, prisoners, slaves, guards, all grow sick, or can be injured. So we have this facility here in order to deal with such eventualities."

Suddenly, Dake realised that on the wooden bench at the centre of the chamber lay Jonti. He raced over to her, and grabbed her and she smiled, but her eyes were distant, as if drugs had been administered.

"Jonti! Jonti, it's me, Dake! Oh, it's so good to see you…"

"What's happening, Dake?" Her words were dreamy. "I had this terrible nightmare, that we had been captured. But now I am in the hospital, and the surgeon says he is able to operate…"

"Surgeon? Operate?" Dake was frowning, mind working like a clockwork engine, and he whirled to see Nak, still smiling, pulling on a grey gown. However, despite the smiles, his face was deadly serious.

"What are you doing?"

"I am Nak. They call me the Surgeon. I am about to perform an operation on your good lady wife…"

"What? No! No! She cannot be healed!"

"You wish me to allow her to die?" Nak looked confused.

"No, yes, what I mean is, the best doctors in Vagandrak have examined her, she has been cut open on three occasions and all are in concurrence; Jonti cannot be healed, not by surgery, not by medicine, not by magick!" He was weeping openly now, and took hold of Jonti's hands, squeezing them tight.

"You know what we want here, don't you?" said Nak, and the smile dropped and he turned, gesturing to the three big dwarves, who came over swiftly, grabbing Dake, dragging him back, restraining him in powerful grips.

"Yes, yes, you want us to work in the mines…"

"And we need your total obedience."

"Yes, of course…"

Nak pulled back the sheet covering Jonti. She was naked. Her body was athletic, perfectly formed, and appeared in the best of health. And that was the irony; for despite outward appearances, she was disintegrating from the inside out.

"What are you doing?" screamed Dake, suddenly, as Nak moved to the edge of the room and the steel benches. He picked up a small iron table, bringing it back with him to stand beside Jonti. On it, Dake saw the gleam of saws, knives, and a host of other intricate steel equipment.

"No, no, what are you doing?" he screamed, again.

"We want your obedience," said Nak quietly. "We overheard you. In the carts on the long journey here, to the Five Havens. We know that Jonti is ill. Seriously ill. We know you came here to find…" he smiled, "the Dragon Heads in order to save her, to heal her; to make her immortal? Possibly. I am simply offering to operate on your good lady wife."

"But… the cancer is in her bones?"

Nak smiled. With a thin piece of charcoal, he drew a line across Jonti's left wrist, then a long line up the centre of her arm, forming a very long, extended T. "Precisely. I am offering to remove her bones."

Dake started to struggle, but the solid dwarves pinned him back, securing him. "Don't you dare," he snarled. "Don't you dare harm her, or I'll…"

"You'll what?"

"I will not be responsible for my actions."

A silence followed, where Dake and Nak stared at one another, Dake with open animosity. Then Nak selected a scalpel from the small table, and placed the razor edge against the flesh of Jonti's arm.

"NO!" screamed Dake, struggling again with all his might. But the dwarves holding him were simply too powerful – and experienced in the art of restraining others with minimal fuss.

Firelight gleamed from the small scalpel in Nak's powerful hand. The silver shone, as the blade pressed down just a little. A pinprick of blood appeared, a tiny crimson bead. Dake was weeping, and slumped against his captors.

"No," he said again, less forcefully.

"Is that an instruction, or a request?" said Nak cheerfully.

"It's a request. Please. Don't hurt her. I'll do anything. *We will do anything.*"

"The outcome for which I was hoping," said Nak, dark

eyes fixed on Dake. "After all, she has very little time left to live, so these, your final moments together, must be precious indeed. It would be such a shame to perform a life-saving operation like this, the removal of cancerous bones, because as we know well in the medical profession, these things can often go horribly wrong, and the patient is dead before she, or he, leaves the table."

"You will have our obedience," said Dake, tears coursing down his cheeks.

"Good," said Nak, and removed the scalpel.

Sakora paced in her cell, waiting for the inevitable. Each movement of her tall, elegant frame was gracious and powerful. Although she still wore her travelling clothes, a silk scarf was wrapped around her throat, and her long brown hair was tied back, tightly now, with various ribbons. In readiness, she kicked off her boots, allowing her bare feet to touch the cool soil deep under the mountain. She closed her eyes, steadying her breathing, and her beautiful face, pale like porcelain, was composed as she recited various mantras and ran through a series of stretches. They would not take her without punishment.

The door opened, and a broad-chested dwarf entered. He was wide of shoulder, narrow of hip, unlike many of the Harborym she had so far witnessed, who seemed more portly, like barrels. He wore a simple cotton tunic, and his hair was tied back tight, braided with beads, his beard trimmed close to his face. He closed the door behind himself, and gave a short bow.

"You are Sakora?"

"Yes."

"I am Jakkanda. You are Kaaleesh. We trained under the

same yallan yend'hah. Your reputation precedes you."

She stared at him, stunned. "A Harborym *Dwarf* has trained in the art of the Kaaleesh? I find that very hard to believe. In Vagandrak, your race is thought to be extinct. Nobody knows you exist!"

Jakkanda smiled, and walked sideways, across the room, pacing. He placed his hands behind his back, like a professor about to perform a lecture. "Look closely at me, Sakora. I am what they call *half-breed*. I am Harborym in blood, yes. But my mother was a woman, just like you. And whilst this puts me at a disadvantage in many areas of the Five Havens, it means I am more… aesthetically *human* than you give me credit for. Look closely at me, Sakora, and tell me what you see? A slender, tall dwarf, or a…"

"Smaller, slender man." She nodded. "You move amongst our people?"

"Some of us, a select few," said Jakkanda. "We work under direct supervision from the Church of Hate. Our leader, Cardinal Skalg, does not like surprises. And Vagandrak is close enough to, maybe, one day offer us very nasty surprises. We like to be informed. We like to be well prepared."

"Why would the people of Vagandrak offer you hostility?"

"Because of our incredible wealth," said Jakkanda, words gentle. He stopped, and she noted he wore soft shoes, not boots like the other dwarves. He faced her, and placed his hands together before him, almost as if in prayer. "Now then. To business. You are here as a slave. And yet I know you, because we are the same, you and I. You will not back down. You will fight."

"Yes, I will fight."

"If I challenge you to hen'yah combat, if I win, then you

become my subordinate, as is Kaaleesh Law."

Sakora frowned. "Nobody obeys the hen'yah rulings. They were outlawed hundreds of years ago, for those not honourable to our traditions would and did abuse them."

"It's trial by combat, Sakora; or something much worse."

"Shock me."

"They know your training, and they know how to hurt you." His face looked compassionate. "They would hobble you, Sakora. They will break your ankles with sledgehammers, and strap you up whilst you work. But you will never walk properly again. You will need sticks. Your balance will be destroyed. And it will break your spirit, for your body will be ruined. You will no longer be a practising Kaaleesh."

Sakora paled a little, but lifted her face; her pretty face. "Then I will kill those who come at me."

"They said," and here, Jakkanda appeared almost as a conspirator, the human part of his half-breed biology taking over to help this, a fellow human, *"they also said, if you did not comply, they would put out your eyes."* It was delivered as a whisper, accompanied by great regret. "I am sorry. All I could do, to help a fellow Kaaleesh was offer this chance at trial by combat. Your choice."

He stepped back, ending the discussion.

"What if I win?"

"You will not win."

"Arrogance is not a trait of our kind."

"It is not arrogance, but simple fact."

"What if I win?"

"If you win, then you will be released; back into the mountain. You will not be given aid, but at least you will be free to find your own way from the Five Havens."

Sakora stared at him. Her lips compressed in a narrow line. She did not believe him, but then, what choice did she have?

"Hen'yah. So be it."

"Prepare yourself," said Jakkanda, and approached, warily, both arms extending forward, fists clenched, left foot forward, head lowered a little, eyes fixed on Sakora as if his very life depended on it. Which it did.

Sakora attacked, in silence, like a striking cobra. A quick succession of horizontal and vertical blows, hands moving in a blur, then leaping back as Jakkanda blocked and performed a low sweep.

"You are fast," he said, and smiled.

Now Jakkanda attacked, and Sakora blocked with left and right forearms, a series of heavy quick smashes and slaps that had her backing away. A side-kick came at her, but she twisted, grabbing the leg, levering up. Jakkanda leapt, twisting, wrenching his leg from her grasp and landing lightly, then springing back as a front-kick ended where his face had been.

Sakora charged, and for long minutes they fought, neither landing a blow other than against defensive blocks. Punches, side-kicks, sweeps, roundhouse kicks, a stunning display of perfect timing, superior training, years of expertise thrust into that tiny room deep within the mountain lair of a hidden race.

Suddenly, Sakora landed a chop to Jakkanda's throat, and he staggered back several steps. She leapt in, blows raining down, and a side-kick caught him in the chest, hammering him back against the wall. He managed to ward off the next few blows, but a punch to the temple dropped him to one knee, and a knee to the nose laid him out flat.

Sakora stood, light-footed, a narrow smile taking hold of her face...

The door opened, and a group of armed dwarves stormed in. Krakka followed, his face hard, and he halted beside the unconscious body of Jakkanda.

"He said I would be released. Back into the mountain."

Krakka looked up, and his eyes were dark. Sakora could not read his intent. Then, slowly, he drew his short sword, which hissed as the oiled blade cleared its scabbard. The iron was dark, and inlaid with three tiny emeralds. They shone.

Sakora took a step back. She glanced at the other guards, and licked her lips.

Krakka plunged the blade into Jakkanda's chest, and his legs kicked, body spasming. His eyes opened for a moment, meeting Sakora's, and then he twitched and went still. Krakka pulled the blade out, wet with blood, a dark stain of death.

"Why?" she hissed, eyes wide.

"He could not control you. Fucking half-breed was useless to us. Now, we have to use a different tactic."

"What tactic?" She started to back away, as the guards rushed at her. She started fighting, but a club caught her temple and she went down hard. When she came to, the dwarves were pinning her down, and Tallazok Mentir stood demurely to one side, watching her.

"You have ideas?" growled Krakka.

Tallazok nodded, and unpacked a small velvet roll, which he laid out on a small steel table beside him. "She is a pretty one, all right. But does a woman really need so much skin?" He unrolled the cloth, and selected a scalpel.

"What are you doing?" cried Sakora, struggling madly. But the guards held her tight, their weight, and strength, pinning her down.

Tallazok knelt by her side, and the blade came towards her, glinting like sunlight. She flinched, turning away.

"Now keep still, pretty one," he said, smiling kindly. "This is as delicate as peeling a grape. And I wouldn't want to put out your eye."

Outside, across the busy mine, Sakora's scream cut through the air like a serrated dagger.

Talon was seated on his low bed when the three dwarves entered. They were hefty, and armed with slender black clubs. Their eyes looked hungry, and Talon stood with a smooth movement. He had to admit, his nerves were crumbling. He had heard many shouts and screams over the past few hours, and it would appear he had been left until the last... it certainly felt that way. He had identified the screams of both Beetrax and Sakora. Now, his heart hammered in his chest like it was made of iron.

"My turn, is it, chaps?" He gave a narrow smile, and nodded to the clubs, his eyes shining.

"Shut up, bastard. I am Kelda. This here is Lungir," Kelda gestured, "and Stone." The swarthy dwarves grunted, all eyes fixed on Talon.

Talon shrugged. "You all look the same to me. Maybe if you washed and shaved, I might be able to tell you apart." His eyes narrowed. His hands and feet were still shackled, and the chain jangled as he shifted. He nodded to the clubs. "What you going to do with those, lads?"

"You're a pretty boy, ain't you, Talon? A proper noble warrior, respected by everybody. Well every man, even a delicate little girl like you, has a breaking point. So we thought we'd show you a bit of, you know, Harborym hospitality, so to speak."

They rushed him, and Talon's hands flashed up to protect himself, but were beaten out of the way. Three blows saw Talon slammed backwards, but the dwarves followed in, clubs beating down relentlessly, forcing Talon to his knees, arms up trying to protect himself. This went on for a minute, then the dwarves took a step back. They were grinning. Talon was panting.

"Well, you're harder than you look. But let's see how much you can actually take, you human bastard," growled Lungir. "Because we can *give* you a lot." The beating continued. And it went on. And on. And on. Until a welcoming black blanket of unconsciousness took him.

Eight guards sat in the barracks' central room. There was a long iron table, and various chairs, all fashioned from iron. They were broad, heavy dwarves, with a range of beard styles and armour, each wearing his own preference of mail or plate armour, and a mish-mash of different styled helmets. They were playing a game using cards, small squares of flattened alloy, and knuckle bones with inscribed numbers. There was a great deal of coin on the table, along with flagons of wine and ale.

"Your turn."

"Fifty! That's you fucked."

"I'm not as fucked as those human scum."

"Go, Degs, it's your fucking turn, you halfwit."

"Call me a halfwit again, and I'll crack your fucking skull!"

"Calm down, there's enough fighting up in the city, don't want to be risking your job down here, eh? Go on, fifteen slates; you putting same in? Watch him, he's a slippery bastard when it comes to bets."

"Go on."

"Brilliant throw! For me, har har."

"What about the other one?"

"Which other one?"

"The young lad they brought in."

"Ach, he won't last a fucking week. He's frail, like a chicken wing. Weak. They'll crack him open like they cracked open Talon's arse, you mark my words."

"But he's only a young 'un; isn't that a bit cruel?"

"The *Scriptures of the Church of Hate* speak of a time when we were abused by the southern bastards known as men; enslaved, we were, treated like animals, forced to work the mines – our own fucking mines! – not as free dwarves, free spirits, but as animals, earning wealth for others, for those of non-dwarf persuasion. We were beaten, whipped, tortured, raped and murdered. They abused us for centuries. They fucked our females, our wives and daughters, and we were not allowed to marry, not allowed to have relationships; they tried to breed the dwarf out of the dwarves with their deviant fucking ways." He took a long drink, and smacked his beard, down which a goodly amount had poured. "I tell ye, comrades, we were slaves to these bastards for centuries – so don't go getting all soft on me, and on them, when you think about a bit of pain they might be going through. They did it to us first. We are supported by the Church of Hate and the Great Dwarf Lords in this matter. So don't you ever forget it."

There was silence for a while, with only the hiss of sliding metal cards and the rattle of rolling bone dice.

"Did they say what they were going to do to the young one? To make him comply?"

"Yes." He grinned, showing black teeth. "It's highly amusing."

Jael lay shivering on his bed, wondering how they hell he'd managed to get himself caught up in so much trouble. His life, he realised, had simply gone from bad to worse. Whilst growing up, times had been extremely tough, and he knew he was a lad of simple pleasures. All he'd wanted out of life was a job good enough to put food on the table, and one day, hopefully, he'd meet a lass, young, plump, large breasted, with childbearing hips; and they'd be wed under the Storm Oak, and she'd bear him proud strapping sons and he'd bake them bread, or make leather belts and boots, or work with his father out in the woods, felling trees to build up the winter stores for the village.

That was all gone, now.

Dead and gone.

Simple dreams, killed by ex-soldiers abusing the weak.

Dragging him through the woods, twigs tangled in his hair, punches to his face, his head, his ribs.

Tied to a tree.

Rescued!

Travel. Then hunted by a terrible beast, and now here, imprisoned, listening for hours to others screaming; to Beetrax, his hero, screaming, screaming, and then finally it was over, and Jael sat up and listened, shivering.

He shuddered, feeling as if he was going to vomit. Beetrax screaming. That was not a sound he'd ever thought he would hear in his darkest nightmares.

Now the sounds of pain had stopped, and there were just the ambient sounds of the mine, something he'd noticed but quickly become accustomed to during his few short hours there. There were chipping sounds, metal on rock. Heavier thuds, of sledgehammers. The clink of chains. The occasional crack of a whip.

What will they do with me?

Will they come, with their knives and torture equipment?

They want to break us, don't they?

They want us to be good prisoners; to behave and not cause any trouble.

What will they do to me?

He heard boots thudding the stone outside. They stopped. A bunch of keys jangled, a key slid noisily into the lock and a heavy mechanism went *click*. The door opened and Jael cowered back on his low bed, head lowered, presenting a truly submissive figure. He could see his own fingers. They were trembling violently, and he felt ashamed. Images flickered in his mind. Memories from back in the forest, tied to the tree, waiting to die...

"I bet you thought we'd forgotten you, eh lad?" boomed a voice, and it was Krakka, squat and powerful, flashing a smile filled with black and gold teeth. He stomped in, and another dwarf came in behind, carrying a chair that was placed in the middle of the floor with a thump.

They're going to torture me on that, thought Jael, and tears came to his eyes. *They're going to tie me to the chair, and cut me open with blades, burn me with fire.* He shuddered as images flashed through his mind. *What can I do to convince them? How can I get out of this situation alive?*

Krakka moved over, sat on the chair, and looked down at Jael.

"You know what we have here, lad?"

"What?"

"*Dragons.*"

Jael stared at the dwarf, who grinned at him from a position of superiority. "Now then, you've been listening to the others screaming, right? And you're wondering when it's your turn, and what we've got in store for you, yes?"

Jael nodded.

Krakka shuffled a little closer, chair legs clacking. "Well, I'm going to let you in on a little secret, boy. On the way here, in the donkey-pulled cart, we was listening to you lot, all the time. And it soon became obvious you, little Jael, are not part of these money-grabbing bastards who were intent on robbing the Great Dwarf Mines for everything they could get their grubby hands on. We heard how you got picked up on the way, and had no other option but to join their little band or perish out in the wastelands. Yes?"

Again, Jael nodded.

"Well I have a proposition for you." Krakka sat back, putting his hands on his knees and beaming, as if he'd already made Jael an offer he could never refuse.

"Yes?" Wary.

"Most slaves end up in the mines doing hard labour. But we have a small, select group who tend to the wyrms. It's very basic needs, like clearing away bones from the Dragon Pits after they've been fed, making sure their fresh meat has been cleared of beaks and claws, that sort of donkey shit. But still, considered a privileged position down here in the mines." His eyes gleamed. "Something to which the other slaves aspire, because it keeps you out of the whipping and beating."

Jael nodded. "Your offer sounds... interesting. But why me? Just because I'm not part of the Vagandrak group proper?"

"No. In return for a lack of torture, and a lack of backbreaking manual labour, I expect you to listen and watch the others. You will be barracked together. If there is any talk of escape, you tell me. If there is any talk of insubordination, any plans whatsoever, you tell me."

"That would be hard. They saved me! I don't know if I could speak about them behind their backs like that," said Jael, voice gentle. His head had lowered, like a beaten dog in submission.

Krakka stood. His demeanour suddenly changed, any sense of friendliness evaporating like steam from a dragon's nostrils. Now, he appeared very angry, and very threatening. "The alternative is this, young Jael. I get a few heavy dwarves in here; they're rough types, been locked down here for a long time, only a hair's breadth away from being slaves themselves. Trouble is, when you're down here like that, you are denied the basics of living, like the soft touch of a quim, the joy of inserting your cock into that willing, quivering honey pot and enjoying a bit of baby-making. So instead, they're willing to shove their cocks in any bit of young flesh, and you look so very young and sweet, Jael; your skin is soft, your hole will be tight and clench like a virgin when she's first taken. And for dwarves like this, with very little pleasure, all they have to do is squint their eyes a little bit, and you're the young female dwarf they could never have. They'll split you so wide open we could drive a donkey-cart through. And if that doesn't work, my dear young lad, well, we'll start with the coffin hanger – it's a metal box, a metal *coffin*, and you lie inside and there are various holes through which we can pour boiling oils, or bring in rats which will eat parts of you whilst you scream and thrash, unable to move your hands to ward off their gnawing teeth. Now you think about that. Think about being eaten alive by rats." Krakka paused, panting a little.

He licked his wet lips. Jael's eyes were full of fear, hands trembling violently. "Or then, we have the Brazen Dragon. A hollow dragon made of brass it is, and we strap you inside and light a fire underneath. Get the coals nice and hot. You cook, Jael, you roast and scream, your fat bubbles, and eventually the skin falls from your flesh and your tender meat – oh what a fine smell it is – will be succulent and beautiful when it peels from the bone like the finest donkey steak." Krakka moved forward, and squatted, and reaching out, took Jael's chin, lifting his eyes to meet the brutal dwarf Slave Warden's own burning coals. "Or if you really displease me, and won't help me in times of… distress, then I can simply feed you to the wyrms. I confess, they have moderately delicate digestive systems… so first we use rock hammers to knock out your teeth, then pliers to remove your fingernails and toenails. Then we have to pulverise your hips and pelvis, your knees and elbows, so that they are smaller particles within the sack of your bruised flesh. Finally, we beat your skull until it's cracked in multiple places. But you are still alive through all of this. Still alive, a sack of pulp, ready to be fed to Moraxx, Kranesh and Volak." His voice had dropped to a husky whisper. "You have five minutes to decide, young Jael. I will come back then."

"Yes, yes I'll do it," said Jael, tears streaming down his cheeks, his head hung low in shame.

Krakka's boisterous laughter boomed through the mines.

Internal Politics

"Please repeat that," said Cardinal Skalg, his voice colder than a frozen corpse. He was sitting, naked, beside a pretty young female dwarf, who he was currently in the state of undressing. She looked bleary eyed, as if drugged, and by the side of the huge bed, with black satin sheets, stood a brass bowl of crushed gangga leaves in boiling water, the steam rising in tiny swirls.

Razor looked Skalg coolly with that single eye, glass dark and unreadable, and gave a small cough, as if clearing her throat. "I said, in the last *hour* there have been *three* Church of Hate priests murdered – one at the altar – and now an angry mob is marching through the streets with burning brands, chanting abuse."

The young dwarf had just taken Skalg's half-erect penis in her hand, and was lowering her head towards it, rouged lips puckered, eyes dreamy and half-closed. "Not now!" he snapped, pushing her away with a smack and standing. He hobbled awkwardly to the balcony, pushing open metal latticework doors, and stepping out into the cool breeze at the top of the Blood Tower. He scowled, hands slapping the smooth stone balcony, and endured a flickering flashback; Kajella, beautiful Kajella, mouth open in a long, silent scream as she fell to her death far below.

That bitch deserved to die. And anyway, for a First Cardinal as powerful as I, there is always a long queue of willing entertainers.

"Cardinal?" Razor followed him out onto the balcony. The city of Zvolga swept before her, and if she had been more naïve, she might have gasped, for this was the first time she had been allowed into Skalg's apartments; promoted, one could say, after Granda took a crossbow bolt in the guts.

"Wait, wait, I'm thinking." And then he saw them, far below in the dark stone streets. They carried burning brands, and were making quite some noise. Skalg's eyes widened, his lips quivered, and a long umbilical of drool detached from the corner of his mouth, spooling like a strand of silver spider's web, to connect him to the balustrade of the Blood Tower's highest vantage point. "There are hundreds of them!" he squealed, suddenly, voice high-pitched, fists clenching and unclenching. "Look at them! The bastards! What are they doing? Where are the City Guards? Where are the Church Wardens? *Where are my fucking Educators?*"

"Calm down, Cardinal." Razor's hard voice was like the crack of a whip, and she looked half ready to deliver a slap across the First Cardinal's face, but managed to restrain herself at the last moment. "Please. You must remain calm. The City Guards are on their way, for this is a civil dispute, and I have instructed a hundred Educators to be at the ready."

"We cannot have this outrage in our city!" roared Skalg, red in the face, froth on his lips. "How dare they? Ungrateful dwarf bastards! How *fucking dare they*!" He paused, breathing fast, then his eyes became bright and connected with Razor's appraising gaze. "What do they want?" he wheezed.

"You remember the prisoner, the one suspected of burning down one of the churches? We, er, met him at the firehouse, and you instructed the Educators to carry out various unpleasant activities on his person until he… died."

"Yes yes, what of him?"

"It would appear word leaked out concerning his innocence with regards his lack of any connection with the Army of Purity, and of his treatment in search of information at the hands of the Church of Hate."

Skalg stared at her. "*Treatment*? How could anybody possibly have found out?"

"Fire Sergeant Takos, apparently, wrote to the king about the 'disgrace he witnessed'; apologies, Cardinal, I am simply quoting what was told to me."

Skalg stared at her, eyes narrowed. "I thought you warned him, when you escorted him home?"

"I did." Razor gave a narrow smile. "I warned him with threats of retribution against him, his wife, and his children. Believe me, he was terrified. He pissed all down his leg. I had to step away from the puddle."

"Hmm," growled Skalg. "I see. So… who are these people I see below me now, flouting city law? Flouting *church law*?"

"That would be the family and friends of the man we killed during torture, Cardinal Skalg. Plus outraged hangers-on, judging by the numbers."

"How many?"

"Three hundred, I believe."

Skalg swallowed. *I simply do not believe this is happening! I do not believe that back-stabbing bastard Fire Sergeant Takos went above the church to Irlax. Does he not realise what the Church of Hate will do to him? To his wife, his children, his cousins, his aunts and uncles, his fucking dog?*

"Very well," said Skalg, regaining a little of his composure. "I will dress, we will meet with the Educators, and we will formulate a plan to help get us out of this mess."

Razor stared at him. "I think it unwise you travel out. I have merely brought you the information, knowing you were otherwise engaged, and have instructed various Under-Chief Educators to manage the rest. I have come to *stay with you here*; to protect you."

Skalg felt himself go a little cold, remembering the recent events with the carriage and burning barrels and a certain notorious assassin.

"I do not need protection," he said.

"At this moment in time, the mob will tear you apart if they get their hands on you." There was something about the cool, detached way Razor said the words that left Skalg standing there, lips flapping, cock limp and useless. Cold reality sank in like molten iron poured into a mould – and then solidified, to create a permanent, solid fact. *They would kill me. The people of Zvolga would kill me. ME! Their First Cardinal and leader of the Church of Hate. How DARE THEY?*

"I will not be imprisoned in my own chambers," said Skalg, his voice a little strangled.

Down below, a cheer went up. Something was burning. It was a Church Warden outpost, many of which dotted the city and afforded groups of up to twenty wardens a base from which to patrol.

"You wish to be burned?" said Razor. "You wish to die without trial, like the dwarf you tortured to death? There has been writing on walls, houses, churches, bridges, appearing all across the city."

"What kind of writing?"

"Five letters. HTCOH."

"What the fuck does that mean? HTCOH?"

Razor gave a narrow smile. "Hate the Church of Hate.

Army of Purity propaganda, but it is getting bigger. The Army of Purity's message is gaining momentum."

Skalg stared again, mouth open, breathing fast, then turned and stared down at *his city*. The City Guards had arrived, and the noise from the mob died for a little while as words were exchanged. Then a roar went up and angry dwarves started punching their burning brands and fists into the air. With military precision Skalg watched the guards form into a wedge, drawing swords, and he could almost see the words trip from the sergeant's lips as... the guards charged the mob, swords stabbing out, slashing down, and suddenly a vicious brawl ensued. The mob fought back, drawing their own weapons, beating down with burning brands and setting several City Guards on fire. Flames passed from dwarf to dwarf and Skalg could hear them screaming as they fought to get out of burning tunics pinned to them by heavy chainmail coats.

Razor moved in close behind Skalg, careful not to touch his hairy buttocks. Almost in his ear, she whispered, "The Church of Hate is losing favour with the populace; the church is losing its grip on power. Instead of rushing out there and threatening *fellow dwarves*," one could not escape the cynicism in her voice, "you must think long and hard, Cardinal Skalg, about what wins over the sweating, downtrodden mob. How do you win them back to your cause? Because the way it stands, you are giving King Irlax your head on a plate."

"King Irlax?" Skalg raised his eyebrows.

"You think I am so foolish I cannot see the struggle for power between you two? You think, just because I am an Educator with black teeth, a ruined eye, and a penchant for cutting off the pricks of dirty dwarves who dare come near me, you think that means I have a lazy brain?" She gestured backwards into Skalg's chamber. "You have spent too long with butter-brained idiots, Skalg. I believe in the Church of Hate. And I believe in Cardinal Skalg. It's taken a long time for me to progress, to get this high in our... religious organisation. But trust me when I say the church saved my life; *you* saved my life, and I owe you a debt of gratitude, my undying loyalty, and a willingness to see this thing through to the end. With, or without, King Irlax's blessing."

Skalg had turned. Razor was careful not to get too close to his flaccid cock.

"An eloquent speech," he said, thoughtful. In the background, more flames roared and more dwarves – both guards and the mob – burned, flames licking at flesh, scorching fat, and igniting beards. In such close proximity, the fire soon raged amongst the combatants. It was a grisly sight from even this great altitude; on the streets of Zvolga, the gutters ran with hot dwarf fat. Skalg looked Razor up and down, as if seeing his Educator for the first time. Truly, for the first time. "I think we need to talk."

"Come back inside, let's get rid of your entertainment, because I have a plan you might be very interested in."

In the city, dwarves screamed and buildings burned. Guards charged, hacking limbs from bodies, and the mob retaliated, hurling cobbles and bottles, using their own swords and war hammers, and all the time chanting –

"Jus*tice*, jus*tice*, jus*tice*..."

And, "Hate, hate, hate..."

Skalg lay in bed, restless, tortured. Faces flickered past his mind's eyes, faces of those he'd murdered, or ordered murdered; the old, the young, male, female, children, babes, their faces flickered faster and faster as if on some distorted, glowing wheel, each presenting themselves with an open mouth like a black tunnel, screaming abuse, screaming at him, Cardinal Skalg, for providing them with death.

He awoke confused, in pain, and angry. Angry with himself, angry with Irlax, horseshit, angry with the entire nation of the Harborym Dwarves. *How can you all be so blind? How can you all be so stupid?*

He was about to get up, but didn't, instead resting back, allowing the pulses of pain – of which he was so used – to flow through him, to settle through him like ash from a pyre of burning corpses. And he thought; he thought about the priests, and he thought about the church burnings; he thought about the Army of Purity and their ridiculous demands, and he thought about…

Irlax.

King Irlax.

Of course! How could I have been so fucking blind and stupid and ignorant?

It's King Irlax. King Irlax is behind the Army of Purity. King Irlax is behind the goading of the mob. He knew all about the torture of the innocent man in the firehouse, even before it was reported to him; he knew that I was breaking the rules in a need to get to the bottom of the perceived insurrection. Irlax was tired of my interference, in his… in his fucking insubordination against the crown. What King Irlax really needed was a puppet cardinal; somebody weak-minded, who would do what they were told, and not be a challenge to Irlax's plans…

So then, think!

What does Irlax want? What are his plans?

Like a chill wind through his soul, Skalg realised with a sudden primeval intuition. King Irlax would combine the crown and the church. Irlax would become the first Cardinal

King. He would merge the two most powerful organisations of the Harborym Dwarves, which had traditionally always been at some low-level war since the days of the Great Dwarf Lords. In one swift, decisive action Irlax would remove any challenge to his authority – now, and for all time.

It was genius. *Genius*!

Skalg sat up in bed, his twisted hump stabbing him with knives of fire. But for once the pain did not bother him. Not in the slightest. Instead, his mind was whirling and spinning like a tornado in the southern desert lands of Zakora.

What a clever plan. Stage assassinations and the burning of several churches. Goad Skalg into doing something stupid, something brutal – as his reputation proclaimed. Then gather support from the people, build up rage in the mob and hate for the church, so that the removal of Skalg would not be an act of blasphemy, but a genuine act for the people. Then a short rigged election, Irlax has all the power in the Five Havens. Janya, Keelokkos, Sokkam, Vistata… and Zvolga. All under the ultimate authority of one Cardinal King.

Skalg's mind was reeling.

How was I so blind? How did I stumble into this rancid donkey shit like a drunk adolescent chasing fresh young quim? How did I not see the warning signs? How did I let that dumb dwarf bastard get such an easy upper hand?

And the answer was there, staring him in the face, and truly, it was a bitter pill to swallow.

You believed your own hype.

You believed your own ego.

You swallowed your narcissism.

You considered yourself untouchable.

You thought yourself fucking invincible, First Cardinal Skalg, you arrogant, arrogant bastard of a bastard of a bastard.

Skalg climbed out of bed, and wrapped himself in a purple robe, and moved to the door, pushing it open and stepping onto the balcony of the Blood Tower.

Far below, the guards should have easily got everything under control from the chanting, violent mob. And yet, amazingly, they had not. Pockets of violence were erupting all over the city. Skalg squinted. He could see eight or nine areas where fires now burned, accompanied by large groups of agitated, chanting dwarves.

The city is crumbling, he realised.

Law and order is breaking down. For the first time in thousands of years. The mob has overcome its fear of the Church of Hate, and for the very first time is fighting back. And it was all my fault, thanks to Irlax's engineering. I blundered into the trap like a baby rabbit into a razor snare.

Skalg licked his lips.

Evil thoughts wriggled in his mind, the ejaculation of demons.

The question was…

What did he do next?

Granda, Chief Educator for the Church of Hate, lay in the bed of the low-ceilinged hospital barracks. The bolt in his belly had been removed, but it had gone deep, deep, *deep*, requiring internal stitches, then stitches on top of the stitches. Granda had lost a lot of blood, and even more of his sense of humour.

"That little bitch," he muttered to himself, often.

The nurses who tended him were squat, middle-aged beasts, many with beards themselves, waddling around in sturdy boots and starched uniforms, scowling at him as if he was an annoying toddler who refused to take his medicine or do what he was told. He wanted to scream, *I'm the Chief*

Fucking Educator for the Church of Hate! but he knew they knew, and he knew they did not actually care; to them, he was just another bundle of injured flesh who needed help and drugs and a few shushes to get him to sleep at night – there there who's a good boy then?

Pain pulsed through him, deep down in his abdomen. It made him feel instantly sick, like somebody had driven a triangular dagger into his guts. He closed his eyes, and waited, but the seconds ticked by and sweat emerged on his brow, under his arms, soaking him within a few minutes.

I need my drugs. I need my pain killers. I need my drugs.

Slowly, the world receded. The Five Havens, the Harborym Dwarves, the cities, the church, the king, Skalg, more than anything fucking *Skalg*, that evil little back-stabbing bastard... No, everything became secondary as the pain took hold and he knew he needed help.

"Nurse!" he cried, finally, when he could wait no longer. "Nurse!" Waves of pain washed over him, getting worse and worse, great oceans of blood which swamped his mind until nothing else existed, only the Pain, and the Pain was the World.

"There there," she said, and she was by his side.

"Thank the Great Dwarf Lords..." mumbled Granda, rolling onto his side. He felt the stitches pull tight, including the ones deep inside him. *Felt them.* Nipping at his internal muscles. It made him cringe. He groaned.

"Don't you worry, we'll soon get your medication for you," said the nurse. Her face zoomed in and out of focus. Granda vomited from the side of the bed, drooling, but he really did not care. He was very much past caring.

"Thank... you..." he managed, disgusted by his own feeble state, and yet unable to do anything about it. This was his existence. This was his weakness. Eternal, shameful, physical pain which he could not control.

"Just one minute," said the nurse, smiling down at him.

Gods, he thought. *That's a savage beard! Why did she let it get so long? Normally, they're so good at keeping them under control…*

He blinked. He was staring at the nurse's boots. They looked wrong, as Granda puked onto the floor, but he could not work out why.

And then it clicked.

The laces were crisscrossed, like in boots they used in the dwarf army. Granda frowned. Why was the nurse wearing army boots?

He looked up – into a pillow, which swamped his face and pushed him back onto the bed. He started to struggle, but was so weak, already full of pain, each movement an agony; but fury swamped him as he realised – fuck, they were trying to kill him! An assassination attempt!

Him! *Chief Educator for the Church of Hate*! *Did they realise who he was*?

His struggling became stronger, suddenly infused with anger and disgust that they would even *dare* target him. But then, maybe that's exactly *why* they'd targeted him.

His struggling turned into a full fight as panic kicked in. He was launching blows, but the nurse was absorbing them. It suddenly occurred to Granda how incredibly strong the nurse was, for a nurse. From beneath the pillow he heard her speak, but could not make out the words. His vision was flashing now and he felt his tongue sticking out as he tried to suck oxygen through the pillow.

A great weight fell across his legs, pinning him down. Strong hands grasped his wrists, and he was held tight by a second figure as the first applied yet more pressure to the pillow over his face.

Images flickered through Granda's mind.

Acceptance into the Church of Hate.

Promotion.

Yullanga, her sweet face, big eyes looking up at him...

Granda went still. Warily, the pillow was removed.

"Is he gone?"

"Yeah."

"Let's get a move on, then. There's more work to be done."

Fire Sergeant Takos, hair scraped back, beard singed, face marked with soot and burns, his uniform scorched and tattered and hardly recognisable, opened his front door on Silverlode Street and stepped into the cool, welcoming interior. It had been a long night. A night of fighting fires and rescuing stranded dwarves; a night of watching innocents burn and angry mobs attack. He was exhausted. Totally drained, every muscle aching, his mind a dull ache.

How did this happen?

How did our world turn suddenly so insane?

He moved down the hallway and stopped at the foot of the stairs, listening. Kloona would be asleep up there, probably had Jeshael in bed with her, because neither liked to sleep alone when Takos was out on a night shift. But it was part of his job. Part of the task of saving lives and fighting fire.

He would catch a couple of hours sleep to stave off exhaustion, change his uniform, then head back onto the streets. The worst of the fires had been dealt with, but Takos had a sneaking suspicion there was more trouble yet to come. Bad trouble. Events in Zvolga had taken a turn for the worst, and he was damned if he knew what he could do about it.

Deciding not to disturb his wife and son, he moved to the main living area. There were thick rugs on the rock floor, and he knew he could catch a few hours' sleep there before heading back out.

Except… he stopped. In the corner of the room, seated on an iron chair, was a figure shrouded in darkness. And what Takos *could* make out was a small, oak crossbow. The tip of the bolt gleamed like a dark eye and he fixed on it for a few moments.

Fire Sergeant Takos stared at the seated figure. "Who are you?" he said quietly.

"That is not your concern," came a deep voice with an accent from one of the higher cities; Keelokkos, probably. So. A mercenary, then. A killer for hire.

Takos swallowed. His mouth was dry. "Whatever you plan to do to me, I accept. But please, do not harm my family."

"Sit down."

Takos took a chair, and seated himself, eyes still on the crossbow. It was unwavering. The dwarf who held it made no show of nerves. Takos found that his legs were trembling, his hands shaking. He placed them flat on his thighs, noticing the skin was marked with tiny burns and swirls of charcoal.

"Are you here from the Church of Hate?" asked Takos, quietly.

The intruder paused. "You wrote a letter to King Irlax decrying the actions of Cardinal Skalg. I need to know if you wrote to anybody else. Is there any other proof of what you witnessed?"

"No, I… no. As a senior Fire Sergeant, I deemed this information important for the good of the Five Havens.

We cannot have a corrupt church. We cannot have dwarf torturing dwarf. This is not the will of the Great Dwarf Lords."

"I see. How much does your wife know?"

"I have told her nothing." But the words came out too fast. Takos felt the intruder smile in the darkness.

"Look. Please. I have money. I can pay more than your... current employer. I will buy your services." *And send you back to murder him...*

"I'm sorry," said the intruder.

Takos saw him tense.

"Wait, no!"

There was a click and a whine. The bolt slammed into Takos' chest, smashing him and the chair backwards. The intruder stood, and slotted another bolt into his crossbow, winding back the tensioning mechanism. He strode over and stared down at Takos. Blood stained his lips and chin. His chest was a concave mess. He was still breathing. Just.

"Not... my family. Please," he wheezed.

The killer looked down with hard eyes. "I'm sorry," he said.

"No!"

"King Irlax thanks you for your contribution to the good of the Five Havens."

"Irlax? But... why?" Blood bubbled on his lips and the light was fading fast from his eyes. In his mind, he remembered teaching Jeshael about the many different types of precious metals, watched with wonder as the young dwarf's small fingers explored gold, silver, platinum...

The killer smiled. "Let's just say this is a tying up of loose ends."

●●●

Skalg came awake to the sound of battle, and it was the most disconcerting thing he had ever experienced. His eyes opened, pain slammed through his twisted back, and fear crawled instantly into his mouth and sat there, a dead rat on his tongue. Metal crashed on metal, and there were various thumps. A slapping sound, then a crash as a metal stool rolled across the floor.

Skalg climbed out of bed and pulled on his robes, kicking feet into silk slippers and

grabbing a short blade from its place beside his bed. In the chamber outside his bedroom the fight continued, and he padded forward and eased the door open a crack.

Razor was fighting three slender dwarves, all dressed in simple black, their faces hidden by hoods. Even as Skalg watched, Razor ducked a blow and backhanded her blade across a dwarf's throat. His hands came up, clutching his opened windpipe as he gurgled and blood spewed out in a gushing torrent. Razor leapt at the other two, a blade in each hand, her good eye focussed on these assassins. They backed away, each holding their own long, curved knives. But they were professionals. Even the sight of their comrade with his throat cut, twitching on the ground, did not give them pause in their actions.

They attacked as a unit, launching from opposite sides. Razor crouched a little, then rolled her upper body under one blade, boot stamping sideways at the attacker's kneecap and dropping him with a crunch. She swept into the path of the other, but he leapt back as her blade slashed by his eyes, then shifted sideways, leaping, kicking from the wall into a high jump, left arm batting aside one of Razor's daggers, his left hand slamming down, his blade entering her neck even as her second blade slammed up into his groin, twisting.

Razor dropped, blood gushing from the neck wound, and the attacker slumped atop her.

With a squawk of disbelief, Skalg opened his bedroom doors and ran out, dragging the wounded attacker from Razor and kneeling beside her. He tore a strip from the edge of his robe, folding it and holding the pad against the neck wound.

"Razor! Razor! Hold this!" He guided her hand to the pad, and she coughed, pink froth on her lips.

The attacker with the broken knee was dragging himself away, and Skalg hobbled towards him, leaping on his back and plunging his dagger down, double-handed. The blade went through the dwarf's spine, and the attacker went limp like cut elastic.

Skalg returned to Razor, and cut the throat of the attacker lying by her side, just to be sure. He gurgled and bled on the tiles.

Skalg knelt carefully beside his Educator, eyes moving up and down her. Her knees were drawn up, fingers stained with her own lifeblood.

"Horse… shit…" she bubbled.

"Don't die on me, Razor! I fucking order it!"

"He got me. That… bastard."

"I am instructing you to be the hard bastard I know you are!" Skalg snapped. "You are not going to die on me. We'll get that wound stitched up, we'll get you back on your feet, and you can help me get to the bottom of this shit with Irlax! You hear me?"

Razor's dark eye didn't move, it simply lost a… quality. There was a simple moment. Her eye went from being alive, to being dead. Her eye was open, but it did not see. And her chest fell, for one last time, and Skalg squatted there, staring down in disbelief, tears in his eyes.

"No," he muttered and then looked around, and suddenly realised the seriousness of his position. Three assassins sent to kill him. In his own fucking home. What about all the guards downstairs? What about his Educators? And sent by whom? The Army of Purity? King Fucking Irlax?

By all the Gods, he thought suddenly. *This goes all the way to the top. My Educators have been killed. My church wardens are being slaughtered. I was right. Even though I did not believe it, I was right. Irlax is exterminating the Church of Hate – and he intends to take over! Total power. Total control.*

What can I do?

What in the name of the Great Dwarf Lords can I do?

And a little voice spoke to him from his twisted back; the demon in his hump; the devil in his own disjointed, broken flesh and bone.

And his dark twin said,

You must kill King Irlax.

And how the fuck am I going to do that?

Your first step is survival. First, Cardinal Skalg, you must survive.

Head down. Down, where it is warm.

Down to the Dragon Engine?

There, you will find answers.

Skalg threw off his robes and dressed as quickly as his deformity would allow. Simple trews and boots, a loose shirt, no robes of state or identifying church colours. He loaded his belt with a variety of knives and a short-handled war hammer. He pulled on a specially adapted mail shirt, which he'd had made at very great expense (to the church coffers), and finally pulled on a helm. It was the best disguise he could think of, and yet was painfully aware there weren't actually that many hunchbacked dwarves in a city like Zvolga. He might as well have had "Cardinal Skalg" tattooed across his forehead. Finally, he moved into his armoury. The smell of leather, wood, polish and oil was strong. He moved down one wall, and selected a belt of very expensive, extremely finely made throwing knives. This, he draped over his neck. Then he grabbed a short, vicious looking straight-edged sword and shoved it through his belt. Finally, moving to the back of the armoury, he unlocked an oiled wooden chest, and opened it almost with reverence. Inside was a small steel crossbow. A Krakkok & Stulliver, gleaming silver. It was truly a weapon of beauty, sculpted, without an ounce of excess metal. It was formed from curves and struts, and was absolutely, totally functional. But better than that, it had a three-bolt loading mechanism on a shaft, tensioned by a spring and locking levers. It was a very, very clever piece of engineering created, again, at very great expense to the church coffers. At this moment in time, Skalg was not only extremely pleased he'd commissioned the weapon's creation, he felt as if his life might depend on it.

Tooled up, the cardinal moved back past the body of Razor, glancing down at her, a glance of regret. Not something he felt often, and this time it was an actual novelty. *Horseshit. She was a good woman. No. Strike that. She was a lethal killer, merciless, bordering on the edge of psychopathy.*

A little bit like me…

Wiping away a tear, he moved through his chambers and stopped by the main doors, slightly ajar. He hefted the Krakkok & Stulliver, feeling the precision engineering, the perfect balance, and he pulled the lever which tensioned the firing mechanism. There were several slick clicks. Subtle, yet powerful.

Skalg breathed deeply, and stepped out into the hall.

A dwarf ran at him, sword drawn, and for a moment Skalg stood, stunned into motionless disbelief. *How can they attack me? I AM THE FUCKING CARDINAL OF THE CHURCH OF HATE!*

He aimed the crossbow almost casually, and pulled the trigger. There was a low click, precise, and a whine. A bolt shot out, cut through the dwarf's chainmail vest, and destroyed his heart. He ended his run sliding across the floor on his back, blood pumping in little fountains from his chest.

Skalg took a deep breath.

"Shit," he said, and for some reason, even after everything he'd seen, everything he'd witnessed from the grassroots street level and up in his eyrie, from the balcony, all the torture he'd inflicted, all the deaths committed in his name, now, it felt *real* for the very first time. Like first love. Like losing his virginity. Like killing his first victim. Like his first gold coin stolen from the church treasury. Like his first verbal abuse of the king. The king. That fuck.

Skalg ran down the sweeping, swirling staircase, hobbling past various dead guards, each one of whom he'd interviewed himself, whom he trusted personally, had vetted personally – after all – how much faith could you put in cunts you hadn't vetted?

No more attacks came.

Skalg still paused. Cautious. He edged towards the next set of steps. And peered… *down.* Down went a long way through the inside of the Blood Tower. A *long way*. A cool breeze drifted up, chilling his flesh.

Normally, he'd have slaves lift him in the brass carriage, but all of a sudden, he did not trust a fall of a hundred floors.

He was pretty sure he'd be a dead Skalg by the bottom. Crushed and pulped into chunks. Cubed Skalg! Ha ha!

He began the descent, and wished for the hundredth time that there was an alternative. Amazingly, no other attack came, and Skalg's lips curled a little. *What? I'm so fucking easy to kill, am I? Four cunts to take out the First Cardinal of the Church of Hate? What a fucking insult!*

He hobbled down the steps, taking them one at a time. His destroyed back would allow no more, and he was panting on the descent. He grinned to himself, then. *Irlax, you are a fucking disgrace to everything that being a dwarf stands for. Broadchested. Powerful. Loud. Brave. Raucous. Rowdy. Ale-drinking. Narcissistic.* He grinned. *And look at who ended up ruling the Church of Hate?* Crippled Skalg. Weak Skalg. Ugly Skalg. Well, surprise, fuckers, because this fucking hunchback taught your society a thing or two about humility, and begging, and torture, oh yes, the fucking torture. Any civilised society can only operate with a decent secret police in place. A dirty, backdoor, nasty fucked-up organisation willing to do whatever the fuck has to be done, just to get the job fucking done. Every society had one, whether they fucking admitted it or not. Only now, *now,* that cunt Irlax was trying to close him down. Close down the church. Take it over. The bastard. The *BASTARD*!

He reached the bottom of the massive stairwell.

A big dwarf stepped out in front of him, and the Krakkok & Stulliver clicked and whined. A bolt in the belly. The dwarf fell to his knees, blood drooling from his lips. Skalg cared little whether he was friend or foe. He was simply–

In. The. Way.

Distantly, there were sounds of civil unrest.

Looking around, Skalg hobbled off into the night.

Hard Labour

The mine ran like a well-oiled machine, and the slaves who worked it were the integral cogs that kept the machinery turning. The whips the dwarf overseers used with relish were the mechanisms that forced the cogs to turn. This large section of mine was permanently lit by fire-bowls, piped through an intricate brass system fuelled by the imprisoned dragons themselves, and connected to the main furnaces and boilers which indeed powered the five cities above.

Beetrax hoisted the sledgehammer, and brought it down with a crack. Another five blows split the large rock into lumps, which Talon then lifted, throwing them into a cart which sat patiently on rails; the dead-eyed donkey in the traces had its head lowered and was unmoving, a beaten, broken beast of burden.

"BREAK!" bellowed a hefty dwarf named Gulga, sporting a perfectly round pot-belly, like a small, hard pregnancy, and wandered off for ten minutes to chat to the other whip-wielding overseers.

Beetrax, his brow lathered in sweat, lowered himself onto a rock with a wince and lowered the head of his sledgehammer to the ground with a thud. He glanced at Talon, whose face was grey and grim, his frame thinner now, harder, after three weeks of solid manual labour down in the mines.

Talon saw the look and forced a smile. "How you feeling, Big Man?"

"I don't feel so big anymore."

"I mean... down there."

"I don't want to talk about it."

Talon, running a hand across his still-bruised face, came and dropped beside Beetrax. He untied his long blond hair, repositioned it and tied it back up. Then he gestured to Jonti, who was bringing round a bucket of water, the wooden sides sporting hooks from which several cups wobbled.

"Beetrax, Talon, I hope you're well," she said as she approached, nodding, and halted, boots scraping rock. "How you feeling, Beetrax?"

"As I keep saying, *I don't want to fucking talk about it*. Don't you people listen?" He shifted, with a jangle of shackles and chains.

"There's lots of things we all would rather not talk about." She gave a thin-lipped smile. "But we're here now, and this is the way it is; you know, Beetrax, you bloody *know* we'll have to get used to and support one another. You know that." She pointed, catching his gaze. "So stop being a bloody martyr, and talk to me."

Beetrax looked at her, then looked away. "I'm fucking sore, is all. It's better than it was, but a long way from where it should be." He turned back, and glanced *past* Jonti to where the overseers were laughing over some joke probably relating to the pain of the slaves, or a particularly fine crack of the whip. His voice lowered. "We have to do something to get out of this mess."

"You know what they promised to do to you?"

Beetrax shrugged. "Better they castrate me then, because this ain't no existence for a man like me. Or any man." He turned to Talon and elbowed him rudely. "You still getting the beatings?"

Fury raged across Talon's face for a moment, before disappearing, to be replaced by something close to despair. "Yes," he said, quietly. "Not every night, but I don't even sleep anymore; I jump at every fucking sound I hear. I agree, Trax, this is no way to live. I'd rather die. Truly. I'd rather die."

"Problem is, they have us locked down tighter than any other slaves." Jonti filled two cups and handed them to her friends. "They know exactly who we are. You'll note Beetrax is the only sledgehammer wielder to still wear shackles? They know who we are, and what we're capable of. If we can work out how to remove the irons, then we're one step closer."

"I have this," Beetrax rattled the sledgehammer.

"And what would you do with that?" said Talon.

"You put your hands on a rock, and I'll break open the shackles. Hit the pin, break it open."

Talon stared at him. "You really believe you're that accurate?"

"Yeah, lad, course I am."

"And if you miss, you crush both my wrists and guarantee my death?"

"Er. Yeah, I suppose I do."

"Not the best plan you've ever had."

"You got a better one?"

Talon thought. "Not at the moment," he said, voice hushed, eyes lowering to stare at the rocky floor of the mine.

"Tonight," said Jonti, taking back the cups and refilling them, "is Meat Night. We'll get longer before lights out." Meat Night was the one day of the week when, as a "morale booster" the dwarf overseers dragged a large iron cauldron into the middle of the barracks compound and cooked up a foul stew of rancid offcuts; the only meat the slaves received on a weekly basis. The stew took longer to cook than the usual rations of black bread and mouldy cheese, and was usually accompanied by alcohol for the overseers which relaxed them and allowed the slaves a little more time to interact. "Now that..." she fought to choose careful words, "*those who were injured* have started to make some kind of recovery, at least enough recovery to start thinking about escape, then we need to start talking. See, Beetrax? That's the first time you've come up with a plan. I confess, I thought they'd kicked it out of you."

"Crushed it out of me, more like," he said, voice low. Images flickered through his mind, scenes from his torture which came back again and again and again. The cackling face of Tallazok Mentir, his naked flesh with its tattoos of pain and horror, the eyes which showed nothing but genuine pleasure at plying his trade. These images came back to haunt Beetrax, usually when he was lying on his own bed, alone, in the small hours, shivering with fear. But he'd come to realise over the last few nights that there was only so much fear he could take; after a while, a man begins to fear the fear itself, and either has to do something about it, or allow his mind to break. Beetrax would not allow his mind to break. If it was the last thing he did with his breath on this planet, he would teach Tallazok about proper fucking pain; closely followed by Val, the dwarf who had abused Lillith. Beetrax cracked his knuckles as frustrating

images of non-explored violence shimmered in his mind.
Gods, there was going to be a reckoning one day.

Beetrax realised his breathing had accelerated and he
forced himself to be calm. He looked up at Jonti then, and
she was thrilled to see a new light shining in his eyes. "I
have a better idea."

"Yes?"

"Instead of talking about it tonight, let's do it."

"How?"

"I have a plan. And it involves the cauldron. Can you get
word around?"

"I'll warn everybody. Just... don't do anything stupid,
Beetrax."

He scowled at her with his one good eye. "Do I look like
the village idiot?" he growled.

Lillith was on the sorting benches, her fingers moving deftly
between the small crushed rocks, analysing and dividing
into different categories by potential metal content. As
she worked, her mind blotting out the clanking of pulleys
and chains that drove the conveyor surface which was
constructed from polished iron slats, tears stained her
cheeks. Jonti tried to console her, hugging and kissing,
holding her whenever she had the opportunity; but it did
no good. All Lillith had to do was picture his evil face,
grinning down at her. That narrow, evil face, with close-
cropped beard and emotionless eyes. Like the eyes of a dead
fish. It was a face that would haunt her until her dying day.

Jonti approached with her bucket of water, and they
looked at one another in silence, and Jonti reached out, her
hand closing over Lillith's, and Lillith looked away, biting
her lower lip, more tears springing to her eyes.

This trip was a voyage of discovery. It was a reawakening of an old flame; an old soul mate whom I should have never let go in the first place. And yet now, this journey has turned from amusing jaunt, exciting exploration, into a living nightmare. And I am not the same person. I can never be the same person again. I have become tainted. I am filled with darkness.

I will kill. I will kill. I will kill again… like I said would never happen.

"Are you well, Lillith?"

"I am not, Jonti."

"You need to be brave, my love. Tonight, we will work on an escape."

"Tonight?"

"Beetrax has a plan. He has had enough. We have all… had enough."

Lillith's face hardened, and her eyes met Jonti's. "I am ready, and I am willing. And I will fucking die trying. I will fucking *die*."

"Good girl," said Jonti, without an ounce of condescension.

Jael sat by the edge of the barracks, watching the others idly, or so it appeared. They moved at random, going about various tasks, and yet he *saw* them, talking, passing messages, collaborating. *Collaborating.* Jael licked his lips.

You are not one of them, reminded his conscience.

You are alone in this, said his soul. *It is your survival that matters.*

He watched items changing hands; from Beetrax to Talon, from Dake to Talon. And he watched as Beetrax moved to a certain, planned, position, and lean his sledgehammer against the wall of the barracks.

He watched Talon, sat with his back to the barracks, rubbing something on the rocky ground.

He watched Dake, chatting to Sakora, whose newly carved face bore fresh, pink, stitched wounds. When she smiled, it brought a wince of pain, and Jael's heart went out to this once beautiful, noble woman, who now carried the blade-slices of slavery on her face. She would never be the same again. None of them would.

His eyes wandered past the compound, over to the overseer barracks. He could see Krakka there, and his heart leapt into his mouth, as it always did when he saw the squat, powerful dwarf. The bastard had done his work well on Jael; infected his mind with a powerful fear, with a clever control mechanism. Jael watched Krakka walking around, issuing orders, ever-fearful the dwarf would turn and lay eyes on him, or even worse, approach him. And then, the torture would begin...

Jael turned his attention back to Beetrax. There was definitely something suspicious going on, something which was out of the ordinary. The question was, did he approach Krakka and tell him? Try to save his own worthless hide by condemning his friends?

His friends.

Were they his friends? Truly? They had saved his life, yes, but Beetrax had made it clear he had no enjoyment in teaching the young man the Way of the Axe. But then, why should he? In all reality, Jael was a stranger to him. Known for barely a few weeks. Why would he give up his important free time?

But Lillith and Jonti, they had been the kindest. Especially Lillith with her amazing healing powers, her knowledge of herbs and medicines. She had cooed over him like a mother over a wounded son. It had been a great kindness, and she'd helped rebuild him mentally as well as physically.

But if you don't tell Krakka, he will break you. He will torture you beyond all recognition. You won't be a human being any longer; you will be a stripped and broken shell. And then Death will come for you, long claws hooking into your soul and dragging you down to the Furnace, where all evil souls are tortured…

Jael covered his face with his hands, and realised he was shaking. What to do? Betray his friends or lose his soul?

"Are you all right, Jael? You look… terrified." It was the soft voice of Lillith, of all people. She reached out, her hand touching his shoulder with great gentility.

"Yes, yes, as well as I can be in this place." He shuddered. Then his eyes met Lillith's. "Is something happening here, Lillith? Something I haven't been told about?"

A strange hard veil fell over the woman's face then, and her eyes narrowed a little. "Do you realise what is happening to me in this place, Jael? Do you understand what humiliation and what abuse is being heaped upon me? I have never felt so low. I have never felt so degraded. It is the sort of thing that breaks a woman; breaks her mind, sweet, young Jael. And something needs to be done. Something important. But I fear allowing you to know would put you in very grave danger; best to let us deal with this." She smiled then, and the hardness leaked away.

She is protecting me, realised Jael. *They are keeping me out of the plan so that I cannot be held accountable. And yet I am here, and I am part of their group.* His mind teetered. He was not sure whether he felt flattered or humiliated. Did they not trust him? Did they think he'd go running to Krakka and puke out their plan?

And he realised, with great shame, that they were right. He was the weakest link in the chain.

"I accept that," he said eventually, and Lillith smiled, and moved away, talking to Jonti in serious low tones.

Jael watched Beetrax approach the cauldron, where various dwarf overseers were taking great pleasure dropping miserable grey chunks of bone and meat into the "stew". He started talking to one, and there seemed to be some lighthearted banter. Jael could hear the jangle of Beetrax's shackles, and the big axeman boomed his trademark laughter across the barrack compound. He seemed in very good form for somebody who had been so recently tortured by these bastards. Maybe he was adapting? Or maybe it was some kind of trick…

Jael turned and Krakka was watching him. Jael felt his heart skip a beat. Krakka lifted his hand, and from across the large space, gestured for Jael to approach.

Jael started walking, and felt both Beetrax and Dake observing his travel. *They know,* screamed his mind. *They know I'm going to tell Krakka everything, tell him even the smallest detail of what I've been watching them do, just in order to save my own skin, to save my own potential future pain and worthless fucking hide…*

He passed five armed dwarves. One was sharpening his axe with great, sweeping downward strokes, the whetstone making a metallic hissing sound with which Jael was extremely familiar from his days helping his father fell trees. The five dwarves watched him pass with suspicious eyes, their brows creasing; one moved his hand to the hilt of a long knife below his mail shirt. Jael shivered.

Jael's boots thudded on rock. He glanced right, past the compound, to the slope which led to the underground lake. The water was like black glass. Motionless. His nostrils twitched at a slightly metallic smell.

Krakka was waiting, his face in a broad grin.

"Jael!" he boomed, and slapped the young man on the back. Jael winced, for his ribs were still sore from his beating back in the forest. "I see that your Vagandrak friends seem... upbeat. Maybe we didn't torture them enough, eh lad?" He boomed with laughter, and slapped Jael on the back again, nearly pitching him to his face. Krakka was powerful indeed, his hands like shovels.

"I don't believe in torture," said Jael, lowering his eyes.

Krakka loomed close. His breath stank like the final exhalation of a corpse. "Well, lad. I think you have some information for me," he said, and patted Jael on the arm.

The night was moving slow. The slaves were allowed gentle exercise around the compound whilst the cauldron of rancid meat bubbled. Beetrax, Dake, Jonti, Talon, Lillith and Sakora walked with other prisoners, most of them dwarves, a couple of them weak and filthy human specimens who had, by various means, found themselves in the hands of the Harborym.

Dake walked beside a ragged specimen, late fifties, long grey hair, straggled beard. Although his body was hard, he lacked body fat, and was looking stretched, weak and wasted.

"How did you end up here, old man?"

"I lived in one of the villages at the foot of the Karamakkos. Like you, I didn't know the dwarves existed; I thought the Harborym extinct. All of us did. It is a common misconception!" He gave a bitter laugh through cracked, blackened lips. His bare back bore the brunt of many lashes, healed now, but showing a rebellious, earlier life as a slave.

"How were you captured?"

"I was out fishing, on the River Makkos. Fresh water comes down from the mountains, rich waters for mackerel and trout." He sighed, plodding in the wide circle around the barracks. "I was daydreaming, as you do in these situations. I had two bites sat in a bucket. The wife and my daughter, Lanna, nine years old – well, she was nine back then – they were going to have a fine supper! Except somebody snuck up behind me, hit me with a club. I woke up in a cart on my way under the mountain."

Dake looked at him. "How long have you been here?"

"Three years." He smiled, but there was not one iota of humour. "My little girl will be twelve now. And still wondering what happened to her father."

"Why you?" asked Dake, his voice gentle with a creeping horror.

"Why not? When these bastards are running low on slaves, they send out teams into the villages and towns surrounding the mountains. They are careful who they take. The dark rumours are of mountain goblins – but there are no bloody mountain goblins. Just these bastards looking for fresh meat to work the mines; to keep the gold flowing."

"Have you tried to escape?"

"Twice. You see the scars on my back? They said next time I'd be food for the Dragon Engine." He grinned then, but his eyes were dark, hooded, filled with a casual desolation. "I want to see my daughter again. Just one last time before I die. I don't care if I die, truly, but I just want to see her face; to witness what kind of young woman she has become."

"Did you not try to petition the king? King Irlax? I have heard he is a fair ruler, from the other slaves."

"Aye. He is a fair ruler to the dwarves. But what does he care about our kind? In their history books, we – us humans – kept the dwarves as slaves and had them work the early mines under atrocious conditions for *hundreds of years*. These cities under the mountain, they were built with dwarf blood. They see us as natural enemies, right down to the bone. They see themselves as victors over a cruel master race; and now every man they bring here is another small victory for their ancestors, for their honour. We are scum to them, Vagandrak man. They love to see us suffer."

"Does this King Irlax ever come down here? If I could just get to speak to him... the trade we could offer with Vagandrak..."

"They don't want to fucking know, boy," snapped the old man, flashing Dake a look of annoyance. "You think they don't understand the value of their gold, their jewels, their alloys, the iron they smelt in huge furnaces powered by the mindless dragons? Of course they know. They simply fucking hate us. Hate us to the bottom of their hearts. They don't want our trade. They want our slavery, our obedience, and our blood."

"Oh," said Dake, and felt totally deflated. They carried on walking, and Dake looked over to the cauldron. Steam was rising from the stew. It smelt like rotting corpses on a week-old battlefield.

To one side of the cauldron, five dwarf overseers were cackling at some joke. They held flagons of ale, and golden droplets painted their beards. Further back by the barracks, several other overseers were attempting to fix some kind of hydraulic engine, full of brass pistons and large, multi-toothed cogs. Their hands were covered in oil. And Krakka stood by the barracks, axe on his back, laughing at some joke he had cracked to Val, the point-faced dwarf who was still abusing Lillith. They were both leering over towards the slaves, and Dake's face went hard. He could only guess at which perverse, sickening anecdote the rapist dwarf was regaling his superior.

But that's all right, he thought.

Because things are about to change...

"Stew time!" bellowed a dwarf overseer, standing on a crate and holding a big, black, evil-looking ladle which was more weapon than food-serving implement. His cheeks were flushed red with the after-effects of quaffed ale. At this moment in time, he looked particularly jolly. There was a certain relaxed atmosphere. Beetrax and Talon were laughing at some joke, and Beetrax swaggered over to the cauldron on its iron stand above the fire. Steam curled. The contents bubbled, stinking bad.

"Hey, would you like me to serve it up?" said Beetrax amiably, a big smile edging through his beard.

"Ha! I see you, Beetrax. The limp is getting better."

"Yes," he winked, "my bollocks are made from iron. But seriously, anything I can do to help. It would be my pleasure."

The dwarf, named Pleddo, considered this. "All right then, get yourself up here on this crate. But be warned, we'll be watching the fucking portions! Too many lumps on any one plate, I'll be forced into giving you twenty lashes!" He patted the whip at his belt and roared with laughter, as if physically punishing humans was one huge moment of comedy.

"No worries there, my friend," said Beetrax. "I've learned my lessons. You know I have. I'm a good boy now. Don't

want to be a fucking eunuch in this lifetime, nor the next!"
He hobbled forward, and looked up at the dwarf on the
crate. The dwarf stepped down, and handed the ladle to
Beetrax, who took the iron implement and stared at it, his
shackles rattling.

"Now you be sure to give fair portions, Vagandrak man,"
Pleddo grinned.

"I will," nodded Beetrax, still smiling. "Beginning with
yours."

"What?"

Beetrax reversed the ladle, and rammed the long, iron
handle into Pleddo's eye, driving it deep past eyeball and
soft, squishing flesh, and pounding it into the brain beyond.
Pleddo dropped like a sack of coal, Beetrax following him
down, kneeling with him, and withdrawing the ladle with a
schlup of pulped brains.

"Talon, I need you!"

Talon grabbed the sledgehammer from the wall of the
barracks and sprinted forward. Beetrax held his hands
ahead of him on the rock floor, and Talon skidded, the
sledgehammer whirring up and over, the head whistling
down to crack against the shackle chain.

"Again!" screamed Beetrax.

Talon hefted the sledgehammer, and swung it once
more. It whistled a thumb's breadth from Beetrax's nose,
and slammed into the chain, breaking it.

"Sort the others," growled Beetrax, climbing to his feet
and lifting his stew ladle. It gleamed black, like the deadly
cooking implement it was, dripping mashed dwarf brains.
He turned on the four shocked overseers, as they stood,
tankards held limp, mouths open in disbelief, staring at
their fallen comrade.

"You bastard!" screeched one.

"Come to Daddy," growled Beetrax, and charged, ladle in one fist, length of chain in the other. The four overseers were unprepared, but still hard bastards wearing chainmail and helmets and bearing swords and axes. As behind, Talon cracked open the chains of the other Vagandrak heroes, his aim as true and perfect as his archery skills, so Beetrax felt the pure fucking joy of battle surge through his veins like a drug, and all his anger, all his frustrations, all his hate, erupted as pure and unadulterated

Violence.

They were dragging weapons from scabbards as he struck. The ladle hammered into one throat, making the dwarf choke and stumble back. Beetrax lashed left with the shackle's length of chain, which whipped across a dwarf's eyes making him cry out, grabbing his face, sword half-drawn. Beetrax grabbed the sword, front-kicking the dwarf away and drawing the blade in the same movement. He turned on the other two, grinning, fury raging through him like an ocean tsunami swell. He rolled his neck, tendons cracking, and rolled back his shoulders, feeling the power within his muscles, within his frame, and understanding the total fucking annihilation he could bring against other living organisms. With joy. With love. With wrath.

"Come on, you cunts," he growled, and charged. His blade hacked down, was blocked, but swept down in a low loop that hacked the dwarf's leg free beneath the knee. He hit the ground screaming. The other swung his blade, but Beetrax blocked the blow, twisted his wrist and plunged the point forward. It was an old battlefield trick that worked well against mud-orcs. The point entered above the dwarf's Adam's apple and Beetrax leant forward, putting his weight into it, watching the point explode from the back of the dwarf's neck in a shower of gore. Blood pattered like rain. The one-legged dwarf was screaming, and Beetrax withdrew his blade and smashed it down on the screaming dwarf's head, three times, splitting the skull in half like a crushed melon. Brains leaked out in a long stream, peppered with skull shards. The dwarf choking on his knees from the ladle-blow got the sword in the face, ending his life. The one remaining from the five stared at Beetrax, and held up his hands in horrified submission. A left slice removed seven fingers, which pattered on the rocks, and the following overhead blow smashed his steel helm *into* his skull, folding the steel into cracked bone and jellied brain, and dropping the dwarf as effectively as any sledgehammer blow.

Silence drifted like ash.

"Come on!" screamed Beetrax, and the others, their chains broken by Talon, ran forward and scooped up the swords and axes of the killed dwarves. Lillith approached Beetrax, holding out a double-headed axe, for which Beetrax swapped the short iron sword. He looked down lovingly at the butterfly blades. Some dwarf had given this weapon love and care, sharpening and oiling, oiling and sharpening. Beetrax kissed the blades. "Don't worry," he whispered. "I'll do you some justice."

From the barracks poured thirty grumpy dwarf overseers, many still carrying their whips, to find themselves facing a fully tooled-up company of battle-hardened ex-soldiers.

Talon came forward; he was the only one still wearing his shackles chained together.

"Come here, lad, I'll sort you," said Beetrax.

"Er, I'd rather have somebody with two eyes make the strike. Sakora?"

"Pleasure."

The sledgehammer whirred, and split the chains. Talon caught the short sword and weighed it thoughtfully. "Just like old times?"

"We have some cunts to kill," growled Beetrax.

Over by the overseer barracks, Krakka was purple with rage, apoplectic with fury, and dancing around like a dwarf under the influence. "KILL THEM, KILL THEM ALL, YOU FUCKING USELESS BASTARDS!" he screamed. Disorientated, filled with ale, the overseers moved forward in a ragged line towards the Vagandrak men and women, the battered heroes, the abused, who stood their ground and grinned unnervingly, their eyes full of uniform hate.

The other slaves had shuffled backwards, away from the arena of slaughter. Jael was amongst them, his face grey, his eyes shining, his face unreadable, licking his lips, his fists clenching and unclenching.

"KILL THEM ALLLLLL!" screamed Krakka, as Val hid behind him.

Beetrax frowned. "I reckon that's five each," he said.

Talon glanced at him. "Well, you already did five."

"They don't count. How's this – if I beat you, you buy the fucking wine?"

"Agreed."

The dwarf overseers charged, chainmail clanking, and were amazed when the slaves did not break and run. In fact, they were even more amazed when Beetrax strode towards them, with great loping strides, and faced the lead overseer – a broad dwarf named Loppa, renowned for violence and bad temper – who charged at Beetrax, his axe sweeping up, his stroke experienced, his cold blue eyes fixed, his mouth a grim line. The axe swept down, and Beetrax... *twitched* to one side, the smallest and most accurate of movements, the enemy axe slicing past him as his left elbow struck out, breaking the dwarf's nose, his axe slamming low, cutting through tendons to hamstring the overseer. He hit the rocks, sliding, screaming suddenly, grabbing at his folded leg as Beetrax loomed over him.

"That fucking hurts, eh laddie?"

"Fuck you, slave."

"Slave? You reckon?" Beetrax's axe slammed down, splitting the dwarf's face in two. It was not a pretty sight. "You're a slave to my fucking axe," he said.

The two forces clashed in that underground mine, as the other slaves cowered and watched, and the lake lapped softly at its inky shores. Axes and swords rose and fell, the strike of clashing iron echoed out, reverberating, so different to the usual clank and smash of sledgehammers on rock, the rattle of chains from the carts, the bray of an occasional stray donkey.

The dwarf overseers were tough bastards. But they were more used to whimpering slaves cowering under whips, no matter what background they'd originally crawled from. And each of the Vagandrak heroes had spent the last twenty years as soldiers, bred and honed and experienced in battle.

Dake fought with a mechanical precision, almost dancing between the enemy, his sword the master of the sneaky cut, the swift stab, the backhand cut from nowhere. Jonti moved as her reputation described. She was *The Ghost* once more. Dwarves wondered how the fuck they died. Talon, like Dake, was accurate, a machine killer, but out of his comfort zone with a blade. What he really desired was a good yew bow and fifty straight arrows…

Lillith, ever the pacifist, stayed to the rear, helping

where she could, defending where she could. But she had developed a new coldness, and on two occasions plunged a dagger through a dwarf overseer's eye and stepped aside as he puked blood onto the rough stone ground.

Sakora danced, beautiful moves, a knife in each hand becoming an extension of her athletic blows; an exotic dance of death, her movements underlined with a new hate.

And Beetrax led the battle, his sheer brute power, his massive hate, his raging fury like an unstoppable machine, an insane lion enraged with hunger, ready to kill, embracing the slaughter.

Beetrax's adopted axe cut left, slicing a dwarf from clavicle to hip, despite his chainmail. Rings popped and pinged. The blade's point opened his flesh like a crazy zip and his insides unfolded slowly onto the rocky ground like so much butcher's offal. His scream was cut short by the stamp of a boot.

The return backhand strike opened another enemy's throat, so that blood spewed from this impromptu tracheotomy. The dwarf fell to his knees, lips working noiselessly as his newly formed second mouth made bloody hissing sounds.

Swords rose and fell. Blood and body parts hit the ground with wet thumps. The Vagandrak soldiers, high on a drug of frustration and hate, worked in perfect harmony; an efficient, oiled machine, tighter than they had ever been. They covered one another. Watched one another's backs. Killed for each other. Defended each other. Sparks flew. Swords clashed. Blood spattered the rocky ground like crimson rain. Blades cut through arms and legs. Dwarf skulls were crushed. Eyes sliced. Throats cut. Bowels opened, allowing intestines to slop to the ground.

And then it was over.

They stood, panting, barely a scratch upon them, spattered with blood globules, a shocked look on all their faces which appeared after any sudden encounter, after any battle; the glances around, searching for loved ones, searching for brothers and sisters, to check they were good, and alive, and whole; to check the whole party hadn't descended into rat shit. Into blood, and dark death.

"Lillith?"

"Beetrax."

"Check the bodies."

"Yes."

Beetrax whirled around, could see the rest of the slaves still cowering. His eyes roved over his friends. All were standing. Nobody was on their back puking blood. All had looks on faces that suggested... life. Then his gaze shifted to...

Krakka.

The Slave Warden.

He was rooted to the spot, frozen suddenly, as if caught in an embarrassing position from which he could not escape.

"YOU!" bellowed Beetrax, pointing across the open space between the barracks, and Krakka stared at him. "I want YOU, you fucking cunt. Right here, right now."

Suddenly, from the surrounding tunnels which led to the mine came a great commotion. It was a stomping of boots, the clanking of chainmail, many boots, many chainmail coats, and from the tunnels emerged an army of armed and armoured dwarves. They carried loaded crossbows, quarrels gleaming, stocks oiled, hands steady as these soldiers streamed from the tunnels and spread out.... Ten, twenty, forty, sixty, a hundred fucking dwarves, heavily armed, crossbows targeted on the Vagandrak slaves.

Beetrax, Jonti, Talon, they looked around, spun around, watching in horror as so many enemies emerged, all with projectile weapons. With military precision, boots stomped and crossbows levelled. Beards bristled. Fists clenched. Fingers tightened on triggers as eyes sighted and they took aim.

Silence fell. The silence of a child's funeral. The silence of a mass burial. The silence of the tombworld.

Krakka was almost bouncing. "Throw down your fucking weapons!" he screeched. "Throw them down, or we'll cut you down! Do it! Do it FUCKING NOW!"

Dake tossed down his sword, which clattered on the stone. He eyed the dwarves coolly, but he knew impossible odds when he saw them. Jonti followed, tossing down her own blade, followed by Sakora, and Lillith and Talon, who gave a twisted grimace of despair. *We were so close. So close... where did these bastards come from? How did they know?*

Finally, only Beetrax stood, clutching his butterfly axe in both hands, a great scowl on his face as he faced a hundred crossbow-armed dwarves. Rage passed across his features in various stages. Slowly, he mellowed, and seemed to relax. Despite their bravery, despite their killing, they were well and truly outnumbered.

"Wait." Beetrax's voice was low, and deep, and unafraid. He looked up, and around. He stared at every man, and slave, and dwarf present. And he grinned, showing hate, showing his total defiance against the Harborym Dwarves. "You are a warrior race, right?" he bellowed, voice roaring out, words reverberating back from the jagged mine walls. "You are fighters, and you are killers! Well. So am I. And I challenge the dwarf cunt who has wronged me, I challenge Krakka, that cunt over there," he pointed, "and I want to see if he needs to hide behind all these dwarf-scum soldiers, I need to see if he is a proud warrior, or just the type to hide behind women and children. Does Krakka hide behind his mother's poxed cunt? Does he hide behind his father's wart-riddled cock? Does he hide behind children, behind mewling babies, behind the living shit who inhabit this hole in the ground?" Beetrax turned, and spread his blood-speckled arms apart, axe in one great fist, broken chains dangling from his wrists, face uplifted in glory and joy and necessity and a need to do what he had to fucking do.

Slowly, his great head lowered, like the head of a lion, and he stared across the space at Krakka, Slave Warden.

Beetrax's words were low, but all heard them, like a pin dropping on frozen steel.

"Or is Krakka a coward?" he said.

A roar went up from the dwarves, a roar of warriors, and Krakka felt Val leave him, stepping away, and the rest of his overseers leave him, and he was alone. Alone amongst his peers. Alone amongst the crowd.

Krakka took a deep breath, and threw down his axe, and ripped off his chainmail vest, tossing it outside with a clatter and shower of sparks.

Silence fell. A natural fallout.

"I accept your challenge, Vagandrak scum. I will fucking break you. I will fucking kill you. This, I swear."

Beetrax grinned, but his eyes were hard, fists clenched.

"Show me," he said.

The dwarf soldiers closed in, forming an arena ringed by aimed crossbows, containing the slaves and the remaining overseers, and the bubbling cauldron of rancid meat. Beetrax stood, staring, as Krakka approached.

"Throw down your axe."

"Scared of fighting with proper weapons, you rancid little shit?"

"No. I want to beat you to death with my fists, you hulking ugly fat son of a bastard."

Beetrax dropped the axe with a clatter, and leapt at Krakka with a snarl. But Krakka was already moving, and they clashed, a flurry of quick heavy blows raining down. Despite being much smaller than Beetrax, Krakka was broad, and powerful, and smashed a right straight to Beetrax's sternum, making him grunt; Beetrax returned with a left hook that caught Krakka in the side of the head, staggering the dwarf. Beetrax front-kicked Krakka in the chest, and the dwarf reeled back towards the bubbling cauldron, but as Beetrax advanced, Krakka dropped to one knee and punched Beetrax in the balls. Panting, red in the face, Beetrax launched himself forward, grappling for a moment and grabbing Krakka's head and dragging him towards the cauldron, where he suddenly stooped, one hand clamping between Krakka's legs making the dwarf cry out. Beetrax lifted him up, and launched the dwarf, who smashed against the cauldron, rocking it on its iron legs. Stew sloshed out, running down the sides like pus from an infected wound. Beetrax's boot came up to stomp Krakka's head, but the dwarf grabbed his boot, twisting Beetrax's knee and bringing the huge man crashing to the rocky ground. They wrestled for a few moments, scrabbling around trying to get a hold on one another, before Beetrax slammed an elbow into Krakka's nose, breaking it. He wriggled, and managed to get atop the Slave Warden. He smashed a punch into Krakka's face, then a second, and a third. "Treat us likes slaves, will you?" he screamed down into that bloody face. "Whip us and torture us and rape us?" He crashed three more punches, knocking out teeth, and Krakka groaned.

Beetrax stood, panting, chest out, eyes on fire. All around him, around the ring of aimed crossbows, there was silence. Beetrax glared at the dwarves, spinning around. "We could have been fucking comrades," he snarled. "But you took us prisoner and tortured us. Why? WHY?"

He moved away from the cauldron, growled some curse in mud-orc, then shoulder-charged the huge iron pot. It rocked on its legs, and boiling stew poured out over Krakka, who suddenly screamed, thrashing. Beetrax charged it again, and the cauldron rocked off its legs, pouring rancid meat and boiling gravy over Krakka, who thrashed, as the cauldron rolled over the stricken dwarf, and went clanging down the slope towards the still, black, underground lake.

It didn't quite make the water's edge, and came to a rest, rocking, behind it a great slimy, steaming trail.

"Bastards," said Beetrax, as Val and the hulking figure of Galog approached, swords in their fists, intentions obvious. Krakka was still on the ground, moaning, hands covering his burned face and beard full of gravy.

"Get down on your knees, fucker," snarled Val, gesturing with his blade. "You've had your fun. You've had your little revenge. But now it's *our fucking turn*... somebody call for Tallazok Mentir, we have a man here who no longer requires his balls!"

"Wait."

The voice was a low, hoarse whisper, and all eyes turned on Krakka. He was kneeling up, his eyes filled with rage, both fists clenched. He staggered to his boots, righted himself, and pointed at Beetrax.

"You're going nowhere, cunt. You stay until the job is done."

Beetrax grinned, turning back towards the powerful dwarf. "I'm starting to like you, you plucky little bastard."

With a scream Krakka charged, and Beetrax launched a flurry of punches but the dwarf charged through the blows, grabbing Beetrax around the waist and powering him to the ground, where his head cracked against rock, stunning him. Now Krakka sat atop Beetrax, pounding blows against the axeman's skull with great solid thuds. Stunned, almost at the point of unconsciousness, Beetrax groaned, rolling in confusion, hands coming up to his face as Krakka jacked himself backwards, up, and staggered away a few steps. His huge fists were bleeding and swollen, and he stared down at Beetrax with contempt, his own face red raw, skin peeling free where the stew had quite literally burned parts of his face off.

"Bastard."

He ran at Beetrax, delivering a harsh blow that cracked a rib, and sent the axeman rolling partway down the slope towards the underground lake.

"You want to fuck with me?"

He ran again, delivering another kick that sent Beetrax rolling further, blood pooling from his mouth and nose, his hands waving weakly, trying to fend off the attack.

"Well, I'll fuck with you all right," snarled Krakka, and ran, delivering one final, mighty kick that sent Beetrax rolling, splashing down into the calm edges of the lake.

"No!" hissed Jonti, and started forward. Five crossbows turned on her, and Dake grabbed her, holding her back.

"There's nothing we can do for him now," said Dake.

Talon stared at the ground, tears streaming down his cheeks.

Krakka moved to the mumbling form of Beetrax, and grabbed the axeman's head between both hands, dropping to his knees, pulling Beetrax's face close. "I'm going to kill you now, you piece of Vagandrak shit. And then all your friends are going to die. Do you hear me, deep down in that thick skull of yours? Do you comprehend?"

He plunged Beetrax's face under the water, and Beetrax started struggling, legs kicking, as bubbles erupted.

Lillith ran forward with a cry of "No!", unable to take any more. But Val sprinted forward to intercept her, grabbing her arm. She whirled on him, punching him in the face. He laughed, and backhanded her onto the slope where she rocked, cradling her bruised cheek and bloodied lips.

Krakka dragged Beetrax's head up, and the axeman spluttered, choking, and his eyes opened. The dwarf loomed close. "Good! You can see me for one last time! Me. Krakka. The dwarf who is going to end your miserable, worthless fucking life."

Beetrax was staring up, his friends and the gathered dwarves looking on from the top of the slope. His hands were clawing weakly at Krakka's arms, but the dwarf was in his element, powerful, dominant. Beetrax was weak, dazed, beaten.

"I'll see you on the other side of the Furnace," growled Krakka, and tensed to force Beetrax's head under the sloshing lake waters one last time. Instead, Beetrax's face jerked forward, mouth opening, and teeth grasping hold of Krakka's bottom lip. Krakka screamed, his fists beating at Beetrax, but Beetrax held on for his life, as Krakka's lip stretched away from his face in Beetrax's powerful bite and he screamed and screamed, his scream taking on a warped, distorted sound, rising in pitch, past that of any woman. Beetrax kept pulling, and the dwarf's lower lip seemed to stretch impossibly far, before finally, with sickening crunching sounds, detached from his face and he slumped forward, dropping under the splashing lake. Beetrax scrabbled for a moment, then rose above Krakka, and placing his knee on the dwarf's head, held the Slave Warden under the inky waters.

Krakka fought for a while, as Beetrax slapped away his fists and ever-weakening struggles, and then Krakka was still, and finally, it was over.

Beetrax looked up through waves of pain and disorientation, to see Val and Galog there. They were wearing curious expressions, and in a moment of intuition Beetrax realised how it worked with the dwarves. Dead Men's Shoes. They had not intervened, because now there was a new position available. The mine needed a new Slave Warden.

"Guards! Over here!" bellowed Val, and crossbows were levelled at Beetrax, who was too weak to struggle as fresh shackles were placed around his wrists. They did not even bother to remove the broken ones.

This action was performed on the other Vagandrak heroes, and their heads lowered in submission and defeat.

"Well, you won your little victory," said Val, smiling his nasty smile, the smile which haunted Lillith's dreams. "But the penalty for murdering a dwarf by any slave is death. I condemn you all to death." His head turned and eyes fixed on Lillith. "Except you, little princess. Lock her back in the barracks. The rest of you?" Val grinned. "We're going to feed you to the Dragon Engine."

Wyrmblood

Chief Engineer Skathos, Jengo, Hiathosk, Kruallak, Lellander, Yugorosk and Kew sat in various positions on the great sweeping spiral staircase that led down into Wyrmblood, and stared with open mouths, rubbing grit from their eyes, coughing occasionally, their faces like those of an amazed young dwarf on his birthday.

Skathos was the first to get to his feet, and he stamped his boots on the great staircase, as if testing it for solidity. He was nothing if not thorough, and having a brain which worked like an engine, understood machines, *developed* machines, he found this staircase mechanism most unnerving.

Jengo jumped up, and placed his hand on Skathos' arm. "Shall I run back? Tell Cardinal Skalg? Tell the king! You will go down in history for this discovery, my friend." He was staring at Skathos with shining eyes.

Skathos breathed deeply, his own eyes wet with tears. This place, *Wyrmblood*, was a myth. Said to be a tale to tell little children, a place where the dragons which powered their cities had originally ruled.

Without answering, Skathos started forward, boots clumping down the steps, face lit with the reflected gold of the dulled, precious buildings spread before the group in this vast, titanic array of opulence.

Jengo stared at the others. Hiathosk shrugged, and
started down after the Chief Engineer. After all, he was in
charge.

The others followed, and Jengo ran down several steps
until he was behind Skathos, who was picking each step
with care, his head swinging slowly from left to right and
back again. In the background there was a gentle, low-
level hissing sound, and they realised it was the flow of the
molten platinum river.

Skathos reached the bottom of the steps, and paused,
staring at the golden cobbles which snaked away before
him in a wide, winding road, as if perhaps thinking this was
all some mirage, some ale-induced dream, and when he
stepped onto the cobbles the road would vanish and he'd
go toppling, screaming and flapping, into some great black
void.

His boot came down with a thud. Skathos knelt, and
his fingers stroked the rough, uneven surface of various
cobbles, each one subtly different, his fingers spread out,
examining the textured surfaces by touch.

"They are warm," he said, and stood again, looking back
at the other engineers. "The roadway is warm."

"I think we should head back and tell Cardinal Skalg,"
said Jengo, uneasily.

"Why?" It was said with such a casual air, Jengo was left
flapping his lips for a few moments before he frowned.

"Because... *because* he's the First Cardinal of the Church
of Hate, and this is the most important find in the last ten
thousand years! Don't you see, Chief Engineer? We have to
tell the people in power! We have to tell... those who are
our betters, and who can make the right decisions!"

He stared at Skathos, who stared back. Slowly, Skathos smiled. "I am the Chief Engineer," he said, voice low, soothing, as if he were talking to an injured infant. "This is our engineering find. We don't *know* this is Wyrmblood. We certainly need to explore first, in order to ascertain what we are dealing with. Don't you agree, Hiathosk?" He said it without turning.

"We wouldn't want to look like fools by making an incorrect diagnosis," rumbled Hiathosk, carefully. "And I, for one, would like to be one of the pioneers who first inspected Wyrmblood, if this is Wyrmblood, so that my name, too, goes down in the history books for future generations to see and for my family to be proud. I would be making my mark on the world." He gave a sideways look at Jengo. "Aren't you even the slightest bit curious?" His arm swept out, gesturing towards an array of low buildings. Now, they could see the very building blocks of the structures were fashioned from bricks of gold and silver. Windows glittered like polished crystal. High pointed roofs met, and were crowned by rubies and emeralds. "Don't you want to see what's here before Skalg and Irlax banish us, never allowing us to return to what they may deem a Holy Place? Because that's a very real possibility. They might keep this place for themselves."

Jengo looked torn. "I- I'm not sure…"

Skathos patted him on the back. "I tell you what, faithful Second Engineer Jengo, you head back now and tell Cardinal Skalg – if that is what's in your heart. I will not complain. Indeed, I give you my most heartfelt blessing! Because you are correct, we should all honour the Church of Hate."

Jengo nodded, and gave him a nervous smile. "Yes, yes,

Chief Engineer Skathos. Thank you for your permission. You know how I respect the Church of Hate above all else; I could not for one moment allow Cardinal Skalg to believe I did not go to him at my earliest convenience in order to share our wondrous find. After all, this does not just affect us few engineers – it affects the whole of the Harborym Dwarves! The entirety of the Five Havens!" His eyes were gleaming with a pious light.

"Go then, with my love," said Skathos, smiling and pointing.

"Thank you, Chief Engineer. Thank you."

He turned and placed his boot on the spiral staircase, turned and gave a nervous smile, then started to climb, boots clumping, the metal of his chainmail glowing almost golden from the low-level warm light which filled this place.

Skathos watched for a while, until Jengo had climbed maybe twenty steps, and he turned to Hiathosk, who was watching him from behind heavy, hooded lids.

"Hiathosk."

"Yes, Chief Engineer?"

"A No.3 Goolak Throwing Hammer, if you please."

"Yes, Chief Engineer." He unhooked a small, specially weighted hammer from his belt and handed it to Skathos, who weighed the weapon thoughtfully, a frown on his face as he made several decisions. Then he rocked back on one hip, half-closed one eye, tensed with the throwing hammer in his grip, and launched a powerful throw which spun, the hammer turning end over end as it whipped through the golden air.

The No.3 Goolak Throwing Hammer caught Jengo in the back of his unprotected skull, bouncing off to clatter to one side down the black spiral steps. Jengo hit the steps flat on his face and did not move.

"A fine throw," rumbled Kruallak. "Worthy of the Underworld Championships, no less."

"Thank you," said Skathos. "Hiathosk. Go and check he is dead, and fetch your hammer."

"Yes, Chief Engineer."

"And Hiathosk?"

"Yes, Chief Engineer?"

"Congratulations on your promotion to Second Engineer."

The engineers moved down golden cobbled roads, past low buildings, then turned onto a street filled with towering temples. Spires and minarets soared and sparkled above them, the structures vast and much bigger, much taller than any human city. They moved to one, where an iron door ten times the size of a dwarf door sat encrusted with precious gems, and Kruallak placed his hand on the great handle, glancing back at Skathos for confirmation. Skathos nodded and he weighed down the lever. The door swung open on silent hinges, great and ponderous, revealing a cool interior, again lit by some low-level ethereal glow. Benches were arranged in formations, leading to a magnificent opulent altar, sporting many golden religious statues and symbols, each one a complex masterpiece in its own right.

"I have a question, Chief Engineer," said Hiathosk. He was frowning. "If this *is* the lost city of Wyrmblood, City of the Dragons, then why is it so... human? There are doors, temples of worship, roads. What use does a dragon have for roads? Or door handles, for that matter?"

Skathos frowned. "I had not considered it, but you are correct. This is more like a human city, but on a vast scale."

Yugorosk gave a cough. "Maybe, Chief Engineer, it was to accommodate the slave race?" The group stared at him, and he coughed again, then continued. "In some of the ancient stories, the great wyrms ruled; but they kept slaves who did their bidding, and could be used as food. So, humans kept like cattle."

"And this is where they lived?"

Yugorosk shrugged. "I read it in a school book my youngest brought back a few months ago. I was reading to him late at night. I thought it fanciful at the time."

"We must explore further in," said Skathos. "Let us proceed."

They followed a gold cobbled road which led to the river of molten platinum, and then turned to follow the river's banks. It moved, a sluggish snake of silver, and a pathway along its banks was fashioned from crushed obsidian.

After a while, in the hazy distance, they saw three massive towers. They loomed above all other buildings, and for once, and in contrast to this place, they were black. As the dwarves grew closer, they saw each tower was a simple, smooth, vertical cylinder, but at the top the cylinders arched into one another, in a curiously organic-looking flow, almost like the great tentacles of some vast sea creature. The towers sported no doors or windows, no precious gems, no markings of any kind, and as Skathos finally led the way to the foot of these vast monoliths, they stopped and stood and stared upwards.

"This feels like something of importance," said Skathos.

"I'm beginning to find this whole place creepy," said Yugorosk. He gave a little shiver. "It's the silence. It's unnatural in a place so big."

At the base of the three towers, there were no doors, but massive archways leading to vast, dark interiors. Skathos moved and stood at one entrance, reaching out, his hand pressing against the gentle curve of smooth black. He ducked his head inside a little, and stared upwards.

"What's inside?"

"They're hollow, like chimneys," said Skathos. He turned back to his engineers, each one looking nervous in the golden light of this underground place. "There are iron ladders fixed to the walls."

The engineers stared at him, then crossed and stood under the massive archway, also gazing up.

"That's a long way up," rumbled Yugorosk.

"I can go alone, if you like," said Skathos, his voice low. "But I have a feeling, an intuition, in here," he pounded his breast with his fist, "that up there, at that summit, will be the answers to many, many of our questions. We will learn the secrets of Wyrmblood, my friends. We *will* be the most famous and celebrated Harborym Dwarves who ever lived – do you understand? And not only that," his eyes were shining now, his lips wet, "I also believe we will discover the magick for imprisoning the dragons, *our* dragons, Moraxx, Kranesh and Volak – for I believe this was their home. *This* is where the Great Dwarf Lords found them, and bound them in magick, and created our Dragon Engine. Do you understand?" He grabbed Yugorosk, his hand crushing the powerful dwarf engineer's bicep, shaking him a little. "Do you fucking *understand*? Up there lie the secrets of the Dragon Engine – the secrets of the Great Dwarf Lords. We could change history, my friends. Damn, we are *creating history*!"

The engineers stared at him. More than one licked nervous lips.

"Now isn't that worth some risk?" growled Chief Engineer Skathos.

"I'm coming with, you," said Hiathosk.

"Me too," said Kew.

The others agreed, and they stood there, like a small band bound by blood and honour and an oath deeper than anything they had ever before experienced.

Skathos led them deep into the darkness, and grasping the rungs of the nearest ladder, which was warm under his touch, he placed his first boot on the lowest rung with a metallic scrape, and began to climb.

I shift and swirl, swimming in oil, trapped and patient and weeping for my lost children and my lost family, for my sisters, for my life. And yet I felt it. I felt them break the seal. And this is good. For it means I am close to my memories, or rather, closer to regaining my mind, my body, my soul… all in a unity capable of beautiful destruction. I can feel their petty souls, like tiny specks seen from leagues above the land, where once I rode the warm currents and looked down on those who filled their hearts with so much hate.

I feel like it is raining in my mind, diagonal sheets of icy drops, slanting down, each one a shining memory returning, and I realise that I need these intruders, I need the connection to bring it all back, to make it work.

And so I reach out, and I can feel their tiny minds, feel the wavering in their fragile shells, feel their weakness, their lust for wealth and power and fame, and yet they are ruled by the core lode of cowardice that runs through every fucking creature on the planet. So I conjure an image I remember from my past: cheering crowds lining streets and castle battlements for heroes. I inject these fragile shells with strength, courage, and a need to find out the truth about their history.

You will be famous, I breathe.

You will have endless wealth, honour, female slaves, nobility for your families. You will live forever in the history books. You will be the heroes of your people, the saviour of the dwarves, for you will discover the truth about the Great Dwarf Lords and you will change the hierarchy of your world, of the Five Havens under the Karamakkos; and for this you will become the greatest heroes the dwarves have ever known.

Climb, heroes!

Climb…

The answer to your questions lies above.

Hiathosk paused, curling his arm over an iron rung and hanging there, sweat in his eyes from his lank hair, and sweat dripping from his beard. *By all the Gods, by the Seven Sisters, this is fucking stupidly high. If we fall, we'll be flat dwarf bread!*

"Don't stop now!" growled Chief Engineer Skathos from above. "We're nearly there! And you'll see, we will be the greatest heroes the dwarves have ever known!"

Hiathosk did not reply, he saved his breath, and grasping a rung made slippery with sweat, lost his grip. For a moment he felt himself falling and a great panic swept through him like a tidal wave of blood.

Yugorosk reached over, grabbing his jerkin and yanking him forward. Hiathosk's hands clattered against rungs and he pulled himself tight, panting, licking dry lips with a dry tongue. He glanced at Yugorosk.

"Thanks, brother."

"My pleasure, brother." He grinned.

"Will you two stop fucking about down there!" snapped Chief Engineer Skathos from above. "Do you fucking know how important this is?" It was not like Skathos to swear, nor to become short-tempered. He was renowned throughout Zvolga for his positive qualities. The Chief Engineer was a consummate professional. He had to be; he dealt constantly with both Cardinal Skalg and the King of the Dwarves. It was not an easy role.

"Coming, Chief Engineer," said Hiathosk, and glancing at one another, the two dwarves continued to climb.

I am feeling stronger with every passing second. My mind is feeling clear, but still I realise most of my memories are missing; along with control. But as the climbing dwarves approach, I realise, I realise that I am feeding off them now, extracting energy from them, the closer they move towards my mind.

And with a shudder, I remember my name.

I am Volak.

I am the Queen of Wyrmblood.

And I need to be free.

Chief Engineer Skathos reached the top of the ladder, and slumped onto a flat section of tunnel where the top of the tower arched above him. The floor was smooth and warm, almost organic under his fingers, and Skathos lay panting for a few moments, completely drenched in sweat. His head started to hurt, a pounding that crashed through his skull, obscuring his thoughts. He could taste something metallic in his mouth, and it made him think of insects.

One by one the other engineers came over the top of the iron ladders, and lay in various states of distress. Several had dumped mail vests and weapons during the climb, tossing them unceremoniously down into the vast empty tower beneath them in order to make the horrendous climb just that little bit easier. Now, as they all slowly recovered, Skathos realised that Hiathosk, also, was complaining of a headache.

"Come on," growled Skathos, for it felt like his self-imposed quest in Wyrmblood was nearing a necessary end. *Never* had he felt so motivated. *Never* had he truly believed in something so much.

Without complaint, the engineers climbed to their feet and followed Skathos. They walked along a flowing, rising pathway that formed the inside of the curved tower summit, and then came to a junction where all three towers met. The great chamber was circular and open to the air. Glancing up, high above, Skathos could make out the distant, dark jagged ceiling of the vast chamber in which Wyrmblood lived.

Skathos focussed. At the centre of the circular area there were three great plinths, fashioned from some smooth, black rock, the surface polished and reflective. Above each plinth there was a small black orb, suspended, without wires or stands or anything to keep them hanging there.

Skathos breathed deeply through his nose as the hammer pounded inside his skull. He walked forward, and staggered a little, the metallic taste in his mouth getting worse. This was it. This was the answer...

"Skathos," said Hiathosk, suddenly, some intuition warning him.

Skathos turned, but waved his hand, turning back and moving towards the first orb. A cool breeze blew, oozing across the archway towers' summit. Skathos observed the orb, head tilting a little, and then he reached out and took it.

Under his fingers, it crumbled to dust... to *less* than dust, for the powder that fell never reached the surface of the plinth.

"What… what did you just do?" asked Hiathosk.

Quickly, without speaking, Skathos hurried to the second orb, touching this and watching it disintegrate. Then to the third, which vanished, leaving nothing but a cool breeze easing across the summit platform.

Skathos suddenly sat down, and looked at his hands. He looked up at Hiathosk, a question in his eyes, a frown on his face, and then back down at his hands which he turned over, and over, again, and again, and again. At first Hiathosk wondered what Skathos was staring at, and he moved closer by several paces as the breeze increased. Then he saw the veins on the back of Skathos' hands were turning black, black lines running across their surfaces and up his arms.

"What is it?" cried Skathos, suddenly, in panic.

The black veins disappeared beneath the arms of his tunic, and then reappeared at his neck, racing up his throat and across his cheeks, up his face, across his temples where the other shocked engineers could see the pulsing beat, only now highlighted in black.

"What's happening, Chief Engineer?" shouted Hiathosk, stepping back, loath to touch his superior. Now Skathos' skin started to blacken, as if licked by fire, and Skathos screamed, dragging himself to his feet.

"It's burning! Help me, it's burning!"

Now, it seemed his whole body was infected, and his hands clawed at his face, drawing blood with his nails, which wept from the wounds like tar. He staggered towards the other engineers, who backed away in a circle, holding hands before them to ward off the screaming dwarf, as his beard and hair suddenly ignited, going up in flames.

Screaming, Skathos ran, back down the path they had travelled, his clothing now on fire, head engulfed in flames, his screams high-pitched like some kind of tortured animal. He reached the edge of the tower where the tops of iron ladders poked above the rim, and without breaking stride, sailed out over the black abyss, and fell...

Fell.

The other engineers rushed to the edge, dropping to their bellies and peering over. They saw the glowing flames drop, but then extinguish in a sudden uprush of cold air. They waited, but there was no crashing impact, no thud, as of a body hitting hard earth; no sound of Skathos hitting the ground at all.

The engineers looked at one another uneasily. Each face was lined with panic, even terror, and they fought to not meet one another's gaze.

Eventually, Hiathosk said, "What just happened here?" He was clutching his head, which felt like it was being pounded by a rock.

"I don't know," said Lellander, "but I think we should leave. Right now."

"That's a hell of a climb back down," said Kew, eyes wide in trepidation, finger curling nervously through the strands of his beard.

"Well, the only other way is to follow Chief Engineer Skathos. Care to try it?" Yugorosk's lips were curled back in a snarl. Kew shook his head vigorously, and peered over the edge, at the long, long drop into oblivion.

Skathos fell, swirling through the cool tower air. The burning stopped, and his eyes closed as he waited for impact and death. Instead, his fingers started to stream away from him, and he watched in horror as it progressed to his hands, and arms, and he realised his feet and legs were flowing off above him, like streamers of black sand...

What have I done?

You have absorbed us.

Why?

To free us from the towers. They were our prison.

I will die?

Yes.

And then?

Then we will be free.

Killing Time

Beetrax, Dake, Jonti, Talon and Sakora had been forced down to their knees, hands now shackled behind them, their faces showing fresh bruises from the fists of Val, Galog and a few others. Lillith had been chained to a fence nearby – her face ashen, long dark hair matted and limp in its thick strands. Jael stood to one side, nervously, but was no longer associated with the Vagandrak group. Krakka had seen to that. But now Krakka was gone. Who would give Jael special treatment now?

Val, holding a thick helve, was walking up and down in front of the group, the helve smacking the palm of his right hand rhythmically.

"This is what's going to happen, you murdering bastards. We're going to load you into a cart and go on a little journey. We're going to pass through some very special gates and arrive at the Dragon Shafts, where our three feeble-minded pet wyrms are imprisoned. The wyrms need feeding, and have a *very good* smell for blood. So I'll cut you a little – that will be one of the fun parts – and then we toss you one by one into the shaft of whichever dragon looks the hungriest, and take bets on how long you survive. The dragons toy with their food sometimes, they only bite off an arm or a leg and chew it for a while. We've seen some stunning spectacles, I can assure you."

Many of the extra crossbow-toting guards summoned by Krakka had left, retreating to the city now the Vagandrak heroes were under control; there was talk of civil unrest, and how their weapons were needed in the fight against the Army of Purity rebels. Val hadn't been listening. He was too enthralled in his own rhetoric; busy leering at the frightened figure of Lillith, cowering and pale by the fence. He had an erection just thinking about her.

Other friendly faces had emerged from the wardens' barracks to watch the show.

Tallazok Mentir, the tattooed torturer was there, his intricately tattooed arms folded, a broad smile on his slender face. Nak the surgeon had also made an appearance, standing nonchalantly in his surgeon's apron, a roll of tools held casually – but threateningly – in one hand; plus Talon's array of grinning special friends.

Dake and Jonti were staring with open hostility, but it was Beetrax's face when Tallazok moved towards the group that brought a tight smile both from Dake and Talon. "If you could get your hands on that bastard, eh Beetrax?"

"He wouldn't be fucking chuckling," muttered Beetrax.

"One day soon," said Dake.

"Yeah, mate. After the dragons have finished eating us, eh lad?"

"Silence!" roared Val, whacking the helve with extra force and stopping his march. He pointed the helve at Beetrax. "I could always knock out all your teeth first. Right now. In fact, it'd probably entertain the crowd…" He gestured, and there came a low ripple of laughter from the watching dwarves, many of whom had personally asked to go three rounds with Beetrax after he'd killed Krakka, who had been a hero to numerous slave overseers.

Tallazok stepped forward then, and grinned down at Beetrax. "Val? I know you are now in charge, in, ah, Krakka's absence, but I thought we might have a little fun? I promised Beetrax the Axeman here that if he stepped out of line, I had a further punishment for him." Val looked down at the steel box he carried. The *Ball Cracker*. "Now, far be it for me to tell you how to run the slaves, but I've seen this kind of thing many times before. If we do not carry through with our promises, then what are we? Weak? Here to be taken advantage of by fucking *slaves*? So I suggest a little demonstration."

Suddenly Beetrax screamed, launching himself to his feet and towards Tallazok Mentir. Val tried to intervene, but was shoulder-charged aside as Beetrax headbutted Tallazok in the chest, knocking him back onto his rump, and landing atop him. "Castration, is it?" roared Beetrax, and slammed his head forward, breaking Tallazok's nose in a spray of blood and stunning the slender torturer. "I'll give you a facial castration, you bastard." His teeth clamped over Tallazok's nose, and the torturer suddenly started screaming, legs kicking, as Val and Galog grabbed Beetrax, ripping him backwards – along with Tallazok's nose, which came away with a *schlup* and strings of skin that stretched, then snapped, to dangle against Beetrax's beard.

Beetrax fell back atop Val and Galog, and everything was a sudden chaos. Beetrax chewed thoughtfully and swallowed, eyes shut, teeth clenched, then rolled off Val and landed on his knees, panting, blood in his beard.

"Where's my nose, where's my nose?" squealed Tallazok, both hands to his face in horror. And then realisation dawned. Beetrax had swallowed it so it could never be sewn back on. His face darkened, and he advanced on Beetrax who knelt there, roaring with laughter, as Val scrambled to his feet and hefted his helve, lifting it up in order to knock Beetrax's teeth from his big, solid skull...

"I wouldn't do that, if I were you," came a cold, calculating voice.

Val paused, face contorted in rage, and he turned to stare at...

"Cardinal Skalg? What the *fuck* are you doing down here?" Val blinked, eyes bulging, for the First Cardinal looked *very different* than during his last visit to the mines, where then, he'd been dressed in fancy black and purple church robes. Now, it was as if the hunchback was dressed for battle, ridiculous though that appeared to Val's shocked face and wide eyes.

What's he doing in my *mine?*

What the hell does the First Cardinal want?

Val felt something die inside him. This did not look promising.

"Lower your weapons. All of you." Skalg's voice was low and commanding, his narrowed eyes sweeping over the group of dwarves. On his journey, miraculously, Skalg had managed to find three of his Educators who now stood at his back, in their church garb, bearing Peace Makers in their weighty fists. They were the kind of Educators Skalg really liked – big, meaty dwarves with emotionless eyes like a dead pig and a lack of imagination which made for good killers.

"But... but we have prisoners! They killed Krakka, the Slave Warden! I have stood in his very great boots and taken over, and I have commanded that they be killed! We are going to feed them to the Dragon Engine. After we've

knocked out their teeth and pulped their bones, of course."
He gave a half smile, but Skalg was unreadable, a trick he'd
picked up after decades of dealing with politicians.

"Hmm. Well, *Val*, that may be a possible outcome, of
course, after I have carried out a full investigation–" began
Skalg, but was cut off mid-sentence.

"But... I'm in fucking charge now!" howled Val, face red
with rage, fists clenching his helve, his knuckles white.

Skalg looked at him, and gave a narrow smile. "Danda?"

"Yeah, First Cardinal Skalg?"

"If this... dwarf... interrupts me again, I would like you to
use a Slim and bash his fucking skull. Is that clear, Danda?"

"Is very clear, your Cardinalness," rumbled Danda.

Skalg gave another tight-lipped smile, and gestured with
a hand, his fingers opening like the petals of a flower. He
smiled and looked sideways at Val, as if daring the dwarf to
see how far the First Cardinal of the Church of Hate could
actually be pushed.

Val bowed his head and shut his mouth.

"Good. Thank you. Now, as I was saying before being
rudely interrupted, I will be carrying out a full investigation.
If the crime is serious enough – which I suspect it might
be, because Krakka, *my* Slave Warden," he put a massive
amount of emphasis on *my*, "was a most trusted and loyal
servant of the Church of Hate, and trusted in our realm –
then I will be taking the prisoners into my custody. For,
ha ha, re-education." Many of the dwarves present bowed
their heads. They had heard many backstreet rumours, dark
gossip, about the re-education meted out by the church.

"Now then. You! Big fella! What's your name?"

"Galog, Cardinal Skalg." He bowed his head respectfully.

Skalg shifted for a moment, his hump uncomfortable,

then continued, "You look like a handy fellow with a hammer. I'd like you to help us accompany the prisoners to a room for interrogation. Er. I think that building over there would do nicely."

"That's Krakka's personal quarters," said Val, almost sulkily.

"As I said. It will do nicely. Galog?"

"Yes, First Cardinal." He bowed and mumbled for a few moments, apparently overcome by the power of the moment.

Skalg gave a little smile. "Galog, I like you. And of course, the church is always looking for honest soldiers to serve the Great Dwarf Lords. Do you understand?" Galog nodded, and blushed at the compliment. "Now then! Prisoners? Can you hear me? Can you get up? Galog here will persuade you with a club, if necessary."

Beetrax stood first, blood drying in his beard, his eyes hard. *This is where it gets real bad,* he thought, and readied himself for more beatings; certainly more killing. He was ready for it. Ready to die for it. He was sick of this shit, and wanted out, one way or another.

The prisoners were gathered together, and Skalg turned and pointed at Lillith. "What about her? Why is she chained to a fence?"

Val stared at Skalg, his mouth opening and closing a little. "She is, er, mine."

"She is yours?"

"Yes, she is mine. Er. Cardinal Skalg."

"In what way is she yours?"

Val squirmed for a few moments. "She, er, is my favourite slave, so to speak." He lowered his eyes and would not meet Skalg's gaze.

"Hmm," said Skalg. "You, dwarf, yes, you there with the keys. Unlock her shackles."

"But!" squeaked Val, and Skalg sighed, and nodded, and Danda stepped up behind the dwarf overseer. The Slim cracked down on the back of his head. Val hit the rocky ground like a sack of hardened horse shit.

"Bring them to Krakka's quarters," said Skalg, quietly, his eyes gleaming, and with chains and shackles clanking, the Vagandrak heroes, one-time treasure hunters, and now miserable slaves who had fallen on bad times, shuffled their way towards the iron and wood building.

Beetrax, Dake, Jonti, Talon, Lillith and Sakora knelt on the wooden floorboards, heads bowed, half-expecting execution by short sword. A swift decapitation. Skalg stared around at the dwarfs present, then said, "Everybody out. Except Danda. Danda, wait here with me."

The dwarves looked at one another.

"I really do not like issuing orders more than once." The hunchback smiled a nasty little smile, and raised his eyebrows. "And trust me when I say that they are orders that, for disobeying, carry a death penalty."

The room quickly cleared, and Cardinal Skalg moved forward, and slowly sat down on a chair which had been placed before the Vagandrak heroes.

"You may look up, now, slaves," he said. They did so, with a clanking of chains. Beetrax and Dake glared at him. Talon's eyes were filled with despair. Lillith looked cool, relaxed, and Sakora held a neutral expression on her recently scarred face. But her stance said something different. Here was a woman ready to kill.

Danda moved up close behind Skalg, a hulking Educator,

his broken nose and scarred features grim and evidence of many a battle. He looked across the slaves, appraising them, eyes lingering on Beetrax.

Beetrax sighed. "All right, lad. Let's get it done. Take off these chains and let's get to it. How many of these shit dwarf fighters are you going to put my way before you realise I'll break open all your melon skulls? Hmm?"

"I have a proposition," said Skalg, his voice quiet, his eyes bright.

"What do you mean?" Jonti tilted her head. Beetrax opened his mouth, but she tutted him into silence. "What kind of proposition?"

"I know some of your names," said Cardinal Skalg. "I have my contacts in Vagandrak; in Vagan, Drakerath, Rokroth, Timanta. I know what goes on in the world of men, although I confess, I care little for your feeble politics. Even when the mud-orcs of Orlana rolled over your land, her splice tearing your people apart, I cared little."

"Get to the point, hunchback, lest I break your spine in another three places," rumbled Beetrax, eyes showing anger.

"You hate it here. You hate being slaves. You are heroes, free men and women of Vagandrak! Is this not so?"

"We hate it here," said Lillith, nodding her head. "But it's not like you will let us go, is it, Cardinal Skalg?"

"That depends."

"On what?"

"You require your freedom. I am in a position to offer you this. In exchange for one simple act."

"An act?" said Talon, his eyes coming alive for the first time in weeks. "An act of violence?"

"An act of assassination," said Skalg, and licked his lips.

"Who's the target?" said Jonti. "I am expecting somebody of power, with efficient guards? Killers?"

"You expect right," said Skalg, eyes narrowing. "This is the plan. We get the carriage back up to my city. You come to one of my personal armouries – whatever you need. My Educators escort you through the city to the, shall we say, start point of your mission. You go into the Palace of Iron, and you assassinate King Irlax."

There came a long, stony silence.

"You want us to kill the King of the Harborym Dwarves?" said Dake, face a scowl.

"Yes."

"And in return we get our freedom?"

"Your freedom, the weapons you carry, and as many diamonds that will fill your pockets."

Again, a long silence as this proposition was processed.

"I'm game," said Beetrax, with a cough. "I'm ready to die to get out of this fucking dump. And killing dwarves? Even king dwarves? Well, that's just a fucking bonus in my book."

"Traps? Guards?" said Jonti.

"We have an unfortunate situation in Zvolga at the moment," said Skalg, quietly. "We have a situation which is bordering on civil war. There is much community unrest. Much… violence in the streets. Normally, you would have no chance of getting close to the king. But the guards and wardens are… stretched. All that is my problem, however. All you have to do is kill one dwarf."

"Is he dangerous?" asked Talon.

Skalg looked at him. "Not dangerous enough to dodge one of Talon's shafts," he smiled. "And yes. I do know how good you are, one-time Chief Protector of the Queen. So then?" His eyes scanned the group. "Do we have a deal? I will provide maps of the mines and the city. Before you set off. Just so you know I am not trying to dupe you."

"One kill?" said Dake. "To get out of this hell? Count me in."

"It is immoral," said Lillith, voice gentle.

"Then immoral it is," rumbled Beetrax. "Now take off these shackles."

"When we leave the mines," said Skalg, standing. "After all, one has to keep up appearances in front of the other slaves. We wouldn't like a riot now, would we?"

The journey by chain-pulled carriage was a blur of junctions, intersections and scowling dwarves, all bearing axes and war hammers. They glared at the southerners, until one look from Skalg made them turn away. The Church of Hate was bad news for those who did not know their manners.

Beetrax nudged Talon, as they rattled along in the carriage. "You all right, Tal?"

"I've felt better."

"But now there is hope."

"A little." He smiled, but it was without humour.

"Fuck me, your cup is always half empty, isn't it?"

"Only since we arrived here, Axeman. Lillith? I beseech thee. Tell this oaf to leave me be. I have a lot to consider."

Lillith smiled, and shuffled closer to Beetrax, then leaning sideways she put her head against his shoulder. "How are you, Trax?"

"Better, now we have a fighting chance."

"In all honesty, my love, I wouldn't say we have a fighting chance. One of the other slaves told me there are ninety *thousand* dwarves living down here. That's a lot of killing to get through."

"Providing Skalg doesn't live up to his promise."

"And you think he will?"

"He'd better, or I'll skin the fucker."

Lillith sighed. "Always so savage, Beetrax." And tears ran down her face, and he held her, and he wanted to ask her, *hey, what happened to you with that bastard dwarf Val*? But he knew it was bad, and he knew it was sexual, and he did not have the heart to punish her further by making her live through it by recounting the tale. All he knew was that one day, even if it took a hundred years, he'd find Val and execute him. And so he sat there in the rumbling carriage, with the clanking chains and the smell of hot oil, watching jagged rock sliding past, and he could feel Lillith's warmth and now, at this moment in time, he was simply glad they were alive, glad they were together, and happy they could share a little warmth, no matter how fleeting.

Sakora sat, her fingers still tracing the scars on her arms, breast and face where she'd felt the kiss of the torturer's blade. She had fallen into a well of despondency but knew one thing – she still wanted to live. And if that meant executing one – ten – or ten *thousand* fucking dwarves, she would happily wield the blade. Fuck honour. Fuck the code of the Kaaleesh. She was done with honour, nobility, and everything else in the world. These bastards had carved her flesh, taken her looks, taken her face. She felt vanity bite her like a dark drug, and realised how pathetic she must sound; but she could not help herself.

Talon's hand moved, and rested on hers. Chains clanked, and there was a *jolt* as they changed at a junction.

"I won't ask you how you are, I'll only point out that if things work out, I'll always be there for you."

Sakora glanced up at Talon, tears in her eyes. "Thank

you," she said. And then, in a small voice, "But what I fear the most, and this is terrible, is I fear stepping out amongst the public again. People will stare at me, and people will laugh…"

"Laugh at what?"" said Talon, eyes filled with innocence.

"At my scars," she said.

"We all carry scars," said Talon. "Some on our flesh, some in our hearts. What matters is how we show strength in the face of adversity. Let them laugh! Because I fucking know how beautiful you are, with or without scars."

"I cannot stand to be mocked," she said, in a small voice. "I fear it will break me."

"Anybody who mocks you will get a shaft in the throat. That, I promise you, my princess."

"Princess?"

"Of course a princess, yes. Of the heart and the soul, but also of the flesh."

"They cut up my face, Talon, or are you blind to that?"

Talon moved close, and smiled, and kissed her, a long lingering kiss on her badly scarred lips. "You are as beautiful to me now as you ever were," he said.

Jonti Tal rode the carriage in silence for a long while, being jolted by the bumps and turns and joints in the track. Eventually, Dake took both her hands and looked into her eyes. "What are you thinking?"

"I am thinking we left Jael behind. He deserved more."

"Better he stays there, I'm thinking. Me and Beetrax already had this conversation…"

"And the fat bastard thought it best to leave Jael behind, didn't he? Oh what an amazing fucking surprise!"

"No. Actually. Trax said we were going into the jaws of

death, and it would be very dangerous, with a possibility none of us would return. He said Jael was safer in the mines for now, and that when we were done, on our way out of this place, we would rescue him."

Jonti considered this. "Really?"

"Yes."

"He *really* said that, and you're not just covering for him?"

Dake remembered Beetrax's words. *The spineless, useless little worm. Better he stays here, like a big fucking girl, and let us real men do the fucking killing, and get the killing done. And then I suppose we'll have to swing back this way to pick up the little prick? Yeah. I know we will. Well, let's hope nobody gets killed doing it, eh lad?*

"Of course he said that. Beetrax is a man of honour! And I would never lie to you, never misrepresent him…"

"Hmm," said Jonti, frowning.

"On another note, what do you think our chances are? Of killing this king? Of escaping? Of surviving?"

"Slim to none," smiled Jonti, then squeezed Dake's hand. "But if we die, I know I will be dying by your side. I know your love is strong and true. And in all honesty? I am proud to have been your wife. I will be proud to die with you."

"Thank you, my love."

"And you, my love, for all our years of joy. I never could have imagined a nobler partner. I never could have imagined a better man to spend my days with. You are my lodestone, my rock, my anchor. I am sure we will live together for an eternity in the afterlife."

Dake hugged her, and they continued the rattling journey in silence.

●●●

The carriage station was dark, filled with low iron buildings, and dimly lit by a single flickering fire-bowl as first the Educators disembarked, then Skalg, and finally his still-shackled "prisoners".

"This way," Skalg said, wincing in pain as he limped forward, setting a slow pace. The Educators flanked him, an armour of flesh and iron.

The Vagandrak heroes followed, shackled, growing increasingly annoyed as they moved down a cobbled street, until Beetrax bellowed, "Oy, cunt!" and everybody stopped. First Cardinal Skalg turned and stared at Beetrax, who grinned at him. "Yes, you, cunt. Unlock these shackles right fucking now. We'll not walk through these streets as slaves. Understand, laddie?"

Skalg considered Beetrax. The Educators seemed to shrink back, their faces changing. After all – *nobody* spoke to the First Cardinal of the Church of Hate in such a way. To do so was to die. Horribly.

Skalg's face remained beautifully neutral. Inside, however, watch cogs were spinning faster than fast. *There is a bigger game here. A much bigger picture.* His eyes narrowed a little. *The humans must be used to maximum effect; here and now, I have no church rank, no church authority. Despite the years of struggle, despite my badges of rank, they count for nothing. For this is all about the final destination.*

Skalg nodded to Danda, who moved amongst the prisoners, undoing shackles which clattered and rattled and slithered to the cold cobbles.

"Good," breathed Beetrax, rubbing his injured wrists. "Now then. Take us to the weapons because we've got some killing to do."

Skalg nodded, face still impassive, and they moved

through dark streets, quiet streets. Distantly, the glow of burning buildings destroyed the image of peacefulness. Distantly, the occasional scream or clash of steel on steel disturbed the tranquillity of the night.

They moved on, the Educators looking over their shoulders often. Skalg, to his very great credit, did not look back once.

They saw nobody, although the sounds of battle and slaughter and fire grew ever closer, a symphony of clashes, screams, wails and gurgles; and they arrived at a church, a huge black towering grotesque thing, with iron spikes and spires and corrugated doors and windows more like prison shutters than the portals to a house of worship.

Skalg used a large iron key, and threw open the doors, striding forward.

"Oh, you are not allowed in here…" came an enfeebled, effeminate voice, which then spluttered into silence. Heated words. Skalg was not nice. A priest came running out, black and purple robes flapping around his sandaled feet as he sped down the cobbles, looking over his shoulder, beard flowing in the slipstream.

Skalg appeared, twisted, face showing pain. He stared at the Vagandrak warriors one by one by one, then smiled, and said, "In here."

They followed.

They walked down a black aisle, towards a black altar. The silence was awesome. As if the gods, and the mountain, and the Great Dwarf Lords had nothing left to say. Great hollow peace surrounded them. To Dake, it sounded like the end of worlds. To Beetrax, it sounded like the end of war. To Lillith, it sounded like the end of all civilisation, and made tears stream down her cheeks.

Skalg moved to a small black iron door beside the altar filled with religious iconography, and produced yet another key. He fumbled for a moment, unlocked the door, and led them down two hundred narrow spiral stone steps into the bowels of the church, into the tomb of the mountain.

They emerged in a surprisingly bright room. Fires burned in fire-bowls connected to the pipes of the Dragon Engine. Beetrax gasped, and Talon pursed his lips. Lillith sighed and Sakora made a grunting sound, not unlike pleasure.

They were in an armoury. A secret armoury.

"Take what you require," said Skalg, gesturing.

Beetrax strode forward, hoisting down a massive, double-headed battle-axe. He swept it with pendulum strokes, then glared at Skalg, his confidence returning a little. "What is this place, cripple?"

Skalg's eyes bulged for a moment. "Cripple? Really?"

"You have a crushed, twisted, hunched back. You are crippled, are you not?"

"One deems it impolite to mention such things," said Skalg, words soft.

"I'm done with fucking pleasantries in the world of my enemies," growled Beetrax, knuckles whitening.

Danda took a step forward, but Skalg held up a hand.

"It's all right, Danda."

"Yes," mimicked Beetrax, "it's all right, Danda. Stay back there, lest I split you from stupid fucking skull to your woman's cunt. Straight through the middle. *Slit*. Like a hot knife through pig lard."

"Beetrax!" snapped Dake, and punched Beetrax in the chest. He came in close. "Shut the *fuck up* and let's get the job done. Right?"

"Sorry, Dake," mumbled Beetrax, then looked over

Dake's shoulder to Danda. "Sorry, mate! Didn't mean you, like, had a cunt, nor nuffink. Or you were a cunt. Nor were soft as a cunt. You get what I'm saying?"

Danda growled.

"Stand down... in fact, get the fuck out," snapped Skalg, and gestured to all the Educators, who made a wary retreat. Skalg was left alone with the men and women of the south. The men and women who had been tortured by the dwarves without provocation.

Beetrax breathed slowly through his nose.

Talon surveyed the lightly armed cardinal.

Sakora opened her eyes and licked wet lips.

"This is the deal, this is the mission, this is the *concept* which will not only keep you alive, but which will see you free of this city. That's what you want more than anything, right? To be free of the Five Havens? To never see another fucking dwarf as long as you live?"

"I'll second that," said Talon.

"Although I'd like to decapitate a few thousand," growled Beetrax.

"Take what you need," said Skalg, unperturbed. "King Irlax resides in the Palace of Iron. He has his guards, but they will not be suspecting an attack of any sort *now*. He has great hounds, half-blind, and they love the scent of non-dwarf meat. Have been bred for it, in fact. Raised on it. Human blood, *your blood*, runs in their teeth and in their veins. They yelp for it." Skalg seemed to take control of himself. "Danda will take you to the gates. Then you're on your own. You will know Irlax. He will be enthroned and bitter and screaming. When you have done the deed, return to Danda – I will have delivered maps and special keys to him. The keys will provide you access to various *special places* that in turn will allow you to leave this city. Forever."

They stared at him.

"Do we still have a deal?"

"Why do you want Irlax dead?" said Jonti, a strange look on her face.

"Tax rebates? Religious differences? Because I want to fuck his niece? Does it matter? One death and you have the means to escape your little group version of hell. I think that's a pretty good deal. I think that's a once-in-a-fucking-*lifetime* chance for a group of stupid blundering fortune-seeking bastards who were about to be fed to the Dragon Engine, minus teeth and knee joints."

They stared at him some more.

"Do we *have a deal*?" Cardinal Skalg was looking far from healthy, happy or personable.

"We have a deal," said Lillith, stepping forward. "But do not get in our way afterwards, *Cardinal*, because your corruption is more sickening than a ten-week corpse being eaten by rancid worms."

Skalg gave a narrow smile, eyes hooded. "Take what you need. I will wait outside."

They wandered around the armoury. It was an amazing place, fully stocked and more so, and wanting for nothing. There were weapons for dwarves, weapons from Vagandrak, elf rat curved swords from Zalazar, spears from the Drakka, even sabres and tulwars from Zakora, the desert people so abused by Orlana the Horse Lady in recent years.

They stocked up well. Swords. Axes. Knives. Talon was in bow-and-arrow heaven, and he packed three sheaves containing a hundred and fifty beautifully made shafts.

They pulled on a motley array of chainmail, greaves, and Dake even chose a helmet. Much of it was just a little too small, but to the vulnerable-feeling recent slaves it was more than big enough. They felt like they were taking back some form of control. They felt like they were taking back their lives. They felt human again. Ready to fight, and die, for their own fucking freedom.

They climbed the stone staircase from the armoury and stood before Skalg, who eyed them up and down, face neutral, eyes unreadable. He was the perfect politician, the perfect churchman. He had been conditioned by lies and immorality for decades.

"Danda will take you now," he said, voice almost a whisper.

"Don't betray us," growled Beetrax. "Or we'll come back for you. You know we will."

"I have much greater enemies than you." Skalg smiled, and there was no sarcasm, and no humour. "Just kill this fucking thorn in my side, and I will be able to return my world to some semblance of normality. I will owe you. Which is why you can trust me."

Beetrax scowled, but said nothing.

Danda led them out of the church, towards the cobbled road.

Skalg sat down on an iron pew, and stared up at the massive crystal depictions showing scenes from the *Scriptures of the Church of Hate*. He put his head in his hands, pain from his tortured spine sending waves of nausea and agony and confusion racking through his rocking, drooling frame. "May the Great Dwarf Lords watch over you," he whispered, and began to cry great tears like molten silver.

Danda stood, and looked Beetrax up and down. He gave a nasty grin, and rubbed his beard, and then glanced at the rest of the Vagandrak heroes. Then he looked up, and around, at the black cobbles and the streets made from black stone mined from underneath the mountain. There came a distant roar of fire, and several screams. It was a soundtrack of misery from an interpretation of the Chaos Halls.

"Hope you're up for this, you lanky outworld bastards."

Beetrax blinked slowly, and lifted his axe just a little. He smiled then, and pointed with the twin blades. "Just show us the way, lad, and stop trying to think. That way lies decapitation for your sort."

Danda shrugged, and set off down the street, one hand on the head of his war hammer which was lodged into his broad leather belt. Houses flowed past as they set a fast pace, most with shutters or curtains closed; the good dwarves of Zvolga obviously waiting for the violence and insurrection to pass whilst thugs and troublemakers roamed the streets. The street curved in an arc, narrowing, and as they came round the bend there were seven heavily armed dwarves standing in the street, their unsheathed weapons bloodstained, their eyes wide with battle lust.

"I'll handle this," said Danda, trusting to his church colours. He stopped, and lifted his hand. "Friends, we are on church business! You must allow us to pass in the name of the Church of Hate!"

"Fuck the church," hissed one, and the seven dwarves charged, brandishing axes and short black iron swords.

Beetrax strode forward as Danda unhooked his war hammer, and even before they struck, Talon had touched a fletch to his cheek and there was a hiss, an arrow flashing between Beetrax and Danda and punching into a dwarf's eye, slamming him backwards with force so that he sat on the cobbles for a moment, stunned, both hands coming up to grab the shaft. Then he toppled sideways and blood leaked from the puncture wound to his brain.

The others screamed a dwarven war cry, as they met Danda and Beetrax at a charge. Trax sidestepped a downward sweep, rammed his left fist into the dwarf's nose, then hacked his axe one-handed into the dwarf's neck between chain-mail shoulder guard and helmet. Blood fountained. The dwarf went down on one knee. The other's sword slammed for Danda, who blocked the blow clumsily with his war hammer and staggered back. The blade came down for a second – killing – blow, but was caught on the butterfly curve of Beetrax's axe, which he turned into an immensely powerful overhead sweep, an axe blade crashing through the dwarf's steel helmet and into the skull below. The dwarf screamed, and gurgled, and Beetrax tugged free his axe with grim face and murderous eyes and charged the four remaining attackers, who had stopped, shocked by the sudden carnage.

"There he goes again," said Dake, almost bored.

"Just like on the Walls of Desekra," nodded Jonti.

"There's no stopping some killers," said Sakora, smiling for the first time in weeks.

"Not when you get their hackles up," agreed Lillith, face a haunted petal of sadness.

Beetrax's axe slammed left, where an arm was raised with a sword. The arm was severed at bicep, dropping to the ground with a *slap*, sword clattering on cobbles, as blood fountained out and the dwarf stared in disbelief. Trax ducked a double-headed axe sweep, and stamped out, breaking the dwarf's knee, folding his leg sideways with a crunch. His axe jabbed forward, slamming into the eyes of the third dwarf and making him scream, dropping his sword, and the fourth had backed away, hefting a heavy war hammer, his eyes focussed now, the battle lust gone, a need for survival kicking in.

Beetrax grinned at him through his beard.

"Come on, lad, let's have it then."

The dwarf charged at the same time as Beetrax, and they clashed, Trax deflecting a blow, axe slamming round to be blocked, shaft on shaft, by the hammer. Both strained at one another, coming close, growling, and the dwarf was immensely powerful, if short, and Beetrax suddenly twisted to the side. The pushing dwarf staggered forward and Beetrax hit his fist on the helmet. The dwarf fell to his knees, and Beetrax's axe swept round, cutting his head free.

It rolled down the street, helmet clattering, blood spewing from the neck where tendons trailed, along with a short section of wriggling spine segment.

Beetrax moved to the two injured dwarves. He stamped on the skull of the one with the broken leg, and the one with the severed arm held up his remaining hand, pleading, whimpering, weeping, tears streaming down his broad swarthy face and into his sodden beard.

"Don't! Don't kill me! I support the Church of Hate, truly I do!"

"Well I fucking don't," snapped Beetrax, and embedded his axe in the dwarf's neck. The dwarf gurgled for a while, twitching, an upright marionette, and then he died. Beetrax kicked his corpse from his axe with contempt, spitting, and turned on Danda.

"You!" He pointed with his axe. "If you're going to be so fucking useless, just keep away to one side, will you?"

Danda was staring at Beetrax, eyes wide. "Now I know why Skalg wanted you to do this," he said, in a low, awed rumble.

"Yeah, well, that's just a bit of what I can give. Now take us to the palace so we can do our job."

Dake moved forward, and slapped Beetrax on the shoulder. "You just killed the seven dwarves!" he grinned, and found it hard to keep the joy out of his voice.

"Good," said Beetrax. "They stink as bad as a ten fucking day skunk corpse."

"Actually, technically, I killed one of them," scowled Talon.

"Well, we ain't keeping scores, lad. Unless you want a thrashing?" Talon's scowl deepened. "A bit more of that archery skill wouldn't have gone amiss. You left me with six of them to murder, you miserable, man-loving bastard!"

"Ha! I believed that one with an ego such as yours wouldn't have thought it too many."

Dake looked sideways at Talon, and without a single ounce of sarcasm, said, "He didn't think it too many."

"Time to move," said Jonti, pointing back down the street from where they had just travelled. A rumbling sound was coming, as of many disjointed, angry voices. It was some kind of gathering, a mob of armed civilians. Flames flickered and there were several shouts.

"This way," said Danda, and cut down a narrow side-street, so constricted that Beetrax and Dake struggled to squeeze between the two high walls of smooth stone. They emerged into a large square, surrounded by trees of sculpted iron which made all the southerners blink at this emulation of the outside world; the *real* world.

"Too weird," said Sakora.

"The Iron Square," said Danda, looking around warily. "We are not far from the palace of King Irlax."

"Can you get us inside? Past the guards?"

"Possibly. They know me. But it will be a great risk."

"How many guards are there?" rumbled Beetrax.

"I don't know."

"Fat fucking use you are."

Danda glared at him, but said nothing. He'd now witnessed how lethal Beetrax's weapon truly was. How deadly the axeman could be in battle. And he was deadly indeed.

They crossed under the carved boughs of the iron trees, hearing the distant sounds of fighting, screaming; of terrible slaughter; dwarf killing dwarf.

They moved down a paved avenue lined with trees. Rusting, metal trees. The ersatz branches wavered, and a cool breeze hissed through iron leaves, which were little more than iron shavings. Beetrax paused, glancing up, and scowled. *There's nothing natural about that*, he thought. *This place. It's just plain wrong. Mimicking the real world above. Why not just live above, instead of burrowing down like moles under the earth? As if you're afraid of everything, terrified of the real world above. Burrowing down down down, as if you're searching for... what? Hell? The Furnace? Well, you found a version of hell all right. And you enjoy living in it, that's for sure.*

"The Palace of Iron," said Danda, voice soft, and pointed.

High iron fences, complete with points. Dake squinted, could make out the gate. Ten guards outside a guard hut. *Ten.*

"This is where I leave you," said Danda.

"Oh no," said Dake.

"Eh?"

"There's ten guards there, my friend. You wear church robes. You will be a good opening distraction."

"This *cannot* be linked to the church!" hissed Danda, eyes wide. Although he was less than bright, this was one thing which had been drummed into him. Drummed in with threats of iron and fire and death.

"You would rather we fail before we begin?" said Beetrax, voice level. "You can get us inside. Without a fight. If we kick off now, at the gate, it will attract more guards and we'll never find the fucking king."

"This was never part of the plan," said Danda.

"There was a plan?" laughed Beetrax. "The only plan I saw was a plan of fucking panic. Skalg is a headless chicken, mate, running around and hoping for the best. We're making this up as we go along, but you can help us make Skalg's dream a reality. In fact, I insist." Beetrax grinned, and his knife pressed into Danda's ribs.

"That would work," said Danda. He gave a narrow smile. "A hostage situation. If things go wrong."

"Good. Let's do it."

They moved down the iron fence. Sounds of disturbance, fighting, rioting echoed from streets which led away. Beetrax watched the guards behind the gate as they approached. They looked on edge. Beetrax knew the signs. He'd spent enough years in the army waiting to die.

Danda had Beetrax and Dake before him, now, no weapons displayed, and the guards eyed Danda warily.

The group stopped. Nearby, flames roared into the sky as the roof of a house ignited. They could all smell burning. A mob could be seen, sticks smashing at one another. Dwarves went down, arms up to protect themselves.

"What do you want?"

"I am here on church business. You know me. You *know* I am in the employ of First Cardinal Skalg. We have been summoned by King Irlax. These prisoners have important information."

More screams went up, and more flames. Ten dwarves ran down the street and were trampled underfoot, screaming. The mob seemed to be on its way towards the gates; a huge gathering with burning brands.

"Right, Danda. Get in. Quick."

The King's Guard opened the gates, ushering in Danda, Beetrax, Dake and the others. The mob was accelerating towards them, and the guard slammed shut the gates, throwing thick bolts across. There were clicks and whines from a complex locking mechanism.

"Move along," said another guard, and gestured with a Peace Maker. A *crusher.*

They moved along, and Danda caught up with them.

"Don't stop now," muttered Beetrax.

"This was never part of the plan," hissed Danda. "I should not be here. I'm *Church of Hate!*"

"We'll get to a clear section, then you can *fuck off,*" snapped Beetrax. "Trust me on this, Danda, you will be no loss to our party."

"But you need me. Later. For maps. To let you escape from the Five Havens. I have to meet a certain dwarf, for an exchange. Then I meet you back here, outside the gates. You see the sequence? The things that need to happen for your escape to work?"

Beetrax considered this.

"Cut him free now," said Jonti.

Talon and Sakora nodded.

"When we get to *that* archway," said Beetrax, pointing to the nearest point of cover. "Then the maggot can do whatever flying fucking horseshit he wants. Yes?"

"As you wish."

They moved, hackles prickling, feeling like they were

going to get a crossbow bolt in the back at any moment from an overzealous human-hating guard. The mob crashed against the gates, and were warned, and ignored the warnings, and swords stabbed through gaps in the fence, stabbing dwarves through the throat, through the groin, through the eyes, through the heart. Blood trickled in the royal gutters. Dwarves were shouting. Dwarves were killing dwarves.

"Come on," growled Beetrax, and they ducked under a large archway, pausing. Beetrax's fingers brushed against cold iron. It was finely sculpted, crafted with loving workmanship. But then Beetrax's cynical side kicked in. *Yeah. Built on the backs of slaves. Built on the backs of misery. Built on the crime of torture and death. The bastards.*

"I will wait here, then leave by another route," said Danda. "When you escape the palace after... your mission, take the first left at the first alley you come across. I will be waiting down there at the house with a blue door with packs, maps, and provisions for your journey out of here."

"Don't betray us," said Beetrax, eyes gleaming. "Don't make me come looking for you. I'm starting to get a taste for killing dwarves. You really don't want me looking for you."

The stocky Educator swallowed, and nodded, and backed away.

"Come on."

They ran down wide, high-ceilinged corridors. There were vast, intricate tapestries depicting ancient dwarf battles, many of them underground, fighting ancient monsters in the dark of the mines. They passed one, perhaps fifty feet long, showing a war scene where mining dwarves fought huge scaled beasts released from underground lakes. They made Dake and Talon shudder as they thudded past, weapons in sweat-slippery fists.

They stopped at a junction of corridors.

"It's getting warmer," said Jonti, panting, sweat dripping from her brow. "Is it just because we're in the palace? Or is there... something else happening?"

"Could be all the fires in the city," said Dake.

"They're sure trying to burn this place to hell," said Talon.

Beetrax fixed him with a steely glare from his one good eye. "We're already in hell, mate. No need for them to make it worse."

Jonti looked at the rough map supplied by Skalg. She orientated herself. "This way. Follow me." And with curved sabre, sprinted down the obsidian tiles, soft boots near silent, sweat running down her face.

There were two guards before twenty-foot-high gold doors, intricately decorated, sparkling with jewels. Talon's arrow slashed into one throat, and the dwarf grabbed the embedded shaft, eyes wide, vomiting blood. Sakora's hurled dagger took the second in the eye, and he dropped to his knees, staring at the group in disbelief, sword clattering to the tiles.

Beetrax put his shoulder against the massive gold doors, and heaved. They swung inwards, silently revealing a truly awesome space. It was a throne room of incredible simplicity. A gold throne sat on a high dais at the far end of the chamber. A single fire-pit burned, illuminating King Irlax, who sat, slumped back in his throne, face filled with sadness, hands on his knees, fingers splayed wide. By his side was a near-empty crystal flagon of wine.

Beetrax glanced around. The edges of the chamber were in darkness, although parts glinted with glass cases containing relics from the dwarves' long past. He nodded at

Talon, who sent a few exploratory shafts whining through the gloom, where they clattered and sent sparks showering from bare stone walls.

"Where's all the gold and jewels and shit?" said Beetrax.

"A king of simple pleasures," muttered Dake.

"Come on," said Beetrax. "Let's get it done."

They moved warily across the large throne room towards King Irlax. His eyes were unseeing, as if he gazed beyond reality into another world; a dream world; a tomb world of his own creation.

Beetrax led the way, the others fanning out, checking the shadows, peering into the darkness. Again, Talon sent several shafts humming to strike sparks from the walls. But there was nothing there. They were alone with Irlax, King of the Harborym Dwarves.

Beetrax stopped, and rested his axe against his shoulder. He eyed the king, who seemed suddenly to come around; to awake, as if from a drunken dream.

King Irlax eyed the six southerners, but his eyes showed no fear. Instead, his lip curled into a sneer and a look of hate passed across his features; not just a casual hate, but something deep, from the heart, from the soul.

"So," he said.

"Irlax?" snapped Beetrax. "I'll not give you any horseshit. We're here to kill you. You got any last memorable words, or shall I just put my axe through your fucking dwarf skull right now?"

"You expect me to beg?" growled Irlax. And he started to laugh, a deep bellowing that came up from his belly; he laughed, and laughed, laughed so hard it looked like he would puke, or maybe have a coronary. Beetrax scowled. The others looked warily about.

"Here you go," said Beetrax, scowling. "I'll give you something to laugh about."

"Skalg surpassed himself," said Irlax, finally controlling himself from his body-wracking mirth. "Slaves from the fucking mines? Really? Did he *really* think I would not expect an attack? Did he *really* think I wouldn't work out that *he'd* worked it out? That fucking hunchbacked imbecile. The Church of Hate? I'd call it the Church of Basic Stupidity if I had my way."

"All this is academic," rumbled Beetrax, and proceeded forward, axe raised.

"Wait! What's he paying you? What's the little bastard offered you? That poisonous toad. I'll have his bowels extracted an inch at a time over a period of fucking *months*. What did he offer you? Freedom? Do you know how many security checks you'd have to pass before here and freedom? You're in the bottom, most wealthy city – Zvolga. You'd have to pass upwards, through Vistata, through Sokkam, through Keelokkos, and finally, through Janya, which, ironically, has the highest level of security despite being the poorest slag-iron bunch of poor bastard dwarves you'd ever not want to meet." He started to laugh again, tears rolling down his cheeks.

"I've had enough of this. Talon?"

"Trax?"

"Put an arrow through his eye. Then I'll finish off whatever's left, and we can get the fuck out of this shithole-cesspit-fucked-up dwarven whore-hole!"

Irlax laughed even harder.

And from the shadows, came his elite guards…

There were thirty of them, emerging from hidden alcoves with sliding doors, and armed with swords and axes. Their faces were grim, and they wore light armour. They moved forwards, warily, fifteen to each side of the king.

"Oh, you crafty, crafty bastard," said Dake.

"We've been set up," said Beetrax.

"Let's do it," said Sakora – and to the dwarves' amazement, the Vagandrak warriors attacked.

Arrows hissed through the air as Talon reacted, firing arrows as fast as he could slide them from the quiver. Every single shaft found its target, eye, throat, groin, and punched dwarves down in a quick flurry of death. Jonti Tal leapt in amongst the enemy, sword blocking, cutting, piercing, and she drifted through these elite guards, her sword causing chaos as it flickered like an eldritch wand. Sakora leapt forward bearing two knives, cutting and stabbing, aiming for eyes and groin, her mercilessness a rabid creature to behold. Dake fought like the efficient soldier he was, blocking, spinning, cutting, stabbing, his mind clear at last, his soul back on the battlefield of Desekra fortress, facing his greatest enemy, his greatest nightmare, the mud-orcs, and slaughtering them all. Lillith stayed back, watching the fight with care, whereas her lover, Beetrax, waded into the dwarves and made himself well known, axe slamming left and right, cutting arms and legs from bodies in vicious accelerated slashing arcs, cutting heads from necks with thudding ease. A sword hissed by, slicing Sakora's upper arm and making her gasp. She dropped to one knee and rammed a dagger up into the dwarf's groin, twisting the blade and withdrawing it in one smooth movement. Blood pissed out and the dwarf keeled over. A short black blade cut into Dake's side, and he grunted, feeling a rib snap. His own blade hammered down on the attacking weapon, knocking it from the dwarf's grasp. The attacker lifted his hands before his face, pleading. Dake cut his sword down through thick fingers and into the face beyond, hacking him to the ground. He screamed. Dake stabbed the point of his blade into the dwarf's throat, silencing him.

Talon was happily firing away. Then, almost subliminally, he *heard* the *twang* of a crossbow. He flinched left through instinct, and the bolt cut a fine line across his cheek. Annoyed beyond belief, he drew a shaft, focussed through the darkness, drew back to his bleeding flesh, and released. The shaft took the crossbow wielder through the mouth, and he choked for a while, dropping to his knees, before he fell on his face and was quiet.

Finally, Beetrax fought like a bastard possessed. Until he came to a big, dark-skinned dwarf with bushy grey beard and mean green eyes. They fought in grim silence for a while, as all around them the battle whirred like some deviant clockwork machine; but they were the epicentre of the storm, hacking, swinging, blocking, axes grinding together in spark showers, heads clashing, fists punching, boots kicking, but for once Beetrax had met his match and they fought each other hard, fought each other to a standstill.

Gradually, all the other dwarves were killed and dead, their blood leaking onto the tiles of the palace throne room.

Beetrax and the broad-shouldered dwarf veteran backed away, panting.

"I'm going to gut you like a fish," growled the dwarf, getting a good hold on his axe. "I'm going to feed you to the fucking dragons."

"You finished?"

"Aye."

"Talon?"

"Yeah, Trax?"

"Left eye."

The shaft hissed, punching the dwarf from his feet. He lost grip on his axe, and his fingers scrabbled at his face, and were soon covered in blood, slipping and sliding on the shaft buried in his skull.

Beetrax moved forward, and put his boot on the dwarf's chest.

"You bastard!" he was spluttering. "That was unfair! Unfair I tell ye!"

Beetrax shrugged, and grinned. "Life's unfair, cunt." His axe swept down, cutting the veteran's head from his shoulders.

Silence fell like drifting ash.

They turned, and looked at Irlax, still slumped on his throne, but who had now gone pale.

"No," he said.

There came a cough. And a whimper.

Focus changed. Shifted. Like sunlight through a blind, as the clouds cover it. The sunlight faded. Dust motes spun, like they would for an eternity.

"Jonti!" yelled Dake, and sprinted across the tiled floor, skidding on his knees to her side. There was a rose petal of blood over her ribs. She was breathing, fast and shallow, a hissing sound like an attacking cobra.

Dake pulled at her, uselessly, until Lillith arrived and smacked away his hands.

"Jonti?" she said. "Can you hear me?"

"Yes."

"The wound, is it deep?"

"Yes. That bastard."

"But... you're the *ghost*! You're untouchable!"

"Nobody is untouchable," said Jonti, and smiled then, and coughed, and her eyes were gleaming, full of tears which released, and fell down her pretty high cheekbones like pearls down a coral reef.

"No," wept Dake, grabbing both her hands. Jonti coughed again, and blood speckled her lips. He looked down. "The wound cannot be much!" he said.

"It is enough," she said, and squeezed his fingers.

"But I love you! We were going to grow old together! We were going to die together!"

"You know that was never going to happen," said Jonti, and coughed again, blood bubbling at her lips. "I had a few weeks left. At best. This cancer. It has made me weak. Made me slow. That's why the bastard got me."

"But… but I love you!"

"I know that, you idiot," wheezed Jonti.

"I don't know what to say…" He bent and kissed her bloody lips, staining his own with her lifeblood.

"Say you'll remember me."

"I will remember you."

"Say you'll light a candle for me."

"I'll light a candle for you."

"Say you'll drink a toast for me."

"I will drink a toast for you, Jonti, friend, lover, wife…"

"Say you'll never forget me."

"I will never forget you," said Dake, tears coursing down his face.

Jonti made a rattling sound, and went still. Her eyes glazed. Her trembling hands became porcelain. Her face seemed to lose its colour, becoming instantly ashen, cold, tinted with blue. Human marble.

"No!" screamed Dake, tugging at her shirt, "No, I don't

believe it! This cannot be!"

"Calm yourself," rumbled Beetrax.

"Why? Why the fuck should I calm myself? My wife is dead!"

"Because," said Beetrax, his voice steady, "there are thirty crossbows aimed directly at us."

"Lay down your arms!" screamed Irlax, leaping from his throne like an ignited devil.

Slowly, the remaining Vagandrak heroes placed their bloodied weapons on the ground.

"Bastards," snarled King Irlax, stalking amongst them. Around him, his armed and armoured guards held steady crossbows. Thirty quarrels pointed directly at Beetrax, Dake, Lillith, Sakora and Talon. "You fucking scum, you came from Cardinal Skalg, and those here can bear witness, you came to kill the king on behalf of the church – and you slaughtered my guards! Well, now, hear this, I can promise you all a swift execution. Get down on your knees. I SAID GET DOWN ON YOUR FUCKING KNEES!"

Slowly, they knelt, one by one.

Dake was crying; uncaring.

Sakora had a poker face. She had accepted her fate.

Lillith lowered her eyes to the ground, filled with a great sadness.

Talon was filled with despondency. The world had turned against him once more, and now he was to die in this godforsaken place.

Only Beetrax stared up, defiant, a snarl on his face, hate in his eyes, hate in his soul. "Make it count, Irlax. Because I'm going to fucking slaughter you, in this life or the next! You hear me, you hateful piece of donkey shit?"

Irlax gave a short bark of a laugh. A light of insanity

shone in his eyes. "I find that… improbable. Because shortly I will rule the entirety of the Five Havens. Skalg will be dead – I will have seen to that. The Church of Hate will be under my control! And I will be *all powerful*. So, feeble axeman, enjoy your invectives, because I am immortal. I am the resurrection of the Great Dwarf Lords! I am in complete control! Now bow your shameful heads, and ready yourself for execution. Beetrax, Talon, Dake, Sakora, and Lillith – I hereby sentence you to death. Guards? Take aim, and fire when ready." He smiled. "I want at least ten bolts in each fucking body. Just to make sure."

Anarchy Rising

She awoke.

She'd felt the passing of ages; millennia, tumbling away like crushed ice as her mind filtered through the atmosphere, tiny, microscopic particles finally released from their Equiem magick imprisonment. They rushed into her brain, and she gasped, and flames licked around her snout. She remembered.

She remembered it all.

The Chains of Skaltos.

The Iron Betrayal, with those huge machines like jaws...

The Great Dwarf Lords, those cunning bastards; and the fall of Wyrmblood, the isolation, the imprisonment, followed by thousands of years of half-remembered dreams, like so much black snowfall; fallout from a destroyed and burning city.

She felt the rage course through her.

She opened her eyes.

And roared...

The Dragon Pits. Three shafts of monumental proportions, drilled down through the deepest rock of the Karamakkos; perfectly smooth cylindrical walls rising for five hundred yards. At the top were massive steel collector bowls and various funnels, heat exchangers and hundreds of pipes – so that every time one of the three wyrms *sang*, their fire could be collected, harnessed, stored to heat and power the five cities above. And when they sang, they could sing for *hours*...

Jael stood before the iron door, and another slave handed him a shovel. He was on a three-man shift to enter the base of the shaft and shovel the remains of former victims that had been fed to the great slumbering beasts, but also to scoop up their shit into thick sacks, so it could be transported away from this place.

"You've come up in the world, lad!" laughed a slave, an old, bent human with blackened, rotting teeth. He slapped Jael on the back.

"But – I'm just shovelling dragon shit, Hanno. How is that coming up in the world?"

Hanno lowered his voice a little, and thumbed the slave warden who sat against the far wall, picking his nose. "Beats working with the other slave wardens in the mines. At least this one doesn't whip us."

Jael nodded, and hefting his shovel and handful of rough sacks which stank worse than any cesspit he'd ever encountered, he climbed rough iron steps with Hanno and Yailem.

"You have to listen for the beginnings of the song. If you hear them, then you know it's not safe to enter."

"And what does this song sound like?" asked Jael, frowning.

"You get used to it. I'll teach you. Either that, or you'll be burned alive and they'll have to find another slave to replace you."

"You there!" rumbled the nose-picking slave overseer. "Get on with your business." He grinned through his food-encrusted beard. "Get in there and shovel the shit like you're supposed to."

"We're just listening for the song, sir," whined Hanno, voice rising several octaves in an affectation of submission. "After all, we wouldn't want to get burned to a crisp."

"Well, one more dead slave matters to nobody down here," the overseer grumbled, and went about inspecting his axe.

Hanno moved to the iron door and listened. There came a scraping sound from the bottom of the Dragon Pit. Hanno turned back to Jael and grinned, thumbing the door. "This one's Volak. The biggest of the three bitches."

"Bitches?"

"Didn't you know? They're all female. Damned if I know how they used to reproduce. But yeah, female. And this bitch sounds like she's about to take a huge…"

The iron door exploded from its frame, tearing free with a screech of sudden, twisted iron and blasting across the space, missing Jael by an inch and spinning rapidly before thudding into the dwarf slave overseer, effectively cutting him in two. The door clattered to the ground with a heavy, deep clang. The dwarf, blood pouring from his mouth and from his two body halves, where he'd been bludgeoned in half just below his breast bone, slithered in opposite directions, slopping to the ground in twin heaps of pulverised bone and muscle and peeping organs.

"By the Seven Sisters!" said Hanno, eyes wide, staring at the overseer. Then his gaze whipped back to the Dragon Pit, and the huge whipping tail as wide as any house, the length of it containing huge spines, each spine the size of a warrior's spear. The tail whipped again, and there came a deep, reverberating *whump* and the sound of crumbling rocks.

"It sounds..." began Jael, but was cut off by the unbelievable, deafening, roaring scream that slammed up from the base of the Dragon Pit. The noise was greater than anything Jael had ever experienced, and he dropped to his knees, arms wrapped around his head, face contorted in pain as the noise seemed to go on, and on, and on...

Suddenly, the noise ended.

"... awake," finished Jael.

The flat of Hanno's hand slammed into Jael's chest, sending him sailing back from the platform. That saved Jael's life. Flames roared in the chamber, a huge bright ball of fire which soared upwards, turning from orange to green to blue. Flames spat from the smashed iron doorway, a jet of pure blue like no fire Jael had ever seen. Hanno hit the ground beside him, covering his head. Jael's mouth hung open, and suddenly the fire stopped.

The world seemed suddenly crisp and black.

Inside the Dragon Pit, Jael saw movement. Matte black limbs and a mammoth tail, circling around, like huge tentacles in oil. Then there came a deep, slamming *thud*. And another. And a third. The whole chamber shook under each impact, and stones and dust trickled down from unseen high recesses above...

God, it's big, he thought, panic settling through his chest.

He turned to Hanno, whose face was a frozen rictus of terror.

"It's... climbing," said Jael.

"It should be sleeping!" screeched Hanno.

"Well, she's awake. Awake, and climbing..."

"By all the gods, we need to run," said Hanno, and he looked over to the pulped body of the slave overseer. Then he looked at Jael. "Listen, lad. Things are going to turn bad. If that dragon has woken up, after being imprisoned for thousands of years…"

"Yes?"

"Well, she's going to be pretty pissed. Wouldn't you be? Go, lad. Run. Escape! There'll be no fighting this when it kicks off proper."

Volak climbed the Dragon Pit, fury swamping her mind like a red-hot brand through the centre of her huge, elongated skull. She shook her long, tapered head and snout, then looked up, slanted black eyes squinting as they made out the collectors and pipework above.

Kept as a slave for thousands of years.

You killed my children!

Destroyed my world.

Now, you betraying dwarf fuckers, it's my turn…

The Dragon Pits had been designed to be massive, smooth, vertical shafts set deep down through the hardest of granite, with the idea being if ever one of the wyrms awoke – Great Dwarf Lords forbid! – the sheer size and smoothness of the walls would be an imprisonment in itself. The reality of the matter was that Volak simply smashed her claws into the walls, gouging holes, creating her own steps, in the same way an ice-climber kicks steps into a frozen waterfall. Up she moved, a creature so vast she could eat a Shire horse with a single bite, her body from snout to tail perhaps a hundred yards, her wings when fully unfurled nearer to two hundred. Volak was big, her armoured skin a dull, matte black, with curved horns atop her head and spear-like

spines running down her back and long, barbed tail. This
was not some cuddly dragon from a child's illustrated story
book; this was a machine built for killing, for slaughter and
death on a grand fucking scale. This was one evil bitch. This
was a creature at the top of its food chain.

Volak lifted her leg, and with three blows punched a hole
in the wall. Another leg up, claws grinding through granite,
and bang, another hole created. She continued to climb,
and suddenly paused, huge head tilting to one side.

A crooning sound reverberated around the deep shafts in
the bowels of the mine. Volak breathed deeply, for she knew
now that her sisters were awake – Moraxx and Kranesh,
shaking themselves into wakefulness after centuries of
enforced slumber.

Volak sent up a cry, her throat ululating, and this was
returned with similar high-pitched screeches, some of the
notes way beyond human hearing. And they spoke to
one another, these ancient dragons; communicated in a
language tens of thousands of years old.

With renewed vigour Volak surged her way upwards,
tail thrashing, and smashing extra holes in the walls of the
Dragon Pit which had been her prison for so long. Huge
chunks of granite tumbled down, thudding on the ground
far below, amidst the bones of a hundred thousand corpses,
amidst her own faeces, crushing her recent cell.

You think to control me? she thought.

You think your world will EVER be the same again?

Above, various engineers and guards had gathered.
They watched in horror as the vast black dragon surged up
towards them, tail whipping.

"Get some weapons!"

"What kind of weapons?"

"I don't know, any kind of fucking weapons!"

"Get crossbows!"

"Crossbows won't fucking work ON THAT!"

"Get spears!"

"They'll have to be BIG FUCKING SPEARS!"

Some wardens were throwing rocks, huge heavy cobbles, which bounced from the accelerating dragon's hide without effect. Five dwarves manhandled a huge boulder, and heaved it up onto the lip of the Dragon Pit shaft. They timed it with care, and rolled it off. It fell, weighing perhaps the same as three or four horses, and bounced from Volak's long tapered head, bouncing free and tumbling down the shaft.

Volak paused, glancing up, her black eyes narrowing. She breathed in, absorbing oxygen, and fire blasted out, scorching up the shaft and setting various dwarves on fire, their beards and hair going up as if they were soaked in fish oil.

Volak continued, and reaching the lip, snarling and growling, she bit and snapped and chewed at the heat exchangers and fire collectors. Her great fangs tore through huge pipes that would take a hundred dwarves to lift. There were screams of high pressure steam, blasting out. Boiling water rained down the shaft, tinkling, and pipes gurgled and emptied. Snarling, Volak heaved her bulk upwards, front claws grabbing the lip of the shaft, crushing granite, and her huge head reared up, coming face to face with perhaps thirty dwarves.

Silence fell like a widow's floating veil.

Volak grinned at them. "Surprised, you little dwarf fuckers?" she growled.

They screamed, and as one mass, ran away, pummelling and smacking one another to fit into the corridor leading from the chamber.

Volak dragged herself into the tight space at the top of the Dragon Pit. Her head swept around, hissing through air, as understanding filtered through. *They got me in here. But then they closed up the tunnels? I will find those tunnels again. They must still exist. Hidden, like my mind.*

She took a deep breath, and fire roared. Her lungs worked like bellows, and the fire turned into fierce blue jets. The stones of the wall started to glow, and Volak moved forward, claws smashing through stones and rocks until she uncovered an ancient, disused tunnel. It had indeed been sealed up, by those who had imprisoned her, and dust lay thick on the ground, amidst piles of rubble. Thick webs swung from above, and one single blast of purifying fire cleansed the tunnel of ten thousand years of debris.

Volak stood there, panting, her black eyes glowing like molten coal.

Then she strode forward, down the tunnel through which she had entered her imprisonment, her claws raking the rock through ancient grooves she had left on her way in, trapped within a huge iron cage of the Great Dwarf Lords' devising. She remembered. Oh *how she fucking remembered.*

She could hear her own screams, now.

And the screams of her murdered babies, freshly hatched from eggs, writhing pitifully as the oil swirled around them. But the pitiful sight had not stopped the dwarves with huge war hammers, striding amongst her babies, the heads slamming down, crushing baby dragon skulls, pulverising the brains of the newly hatched into so much egg yolk. And then the fire. Flames, as her babies burned…

I remember, thought Volak.

I remember.

Her head twitched left, and she heard Kranesh fighting

her way up from the Dragon Pit in exactly the same way Volak had escaped. *Come, sister. Come to me*! And then more cries, and she heard the soothing croons of Moraxx... Moraxx, *so many years, so much time lost, but now we are free, now we will bring back our sovereignty, now we will show these fucking dwarves who are in charge of this world...*

Ahead, in the wide, ancient tunnel, twenty dwarves ran towards her. Many carried crossbows, but three wheeled a heavy, mounted crossbow – a siege engine, effectively, with bolts as thick as a dwarf's thigh.

They stopped, and crossbow quarrels fired at her, pinging from her heavy armoured scales.

Volak strode forward as the dwarves fought with the industrial siege machine, all three sweating as they dragged back wrist-thick cables and wound several tensioners with clacking ratchet sounds.

Volak stopped, and her head tilted to one side.

"Unleash the Beast!" screamed one over-enthusiastic dwarf.

A lever was pulled.

The massive bolt thundered towards Volak, who simply shifted, moving her right shoulder, her right, folded wing, and the bolt slammed past, and brought down part of the roof. Rocks fell, amongst small tumbling stones and an inverted mushroom cloud of dust.

Volak looked back to the gathered dwarves, who stood, dumbstruck that they had missed.

"You will have to do better than that," rumbled Volak, and the dwarves thought they saw the black dragon grin, although it shouldn't be able to grin because it was a dumb, mindless wyrm and it shouldn't even understand humour, let alone fucking *speak*...

Fire screamed down the tunnel, a roaring jet of superheated energy. The dwarves turned to run. They ignited. Some were picked off their feet by the blast of fire, and accelerated down the tunnel, their armour glowing as they screamed within their molten cages, metal running into scorched flesh, helmets turning fluid and flowing into eyes and through flesh and skulls, burrowing down into confused brains...

Volak paused, breathing deeply, her great ribcage rising and falling.

Then slowly, she walked towards the end of the tunnel. A myriad of constellation starlight glowed from thousands of fire-bowls to meet her curious gaze, as she looked out over the darkly beautiful panorama of Zvolga.

Volak's black eyes swept left, then right, taking in the entirety of the city from this lofty, ancient, forgotten eyrie.

She waited, patiently, her breathing slowing as she regained her composure, channelled her rage; controlled her hate.

Behind her, claws raked the ancient granite, and she turned.

Both Moraxx and Kranesh appeared to be made of metal, their scales overlapping, their huge horned heads reflecting the firelight from a hundred burning fires, burning dwarf corpses, and glowing rock. Moraxx glowed the most, being the colour of brass, a deep golden red, her scales beautiful and shining under firelight. Kranesh was silver, like hardened steel, her scales less romantic than those of Moraxx; more like a warrior, a siege engine of living, breathing flesh.

Only Volak reflected no firelight, her scales matte black.

Her eyes stared at the city below them.

"Welcome, my sisters."

"They have made a mockery of our kind," said Moraxx.

"They have pissed on our nobility," said Kranesh, her anger barely in check. She was always the most violent of the three. The most psychopathic.

Volak grinned, as she stared down at a city housing perhaps twenty or thirty thousand dwarves.

"I believe," she said, tongue curling over her curved black fangs, "that it is time the slave became the master. Time we retook our kingdom, our slaves, our world. What say you, sisters?"

Kranesh gave a nod of her great, silver-scaled head. Distant fire reflected in the crescent of her curved horns. She grinned, and it was the grin of a killer, not a victim. "I believe now is the time to burn," she said.

All three wyrms leapt from the highest eyrie of Zvolga, unfurled their massive wings, and with *booms* of slapped air, soared up, banked, and dropped towards the dwarves who had imprisoned them so many centuries earlier...

"Guards? Take aim, and fire when ready." He smiled. "I want at least ten bolts in each fucking body. Just to make sure." Irlax was grinning, and the guards, standing in a circle, tensed, their eyes focussed, fingers applying pressure to the triggers of their collective crossbows...

There came a distant, deep crash; a roll of thunder.

Irlax glanced up. Several guards looked at one another.

"Kill them!" screamed Irlax... as a second crash came, a heavy heaving grinding sound, like two houses slammed together. The throne room of the Palace of Iron shook violently, and three guards lost their footing, dropping to their knees in a sick parody of the prisoners arraigned before them.

More grinding, bashing sounds followed.

"Is it an earthquake?" screamed one guard over the noise, as plaster started to fall from high above, along with several dislodged stones. Now, the entire chamber was vibrating, shaking, rocking even. More guards lost their footing. Two crossbows discharged, quarrels whining and clattering across the throne room.

"You five, go and see what's happening!" screamed Irlax. He had stood from his throne, but was staggering as the floor rocked, and his throne clattered over onto its side, tumbling and rolling from the dais.

Beetrax met the gaze of the other Vagandrak heroes. He gave a small smile, and they nodded and as one, as a perfect unit, they launched themselves at the guards. More crossbows whined, and two guards were shot by their dwarf brothers, bolts thudding into a chest and a leg. Beetrax grabbed a guard by the throat, drawing his sword and stabbing another in the face. Dake kicked one in the balls, taking the war hammer blow on his left arm, crying out in pain but still moving forward, grabbing the hammer as the dwarf fell back. The hammer rose and fell, crushing the guard's skull. Sakora danced, hands flicking out like bone blades gouging throats and eyes and leaving a wake of choking blindness as she landed lightly on the rubble-strewn floor. Lillith managed to wrest a dagger from a guard, and stabbed him in the belly, watching him vomit blood to the tiles.

"What are you doing?" screeched Irlax, dancing and staggering around in rage. "What the fuck are you all doing?"

Talon elbowed a dwarf in the face, taking his crossbow. He aimed it across the space and pulled the trigger. A bolt whined, flashing through the fire-lit gloom, and punched a hole in Irlax's belly. The king made a whooshing sound, both hands dropping to the wound, and he fell to his knees, staring at his bloodied fingers in disbelief. He looked up, vision blurring a little. Still, the Vagandrak heroes were fighting, steel rising and falling, cutting throats, stabbing eyes, decapitating guards with a blur of surgical battle experience.

Then a shrill voice cried out, "The dragons! They've escaped!"

There came a pause in the fighting, as everybody looked at one another. The Palace of Iron boomed to the sounds of destruction, and the shaking intensified. Five of the guards dropped their weapons and ran for the huge golden doors, disappearing into the chaos beyond where more plaster rained down from high above.

Beetrax punched a guard in the face, and turned – to stare into the point of a crossbow. The dwarf grinned, but his dark eyes contained not a sliver of humour. He was a killer, this one. A veteran.

"About time you fucking died," he growled, and squeezed the crossbow trigger.

The dragons circled down over the streets and buildings of Zvolga. A young female dwarf looked up, and saw them. She pointed, and screamed. Soon, dwarves were running like ants through the streets as the three massive wyrms circled, and a mob of violent protesters, who had just set fire to a Church of Hate, stood there with oil-filled lanterns and burning brands, looking up, mouths open.

Volak dropped suddenly, wings folding back, a stream of white fire erupting, blasting down the cobbled thoroughfare

and incinerating the mob in a single long howling fiery
blast. Moraxx and Kranesh followed, their flames roaring
through streets, blasting the walls from houses, sending
dwarves running, screaming, burning into their homes...

Volak landed on a Church of Hate, which had just started
to burn, and stood on the high sloped roof with its spires
and turrets, and she grinned down at the sudden chaos
below, at the collapsing buildings, the carts burning in the
streets, the flaming corpses on the glowing cobbles. She took
hold of the massive tower and heaved, and it crumbled,
thousands of tons falling down to fill an entire street below.
Then she glanced down, into the interior of the church,
to see a hundred priests cowering, their black and purple
robes flapping as they started to run in sandaled feet. Volak
breathed, and fire roared into the Church of Hate's interior,
sending the hundred priests blasting into the walls, their
flesh burned from their bones, their screams cut off in one
hot white fiery instant.

"Right, lads, there's fifty of us, each bearing two spears,"
said Sergeant Scalanda. "That's a hundred fucking spears!
Let's be brave now, let's take down these bitches before
they destroy our city!" They crouched behind a section of
overturned carts which blocked the street. Behind curtains
dwarf civilians were twitching, watching.

"Sarge, what happens if their armour is too strong?"

"Come *on*, Gentahosk, a *hundred* spears! There's not a
creature on the planet could withstand that." Scalanda
peeped from between wheel and axle, and watched as
Moraxx banked, and came in low, head rearing back ready
to launch fire. "NOW!" he screamed, and the dwarves
leapt to their feet, arms coming back, each bearing a six-

foot spear, long narrow metallic shafts with tips sharpened to a razor point. The spears flashed through the air at the incoming dragon, a hail of gleaming shafts, the majority striking Moraxx, and clattering from her scales. She pulled up, huge wings giving a mighty great *slap* as she kicked upwards, almost vertically.

"See!" ranted Sergeant Scalanda, grinning from ear to ear. "See I TOLD YOU! BITCH!" He waved his fist, and turned to the lads, who were readying themselves with their second spears for the next attack.

"Sarge, I don't think any managed to pierce her armour," said Gentahosk, face miserable, eyes gloomy.

"What is it with you and moaning about fucking armour?" snarled Scalanda. "You always have to piss on the bonfire, don't you, lad?"

"Er, Sarge?" interrupted another dwarf.

"*What*?" Scalanda turned, but the dwarves were looking up. The sergeant looked up.

Moraxx had risen swiftly, vertically, into the heart of the cavern above Zvolga. Now she dropped back in a vertical dive.

"RUN!" screamed the sergeant, as she flitted through the darkness in absolute, terrifying silence, firelight glittering from her brass scales, tale whipping behind her in fury as she launched herself at her attackers...

They ran, managing perhaps five paces, maybe ten. Fire roared, a massive billow, incinerating the overturned carts, most of the dwarf guards, and melting the cobbles into molten stone for a hundred yard circle. There was a *whump* as her wings cracked the air, claws touching down and sinking into the molten stone which flowed around and over her scaled toes. She turned, tail whipping out and demolishing a row of stone terraced cottages like a huge, powerful tentacle. She eased her wings back, head lowering, tilting, searching, and finally came to rest at the opening of a narrow alleyway at the edge of her destructive circle.

A singed Sergeant Scalanda was there, quivering, having just climbed back to his feet, his spear clasped in two heavy hands, his uniform smoking, his beard on fire. His eyes were wide and he stared at Moraxx up close now. Her head moved forward, snout poking into the alleyway, and her black eyes narrowed to slits.

"There you are, *dwarf*," and the word dripped from her lips like silky poison.

Sergeant Scalanda patted his flaming beard, suddenly realised he carried a spear, and jabbed it out in a quick movement, stabbing Moraxx in the eye. Scalanda wasn't sure what effect this would have, but what happened next was as far from his thoughts as was possible. The black eyeball folded in and down around the razor point of the spear, and *popped*, allowing black slop to run down Moraxx's scaled cheek…

Moraxx screamed, and she leapt back, wings beating, smashing two houses into rubble at foundation level. She whirled about in a tight circle, tail thrashing, wings beating, and fire roared, a massive circular projection as she spun, igniting everything flammable in a two-hundred-yard radius, smashing windows, burning timbers, and she leapt into the air, great wings thumping, and reared upwards to where a huge, arched bridge spanned over the city like a beautifully carved spiral necklace. In her fury and pain, Moraxx crashed into the bridge, and Sergeant Scalanda watched with open mouth as the dragon's huge body connected, crushing a section, and the whole bridge quivered, and seemed to twist around itself, and stones began to fall, tumbling down on the city below, and as he watched, mouth open, still amazed to be alive, the whole bridge shuddered and began to fall, a million tons of well-balanced stone, now nothing more than airborne rubble.

Scalanda watched the bridge fall, amazed at the beauty and horror of this destructive spectacle. And then perspective came rushing back in, and he suddenly realised *how fucking big* the bridge was, and he turned, panting fast, and began to run, sprinting through the deserted cobbled street, away from the falling bridge and, more importantly, away from the huge dragon he had just successfully wounded...

There was a huge, squealing, rending, tearing sound and the world rained plaster and stone as Volak peeled back the roof of the Palace of Iron's throne room and peered down, head lowering on the long neck full of spear-like spines, horns glistening, dark eyes analysing... the room shook worse than any earthquake and the crossbow went *twang*, the bolt skimming Beetrax's cheek and removing his left earlobe. He squawked in pain, then planted his axe-blade in the centre of the dwarf's face, bludgeoning the nose into a concave crevice, splitting the skull halfway down the centre, and allowing blood and brains to spill out around the edges of the razor-sharpened steel.

The dwarf hit the ground, gurgling. Beetrax put his boot on the dwarf's chest and tugged free his axe, before looking up, and gulping, and searching for the others.

"Time to get out of here!" he screamed, amidst the shaking of the room. Lumps of stone thudded all around him, and he glanced over to Irlax, still on his knees but looking up now, staring up at the huge dragon which clambered down into the throne room, into *his fucking throne room*, and his face still registered rage, pure white-hot fury, and the dragon chuckled, a deep-throated rumble echoing through the space.

Beetrax skidded next to Talon.

"But what about the king?" panted the blond-haired archer.

"I reckon he's as good as dead!" snapped Beetrax, eyes sweeping the entire massive body of the ancient wyrm. "How did it get so fucking *BIG*?"

"Time to leave?" said Dake.

"Time to leave," agreed Sakora, and they sprinted for the double doors with the remaining dwarves, all fight forgotten, all orders gone and pissed away on the wind. There were thuds as Volak's claws hit the ground, and curled, chewing through tiles which popped and cracked and spat up shards of stone and cement.

The Vagandrak heroes sprinted for the exit, as behind them, in a fit of anger, King Irlax of the Harborym Dwarves dragged himself to his feet and faced the dragon.

Beetrax led the sprint out into the grounds of the Palace of Iron. And there he stumbled to a halt, Dake running into the back of him and bouncing back, falling on his arse. "You stupid dumb oaf!"

But Beetrax was looking out, and up. And Dake looked, along with Talon, Lillith and Sakora. Their mouths opened. For the world they had left – an underground dwarf city – was now a burning chaos of anarchy. Two dragons wheeled through the skies, dropping fast to lay waste to buildings, streets, churches, palaces, towers, bridges, and dwarves – thousands of dwarves whose screams were cut short in quick hot infernos. They had entered the palace from a city – now they returned to a devastation.

"By the Seven Sisters," whispered Beetrax.

"Let's keep moving," said Dake. "That big fucking dragon is not far behind us."

"I think we have a few minutes," said Lillith. "It seemed to be interested in Irlax more than anything else."

They picked their way across a rubble-strewn lawn, and glanced back. The Palace of Iron was a smashed carcass, its towers crumbled or crumbling, toppling even as they watched; its high chambers were crushed, and now they realised what all the shaking and carnage had been about. Volak, smashing up the palace, burrowing her way down into the heart, to the throne room, for her audience with the King of the Harborym Dwarves – the King of the Five Havens.

"This way," growled Beetrax, and they ran for the gates. The gates were no longer there. Most of the gates, the fencing, the guard houses and the guards themselves were just puddles of molten metal, molten flesh, on the fire-scorched ground.

They sprinted down the street, ducking involuntarily every time one of the circling dragons let out a bloodcurdling roar, fire blasting through the darkness and turning the gloomy underworld into the brightest of days.

"Left, blue door," panted Beetrax, and they turned left, sprinted down the narrow cobbled alley.

They skidded to a halt, weapons in sweat-slippery hands, by the first blue door, which was ajar.

"If that bastard Danda has let us down, I'll wring his fucking neck like a strangled fucking chicken!" roared Beetrax, and kicked open the door.

There was no Danda, but there were five packs in a row. Atop them were various maps folded in oilskin to protect them. Beetrax rummaged through a pack, finding cubes of cheese and strips of dried meat, along with arrows, knives, blankets, and other supplies.

He looked back, beaming.

"Danda did good!"

"And took off when the dragons started torching his city," said Talon, grabbing a pack and shouldering it. "Come on, Trax, we need to move. We need to get the fuck out of this place." Each man and woman of Vagandrak took a pack and stepped outside the door.

Beetrax opened a map and orientated himself. "This way," he said, and started down the street.

"That's the wrong direction," said Lillith.

"No. We need to go up. You see those stone steps against that far wall…" he pointed, squinting down one arm. "That way."

"We go back for Jael," said Lillith, words barely more than a murmur.

Distantly a hundred burning dwarves screamed.

"No, fuck that," snapped Beetrax. "It's our own survival that counts. The lad will have to sort himself out. He's not our problem. He's not *my* fucking responsibility."

Lillith set off down a different street, and stopped, looking back. "I'm going for Jael. Anybody coming with me?"

Sakora moved to stand beside her, followed by Dake, and finally Talon, who gave a little shake of his head.

Beetrax stared at them all, face incredulous. "Are you all crazy?" he said, holding his hands out, palms wide. "You'll get us all killed trying to rescue the pimple-faced little bastard."

"Well, we'll die trying," said Lillith. "We brought him here. We'll take him home."

Mumbling, cursing, Beetrax shook his head and followed them. The group, excluding Dake, moved down the cobbled road as distantly, Kranesh, her silver scales gleaming, went to work dismantling the top five floors of the Blood Tower, home to Cardinal Skalg of the Church of Hate.

Dake watched his comrades move away, and then looked back towards the desecration that was the Palace of Iron – resting place of his wife, his lover, his one true love, Jonti Tal.

"Rest well, my love," he whispered, tears trickling down his cheeks like molten pearls. Then he turned, and followed his comrades into the darkness.

King Irlax stood, barrel-chested and proud, face lifted, eyes meeting the gaze of Volak, Queen of Wyrmblood. Blood pumped from his stomach wound but his fear had gone. He met the eyes of the dragon, and he felt nothing but hate.

"How dare you!" he bellowed, as Volak came about, tail curling behind her, head lowering to ground level so that she might look at him.

"And you are King Irlax, descended from the Great Dwarf Lords?"

"I am!" he boomed proudly.

"Oh how fucking disappointed they would have been." Her lips curled back, and Irlax reddened as he realised the dragon was laughing at him.

"You mock me, slave?" he hissed, eyes filled with fury. "You, who have lived in a pit amongst your own piss and shit for the last ten thousand years. *You* mock *me*? Well, I am King of the Harborym Dwarves, Master of the Five

Havens, and I COMMAND you to climb back down into that fucking shaft and curl up and go back to sleep, I fucking COMMAND it in the name of the Great Dwarf Lords, who imprisoned you all those centuries ago."

Volak stared at Irlax. "I respect your courage," she said, eventually.

"Good! Now get back to where you belong, you fucking wyrm slave." Irlax's voice dripped with contempt, and disrespect, and a true belief he wielded the power of the Great Dwarf Lords, pumping through his veins, flowing with his blood, an embedded magick from the days of the Equiem Wars.

Volak chuckled. "Please. Allow me to explain how this is going to be, King of the Harborym Dwarves; King of the Underworld; King of the Five Havens." Volak hunkered down a little, tail thrashing and scoring a line through stone. "First, I, Volak, Queen of Wyrmblood, and my sisters, Moraxx and Kranesh, are going to destroy your entire fucking city. We're going to raze every fucking building to the ground. We're going to hunt down, burn, and execute every fucking dwarf in this fucking stinking cesspit of an underworld. We're going to exterminate you, King Irlax. Like the vermin you are. Then, we will head up, smash our way through Vistata, Sokkam, Keelokkos and Janya – but we will not destroy them yet. We will let them see the horror we have visited on you, and let them shiver in their anticipation of our return. We will explore the world above, and see what has changed. We will wage war on any we find, for your kind, the dwarves, the men, the elves, all have been an enemy of our blood for millennia. And then, when we have explored, we will return to the Five Havens, and we will take our time, we will enjoy ourselves. It may take us five years, it may take us a hundred. But we *will* slaughter *every fucking dwarf under the Karamakkos*. Do you understand, dwarf? This world was ours long before you came; and now, we want it back."

King Irlax was staring in absolute disbelief. "Th- th- this cannot be!" he stuttered in fury. "You cannot do that! You are our *fucking* slaves... our *dragons... our dragon engine*!"

"No longer." And there it was, that curl of lips, that mocking dragon smile once more. "And first, King Irlax of the Five Havens, King Irlax of the Harborym Dwarves, *first* I'm going to start by executing *you*."

Slowly, Volak moved her head forward. Her great mouth opened, and Irlax could see row upon row upon row of curved black fangs.

Volak jerked forward, snapping down, cutting the king in half at the waist. His legs toppled to the ground with plopping squelches of blood, as Volak chewed thoughtfully for a while, compressing his bones, his flesh, his organs, his armour, all into one smooth pâté – which she spat out into a big pink pile on the crushed tiles of the throne room floor of the Palace of Iron.

"You taste like what you are," she told the empty throne room, turning her head, whipping her body around, one great foot lifting up and coming down, crushing the magnificent regal throne of King Irlax, throne of the Harborym Dwarves for ten thousand years. The Throne which had housed one of the Great Dwarf Lords himself.

Volak chuckled to herself, and remembered her long years of slavery.

"You taste like vermin," she said, and her wings beat with a slap, and she smashed upwards, crashing through roof timbers and up, out, into the fire-bright dancing darkness over the crumbling, disintegrating, burning city of Zvolga.

Beetrax's axe cut left, chopping an arm from the body, then slashed right, blinding the second dwarf. He headbutted a third, and stamped on the knee of a fourth. The others came behind him, swords slamming out, killing the slave overseers where they stood. There was no mercy asked for, and no mercy given.

"Jael!" bellowed Beetrax. "Where are you, you little rat?"

They found him hiding beneath the barracks, and he crawled out, eyes afraid, and then face lighting up when he saw the group.

"You survived!"

"Most of us," said Dake, sadly.

"Where's Jonti?"

"She's sleeping with the angels, lad," said Beetrax, slapping Jael on the back. "Well, look at you, you little cockroach. You survived!"

"I knew you'd come back, Beetrax," said Jael, eyes wide, staring up into his hero's face. "I knew you would."

"Aye. Right. You knew that, did you?" Dake, Talon, Sakora and Lillith all scowled at the axeman, who writhed uncomfortably under their glares. "All right, all right, I know a bloody knife in the heart when I see it. Listen lad. Get your shit together, because we have a long journey, and a long battle, ahead of us..."

"But..."

Beetrax stared at him. "But what?"

"The dragons! They awoke! They escaped!"

"Er. Yeah. We've established that bit. They're causing bloody murder up above, but hell, I reckon the dwarves asked for it."

"I know where they come from."

Lillith moved forward, pushing Beetrax out of the way. "What do you mean, Jael?"

"I overheard an engineer. They were whispering, over there, whilst I hid beneath the barracks. One said they'd found the city of Wyrmblood. And that's why the dragons have awoken. He said it was death for the world; for this world, and the world above."

Jael's words chilled them.

"Right then!" said Beetrax. "Let's get out of this shithole. I, for one, fancy a pint of real ale."

"We cannot," said Lillith.

Beetrax scowled. "What does that mean?"

"It means what I say. We cannot leave."

"Er. I think you'll find we fucking can, and we fucking will."

"You don't understand," said Lillith, looking up at Beetrax, eyes filled with tears. "These great wyrms, these creatures of Wyrmblood – it says in the Scriptures of the Church of Hate that once they ruled the world. All races were slaves beneath them. Men, dwarves and elves."

"Aye?" said Beetrax. "What has that got to do with us?"

"They're free, Trax," said Lillith, voice gentle. "They will seek to re-establish their Empire."

"You reckon?"

"Oh, I am certain."

"Well, correct me if I'm wrong here," he scratched his beard, "but there's only three of 'em, yeah? How can you establish an empire if there's only three of you?"

"That's what we're going to find out," said Lillith, and bowed her head.

•••

It was dark, lit eerily by the flickering fire brand he carried. The steps went ever down, and he limped, and hobbled, and moaned, and whined during the long, long, long descent. Halfway down from the halfway block, First Cardinal Skalg of the Church of Hate paused, leaning against the rough-cut wall, sweating, swearing, and allowing just a little bit of piss to dribble down his leg. Pain rioted through him, and tears stained his cheeks. His drugs were back in the Blood Tower, but when he'd arrived to grab necessary provisions and possessions, a dragon was busy taking apart the top floors of his home with furious anger – and so he'd left in a hurry, slinking away like the threatened rat he was.

Now, however, down here, he would be safe.

He'd left his Educators at the halfway point, called the Block. They, probably, would be safe. But Skalg was saving the best hideaway for himself. Here. Now. Deep, deep under the Cathedral of Eternal Hate. Deep down. Entombed in the bedrock of the mountain. Buried, deep within the Iron Vaults.

Skalg continued, stumbling, cursing, sweating, pissing, pain his mistress, fear his lover.

The Iron Vaults.

Built by the Great Dwarf Lords.

Down, he continued. And noted when the steps turned from rock to iron. And his boots made hollow clanging sounds. And he reached the first vault door, and trembling hands shook with the keys. He unlocked it, went through, and locked it behind him. And this happened another six times. Seven doors, seven sub-chambers, all leading to the vaults.

Finally, he started to feel secure. Deep down. Buried. Even the fucking dragons couldn't get to him. *Nothing* could get to him.

Finally, he was safe.

Eventually, a long tunnel led to a massive chamber. In the gloomy chamber was every kind of precious metal and jewel and mineral. The huge, huge chamber, with high-vaulted ceilings, thousands of years old, was a museum. It was an archive. It was a vault. And, at the far end, on a low stone table of rock, there stood the Dragon Heads. Three fist-sized, colourless jewels, on simple plinths of basic rock; ancient, hand-carved, and priceless.

Skalg walked slowly towards the three jewels. They glinted, altering the light in a strange way. An impossible way.

Skalg smiled, then. He reached out, and touched one, and closed his eyes, and felt the ebbing throb which ran through his fingers. It calmed him. It soothed him. It made him feel… in control.

He breathed deeply.

His eyes opened.

"The Mountain gives," he said, his smile broadening, "and the Mountain takes away."

And First Cardinal Skalg, of the Church of Hate, considered the future.

Epilogue
TIME TO BURN

The Karamakkos Mountains. Untamed, vast, eternal. Ice-locked, brutal, merciless. Friend to no man, dwarf, or elf.

On the peak of Makkos, the sun sank, a huge red orb dominating the horizon and sending liquid blood shadows spilling through the valleys, the crevasses, the frozen tarns, blood shadows creeping across snow-locked slopes, across rocky, ice-encrusted peaks, across ancient ravines and rocky ledges as old as the world. Here, three shadows were outlined in black.

They sat, motionless, ink paintings cut out from the sky.

And then one moved, uncurling slowly; great wings unfurled, and gave a heavy, slapping *wham*, as it leapt up, and soared, banking, to drop fast and straight and vertical, deep into a valley where a snow lion hunted reindeer.

The snow lion, coat thick and shaggy due to the harsh winter conditions, felt a premonition and crouched back at the last moment. A shadow fell over the huge beast, great jaws fastened around its mewling, screeching body, and then it was kicking and clawing as the dragon, the wyrm, carried it high into the sky and returned to the solitary peak of Makkos, landing with a thud, claws gouging ancient rock, and chewed for a few moments, before swallowing the snow lion, her teeth shutting with a final, terminal clack.

"What now?"

"There are still many dwarves beneath the mountain."

"We have all the time in the world for those bastards. I want them to wait, as we waited in our Dragon Pits. I want them to feel fear, as we felt desolation in the knowledge our children had been destroyed. I want them to build their futile defences down in their fucking stinking holes, as they survey the carnage we have already inflicted, and pray for the day we will never return. They will plot and plan, and seek to destroy us. They will come to understand Wyrmblood, and they will seek to stop us returning."

"And now?"

"For now," breathed Volak, flames curling around her snout, "for now, we will enjoy the fresh mountain air; we will enjoy the succulent meat the world provides; we will enjoy the freezing wind on our scales; we will free our minds, give ourselves space and time to think; we will explore the land we once knew as our own, the valleys and rivers, the forests and mountains, we will see what cities the men and dwarves and elves have deemed fit to build in our absence."

"You think our domain has much changed?" said Kranesh.

"I think we have been written out of history," said Volak. "I think," and her lips curled into a black grin, "I think we have been *forgotten*."

"Then we must remind the world we exist," said Kranesh, frowning.

"We must show the world that we are dominant," said Moraxx.

"Yes," breathed Volak, with joy. "We will do all those things, my sisters. We will fly, and we will feed, and we will explore, and we will burn, and we will destroy. Are you ready? Are you ready to see what a mockery they have made of our world?"

"We are ready," whispered the mighty wyrms.

And as one, the blood-dark silhouettes detached from the Makkos peak, and with lazy, long wing-beat strokes, these ancient dragons, free at last, headed south... gliding towards Vagandrak.

Acknowledgments

As ever, lots of people (and a monkey or two) have helped with the creation of this book, and I give love and thanks to you all! You know who you are! Have a banana on me. Ook.

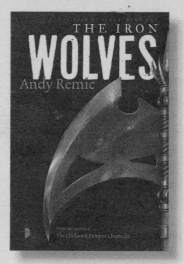

THE CAGE OF SOULS: BOOK ONE
THE IRON
WOLVES
Andy Remic

From the author of
The Clockwork Vampire Chronicles

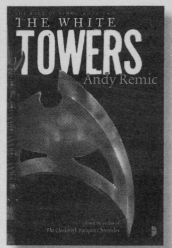

THE RAGE OF SOULS: BOOK TWO
THE WHITE
TOWERS
Andy Remic

From the author of
The Clockwork Vampire Chronicles

*" Andy Remic is the
Tarantino of fantasy,
and if that isn't a
compliment, then I
don't know what is."*

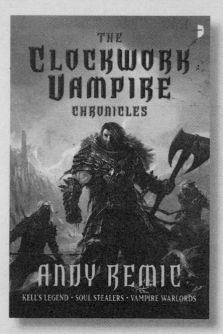

THE
CLOCKWORK
VAMPIRE
CHRONICLES

ANDY REMIC

KELL'S LEGEND · SOUL STEALERS · VAMPIRE WARLORDS